BETWEEN THE LAKE AND THE
MOUNTAINS A KILLER IS WAITING . . .

'I'm going to write a piece about the Jenner
Clinic.'

She frowned and looked out of the window. A
train was crossing the bridge, and its thunder
drummed against the glass. She said, 'I'm not sure
it's a good idea.'

'But it's the kind of thing you're trying to push
me towards. And I'll need your help in setting out
the basic research outline. There's a lot I don't
understand – like, how come Jenner picked such a
remote and inaccessible spot for his labs?'

'He liked the view.'

'And, you know, I haven't the faintest idea of
what actually goes on at a baby farm. Where did
those chimpanzees come into it, for instance?'

She took the paper napkin from her lap and
crunched it up into a tight ball, dropping it on to
her plate. 'I've got to go,' she said.

Carson watched uncomprehending as she stood
up and edged sideways from between her chair
and the table, looking down and not meeting his
eyes. He said, 'But you were going to tell me
about the fertility business.'

'Some other time. Please, Peter, forget the
article . . . don't ask, just believe me. It's better
forgotten.'

Chimera

STEPHEN GALLAGHER

SPHERE BOOKS LIMITED
30-32 Gray's Inn Road, London WC1X 8JL

First published in Great Britain by Sphere Books Ltd 1982
Copyright © Stephen Gallagher 1982

Printed and bound in Great Britain by
Collins, Glasgow

ACKNOWLEDGEMENTS

I'm indebted to a number of people for their help in research. Among them are Miss M. Badham of Twycross Zoo, R. A. Bullers, QFSM FIFireE, County Fire Officer with the Greater Manchester Fire Service, Mike Chafetz of the Texas Christian University of Fort Worth, Nick Ellerton, Assistant Curator of Mammals at Chester Zoo, Dr Roger Gilbert of the Department of Genetics, University of Wales at Swansea, Richard M. Hartzman, Attorney at Law, Mr Bernard McArdle, Casework Consultant for the Deaf with Trafford Borough Social Services, and Dr Jerry Ravetz, Reader in the History and Philosophy of Science, University of Leeds. My thanks to them all, and to Jim Pope for putting me on the map; any credit for accuracy must go to them, but the responsibility for all arguments and contentions is mine.

PART ONE

Special Handling
7 October 1944

M Francois de Menthon
Prosecutors' Office
Palace of Justice
Fürtherstrasse
NUREMBERG   12 August 1945

I will do my best to supply the information that you have asked
me for. It is not, as you tactfully suggest, so difficult to
remember; I only wish that it was. The difficulty is in the
retelling.

You ask me where I was when I heard the explosion. I was by
the gas-chamber elevator, helping to load an old woman on to our
iron trolley. Two of us were working where one could have
managed; she was naked and starved, and no weight at all. Her
hair had been cropped to make felt for German boots, and her
teeth had been jerked for their gold.

The explosion was close by, and it banged the soot off the
crematorium walls. Petrov and I had either end of a plank which
we used to lift the bodies on to the wagon, and we held it as we
tried to listen over the throb from the drawing fans which heated
the brick ovens. The tiny windows were still rattling in their
frames when the gunfire started.

I looked across at Petrov, but he was no more certain than I
was. He was nineteen, almost the same age as me, but he looked
much younger. He shrugged, and we tipped the plank so that the
woman rolled on to the trolley with the two children. Then we
stepped over the rails and put our weight behind the carriage to
start it rolling towards the incinerators.

I know it sounds commonplace. It was commonplace. I'd lost
count by then of the number of corpses we'd rolled into the ovens,
the grandparents and the children and the skeletal musulmans
from the Auschwitz K.Z. across the railway track. We were
Sonderkommando, pressed labour for the S.S., alive and fed

3

only as long as we worked. I'd had four months in the Kommando of the living dead, and my only tears were for the burnt-flesh odour of the ovens.

A siren had started up, somewhere on the Birkenau side of the camp. Still the gunfire went on, peppered here and there with louder blasts and an occasional hoarse command. Two of the S.S. men were at a window, trying to get some sight of what was happening, but I doubt if they could have seen much more than a haze of smoke over the pine trees.

We got the trolley on to the turntable in the middle of the Krema, and I looked around for an order; without an order, we couldn't know which oven was the next to be loaded. But the S.S. were preoccupied, and one by one the incinerators were being left unattended as the labour group started to gather at the far end of the chamber. The acting guard commander was a man called Voss, and he was still at the window. If the smoke hadn't been so heavy, he would have been able to see that the roof of the number three crematorium had been blown completely off.

Petrov and I were too conspicuous, out there in the middle of the floor. I left the wagon on the turntable, and Petrov followed me over to where everybody seemed to be heading. There was a group of indecisive men growing around Spalinsky, the Russian work boss, and we joined it. I suppose it was inevitable – Spalinsky was one of those who cursed and schemed in the dormitory loft at nights whilst the rest of us were quiet and resigned. Most of the Kommando worked their little rackets and tried not to count off the days towards the final bullet; Spalinsky spread hope like a disease.

The rumble of the fans in the chimneys made it difficult to hear what was being said. I caught some of the threads of the conversation as they ran like rats through straw; rebellion, revolt – do we break out the hidden weapons and fight now, or do we wait? Can we make it through the wire, and if we make it through the wire can we make it to the river, and if we make it across the river will the S.S. find us in the forest?

I didn't join in. I had a bad feeling, and I realised what it was; for the first time in months, I was afraid. I could manage it when

I'd had no future worth thinking about, but now the days ahead were opening up again.

And days were all we had as a Kommando; we'd served our time, and we were due for extermination and replacement. All we had to look forward to was a march into the woods behind the number five crematorium, a moving line for a small-calibre shot in the back of the head and a common grave. And still, there were arguments.

They quietened as Sergeant-Major Voss turned from the window. He saw the unattended furnaces and the idle transport trolley. No S.S. could tolerate discipline falling apart so quickly, not from scum like us; he marched the length of the room, making straight for Spalinsky.

The men on either side of Spalinsky fell back, but the Russian stood his ground. Voss thrust his face up close, and barked.

He wanted to know who had given us permission to stop working. He was carrying the metal-tipped cane that was issued to all the S.S. in the camp, and he slapped it hard into the palm of his hand. Again, he demanded why we had left the ovens.

Spalinsky started to mumble something, but he wasn't raising his voice enough to be heard. The acting commander's cane whipped up suddenly and came down across the Russian's head.

The force of the blow sent Spalinsky down on to one knee, and he fell heavily against the man beside him. The skin of his forehead was split open. As Voss turned away Spalinsky came up again, and as he straightened he brought a short knife from the top of his boot and rammed it upwards under the acting commander's ribcage.

It was the irrevocable step, the trigger to action. The instruction turned into a gurgle and Voss began to sag, his jaw hanging open as he looked down at the knife protruding from the front of his jacket, still gripped by the Russian as he took more and more of the S.S. man's weight on to the blade.

I heard Spalinsky call for the oven door to be opened. Voss was pushing against him feebly, trying to lever himself off the steel. Over by the window the other S.S. was starting forward. He

5

couldn't see exactly what was happening, but he was apprehensive.

Petrov was the nearest, and he took hold of the handle that unlocked the iron door and swung it open. The fans had been on too long and the incinerators were overheating; blistering air poured out carrying soot and sparks and smoke, and most of us had to fall back. But there were three who had a hold of Voss and he couldn't fight them off – he was clutching at his stomach as if he feared that it would all spill out if he let go. They lifted him up by the seat of his pants and hauled him into the oven.

The other S.S. man had covered half the distance, but he faltered when he saw the guard commander's boots disappearing over the rollers. He was fumbling with the cover on his holster, but several of the Kommando men had already produced Walthers and Lugers.

Spalinsky was shouting for everybody to save their bullets, and four of them got to the S.S. man before he'd half-drawn his automatic. One of them wrenched it out of his hand, another booted him in the groin to make him co-operative, and then they hustled him to the still-open oven and pitched him inside.

There was firing then as the armed S.S. by the door opened up. They got a volley of pistol shots which drove them back towards the entrance, and I was just scrambling to cover behind one of the incinerator supports when a grenade went off.

We had more weapons in the dormitory upstairs, machine-guns and grenades hidden in the hollow spaces underneath the bunks. Those of us who weren't armed went up to get them; as we kicked the bunks apart we could hear breaking glass down below.

There was a man with a pistol at almost every window when we returned. I went to the nearest and offered the machine-gun that I was carrying; I knew better than to try to use it myself, even though most of those who were now loosing off shots were far from marksmen. The man at the window was one that I knew vaguely, a lawyer from Sered; he'd been through the not uncommon anguish of discovering his wife amongst the dead in the gas chamber.

He took the machine-gun and gave me the pistol, telling me to load it. The gun felt strange and flat, and it was hot. After digging in his pocket for a moment he came out with a twist of handkerchief with half a dozen cartridges knotted into it.

I managed to find the release, and ejected the magazine from the grip. While I fumbled with the bullets, the lawyer poked out more glass from the window with the muzzle of the machine-gun and started spraying the yard. The noise was overpowering, and he shook with the recoil.

He fell back after a while. I'd filled the clip and reloaded the magazine by then, and I was expecting him to take it from me. But he told me not to nurse it, to find a window and use it; as he spoke, there was an explosion close by outside which shook out any glass that was left. Everybody ducked, and a couple of men fell back with bad cuts. I saw Spalinsky get over to one of the blown-in frames and throw out a grenade; the whipcrack came a few seconds later, and for a short time the gunfire stopped.

Windows were left free as the men with wounds were pulled to safety. I crawled over to one, and tried to look outside. The courtyard was empty, and the S.S. men along with a handful of Wehrmacht had fallen back as far as the perimeter wall. Spalinsky's grenade had dropped well short on the lawn over the chambers.

As I was watching, a line of grey trucks arrived on the camp road. Four of them stopped behind the Krema perimeter whilst the others drove on. The tailgates fell open and out of the first one came the Kommandoführer with a heavily-armed squad of Wehrmacht behind him. As soon as he was recognised, we started firing again; I got a couple of shots away, but I doubt that I hit anything. I was afraid that I'd lose my grip on the gun and let it fall to the cinder path below.

There were more of us now. The men from the basement chambers had come up in the elevator, and there were over a hundred men crowded into the incinerator room. The ovens were still burning and the drawing fans were still rumbling; by that time the firebrick linings of the flues would be melting and breaking up to fall into the ovens.

7

Someone shouted that there were howitzers. I risked a look, and saw that it was true; two cannon being dragged to bear. They were going to demolish the Krema around us. It was a bad moment — we weren't soldiers, we were students, jewellers, tailors, shopkeepers, clerks, and we'd only had a few minutes' practice at resistance. It was Spalinsky who caught the mood and turned it.

He'd bound up the wound in his head with a strip from his shirt. He told us that two of his fellow-Russians had gone out of the back of the Krema with wire-cutters just before the trucks arrived; there should be a way out for us, as long as we didn't wait to be encircled.

The Birkenau sirens were still keening as we moved down to the coke-store corridor. Many of the Kommando didn't know why they were moving or where they were going. Some stayed by the window with grenades, ready to set up a distraction.

A double explosion was the signal. It was followed by heavy gunfire from both sides, and the corridor crowd started to move as soon as the end door opened up to daylight. I was somewhere in the middle, and I was carried with the swell.

No S.S. were waiting outside; all of their firepower was on the K.Z. side of the building as they probably assumed it was the only route open to us. We ran for where the Russians were waiting; several layers of wire had been cut and wound back. We had to slow down when we reached the gap, because it wasn't wide enough to take us all. The Russians were grabbing us and bundling us through, and as I shuffled and waited my turn — a couple tried to elbow in front of me, but I wasn't going to let them — I glanced back and saw the last of our people emerging from the Krema gates. The S.S. on the far side of the building were still keeping up the barrage, and probably hadn't yet realised that their fire wasn't being returned. Then a hand gripped my shoulder and pushed me through the wire.

I'd cheered as loudly as everybody else as we ran from the wire, the S.S. on our tails and the cordon patrols and the river ahead. We were going nowhere, but we were moving. The last man at the wire turned and emptied a machine-gun at the soldiers, and they dropped him before he made it through.

We scattered. Thirteen of us made it as far as the river, the rest were probably gathered in by the dogs and the patrols. We hid in the marshes until the light started to go, and then we risked a crossing.

Spalinsky went first. I'd fixed my sights on him and stayed as close as I could, and the Sered lawyer had done the same. Petrov had stayed close to me, although I didn't realise that he was following me until we stopped. There were also three Russian prisoners of war who had arrived in the K.Z. at the same time as Spalinsky, and five of the Slovak team who had come up in the gas-chamber elevator. The other was a small man named Mayerling; he used to swill the corpse wagon with water to keep it cool. We had three handguns and one machine-gun between us, and none had a full load of ammunition.

The river was low, showing yellowish mud flats. Spalinsky waded out, and the rest of us got into a line behind him. We hadn't dared to wait for complete darkness – we'd never find the far bank – so we were dangerously exposed, and we left a deep trail in the silt. The day had been one of pleasant autumn sunshine but the water was cold, and Mayerling had to be helped. One of the Slovaks afterwards said that he'd peed himself with fear on the way over.

We had another eight kilometres of marshland before the forest. What we would do then, nobody knew; back when the possibility of escape had been suggested, the idea had been to contact some partisans in the hope that they would take us in. But nobody knew for sure whether these guerilla groups really existed or whether they were just a piece of hopeful folklore – some of our guns and explosives were supposed to have come from outside rebels, but the lines of supply within the K.Z. were so well-covered that nobody could say for sure.

We kept moving, with the idea of covering as much ground as we could manage before the next light. By morning the S.S. and the Wehrmacht would have recovered from being stunned by the audacity of a bunch of rebellious Jews, and the search would be better-organised. We'd have to hide in the daytime, and move again at night.

It was about eleven o'clock when we reached a farmhouse, and we decided that we'd have to stop, at least for a while – we'd all been chilled in our wet clothes from the river, and Mayerling was shaking badly.

Even by moonlight it was obvious that the farm was poor and run-down. There was a barn that stood some distance from the main buildings and stables, along a track that was waist-high in weeds at some points and which passed through a broken fence on the perimeter of the yard. Twelve of us stayed whilst the lawyer went to take a look.

For some reason I was afraid of geese as the lawyer led us back, but nothing squawked or flapped up from the grass. The barn was a timber-framed structure that had started to warp and sag with neglect; the planking in the doors was split and they were jammed open.

Inside, it smelled of goats and old straw. There was a four-wheeled buggy filling most of the lower level, jammed in with the filthy cowstalls and leaving us no room to get around. One of the Russians found a ladder nailed to a crossbeam overhead, and by this we were able to get into the comparatively dry hay-loft.

As we were getting settled, Spalinsky asked if we had any doctors amongst us. It was a futile hope because everybody knew that Mengele took all the doctors for his own uses, putting them to work on an odd range of projects that he'd concocted with a particular interest in any twins or dwarves that arrived at the camp. Spalinsky's head had opened up and started to bleed again, so I admitted that I'd had less than a year in medical school before I'd been taken away.

The lawyer had the idea of going to the yard to get water. Petrov wanted to come along, but Spalinsky said no; so it was the lawyer and me.

We found a bucket in one of the cowstalls. It was dented and the handle was broken, but at least it wasn't holed. I remember the strange, hard feel of the ground as we walked towards the farmhouse, beaten dirt that had packed down solid. There was no gate across the yard, where the dirt became ruts and tracks. We could hear horses stirring in a low shed by the main house, but otherwise nothing.

The pump was in a lean-to where the firewood was stacked. I held the pail and the lawyer tried the handle; it made a rusty grinding noise, and the pump did no more than give a couple of dry coughs. When he swung it again the noise was less but the water was still no more than a trickle, and it didn't look clean. I emptied it away, and just got the bucket under the spout again in time for the rush of water that came with the third swing.

The lawyer checked the house before we moved out. The shutters were still up and there was no light showing through. We carried the pail back between us and managed not to lose too much. About two-thirds of it went for drinking when we got it up into the hayloft, and I used what was left to clean up Spalinsky's head. The cleanest piece of rag that I could find was the twist of cloth that had held the pistol cartridges; everything else was filthy with river water. Besides the mud, the Vistula was a common dumping-ground for the crematoria ashes — all of our clothes and the striped burlap worn by two of the Slovaks would be stiff and rough by the morning.

I'm sure that I must have made a very rough job of Spalinsky's hurt, but he didn't complain. I remember feeling proud at the idea of having some identity within our group, and I suppose it was this dangerous glow of self-esteem that carried over to an hour or so later when everybody else was asleep and our water supply was nearly finished.

I decided that the bucket needed to be refilled, and that it was up to me to do it. Me, our doctor, hardly out of my teens and without training or skill — but then I couldn't lead and I couldn't fight, and against the brutality that I knew the rest of the Kommando would be suffering on the far side of the river, I needed to feel that I was earning my place in the group.

When I was sure that everybody was asleep, I put the handle of the bucket over my forearm and climbed down. The little water that was left was cloudy with blood and dirt, and I emptied it away outside the barn door. I was almost halfway to the yard when I heard voices.

I got into the long grass by the path – the cover wasn't as thick as I'd hoped, but there was nowhere else to go. Even though I pressed myself down I could still see the path as far as the yard, and the moonlight picking out the details of the S.S. uniforms.

It was a small party, but a heavily armed one. There were dogs straining at the ends of their leads, and tagging along behind there was a man in rough peasant's clothing – the farmer, I would assume. He must have heard the lawyer and me at the pump, and then waited for us to go before he slipped out to look for a patrol.

I was conscious of the sparseness of my cover, and the possibility that my prison-pale face would show through the grass. It was autumn cover, very dry and brittle, and I had to be careful not to make a noise as I turned my face to the ground and tried to flatten myself into the earth. I could hear boots on the hard ground, and the breath of the dogs as they came down the path only a few yards away. And then I heard one of them yelp as it broke from its leash and came floundering towards me.

The sound was throttled off as the handler took the strain and then let the dog pull forward under control. I hugged the ground harder, and my skin crawled as I waited for the animal's breath to fan my neck. As soon as the patrol knew what I was, there was a good chance that they'd let the dogs have me; there were slower agonies back at the camp but they existed in an indeterminate future, whilst this was a terror of the moment.

There was a sick, liquid kind of sound that I couldn't identify. The handler was wading through the grass, and I heard him curse. There was a bang and the dog yelped, and there was a rough blow on my back. The dog was barking loudly now and trying to get to me; at least they'll be hearing this in the barn, I thought. I'd like to say that it was because I wished them an escape, but all I really wished for was my own rescue.

I waited for the order to get to my feet, but none came. I raised my head, and saw no jackboots; I saw the bucket a couple of feet away, where it had rolled after bouncing off my back. The patrol were moving on down the path. It was the aftertaste of Spalinsky's blood that had saved me, distracting the dog and diverting its handler.

They shot Petrov. He was by the barn doors; Petrov my puppy, who would follow me anywhere and was following me now. I saw the farmer hurrying back along the dirt track to the safety of his house as the first shots came from the hayloft. The S.S. scattered and started to return the fire, and somebody must have rolled grenades through the open doors. There were two explosions, and pieces of the buggy were thrown out high; the rest of it started to burn, and the fire spread to the structure itself.

I was crawling for the trees on the edge of the clearing. The flames moved quickly to the upper storey of the barn, and as they reached it the machine-gun stopped; the ammunition must nearly have gone, because only one handgun continued to fire from inside the building. This also stopped a few seconds later, but then I heard a defiant yelling. Spalinsky was leading the last of the Twelfth Sonderkommando through the flames and on to the guns.

Whilst the attention was away from me, I got into the trees. I ran for half a mile and crossed two narow tracks, and only when the barn was a glow in the night sky did I stop and crawl under some low scrub.

I moved slowly over the next two nights, after unpicking the yellow Star of David from my jacket to make me less conspicuous. I saw no more patrols, so perhaps the fanatical obsession of the K.Z. administrators with roll-calls and numbers had broken down under the mass of people involved in the escape attempt. Being a Sonderkommando rather than an ordinary prisoner I was reasonably fit and adequately clothed, and in preparation for the breakout — the one we'd planned as opposed to the one that had been forced upon us — I carried identity papers and money which I had organised from the belongings of the dead. They gave me at least a superficial legitimacy, and for real emergencies I had two 140-gramme cylinders of gold from the Krema 2 foundry.

What I didn't have, and needed, was a travel warrant. But

when I reached Gleiwitz there was no special guard around the station or the railway track, and I was able to get on a freight train heading south to Dresden. From there it was my idea to get a connection to Ulm, only eighty kilometres from the Swiss border on Lake Constance. In the end, I made it as far as Schaffhausen, where the border was not so heavily guarded and I was able to slip across to Basle.

After I reached England, I heard that there had been no other successes in the escape attempt. Those who hadn't tried to run had been forced to lie face-down in one of the courtyards before being machine-gunned. For the remainder of that first day a steady flow of bodies on pushcarts and shambling columns of wounded had poured into the camp from the surrounding countryside; the survivors were taken out into the birch forests of Birkenau and shot. My own group were brought back across the river that night. They attacked their guards in the Krema courtyard and attempted to seize their weapons, but shortly afterwards they joined their brothers before the crematory ovens.

It was the first and the only organised mass revolt in the history of the Auschwitz K.Z. It shocked and surprised the S.S., who were accustomed to a docile Jewry so starved of hope that they could be led with the emptiest promises to the extent of compliance up to the moment of extinction. I brought the story out with me, but it was given only the credence of a fantasy of persecution until the K.Z. gates were opened to the world. There is now evidence more persuasive than words.

Henryk Liawski
Cambridge.

14

PART TWO

Cumbria

15 October 1987

Chapter 1

The police howler and the horn blasted simultaneously close behind, and when Peter Carson looked in his rear-view mirror he saw the white headlamps and the flashing blue lights closing fast in the rain. There wasn't room to pass on the narrow country road, but the saloon wasn't slowing at all. He wrenched the wheel of the Mercédès hard over to the left; there was an angled grass slope a couple of feet high between the road and the stone wall, and the whole car tipped dangerously as he hit it and braked, tyres riding and bouncing up the verge. The Mercédès threatened to slew back on to the tarmac or else fishtail around and ram the wall, but then the police car was charging through the gap and braking hard into the next bend. The howler cut abruptly and it was gone, swallowed by the turning of the lane.

The Mercédès came to an awkward halt. The drizzle-dampened road and fields ahead were canted across the windscreen, and Carson waited a moment to regain his breath before slowly unlocking his hands from around the steering wheel. He reached down to the floor for the folded map that had slid from his knees.

The engine was off, stalled. The only sound was the muted spatter of rain on the car's body. He unhooked his seat belt and opened the door; because of the angle it fell away and he nearly fell out after it.

Leaves were still dropping from bushes that were pressed against the back of the wire link fence on the far side of the road. The white saloon had ripped at the foliage as it passed, ramming through a gap with only inches on either side. Bastard must have been in a hell of a hurry, Carson thought. Couldn't even wait until there was room to pass.

The wind slapped at his city clothes as he emerged from the

car's warm shell. It seemed to want to make a game of him, the kind of vicious game a belligerent child might devise against a stranger. He turned up the collar of his raincoat and wiped his face of beaded drizzle, circled the car and stepped up on to the bank.

He leaned over to check the side of the car, holding on to the wall to keep his balance on the wet turf. The irregular blocks of slate were stacked without mortar and flecked with yellow moss, and when he put his hand on to the top stones they shifted with a dull clacking sound. There was no sign that he'd actually hit the wall, only whiplash marks of dark sap from where the grasses had beaten against the paint-work.

From here he could see across the road and over the bushes and the wire that were its far boundary. A thinned-out stand of trees ran about fifty yards to the edge of the lake, a flat bright sheen of water which stretched across to the misted towering shoulders of the glacier-cut valley side. The Cumbrian greens were leached of colour by rain and distance but this couldn't take anything from the awesome might of the mountains. Their sides were almost sheer in places, their crags and ridges softened by a rolling cover of heather and ferns, but the softness was deceptive; in places it was broken and betrayed, a curtain that had ripped and fallen with a rain of scree all the way down to the water's edge.

Washed-out jade, wet and glistening greys, the tawny peppered browns of dying bracken on the lowlands, the iron darkness of sky and water; the valley seemed to beckon and threaten at the same time, as if it was in the process of shedding the bright summer disguise that it wore for the tourist season, exposing the harder and less tolerant persona that had always been underneath. The season in this part of the Lakes was obviously over – the fields at the valley's open end had been empty of tents and trailers, and when he'd passed the driveway of a solitary country house hotel a mile or so later the iron gates had been chained and padlocked. From that point on Carson had seen no other buildings besides the occasional block of a hill farm high on the valley slope above him, and no other vehicle until the police saloon had come howling up behind and forced him off the road.

Where could it have been going? The map showed the road on this side of the lake to run into a dead end, following along by the ribbon of water for another mile or so before turning off into a side valley and petering out at a place called Dale Head where the contours were crammed so close together that they almost merged. A little way into the side valley was the hamlet of Langstone, shown on the map as a couple of insignificant grey blocks strung out along either side of the road, no more than two or three buildings in each; further along and set back from the road there was a featureless chapel that didn't even merit a name, and beyond that there was nothing – nothing, that is, apart from the Jenner Clinic, which wasn't shown on the map and which he'd added as a small red cross.

He was stepping down when the second saloon appeared, driving as hard and as fast as the first, and Carson scrambled back to safety as the police driver saw the Mercédès half-blocking the road and swerved to avoid it. Close behind came a dark-blue Land-Rover pulling a caravan trailer which bounced and bucked at speed. The man in the Rover hit the brakes when he saw the tilted obstruction before him but he didn't stop; he made a fast and noisy gear-change and went over against the wire fence, rasping and banging as vehicle and trailer dragged along it, swinging out again as soon as the front of the vehicle was clear. The caravan bounced sideways to follow, sweeping across within a couple of feet of the Mercédès' front fender and rocking unsteadily on its low axle.

Jesus, Carson thought, I'm going to be stuck here forever. He could see himself backing off the verge, straight into the path of another police stampede, more vehicles slamming into the back of the tangle as they came in an endless high-speed stream from Penrith. He crossed the road and tried to look back, but with its twisting to follow the lake shore and its rise and fall it was impossible to see more than a couple of hundred yards.

He slid into the car, and with an eye on the mirror he started the engine and put the shift into reverse. He got all four wheels back on to the tarmac without too much problem, changed through to *drive* and rolled forward, tentatively at first, as he tried to feel for damage in the steering or suspension. No judder, no noise, no pull; with another glance in the mirror he started to accelerate.

Mist began collecting on the screen straight away, and he had to switch the blowers to cold. He was losing the lake now, and the road was becoming more enclosed; the wall on his left was higher and the trees and bushes to the right were much denser, overhanging the road and shading it with greens and browns. Occasionally the wall was breached by a gateway, chained and padlocked like the one before the deserted hotel, and Carson had a brief glimpse of the jointed slabs of field that tilted until they met the sudden upward rush of the valley side. In a couple of them were the formless humps of browsing sheep, but otherwise the pastures were mostly empty and no two seemed to be of exactly the same shade.

It was hill-farm country, hard and functional, the rocks close under the surface like knots in muscle. The rubble of glacial deposits had been cleared and arranged into endless dry walls and the forests had been felled and replanted, but for all the superficial changes of use the tough underlying structures remained the same, only subject to the massive forces of time. It wasn't the most obvious place on earth to site the backup for a fertility clinic.

It was true that they seemed to be everywhere these days, and when Tracy Pickford had told Carson that she worked at a place out in the country he hadn't thought it remarkable; but then he'd automatically been thinking about the sick and anaemic farming belt around London, stitched across with pylons and dotted with commuter developments like cheap crockery packed in dead straw. This wasn't 'the country', somewhere serviceable and handy where you beat the kids and left litter, it was a place that could, without consideration or sympathy, kill. Tracy had told him about a girl who had died the previous February, a lab assistant who had gone walking in the snow in Wellingtons and who had only been found when the spring thaw uncovered her. Tracy had replaced her in May.

She'd told him this after he'd accepted her invitation to visit, and he had the uncomfortable feeling that she was concealing some amusement as she tried to scare him; but when he watched for the signs there were none, and so in spite of the fact that they'd met for the first time that evening, and there were no obvious sparks of attraction flying between them, he'd let his acceptance stand. His monthly cheque had been paid into the bank from his trust fund and there was nothing to keep him in London, which was why he was on this remote valley road and slowing to a halt before a police roadblock.

Toby Knight was a police sergeant, uniformed branch, traffic division. He'd been a sergeant for a number of years and it looked as if he was going to stay a sergeant until he retired. He believed he knew why; the whole complex machinery of promotion was refined down in his mind to one simple principle, they either liked you or they didn't, *they* being the people on high who called all the changes. Mike Schaffer, the force's youngest D.I., had a police college background and was liked; Toby Knight was a late recruit, looked everybody's idea of a hard copper, and was not. In Knight's words, Schaffer could fart and play *God Save the Queen* on a comb and tissue paper whilst Knight himself had all the popularity of dog shit on a ski slope.

They had subtle ways of making their dislike known. They might pull you from your traffic duties at the start of your shift and second you as extra manpower for a major incident; and then, when they'd got you suitably excited at the change in routine and the escape from rosters and reports, they would put you on a roadblock; not even a roadblock at the incident itself, but as far down the road as they could push you and still raise you by radio. Then just to make the torture more exquisite they'd insist you maintained radio silence.

It was a big Sherpa van, quite new-looking, ultramarine in colour with 'POLICE' lettered in white capitals on its side. Knight had Dick Forsyth for a driver, a constable who'd joined his eight-man team fresh and eager from his first four years of general duties, but whom Knight was slowly educating into an agreeably sour outlook on life.

The van was parked at an angle by a farm gateway, straddling the road so that nothing could get past. As Carson pulled in he could see that the windows were misted on the inside but that little wet patches had been cleared, streaky spyholes which gave the occupants a view of the road. After a couple of seconds the nearest door opened and a policeman climbed out, slamming it wearily behind him and trudging over towards the Mercédès. He was wearing a flat peaked cap and a bulky cold-weather jacket, over which he had a fluorescent orange jerkin. Carson wound his window down and looked out.

'Is there something wrong?' Carson called as Toby Knight walked around the car. Thunder rippled somewhere far off, somewhere on the other side of the mountains. A bunch of ragged crows lifted from the field beyond the wall and flapped off over the trees.

'Sorry, sir. The valley's closed off.' Knight was big and square-looking, an impression that was enhanced by the padded jacket. His eyes were pale blue and seemingly devoid of enthusiasm, and whilst his nose and cheeks were pinched and reddened by the October chill the rest of his face seemed drained of colour.

'For how long?'

'We can't say. Will you just turn your car around in that gateway over there and head back towards the main road, please?'

Carson glanced over to where Knight was pointing, following the gesture without really wanting to, and said,

'Wait a minute. At least tell me why.' There were a couple of sheep pressed up against the wooden bars, but they flinched and moved away as a second policeman stepped from the van.

'Ring the information centre in Penrith. We're not allowed to tell you anything.' Sounds good when we don't actually *know* anything, the sergeant thought.

'You're bouncing me back after a four-hour drive from London and you won't even give me a reason?'

'That's right.'

'London in four hours?' the second man said. He was shorter, younger, sharp-faced. 'You must have been over the limit. Get moving before we decide to do something about it.'

'But I've got to meet someone at the Jenner Clinic. Isn't there at least another road I can take?'

The pale-eyed man was unmoved. Beaded rain glistened on his jerkin, collected, ran. 'The valley's closed, I told you. Nobody goes in or out.'

'Look,' Forsyth, the younger driver, added. 'It may not be obvious to you, but we're getting pissed on out here. We've got better things to do than argue with every dummy who can't understand simple English.'

Carson hesitated for a moment and then stepped out on to the road, closing the door beside him. Now he was as exposed as they were although he wasn't as well protected, and Knight was giving him a narrow sideways look that said *you're out after trouble, aren't you, smart-arse?*

'All I want to know,' Carson said, trying not to shiver and to sound reasonable, 'is why you won't let me drive to the Jenner Clinic.'

'It's not the clinic,' Knight explained with all the patience of a man wheeling home a broken bicycle, 'it's the whole valley – the village, the farms and everything. You want to know any more than that, I've told you what to do.'

'I know. Ring some number and get a recorded message that won't tell me anything either. I was elbowed off the road a couple of miles back by a line of your wagons tearing past as if they'd forgotten what their brakes were for.'

'So make a complaint,' the sharp-faced one said.

'I don't want to make a complaint, I want to get to the clinic.'

'Well, you can't.'

There was a honk from back up the road, and all three turned to look. There was another car drawing in, not a police vehicle but a big, comfortable-looking family motor that was just out of its best days and starting the five-year slide to the scrapyard. The brakes squealed as it stopped.

'I'll see to it,' Knight said, and moved off. As he went he looked towards Forsyth and gave a sharp sideways nod in Carson's direction, the meaning of which was obvious; get rid of him.

Forsyth watched his sergeant walk away, and then he turned to Carson. He put a hand on the Mercédès' hardtop and leaned in close. His breath smelled of mint, and little rivers trickled off his shoulders.

'Right,' he said. 'You've been as difficult as you're going to be. Either you turn this car around or I have you booked.'

'On what charge?'

'I'll think of something later.'

The side-window on the second car was down, and the driver was looking out. 'The valley's closed,' Toby Knight was starting to recite as he approached. 'You'll have to . . .' Knight hesitated. Detective Inspector Mike Schaffer was looking at him, eyebrows raised in enquiry. 'Oh. Sorry, sir.'

'It's all right,' Schaffer said. The car was his own. He'd had to sell his battered old Spitfire to get something that was more suitable for a young family. He hated it. 'Stoneley got me on the telephone an hour ago and told me every car was out.'

'I'll let you through as soon as we get this difficult bastard out of the way.'

Schaffer glanced across towards the Difficult Bastard. His eyes lingered for a moment on the Mercédès, silver-grey and sleek, and he felt an ill-repressed twinge of envy. The

Difficult Bastard didn't seem to be putting up any great resistance; he was simply listening to Constable Forsyth and trying to pull the collar of his inadequate raincoat tight around his chest. Forsyth's eyes had narrowed down and he was reinforcing his points by stabbing at the air with his forefinger just a couple of inches in front of the other man's breastbone. Tact in action. Toby Knight certainly knew how to train them.

'What's the problem?' Schaffer said.

'No problem, he just won't turn back. Dick Forsyth's having a go at him now.'

'Is he local?'

'Not with that motor. I'll bet he's driven all the way up from London just to get his tubes tied.'

That was doubtful. Vasectomies were almost a street-corner job these days, and few of the fertility clinics even bothered with them.

'He's asking about the Jenner place?' Schaffer said.

'We haven't told him anything. He saw a couple of the vans tear-arsing down the road to the village and got a bit suspicious, that's all.'

Schaffer nodded. 'What instructions has Stoneley given you about letting people through?'

'Nobody, he said.'

'He probably had other things on his mind. Might not be a good idea to let this one turn around if he suspects there's something going on.'

Toby Knight didn't give an opinion. When it came down to it, orders were orders and they weren't for an under-age Police College snot like Schaffer to mess around with. 'What do you want to do about him?' he said neutrally.

Schaffer opened his door and reached back for the zippered jacket that he'd slung over the passenger seat. 'I'll come over.'

Forsyth was saying that he wasn't going to argue, and that Carson was blocking the road, and Carson was pointing out that it wasn't *his* van taking up all the space, and then Schaffer came around zipping up his anorak and broke in smoothly.

'My name's Schaffer,' he said, 'I'm a Detective Inspector. You're asking about the Jenner Clinic, is that right?'

'I'm expected there.'

'Name?'

'Peter Carson.'

Schaffer looked him over. Shade under thirty, well-dressed but damp. He didn't seem to have the shuffling embarrassment that Schaffer might have expected of somebody who'd driven three hundred miles to play with himself into a bottle; besides which, he was alone.

'Were you going as a patient?' Schaffer asked.

'I'm supposed to be meeting a girl who's on the staff.'

That was more like it. Schaffer had heard that although the Jenner staff lived in, most of them kept rooms or flats in their home towns and spent their leave there. 'You mean a girl-friend?'

'Sort of,' Carson said uneasily, and Schaffer realised that there was nothing to be gained from half-hearted questions in the wind and the rain. The sky had darkened a little more even in the couple of minutes that they'd wasted.

'Right,' he said. 'Move your car over and let me through, and then follow me down to the village. Stay in sight of my mirror and don't try wandering off when we arrive.'

He started to walk away. Carson called after him, 'Are you going to tell me what's wrong?'

'Later,' Schaffer called without turning around.

Forsyth went to move the van and clear the road. Toby Knight caught up with Schaffer before he reached his car.

'What do you want us to do if we get another like him?' he asked.

Schaffer hesitated. He might have made trouble already, but he wanted to be safe. 'I'll try to find Stoneley when I reach Langstone, see what he's got in mind. If he wants to go on turning people away we'll have to come up with some kind of story, a quarantine or a secret exercise or something like that. Quarantine might be easiest with the clinic up on the hill.'

'We've only had a couple of delivery vans so far. Not what you'd call trouble.'

'It'll come,' Schaffer assured him. 'It's about the only thing we can be sure of.'

'I expect so,' the sergeant said, and then tried to approach the subject that was really concerning him. 'Sir . . .' The word tasted bitter for a man several years his junior.

'Yes?'

'Well . . . what *is* it? Have we got a major accident, or a crime, or what?'

'You probably know as much as me,' Schaffer told him, and despite the truth of the statement he still felt some guilt when he saw the ill-disguised disbelief in the older man's eyes. 'I got a call to say my leave was cancelled and to get myself over here, and that was it.'

'Let us know, won't you?'

He smiled. It felt hollow. 'Of course I will.'

Carson started up the Mercédès and made a tight, slow turn to put the car's flat nose into the bay before the gateway. This gave enough room for Schaffer to crawl past, head out of the window and watching his flank. When the two cars had fallen into file and driven off, Forsyth swung the van out to block the road again. Then he cut the engine and watched as his companion walked back through the drizzle and climbed into the passenger seat. The van bucked on its springs as he got settled.

'What did he tell you?' Forsyth asked.

Toby Knight removed his uniform cap and grimaced with disgust as he wiped the rain from his face with a damp handkerchief. 'Nothing. He's pretending he doesn't know any more than we do.'

'The lousy sod.' Dick Forsyth looked down the road after the two cars, but they were out of sight and the rainwater had already seeped into the tracks left by their tyres. 'They'll tell that flash bastard in the fancy car before they'll tell us anything.'

Over on the Penrith side, something moved in the road.

Forsyth switched on the ignition and flicked on the windscreen wipers. The heavy-duty blades swept lazily across and licked the screen clear for a moment but it had gone, probably bounded into the bushes at the roadside. He cut the ignition, and the blower fans and the little coloured telltales on the dashboard all died.

The next driver along the road would be in for a hard time.

Chapter 2

Jerry Crichton had started his career with the Cumbria Constabulary's Eastern Division based at Kendal. He was obviously, in the morose vocabulary of Toby Knight, liked; within six years of service he'd got exactly what he wanted, transfer to a one-man station and the freedom (more or less) to set up his own working schedule. For some it would have been a damnation; farmers' squabbles and trespassers, tourist hassles and firearm certificates, long hours in winter snow closing off routes or setting up searches — but not for Jerry Crichton. He lived in a pebble-dashed house in Ravens' Bridge at the tip of the lake and the head of the Langstone road, a house that was lodgings and station combined. It was on a quiet lane behind the church and there were open fields from whichever window you looked. He had a wife, a small daughter and a white police Minivan. He also had area responsibility for four villages. Langstone was one of them.

Today, Langstone was in chaos.

It was a ribbon of a place, no more than three or four hundred yards from end to end, and fully a third of it was the Langstone Hotel. The hotel was a two-storeyed grey slate building, long and dignified and knitted over with ivy. In the middle of the frontage was a porch with a bay window above it, and fastened to the wall by the bay was a black wooden sign with the hotel's name in gothic. Directly opposite the hotel was the schoolhouse, a one-storeyed, L-shaped building which was big enough for only three rooms, a cloakroom and a classroom and the schoolmaster's office. Next to that was the old concrete and wood structure of the village meeting hall; opened in 1913 and disused since 1962, its windows were boarded and its single door nailed up. The two buildings sheltered Langstone's only telephone box in the angle of the schoolhouse walls, beyond them there was only a short terrace of uneven cottages and the slightly larger block of Hamilton's Store, and then it was back to the open road and the climbing valley.

There were no pavements, as such. The three incident caravans filled the car park at the side of the hotel, and the assortment of Sherpa vans and Minis and Rovers that had descended on the village shortly after dawn had to be parked wherever they would fit. Some had been squeezed into the protected angles behind bays and porches where they didn't block the main – the *only* – route through the village, but most of them were in an uneven line down one side of the road beyond the end of the houses.

Keeping the route clear was the job that had been given to Jerry Crichton. It could have been anybody, but the sergeant had mumbled something about local knowledge before running off to leap for the open tail doors of a moving van, which was taking men and plastic sheeting and ropes to the Jenner Clinic. There were almost eighty men around the village, and most of them were engaged in labour shifts to cover the exposed parts of the clinic's burnt-out shell against the weather. There was a constant van shuttle, bringing exhausted men down the track road and dropping them outside the hotel and then reloading with another force that was hardly any more spirited. There was another shuttle as well, a blue Rover which carried one-way loads. Polyurethane bags, man-sized and full.

The drains had become blocked with dead leaves, making the street into a shallow river that ran fast with the rattling expectorant of downspouts and gutters. Vehicles cut it up into white plumes as they passed through, leaving eddies and ripples that bobbed around in confusion until the slope of the valley got hold of them again.

When Schaffer's car appeared and crawled into the village, Jerry Crichton wondered if the valley roadblock had somehow broken down; as far as he knew the forensic specialists that Stoneley had requested shouldn't be arriving for a few hours, but then, as he signalled a stop and waded across in a crackling of oilskins, Schaffer was holding up his warrant card.

'Where's Stoneley?' he said without preamble.

Crichton thought he'd seen the chief hopping out of the Rover on its last delivery. 'He just got down from the clinic, I think.'

'Isn't he setting up an incident room?'

'Not up there. Not enough room. He's having as much of the clinic as he can manage covered and roped off. There isn't even space to hook up a trailer.'

'Where, then?'

Crichton pointed, and rain sluiced off the arm of his waterproof. 'The schoolroom, that place opposite the hotel. It was the only place big enough to hold all the bodies.'

'Any survivors?'

'None at all, as far as we can tell.'

Schaffer checked his mirror. Carson was behind him, drawing in slowly. He said to Crichton, 'You see the silver Mercédès that followed me in?'

'I can hardly miss it,' Crichton said. There was a mixture of appreciation and envy in his voice that Schaffer could recognise. The car was like a ray of light from another life altogether; it disturbed, dissatisfied.

'He turned up at the roadblock wanting to go to the Jenner Clinic. Put him somewhere so he can't see what's going on, and don't tell him anything. I'll come and find out where he fits in as soon as I get the chance.'

Crichton mused for a moment. 'Back room in the hotel be all right? It's all there is, really.'

'It'll do. But keep an eye open to make sure he doesn't do any wandering around, asking questions.'

Jerry Crichton nodded and took a couple of splashing steps back, and pointed up the road to where the line of vans ended. He was apologetic, but there was nowhere nearer the centre that Schaffer could park. As the saloon moved off, Crichton turned and walked to the Mercédès.

'Back room in the hotel' turned out to be an empty dining-room off the main lobby. It was actually at the front of the building, but any view was effectively blocked by the vehicles that were parked outside the windows.

The room was all dark wood and embossed wallpaper. There was a large fireplace on the far wall, with a dusty embroidered firescreen in the grate and a set of cast-iron pokers and tongs laid neatly in the hearth. There were dining tables – too many of them for the size of the room – laid with crisp, heavy linen that showed no more than a few discreet darns. The silverware was similarly ponderous and was scratched with a generation of hairline scuffs. The overall effect was of a mellowing of bad taste which had, over a hundred years or so, become country chic.

The room was cold, in spite of the radiators. Carson put a hand on one of them; it was vibrating slightly, no more than lukewarm.

The Sherpa van outside one of the windows started up without warning. As it moved away a little more light entered the gloom, but not much. Out in the road a couple of dark shapes flashed past, heads down and running, and then a few seconds later there was the sound of a scramble in the lobby as the two policemen fell in through the open vestibule, past the hand-lettered sign that said *no boots or rucksacks*. The hotel's owner, it seemed, was keeping up a constant supply of coffee, soup and sandwiches, and Carson could sense the life elsewhere in the building; desperate, rushed activity in the kitchens, babble in the sitting-room across the lobby, a dead stillness in the bedrooms above.

There was a Lake Steamer timetable on the sideboard. Carson wandered over and read it, not because he was interested – it was out of date, anyway – but because it gave him something to do. He felt the frustration of non-involvement, of incomprehension, but he seemed to have no choice other than to wait for Schaffer to come back for him. The muffled extracts of conversation that he caught from passing men on the other side of the dining-room door did nothing to help.

He pulled out a chair from one of the tables. The linen cloth whispered across the seat and then flapped down and hung without swaying. He sat and waited.

Schaffer stood aside in the school cloakroom to let two men pass. They were carrying one of the dark grey polyurethane meat sacks on a stretcher, and they were having difficulty with the narrow doorways and tight angles. The sack's contents were shapeless, inert, somehow less than human. A sergeant came close behind the stretcher bearers; he was carrying a file box filled with forms and log sheets, and he led Schaffer through to the office which had been converted for Stoneley's use.

Stoneley was on the telephone but the door was half-open, so Schaffer walked in. Stoneley seemed to be doing more listening than speaking – unusual – and he looked up at the young D.I. After a few seconds Schaffer became un-comfortable under the stare, but Stoneley didn't look away. Schaffer knew that Stoneley's mind was being devoted entirely to the caller on the other end of the line, but he wished that he would lower his eyes, draw back from the brink of recognition until he had attention to spare.

Two W.P.C.s came in carrying ring-files of procedure notes. Neither of them, Schaffer noted with mixed gratitude and disappointment, was Ellen O'Brien. The girl was barely nineteen, still technically in recruit training, and Schaffer did his best to avoid her wherever he could; her effects on his nervous system were severe and seemingly beyond intel-lectual control, effortless and beguiling as they were.

There was a battered old table by the door of the office, and the W.P.C.s added their binders to a number of others that had been stacked on it. Underneath the table there was an untidy heap of papers, exercise books and dog-eared hymnbooks, obviously the result of a peremptory clearing of the schoolmaster's effects to make way for the police incident set-up. It seemed that the place had only recently been cleared of children, and their characteristic damp, sour smell still hung in the air.

Stoneley ended his call and cradled the telephone as the W.P.C.s were leaving. 'It's about time,' he said to Schaffer without any welcome or greeting. 'Where the hell have you been?'

'Don't jump on *me*,' Schaffer said defensively. 'I've been on leave.'

'No leave for anybody until this one's been cleared up. What've you been told?'

Schaffer took hold of the office's only other chair and brought it around to the desk. 'Only about a fire and multiple deaths at the Jenner Clinic. No details.'

Stoneley frowned, trying to fish some unidentifiable gobbet of information from his memory. 'Was it you that was asked to start the enquiry about staff records with the D.H.S.S.?'

'Must have been somebody else.'

'Christ, I hope so. Until we get that information we won't know if we've got a full body count or not.'

'How many?'

'Ten, all told. We think we're still one short, but we can't be sure.'

'And how did it happen?'

Stoneley snorted and shook his head. There was no amusement, just bitter frustration turning under the surface. 'I'm waiting for the report from the fire people, but there are problems with the rain. We can't get enough plastic sheets together to cover the entire site, and the ones we've got won't stay down in the wind. We know that the buildings went up just before dawn and that at least half of the place was well alight by the time anybody arrived.'

'But how come nobody got out?'

Stoneley started to answer, but then the telephone rang. He

scooped the receiver to his ear and listened for a moment, then he sighed and cut in to tell the caller that he'd put them back to the exchange for rerouting to the information centre. He jiggled the cradle a few times and slammed the phone down without waiting to see if the doubtful procedure had worked. Schaffer repeated his question.

'Nobody got out because, as far as we can see, they were nearly all killed in their beds. Somebody crept from room to room with a big kitchen knife and slit their throats, so anybody who wasn't actually dead was at least too cut up to crawl away before the gas tank blew. Six of the bodies had been dragged out and heaped in the courtyard, the other four got burnt up inside – looks like our ripper was as surprised as anybody when the fireworks went off.'

'Couldn't he be one of the four?'

'Nothing so simple. One girl had the strength to drag herself away. She got out of the yard and into a field, but our friend went after her to finish her off. I reckon that's what he was doing when the roof went up.'

'You don't think the fire was deliberate?'

'No – not to destroy the place, anyway, not straight away. He was taking his time, so he didn't think he was in any danger. At least one of the victims was awake when he or she was attacked. We don't know which because the body's so burned, but we're thinking it could have been Jenner himself, working late in a little office on the ground level. Maybe there was a struggle. Maybe they smashed a light or kicked over a paraffin heater – we just don't know. The gas tank was right next door, one of those big propane jobs. It had just been topped up ready for winter.'

Schaffer asked about identification, and Stoneley said, 'Impossible, so far. They were all in night things – at least, the ones that had been dragged out were. Until we can sort out who's who we can't even tell who it is that's missing.'

'You reckon it was one of the staff rather than an outsider? A patient, say?'

Stoneley shrugged, and shook his head. Jenner's main

consultancy was in a Carlisle hospital, and the remote valley clinic was not really a clinic in the conventional sense, but more a laboratory backup where eggs were sorted and graded and generally manipulated under supervised conditions. Maybe Jenner had the occasional dissatisfied customer, but the idea didn't ring any alarm bells for Stoneley.

'So who,' Schaffer said, 'would want to wipe out the entire staff and blow the place up?'

'That's what I intend to find out. I'd be considerably helped if *my* staff would turn up and get stuck in when they're called.'

'The message didn't reach me until late. A couple more hours and it wouldn't have reached me at all.'

'Don't get resentful, Mike,' Stoneley said, changing his tactics. 'I need you.'

Schaffer knew better than to be taken in. 'I'm not resentful, but I don't like . . .'

'I know, I'm sorry. But I've got the Chief Constable breathing down my neck and it was the worst possible time to be without my Scenes of Crime officer. I've had to handle the incident procedure myself, and I'm not very good at the fine detail.'

'What's the Chief after?'

Stoneley settled back in the schoolmaster's chair, as if he were half-entertaining the thought of putting his feet up on the desk. 'I don't know,' he said. 'Somebody's squeezing his, so he's squeezing mine. If you'll take over the set-up of the incident room I can concentrate on fending off all the political interference. He's talking about bringing someone in.'

'Thank him for his confidence,' Schaffer said drily. 'We can handle it.'

'There's some specialist in explosions coming up from Woolwich, I don't mind that. But if he thinks he can bring in a team of Yard men just so that he can claim the costs back off the Home Office, well, he can piss off.'

'He couldn't justify it. Not so early on.'

'He might try,' Stoneley said. It was common knowledge

that the Chief Constable was looking for a post down south somewhere. Stoneley considered that one of the requirements of survival in his job was to keep some kind of track of the ideas and intentions of the force's administrators. To this end he occasionally went around the offices after hours and collected the discarded shorthand pads from the secretaries' waste baskets. An accomplice in the typing pool later made a translation for him.

Schaffer said, 'You'd think it would be more to his credit to keep as much prestige as possible for his own force.'

'God only knows how his tiny mind works. Look, I'll hand all this over to you and then I've got to call him.'

Schaffer looked around the room. He didn't see much that was worth handing over; a stack of boxes of forms, ring-files, loose papers, system cards, a display board on its side. Presumably the Ladybird books in the glass-fronted case belonged to the school and not the constabulary.

'I collected somebody at the roadblock,' he said. 'Supposed to be coming to see some girl at the clinic.'

'Is he local?' Stoneley asked with interest.

'London. Name of Peter Carson.'

'We'd better have a look at him, then.'

'Can I change the orders to the men on the roadblock? So far they've been turning everybody away.'

'Oh Christ, yes.' Stoneley winced at his own forgetfulness. 'I meant to give them some clearer instructions as soon as they were set up, but then I had to go on to the clinic site and I clean forgot.'

Schaffer stood up, pushing the chair back. It seemed to have been designed for discomfort, like all the school equipment of his youth. 'I'll get a message over to the hotel to have him brought. Then you can tell me what kind of stage we're at.'

'That won't take long. We've sealed off the whole valley and put men with binoculars on the ridgetops. No cars were seen going out after the explosion, so there's a chance that our stab-happy friend's lying low and looking for a chance to run.

Most of the effort now's going into an intensive site survey.'

'We'd better make the most of it while we can. Once the press get hold of this, the valley will be crawling.'

'That's why the press aren't going to be told. I managed to get my hands on the local stringer and promised him the earth if only he'll keep his trap shut.'

'Will it work?'

'Course it will. Name's Hamilton, runs the village store. I'm letting him wander around the hotel, but I've warned everyone to tell him nothing.'

'Right.' Schaffer moved to the door. There was a dusty old religious print on the wall by the frame. *Light of the World*, Holman Hunt. 'I'll have this Carson sent over to you, and then I'll call the roadblock. Got any preference on the line we spin?'

Stoneley had lifted the telephone receiver and was dialling. It was an old handset and the dial moved loosely. 'Make it general,' he said. 'We could leave ourselves open to all kinds of criticism if we don't.'

'Okay.' Schaffer moved out to look for some unfortunate of lower rank than himself to send across to the hotel. Some incorrigible devil in a quiet corner of his mind was wondering if Ellen O'Brien would be anywhere around. You ought to be ashamed, he told it, and you with a family. Yeah, grinned the devil, and continued to look around eagerly.

Chapter 3

Carson had become familiar with every pattern on every plate propped on the rail that ran around the dining-room above the height of the doors and windows. At one time they had all been very cheap and they were still very ugly. Most had been broken and, unfortunately, repaired.

He was not only bored, he was cold, and as he sat alone he had the uneasy feeling of being surrounded by ghosts at every table. It was as if the fabric of the place had absorbed the spectres of countless middle-aged couples sitting without conversation at afternoon tea, their children gone, unwilling or unable to learn to live for themselves again, shades that drifted through chintzy cafés and tea gardens in a winding spiral to the grave. When he looked around him sharply the tables were, of course, empty; but when he looked away he could sense that the shades were filtering back, watching him, willing their misery on to him.

In the street outside and the valley beyond, the rain was dying. The thick layers of cloud were breaking and tearing as their energies were spent and they withdrew and regathered for the next attack. Where the weaknesses were greatest pale shafts of light speared down, crisp and distinct against the grey. Nothing bright and nothing gaudy, but the dull and washed-out sketch beyond the window began to fill out and assume a semblance of three dimensions. Drizzle still spattered on the glass, but it was peevish and insincere.

He wandered over to the door and turned his head slightly to listen. The same maddeningly incomprehensible sounds of conversation muffled by layers of wood and plaster, but nothing close by. He didn't think they'd locked him in; there was a keyhole in the door but there was a build-up of gloss paint around it. The lock mechanism was probably a mass of fluff and oil. Carson gripped the doorknob and tried a little pressure; it moved, not easily, but it moved. Encouraged, he gave it a full quarter-turn and felt the door come free. He let it swing in just a couple of inches.

He waited for a moment, listening to the lobby just outside.

Nothing.

Made bold by the silence, he opened the door and stepped out.

Jerry Crichton was staring at him from a chair on the other side of the lobby. He was still wearing his oilskins but his uniform cap with its waterproof nylon cover was on the floor beside him, leaving his hair plastered in damp spikes on his forehead. His hands were wrapped around a half-pint mug of tea and he was leaning forward with his elbows on his knees.

'Where do you think you're going?' he demanded.

'I thought you'd forgotten me,' Carson said lamely.

'No chance. Back in the dining-room.'

'Am I under arrest?'

Crichton continued to stare, his face giving nothing away. 'You're being difficult again,' he said.

'I think I've been more than reasonable. Is somebody dead?'

'Now why,' Crichton said softly, 'should you want to say a thing like that?'

'Forget it. I'll go back in the dining-room.'

Four or five minutes later he heard the chair creak and footsteps move towards the back of the hotel and the kitchens. A few seconds after this they were recrossing the lobby, hollow thuds on thin carpet, and then they stopped abruptly and Crichton's figure passed outside the window. Carson moved to the glass to watch him; he felt that he had a vested interest in Jerry Crichton because besides him there was only an absent C.I.D. man who knew of Carson's presence in the village.

There was a car in the road, a Ford Estate, and there was a constable bending and talking to the driver, who couldn't be seen from where Carson was. Crichton joined him and they exchanged a few words, and then the other constable nodded and set off for the schoolhouse. Crichton was talking to the driver and pointing down the road, and then he stepped back as the Ford started to move off.

Crichton walked out of line with the window, out of shot, and Carson felt cheated; the stupefying ennui of his enforced wait had breathed fascination into the simplest drama. He was again forgotten and ignored, but forbidden to leave. He returned to his table and tugged idly at the fraying edge of the cloth.

After a couple of minutes he heard Crichton's voice in the lobby with another, pitched slightly higher and more insistent. The noise tracked along the wall and suddenly erupted into the room as the door was thrown open. 'In there and please don't argue, Mister Forester,' Crichton said firmly. 'You'll be called later.'

'Don't believe him,' Carson called out sourly, 'it's a trick.'

Jerry Crichton ignored him, and Forester only gave him a quick glance. He was slightly under average height and in his mid-thirties with close-cut, dark curly hair. He was wearing a grey mountain jacket and he wasn't being as co-operative as Crichton would have liked.

'For the last time,' he said, 'will you tell me what's happened at the clinic?'

Crichton was backing away, counting it a victory to have hustled him over the threshold. 'I told you,' he said, pulling the door closed, 'It's no use asking me.'

Slam. Click. Forester looked helplessly at the door, momentarily lost. Carson said, 'He's right.'

Forester turned sharply. His eyes were dark, so dark they seemed like twin black points. 'Have you got anything to do with this?' he said.

Carson shook his head. 'Not me. I only made the mistake of trying to drive around in a free country.'

'Have you been up there? Do you know what's happened?'

'I know as much as you. I was stopped at the roadblock on

41

the valley road and diverted in here. All I've really been able to see is that, whatever's happened, it's big.'

Forester's aggression loosened off a notch, and he seemed slightly dazed as he looked around the dining-room and saw it for the first time. 'I tried to telephone from Carlisle this morning, but the call was intercepted.'

'You tried to call the Jenner Clinic?'

'That's right.'

'And what did they tell you?'

'Now, wait a minute.' The dazed look was gone, and Forester had switched back to *danger*. 'Is this some way of getting answers out of me?'

'Of course not. It's just that I was trying to reach the clinic as well before they stopped me.'

Again Forester relaxed, again not much. 'Jenner didn't show up at the hospital,' he said. 'He's a consultant there, private. We were waiting for an appointment. Then the hospital cancelled without explanation and I wanted to find out why.'

'So you called and couldn't get through?'

'I got the exchange instead, some recorded message.'

Carson said, 'There was nothing wrong with the lines last night.'

'You were able to get a call in?'

'No, but my . . . my girl-friend' (use the word and worry about the niceties of definition later) 'got one out. That's why I came up.'

'Was that it? Why did she phone you?'

'She asked me to come up. She said it was important.'

'Is that all?' Forester sounded disappointed.

'That's all.'

Another shape outside the window, somebody jogging from schoolhouse to hotel. 'There wasn't any hint or clue . . .' Forester began, but Carson cut in firmly.

'Nothing. I'm sure there was nothing wrong at the time – she wasn't upset or disturbed or anything.'

Forester thought about it for a moment, then turned and

walked over towards the window, nodding to himself as he went. 'So whatever's happened, it was either late last night or this morning.'

'It may not be the clinic. It may be something else altogether.'

Forester stopped and looked at him, hard. 'Do you believe that?'

'Not really,' Carson admitted.

'Well, aren't you worried?'

'I suppose I am.'

Forester obviously didn't know what to make of him. 'Jesus,' he said, 'you're an icy bastard. I've got a child up in that clinic and I'm nearly crawling up the wall!'

'I'm saving my energies, that's all. I'm waiting until I find out the facts.'

Forester hesitated a moment longer, trying to make some sense out of Carson's attitude, and then he put it out of his mind and made for the door. 'Wait all you like,' he said. 'I'm going to get hold of somebody and find out for myself.'

The door was already open, and Jerry Crichton was blocking his way. 'I told you to stay until you were called,' he said.

'I'm going up to the Jenner Clinic,' Forester told him stubbornly.

'You're not going to any clinic, you're not leaving this hotel, you're not even leaving this *room* until I say so.'

'What makes you think you can make that stick?'

'Try arguing after I've handcuffed you to the radiator. Just in case you hadn't noticed, we're bang in the middle of an emergency here.'

Carson added, 'No use asking him, anyway. He only directs the traffic.'

Crichton came to bear on Carson who was leaning on the sideboard, his face a blank. 'And as for you,' Crichton said, 'you follow me.'

'You mean somebody's going to talk to me?' Carson said, slightly overdoing the innocent wonder.

'Stoneley's going to listen to you.'

'Who's Stoneley?' Forester wanted to know.

'Detective Superintendent. Don't try being funny with him, Carson.'

'I want to see him,' Forester insisted promptly.

'Wait your turn. This comedian's first in line.'

Crichton led the way across to the schoolhouse and Carson tried to look around as he followed, but really there was nothing to see. The rain had slackened to nothing more than a fine windblown mist.

The slate walls of the school were similar to those of the hotel, irregular blocks that had been fitted together and then planed to present a flat outer surface. The stone gleamed wetly in the brightening afternoon as Crichton and Carson went up a couple of steps behind a railing and then turned through the doorway into the school's cloakroom.

Everything seemed to be scaled-down. Slatted benches designed for elves, rails and coathooks no higher than four feet above the muddy floor; and then, spread and scattered around, the incongruously huge muddy galoshes and fluorescent rainwear of the police.

There was another door at the other end of the cloakroom. It had been chipped and battered and repainted often, and the frosted glass panels in its upper half bore the peeling remains of vinyl stickers of cartoon characters. Crichton led the way through into the one large high-beamed room that served for assembly and teaching and wet-weather play. Most of the room was screened off by a makeshift corridor that had been formed by free-standing partitions and which led to the door of the schoolmaster's office. The partitions also served as display boards for the children's crayon drawings, little blue strips of sea and sky, leaning houses, grinning misshapen heads. Beyond them Carson could hear the stiff rustle of plastic and the sound of men lifting something heavy.

Jerry Crichton tapped at the office door, and Carson turned as he heard footsteps on the bare wooden boards behind him.

44

It was the C.I.D. man, Schaffer. Crichton said, 'This way,' and Carson stepped through into the office.

Stonely was half-way through dialling a number on the telephone. He was using the flat end of a pencil and had paused with it in mid-air as he waited to find out the reason for the interruption. Carson saw a shandy-haired man in middle age, medium height and stocky, who spent money on his suits but ruined the effect with a lousy taste in ties.

'Who the hell's this?' Stoneley said.

'Carson from London, sir,' Crichton told him. 'You said you wanted to see him.'

The confusion on Stoneley's face cleared and he put the receiver down, number uncompleted. 'Have a seat,' he said, and indicated the chair across the desk. As Carson was sitting down Schaffer caught Jerry Crichton's arm in the doorway and asked in a low voice if the constable could find him another chair from somewhere.

Stoneley pulled a notepad across the desk and turned to a clean page. 'You were on your way to the Jenner Clinic, isn't that right?'

'Yes,' Carson told him. 'Doesn't look like I'm going to get there, though.'

'Who were you going to see?'

'A girl called Tracy Pickford. She's a lab assistant.'

Another tap at the door. Schaffer reached to answer and Stoneley said, 'Have you known this Pickford girl for long?'

Jerry Crichton was just outside in the makeshift corridor. He was apologetically offering a chair that was yellow-varnished and flecked with poster paints. It was about the size of a toadstool. Schaffer shook his head wearily and closed the door, and then he folded his arms and leaned on the wall by *The Light of the World*.

'I hardly knew her at all,' Carson was saying. 'We met a few weeks ago when she was in London. We went out a couple of times.'

'Is that when you arranged this visit?'

45

'We didn't arrange anything. I came because she telephoned me last night and asked me to.'

The atmosphere of the interview began to shift and change. It was no longer a perfunctory questioning, there was real interest.

'Last night!' Schaffer said from by the door. 'What time?'

'About nine.'

Stoneley tapped the desktop with his pencil. 'Wait a minute. A girl you hardly know rings up and asks you to drive half-way across the country at a few hours' notice, and you drop everything and run? That doesn't add up, Carson.'

Carson shrugged. It had seemed reasonable to him – well, almost. 'It's what happened.'

'What reason did she give you?' Schaffer asked.

'None. She said she'd explain when I arrived.'

'Didn't she at least give you some sort of idea?'

'She said I might find it useful, that's all.'

Schaffer detached himself from the wall and moved around to perch on a corner of the desk. 'Useful in what way?' he said as he pushed some papers and a small loose-leaf calendar aside.

'I don't know.'

'What about your job?' Stoneley said.

'I don't have one.' And then, seeing an instant flaring of suspicious doubt in their eyes, 'What I mean is, I work for myself.'

'Doing what?'

'I write articles for magazines, and send them to my agent. Sometimes she sells them, sometimes she doesn't.'

Schaffer wasn't wholly convinced. 'And out of that you make enough to live in London and run an expensive car?'

'I hardly make anything out of it. My main income's from money my father left me.'

'I want to get back to the Pickford girl,' Stoneley said, and Schaffer relaxed a little. 'You met her in London – what was she doing there?'

Carson said firmly, 'Before we go any further, how about

giving me some idea about why I'm here? Am I suspected of something?'

'Start being obstructive,' Stoneley told him, 'and you might give us a reason.'

'In that case I want to call a solicitor.'

'All right, Carson,' Stoneley sighed, 'you're not suspected of anything. Now will you answer the question?'

'When you've told me why I can't go up to the Jenner Clinic.'

Stoneley's patience was down to tissue-thin. 'Because your girl-friend's dead and the Jenner Clinic's in ruins, that's why.'

Carson sat in silence for a moment. He knew they were watching him, looking for his reaction. He had nothing to give them. 'Thanks for breaking it to me so gently,' he said.

'You asked for it, Carson,' Schaffer said quietly.

'Now,' Stoneley said, and the telephone rang. Schaffer promptly grabbed it before it could ring again and turned his body away slightly to screen the call. Stoneley went on, 'Tell us everything you know about the set-up here.'

'I know nothing about it.'

'She must have talked about her job.'

'I told you, I don't – *didn't* know her very well. I met her once at a party given by one of the editorial assistants on the *Observer* magazine, and then again by accident in a pub on the river. Then I took her to dinner once, we exchanged telephone numbers and I didn't hear from her until last night.'

'And you're telling me she never even mentioned the clinic?'

'She mentioned it, but not in detail. She seemed more interested in what I did – God knows why, because it sounded pretty dull even to me. I got the feeling she didn't really like me much, so I was surprised when she called.'

Schaffer was back with them. 'When she rang you, what did she say?'

'Only that it was important that I drive up, and that she'd explain when I arrived. Only she can't, now, can she?'

'We think there was one survivor,' Schaffer said carefully, 'but we can't be sure. I wouldn't want to hold out any hope.'

Carson asked, 'How did she die?'

Stoneley shook his head firmly. 'That's not for release.'

'Come off it,' Carson said, 'when the newspapers get on to this . . .'

'They won't. Not until we're ready, anyway. Chances are, whoever did it is lying low in the valley somewhere, and the last thing we want is eager beavers with cameras and notebooks scrambling around and blocking the one access road that we've got to the village.'

Carson glanced towards the door, remembering the jam of cars and vans in the street outside, and said, 'You've managed that job well enough yourselves.'

Stoneley was holding the pencil in both hands, flexing it lightly. He brought it up before him and extended a finger to point at Carson. 'And it goes for you, too, just in case you get any ideas about phoning the story out!'

'Don't worry,' Carson assured him, 'I never do newspaper work. But you are saying it was murder?'

Stoneley raised his eyebrows innocently. 'Did I say that?'

'You said that somebody did it.'

'I don't remember saying that.' He looked up at Schaffer. 'Do you remember it?'

'I think Carson must have misheard you, sir,' Schaffer supported formally.

'All right,' Carson said resignedly, 'I get it.'

There was another tapping on the door, and this time a young W.P.C. looked in timidly. Her hair was drawn back and she was clear-skinned and dark-eyed. For some reason Schaffer took an unusually close interest in the sequence of dates on the desk calendar.

Ellen O'Brien said, 'They're asking where do you want the radio to be set up, sir.'

Stoneley held his breath for a moment as he looked speculatively at the ceiling, then let it all out in a rush. 'In the main room,' he said. 'Tell them to shift all the books and crap out first.'

She smiled her thanks and started to back out, but Jerry Crichton was behind her. 'Super!' he called. 'Can you take a message in the radio car?'

'Where from?'

'It's from the roadblock.'

Stoneley pushed his chair back from the desk, and nodded towards Schaffer as he got up. 'Mike will see to it. I'm handing over the set-up to him. Get it, will you, Mike?'

'Sure.'

Carson was the only one sitting, the only one that wasn't suddenly going somewhere. The fresh page of Stoneley's notebook was still unmarked.

'Does this mean I can go?' Carson said.

'I want you to do us an identification first,' Stoneley said as he shuffled sideways around the desk, his back up against the Ladybird cabinet. 'Come with me.'

Schaffer went off to the radio car, Jerry Crichton went back to the road outside, and Carson didn't know where Ellen O'Brien went although he watched her going with interest.

Stoneley led the way out of the office and around the end of the partitions. The schoolroom was lit by fluorescent strips on the exposed A-frame beams overhead. A few shreds of coloured crêpe hung from the fittings, untidy remnants of Christmas parties and laughter. The room was being used as an emergency morgue.

All of the school's low desks had been pushed together to make trestles for the bodies. There was a long grey meat sack on each. The sacks were all the same size and shape, but the contents obviously weren't. They were lined together down one side of the room, ten in all, and at the foot of each there was a clear plastic bag with a tight seal on the top. The clear bags held watches and charred scraps of clothing.

One police officer and two civilians were attending to the bodies. The civilians wore rubber gloves and aprons. The three were at the far end of the line, looking over a clipboard;

Carson saw that there was a similar clipboard by each of the sacks. Most had names written in black fibretip print on the first sheet on the board, some had names and queries, a few had just the queries and nothing else. Stoneley was walking along the line, and Carson realised he was expected to follow. Fear and apprehension were crawling like twin parasites in his belly.

He forced himself to concentrate, to read the names on the clipboards as he passed. He wished he'd stayed in London.

Horsley, BD, M (Def)
Collison, R, M (Def)
Clarke, TP, F (?)
Noble, K, M (Def)
Noble, E, F (Def)
?
?
Jenner, B, M (?)
Wells, CA, F (?)
?

Stoneley came to a stop by *Wells, CA, F (?)*, and one of the civilians detached himself from the group and came over. He looked too cheerful and dignified to be dressed like a butcher; Carson supposed that he must be the pathologist. His hair was snowy white tinged with yellow, and his eyebrows were brushed out into little peaks. 'Excuse me if I don't shake hands,' he said.

'Might be able to knock off one of those question marks for you, Doctor,' Stoneley said. 'Mind if we take a peek?'

'By all means. I'll warn you, though, some of them aren't too pretty.' Carson's stomach tried to do a flip.

'Just the one,' Stoneley said, and pointed at the sack before him. Barry Lennox, the D.I. who had been assigned to work on identification of the various bodies, came over to watch.

'Lucky,' the doctor said, squeezing into the narrow gap between the desks. 'You haven't picked one of the messy ones.' He nodded towards *Jenner, B, M (?)*, the next one along.

'It'll have to be a dental job for him — assuming its a him. There isn't enough left to be sure.'

The pathologist bent to the meat sack, and started fiddling with the airtight plastic seam. His rubber gloves weren't the five-fingered condoms used in surgery, they were charnel-house thick. The little squeaking sounds they made probed Carson's ears delicately, like the tips of silver dividers. His heart rate was way up and he felt that his contact with the floor was little more than a memory. The doctor slit the seam down a foot or so of its length and peeled back the cover.

It wasn't as bad as he'd feared. In a way, that was worse. The pathologist had drawn the grey plastic back to her chin; Tracy Pickford lay quiet and composed, and the pale bluish cast of her skin lent her strong features a delicacy greater than that they'd possessed in life. There was no horror, no revulsion; nothing. There was nobody home. Nobody would ever be home again.

'That's Tracy,' Carson said.

Stoneley nodded and thanked the pathologist. Barry Lennox took a fibretip pen from his inside pocket and began to alter the information on the clipboard as Stoneley and Carson walked back down the row towards the partitions and the way out.

'You don't seem very affected,' Stoneley commented with a sideways glance at Carson.

'I wouldn't know how I'm supposed to seem. I'm not exactly dancing, am I?'

'You ever seen a body before?'

'Once,' Carson admitted.

'I suppose we forget,' Stoneley said, and they paused by the door of the office. 'It's something you have to live with.'

Carson wondered for a moment if Stoneley was making a joke, but then decided he wasn't. 'Yes,' he said, 'but I'd be careful about dragging that other guy in here.'

'What other guy?'

'Forester. He's at the hotel. He had a child at the clinic.'

'A child?' Stoneley said, completely mystified. 'We didn't find any children at all.'

'It's what he said.'

'There were no patients. The place was a back-up facility. Any patients would have been at the hospital in Carlisle.'

'I suppose,' Carson said, fishing for a contradiction that he hoped he wouldn't get, 'I may as well turn around and go home now.'

'Oh, no. Not yet. I want a statement off you and then I want you to hang around in case we have any more questions.'

'Where am I supposed to stay?'

Stoneley looked at him as he pushed open the office door. 'That hotel across the road,' he said. 'See if they can fit you in. You can afford it.'

Carson met Schaffer in the cloakroom. Schaffer seemed to be in a hurry, but Carson managed to block his way without it seeming obvious.

'What do I do about making a statement?' he asked. 'Stoneley said I should.'

'Find a W.P.C. over in the hotel,' Schaffer said, and pushed on past.

Stoneley was back at the desk when Schaffer found him, licking his thumb and turning over the pages of a pocket address book. Despite his insistence that he was handing over the incident set-up to his Scenes of Crime officer he showed no inclination to leave the office and the telephone.

'What took you so long?' he said.

'Reception problems in the radio car.'

'We'll do better when we've got a decent set-up in here.'

'What does the headmaster say about that?'

'I don't know,' Stoneley said. 'I threw him out.'

'And what about the kids from the school? They'll have to find somewhere else for them.'

There was noise outside, gasping and shuffling, and three uniformed men passed the open doorway laden with equipment and loops of cable. 'It's not my problem,' said Stoneley. 'There couldn't have been more than a dozen of them, and we need the space more. Anywhere's better than those godawful incident caravans.'

There was a clatter and a bang that echoed in the roof space above. A ladder had been raised, and two men climbed past the window with a length of timber and a collapsible aerial mast. Schaffer said, 'Something else has come up, anyway. That's what the message was about. Somebody's turned up at the roadblock, he's showing a very official-looking government pass and he seems to have a pretty detailed knowledge of what's going on here.'

Stoneley snapped the address book shut. 'Oh, no. I bet that creep from upstairs has tipped somebody off.'

'I had to say let him through, anyway.'

'He'll probably keep us tied up with questions for an hour. Then he'll say "keep me informed" and we'll never hear from him again. I can do without it.'

'Do you think he'll try to interfere?'

A tentative banging started on the roof above. Then it became more confident, more regular. Stoneley pocketed his address book and moved towards the door.

'He might try,' he said. 'I'm going to get out of the way before he arrives.'

'Well, thanks!' Schaffer said, but Stoneley was already half-way to the cloakroom.

'You can handle him, Mike,' he called over his shoulder, grabbing his anorak as he went. 'You're more diplomatic than I am.'

There was a car across the doorway, a black four-door saloon. It was spotless, and water had beaded on it in a way that suggested many deep layers of wax, lovingly applied and buffed. Wraiths of steam trailed from the bonnet, and a dark-uniformed chauffeur sat behind the wheel and stared through them as if reading stern omens.

The rear door on the near side was open. There was a small man standing by it.

'Which one of you is Detective Chief Superintendent Stoneley?' he said.

Schaffer pointed. 'He is,' he said promptly.

The small man ignored Schaffer and looked directly at Stoneley. 'Hennessy,' he said, 'Home Office. Is there somewhere we can talk?'

'Come into the school,' Stoneley said resignedly.

The radio men were in the office, so they stood in the cloakroom. Besides being small, Hennessy was the kind of fat man generally called 'portly'. He wore conventional dark-rimmed glasses and shaved all the way up to the tops of his ears. Stoneley disliked him on sight.

Hennessy didn't waste any time. 'Right,' he said. 'First, I want to know who gave those men on the roadblock instructions to say that the valley's under quarantine.'

'Now, just wait a minute,' Stoneley said. 'You may be Home Office, but you don't have any direct authority over me.'

'We'll see about that. The quarantine story is right out, you understand?'

'For what reason?'

'Because it's too damn sensitive in view of the work done at the Jenner Clinic, that's why.'

'I'll bear it in mind.'

'You'll follow it up and no arguments. There's more at stake here than your murder case.'

Stoneley heard the distant flutes and drums of interdepartmental politics, cresting a distant hill and marching straight towards him. 'Did our head man get in touch with you?' he said.

'No. I got in touch with him.'

'So how did you find out?'

'Your club-footed enquiry to Central Records set all the alarm bells ringing. There was a watching element in the D.H.S.S. cross-referencing programme, and as soon as you asked for staff records from the Jenner Clinic all hell was let loose.'

'Mind telling me why?'

'Yes, I would.'

Stoneley was getting ready to walk away. 'I'm sorry,' he said, 'but I've got a multiple killing to investigate and I can't waste time on internal wranglings.'

'*I'm* sorry,' Hennessy said with empty professional sincerity, and he called up a thin tight smile from the diplomat's manual to go with it. 'I didn't mean to come on so strong. I was sent to help you.'

'We don't need any help.'

'I'm afraid it's obvious that you do. That quarantine story, for one thing.'

'There's nothing wrong with the quarantine story, as long as it keeps people out and stops them asking questions.'

'That's exactly what it won't do. Have you any idea what went on at the Jenner Clinic?'

'Of course. Jenner made babies in bottles. You're not going to tell me that a fertility clinic is likely to spark off a plague scare.'

Hennessy gave a little head-shake of exasperation. 'Obviously it's no damn use trying to tell you anything. This was a *laboratory*, Stoneley. Start spreading a story like that, and before you know it every media yob in the country will come crawling in the hope of another Seveso. And you know what they're like – even if there isn't one they're liable to try to boost it up.'

'That's a new one on me. You make it sound like you could start an epidemic with a mucky book and a paper hankie.'

Hennessy looked around the swampy cloakroom, seemingly for somewhere to sit. *Those benches are about your height, shrimp,* Stoneley thought unkindly.

'Jenner didn't just hold a fertility licence,' Hennessy said. 'He had grants to practise basic genetic manipulation with human DNA. Now that's nothing in itself, because there are some DNA experiments you could conduct in the average kitchen with no danger at all. But if somebody gets the idea that Jenner's been doing something like combining human and viral tissue to create a pathogen with no known antidote – you see what I mean?'

Stoneley nodded in reluctant agreement. 'I'm sorry,' he said, 'but I wasn't to know.'

'It's essential that you tell those men on the roadblock to change their story. They wouldn't take the order from me.'

'I'll have Schaffer pass the message on. Perhaps we'll be better off telling the truth.'

'No,' Hennessy said quickly. 'Don't let out any more information than you have to. There's more in this than a straight murder case.'

Stoneley looked at him closely. 'Do you know something I don't?'

'It could be political, that's all,' Hennessy said evasively.

'I told you, that doesn't concern me.'

'It'll start concerning you fast if Kennedy and his genetic lobby in the States can find some angle to start putting pressure on Britain to wind up its fertility monopoly. They're only looking for the chance.'

'We've no reason to believe there's any connection.'

'There doesn't have to *be* a connection. Just give the Friends of the Earth something to work from and they'll take it from there. Then we'll have restraining orders and complaints of public mischief flying around, and the next thing we know, the science unions will be on our necks. Even if we get it all cleaned up in the end, we'll have lost international credibility.'

'All right,' Stoneley said, weakening a little at last under the incomprehensible barrage, 'so I'll accept your advice on public policy. But I'm not prepared to see you interfering with the investigation.'

'I hope it won't be necessary,' Hennessy said smoothly.

'Damn right it won't.'

'Can I see the site of the incident?'

Stoneley considered it for a moment. 'Are you going to push me for it?'

'Not if you don't want me to.'

'Then I don't mind. It's about time I checked to see if the

close search has turned anything up. You can come in my car.'

They re-emerged from the school, and Hennessy talked to his driver as Stoneley walked the hundred yards or so to the hotel car park where Schaffer was supervising the transfer of equipment from the incident caravans. The vans were due to be replaced, and one of them leaked. Stoneley climbed the three aluminium steps and put his head inside the nearest one. Schaffer was kneeling on the floor, trying to wrestle a typewriter into its cover.

'Mike,' Stoneley said, and Schaffer looked up.

'Yes?'

'Wasn't there somebody else to see me? Something about a kid?'

'That's right, Forester. You want to see him now?'

'Look after it for me, will you? I'm going up to the site with that fat dwarf.'

Schaffer stopped trying to force the desk-sized machine into its portable-sized case. 'What's going on?' he said quietly.

'Nothing, only what we thought. Seems they're frightened of losing foreign trade in the baby farms if the word comes out wrong.'

'Is that all?'

'Obviously it's enough to make the pen-pushers dance. As long as he keeps quiet he won't be any trouble.'

The black car had gone, and Hennessy waited for Stoneley by the telephone box outside the blind shell of the meeting hall. He was carrying a briefcase, and there was a light tan raincoat folded over his arm; the unwrinkled sheen of the fabric seemed to suggest that if ever it had to be used Hennessy would dispose of it and buy another. He was as conspicuous against the tough stone of the village and the open vastness of the valley as a hair on an egg.

Stoneley chose one of the blue Land-Rovers in preference to his own saloon. They drove past the cottages and the corner store and the line of empty vehicles which tailed out along the road, and after only a few hundred yards as the route started to curve out of sight they came to a side-road which climbed off to the left, its entrance almost disguised by rowan trees. There was a Sherpa van blocking the main road and a temporary barrier of plastic cones across the turning, but even as the Rover slowed a constable came forward and removed a couple of the cones and waved them through.

The road was steep and the close, moss-covered walls on either side indicated that it was an old farm track; but the asphalt was glossy-black and seamless, laid no more than half a dozen years or so before. Hennessy looked around in obvious discomfort as the valley began to open out and unroll around them.

Although the rain had stopped, small roadside culverts were still spouting with the pressure from wet earth banked behind the walls, flooding the weed-choked ruts that had been scooped out on either side of the tarmac. Hennessy said, 'Have you any idea exactly what happened?'

Stoneley changed down through the gears as the Rover's nose lifted. 'To be honest,' he said, 'not yet. Most of my inspectors have been going over the site. We've had it photographed from all angles and now we're collecting and tagging everything in the ruins to hand over to forensic for analysis. It could have been one person, or it could have been a gang. We're certain that the stabbings occurred before the explosion – the bodies that haven't been carbonised all show knife wounds from a big kitchen job about a foot long. The fact that it looks like the *same* knife in each case suggests an individual, but we don't know for sure. That's why we're very interested in the missing staff member, if there is one. We don't know for sure because we still haven't had a straight answer from the D.H.S.S.'

'There was a security hold on the information. There should have been eleven people working and living-in.'

'Well, we've got four men, four women and two bags of charcoal.'

'Then it's a woman you're looking for.'

Stoneley absorbed the information. 'Aren't we all?' he said dryly.

Hennessy twisted himself around in his seat and looked out through the square window in the Land-Rover's back door. Langstone was out of sight, and the dappled gun-metal surface of the lake was starting to rise into view.

'Bit of a distance from the village, isn't it? he said. 'Aren't you cutting yourself off with a base down there?'

'It's a choice of that or a couple of draughty old caravans right up at the site. Anyway, the less traffic we have up here, the less chance there is of something vital being disturbed. And the village is quiet enough at this time of the year.'

The Rover bounced queasily as the road dropped over the lip of an upland hollow, and the ruins of the Jenner Clinic lay ahead.

It was a converted farmhouse and outbuildings in the shape of an imperfect U, surrounding a central cobbled yard that was open towards the distant lake. The aged shells had been stripped out and rebuilt so that the complex was, in many ways, a modern forgery which preserved the outward appearance of the original; the lines of the walls, where they stood, were too clean and the windows – where they survived – were too large and regular. The left-hand building as they approached was burned and empty, the modern fittings and the renewed roof gone into ashes. The top of the wall had started to crumble into the courtyard, but most of it was upright and blackened. The entire layout, which included an untouched barn a hundred yards or so from the main buildings, spread across a depression where three flat planes of the fell angled together and gave shelter. There were a few trees outside the low containing wall that circled the farm, but beyond them the valley side stretched open and empty.

'Look at that view,' Stoneley said as he steered the Rover towards where a group of vans and a Fire Officer's white car were ranged in a field just off the road. 'Jenner must have had money to burn, to get a site like that.'

Hennessy wasn't impressed. 'He's welcome to it. As far as I'm concerned it can stay on the calendars.'

Stoneley glanced across. Hennessy's façade of confident self-assurance was far less substantial now, as if the open country were squeezing the potency out of it; Stoneley was somehow cheered by the sight, by the way that it gave him a sudden understanding of the source of an enemy's magic. 'You're not a countryman, then?' he said.

'Certainly not,' Hennessy said with feeling. 'All flies and tourists in summer, then the winter comes and it's blocked roads and frozen pipes. Give me the city any day.'

They pulled in through the open gateway and bumped and jarred across the ruts that had been left by turning traffic. The Rover chewed its way across the field without concern and swung about, nosing up to the boundary wall alongside a dirt-spattered Minivan and lurching abruptly as Stoneley hauled on the handbrake and locked the transmission so that Hennessy almost jerked forward off the hard seat.

Stoneley left Hennessy to pick his way delicately through the sodden turf in his town shoes, walking out of the field and up to the farmyard entrance. The tubular steel barred gate had been wedged back, but there was a rope barrier across the entrance. Stoneley ducked under it and went on into the courtyard.

There was debris strewn across the cobbles from where the upper storey of the left-hand wall had started to fold and crumble. Two vehicles, a Peugot Estate and a Toyota, had been parked in the yard, but now they were blackened and blistered and smashed almost unrecognisable by fallen rubble. Broken glass grated underfoot as Stoneley moved in for a closer look; inside the wing seemed to be nothing more than black charring, all the walls, all the beams, all the way up to the open sky. Some of the plastic sheeting that had been spread to cover the empty windowframes was still in place, but the rest had shifted and crept to leave bulging gaps open to the weather. Water was making hollow throttling noises in a broken gutter somewhere.

Most of his men were in the main part of the house, observing, noting, collecting. The upper storey of that section was all staff quarters, and the ground floor was taken up by a small common-room and Jenner's extensive private flat. There was smoke and soot damage, but about two-thirds of the fabric had survived the fire. The stables in the far wing were greyed and streaky but otherwise untouched.

He heard footsteps behind, and Hennessy came level. He was breathing heavily and perspiring after only a couple of hundred yards on a mild slope. In the wrecked wing a dark figure was picking its way through the ash and the detritus, moving carefully towards the light.

'Fire Officer,' Stoneley said and Hennessy, not yet able to speak, nodded.

The Fire Officer was Clive Lord of the County Fire Service. There was a silver Service crest on his peaked cap, but otherwise he was dressed for the rough; wellingtons with steel toecaps and ridged soles, heavy overtrousers and a dark pullover with leather reinforcement on the elbows and shoulders, thick gloves. He stepped through the charred doorway into the yard with obvious relief.

'Starting to get a picture yet?' Stoneley asked. He'd worked with Clive Lord before on a hotel fire and a tanker crash. Lord was fast and decisive in a crisis, slow and considered over the after-effects. He'd been poking around the wreck for more than three hours.

'Too early to be sure,' he said, 'but I think I can make a few guesses. Do you want them now, or do you want to wait for the report?'

'I'm lousy at waiting. Tell me now.'

Lord was pretty confident that the fire had been started on the ground floor, and that it had been deliberately set. There had been a short corridor that ran the length of the wing with a small laundry at one end and a utility room at the other. He counted off the rooms in between, pointing to the remains of now imaginary dividing walls; an office, some kind of changing room with metal lockers and a couple of steel sinks, a small tiled operating theatre with an elaborate jointed bed and a lot of electrical equipment, now burnt out to nothing; next to that some kind of recovery room, and beyond that the laundry. On the level directly above had been three separate lab facilities, each with an elaborate ventilation system, and above that in the attic space Lord guessed that there were more staff quarters.

'I've got the planning permission proposals down in the village,' Stoneley said. 'I could have told you all that.'

'Thanks a lot,' Lord said. 'Where were you two hours ago?'

He showed them the office. 'This is where I think it started.'

'How can you be sure?'

'I can't, not yet. But I think you'll find it's right. There are several pounds of paper ash on the floor. Paper has to be very loosely packed to achieve total burning. Tightly packed paper – like in files or ledgers – well, it chars all the way around but the centre pages are left untouched even in the worst fire. I'd say somebody ransacked the place and scattered all the records.'

'Just stick to the facts, Clive,' Stoneley said. 'Leave the detection to us.'

'It's how they proved arson in a factory in Leicester last year,' Lord added smugly.

'All right, so say it *was* ransacked. How do you know that's where the fire started?'

'Because that room was burning longer than all the rest. Protection in the building was generally good. They had internal fire doors, lots of extinguisher points, a good alarm system. For a while it hardly spread at all. A couple of men with extinguishers could have killed it.'

Unfortunately, nobody was in a fit state to handle a fire extinguisher when the fire started. Stoneley wanted to know how come it had suddenly escalated to swamp the whole wing in flame.

'Fireball,' Lord explained, and showed them the remains of the utility room. He pointed to a twisted and blackened pile of bricks and metal. 'That was the propane tank that fed the boiler and the heating system. The floor was concrete but looks like somebody had stacked a load of magazines and newspapers around the bottom of the cylinder. That isn't recommended. Anyway, it looks like they caught and started to heat the cylinder up and got the gas evaporating faster than the emergency relief valves could let the pressure escape. The cylinder ruptured and took off like a rocket, straight through the internal walls and up through the floor of the second storey. The rest of it's embedded in the wall at the far end of the wing. The engine from Ravens' Bridge arrived shortly after that and managed to stop the fire from taking over the rest of the buildings, but they heard the bang as they were coming up the hill and saw the fireball thrown about a hundred feet into the air. That got rid of most of the gas and they were able to get in close enough to use foam.'

Stoneley thanked him, and Lord promised him a written précis by the next morning with a more detailed analysis to follow. As the Fire Officer went off to his car, Stoneley, with Hennessy in tow, looked in on the detailed inspection of the main building, but he knew better than to stay around long and provide a distraction. He crossed the yard and stepped under the rope, walking briskly downhill towards the Rover.

'Listen,' Hennessy gasped, labouring to keep up and looking decidedly less cool and composed than he had on his arrival. 'I don't want to follow you around like a pet dog. You'd soon get tired of it and so would I.'

'I think we'll be able to manage without you,' Stoneley said graciously. He stopped by the wall opposite the gate to the impromptu car park and looked over; in the field beyond a line of more than twenty men was moving slowly across, each man giving all his attention to the ground in front of him. Occasionally the line would stop with a shout from one of the men, and the supervising detective would run along from the end of the line to check the importance of whatever had been found. After a minute the line would move on.

Hennessy said, 'Will you consult with me before you take any major steps of procedure?'

'No.'

'But . . .'

'I'm prepared to co-operate within limits, but that's asking too much.'

'I could insist,' Hennessy said gently.

'Insist away,' Stoneley said, unimpressed. 'It won't get you anywhere.'

'I thought I'd explained to you how delicate all this can be.'

'You did, and I'll bear it in mind. But this is a multiple murder, and I'm not prepared to hand over any of my judgement and professional responsibility to an untrained civil servant, no matter how delicate or political the issues may be.'

'I'm sorry, Stoneley,' Hennessy said, 'but I can't let it rest at that.'

'I'm sorry as well,' Stoneley told him, blandly insincere, 'but you'll have to.'

The late brightening of the afternoon was beginning to degenerate into dusk. A van-load of policemen passed Stoneley on their way back to Langstone as he walked back across the field to his Land-Rover. Hennessy stumbled after him.

Chapter 4

Carson had found a W.P.C. in the lounge of the Langstone Hotel, and had explained how he was to make a statement. The stocky blonde told him to wait in the lobby, and went off muttering dark things about Stoneley under her breath. She returned after a few minutes with a red folder and, walking a few paces behind and looking a little unsure of herself, the dark-eyed girl who had looked in during the interview in the schoolhouse. They went through into the empty bar and sat on high stools by the counter whilst Ellen O'Brien sat at a low table and listened; presumably observation of the procedure was part of her training programme. She hadn't yet learned to lose the self-awareness that prevented her from easing inconspicuously into the background – but no doubt it would soon come, when like those around her she would know the precise limits of her world and discard her interest in anything beyond.

A form came out of the red folder, and the W.P.C. began by making a note of the time and copying an acknowledgement of caution from a printed card at the back of her notebook. Then, sentence by sentence, Carson watched as she transcribed his story with painful slowness, frowning with a concentration that reminded him of junior school exercises. He wondered if he ought to offer to write it out himself but he hesitated, not knowing the procedure. Ellen O'Brien coughed demurely behind her hand and rearranged her legs a couple of times.

When the 'unwitnessed statement' was completed and given to him to read, he was surprised to find that it was clear and direct with no words wasted, no bias, no embellishment. He signed it thankfully, and regained his limited freedom.

A group of about a dozen policemen were arriving as

Carson moved into the lobby. They shuffled and sighed and sniffed through into the lounge, trailing more mud and dead grass across the tatters of newspaper that had been laid down to protect the carpet. The door through to the dining-room was open, but Forester was no longer inside – probably getting the grilling over in the school, Carson thought. His main concern at the moment was to find somewhere to stay the night.

There was nobody at the reception desk, and he hesitated at the idea of ringing the imperious little bell on the counter. As he looked around, a tall girl of about twenty-three or four came out of the lounge at speed. She was carrying a tray piled high with rattling coffee cups and a couple of jugs. She hurried past the bar entrance, past the reception desk and past Carson without even glancing at him. He fell in behind her.

'Do you know where I can find the manager?' he said as they made a sharp turn into a corridor which led towards the back of the building.

'I think he's getting bread out of the freezer,' the girl called over her shoulder. There was a strong thread running through her accent, Australian or New Zealand. She turned sideways and used her hip to bump open half of a two-way swinging door. It flipped away as if it had been rammed, and she swept through.

'I need a room for the night,' Carson explained as he followed her into a long and well-lit kitchen. The air was warm and yeasty, and over by the door which led to the hotel's rockery garden a middle-aged woman was slicing a huge tinned ham on a hand-operated machine.

The girl dumped the tray on the draining board of a double sink. 'Can you come back later?' she said as she started to run hot water. 'I think he's all tied up.'

'I would,' Carson said, dodging as the kitchen door again swung inwards, 'but unless I get a room I've nowhere to go.'

A thickset man in a shapeless green tweed jacket came

limping through the kitchen door. He didn't even seem to see Carson as he crossed to the work surfaces by the ovens and set down a couple of loaves that banged like rocks and steamed faintly in the warm air.

'Here you are, Lesley,' he said to the girl. 'Wrap these in tinfoil and get them in the oven.'

Lesley cut the flow of hot water and left the crockery. Carson said, 'Are you the manager?' as the man limped past him. Carson had to do another sidestep as the kitchen doors bounced again.

'Yes,' the man said abruptly, 'excuse me.'

There were two uniformed policemen peering in through the open doorway. 'This where we can get hot soup?' one of them said.

'Soup's all gone,' the manager told them. 'We're on tea and sandwiches now.'

'There was supposed to be soup.'

'Your mates drank it all. I've been trying to get more powder from the store, but Billy Hamilton's gone out and left it all locked up.' The manager opened up an exercise book and started to make an entry. Carson could see that he'd ruled the pages off into columns and was making detailed notes of the cost of every item involved in the police operation.

The girl said, 'I saw him in the lounge before. Something about details for the *Advertiser*.'

'Well, he's not there now.'

'You can't keep going in weather like this on tea and sandwiches,' the policeman objected.

'Unless you're going to help me break into the store, that's all there is. We've been cleaned out of everything else.'

The two policemen glanced at each other, and there was a brief and silent communication between them. Then the second one said, 'Is there a spare key to this place?'

'If there is, he hasn't told me.'

'Come on,' the first man said, 'let's take a look.'

The manager sighed and reluctantly moved to go with them, and Carson said quickly, 'Before you go, I need a room.'

'Yes, later. You can see how busy we are.' There was a loud slam as the girl closed the oven doors on the silvered loaves.

'It won't take you a minute,' Carson insisted, seeing his one opportunity sliding away like a live fish through his hands, but one of the policemen gave him a warning look.

'You heard him,' he said.

'Go to the front desk and have a look at the book,' the manager said, spelling it out heavily as if for an obtuse child. 'Sign yourself in and take a key. I'll sort it all out in the morning. Lesley, make a note, will you?'

The girl nodded wearily and said, 'Sure,' as she splashed more hot water into the sink and reached for a pair of rubber gloves that were lying slack and deflated on the window ledge.

'Thanks,' Carson said to the empty doorway, and then followed the three men down the corridor and into the lobby. He considered asking about dinner, but decided to retire with his minor victory.

There was nobody around to object or question as he lifted the counter flap and stepped behind the small reception desk. The checking-in book was a loose-leaf folder that was kept on a shelf under the counter along with several bundles of envelopes, some creased old magazines, a car service manual, a bottle of nail varnish and two coat hangers. He opened it to the latest entry and saw that there had been nothing written for three or four days. Open house.

He glanced up as he was writing his name. He had a clear view down the lobby and across the street to where Forester was standing by the short railings of the school entrance, looking up at the darkening sky. A blue Land-Rover – Stoneley's, if Carson wasn't mistaken – cut across the scene as it passed, and then Forester moved towards the hotel. The interview with Schaffer didn't seem to have assured him at all.

Carson completed the entry and chose a key at random from the hooks on the peg-board behind him. Pinned to the board were a couple of unclaimed letters with postmarks more than a year old. He looked around as Forester came in through the vestibule, and said, 'How did you get on?'

'No hope.' Forester stood just inside the doorway, looking around him as if he found his surroundings inexplicably strange. 'From the sound of it, the place was ruined.'

'But they told me they didn't find any bodies of children. Doesn't that mean there's still a chance?'

'Not for me.'

'But if there was no body . . .'

'There was no body to find. The child hadn't been born yet.' Forester crossed the lobby dejectedly and slumped into the upright chair that Jerry Crichton had occupied about an hour before. 'Jenner was getting ready to do an implant for us. More than thirty tries, and it finally started growing. It was due to be attached in Carlisle this morning.'

'I'm sorry,' Carson said, wary of empty sympathy. 'But it's not like losing a real baby, is it?'

Forester was studying his shoes, legs outstretched. 'Maybe not to you.'

'Can't you try again?'

'If we could afford it, we might. I doubt if we can, after the cost of this.'

'Surely you can claim some of the costs back.'

Forester looked up at him, through him. 'Claim them from where?'

'I don't know. Insurance, or something.'

A shrug. 'It's not only the money. Couple more years and it will be too late to be worth trying. It would have been a boy.'

'I'm sure you'll be able to make a claim.'

It was indifferent news. 'We might, but it will come too late. And I'm not even sure we'd win – even a foetus hasn't got any rights until near the end. What chance have you got for something in a bottle?'

'Well,' Carson said, 'I'm sorry.'

Forester accepted it and ignored it. 'Suppose I'd better go back to Carlisle,' he said, getting to his feet. 'Break the news.'

'I think Stoneley wants us to stay around.'

'Yes, well. I'm not too worried about what Stoneley wants.'

Carson was still holding his key with its oversized plastic tab as he moved around the counter and lowered the flap. 'Whoever did it, I'm sure they'll get him.'

Forester stopped, framed in the doorway. 'Get who?'

'You know. The killer.'

'They told me it was an accident,' Forester said, frowning as this new information began to scramble in and mismatch with the old.

'Oh,' Carson said, suddenly unsure of himself. 'Well, maybe it was.'

'What did they tell you?' Forester demanded as he moved back towards Carson.

'Nothing direct, but they've sealed the valley off and they're looking for someone. I assumed . . .'

Forester cut him off as the hotel manager and the two policemen returned from the village store laden with booty. He took Carson's arm and drew him into the empty dining-room, closing the door behind them.

'The lying swines!' he hissed in a low voice. 'Are you sure of this?'

'I had to identify a girl I knew. She definitely wasn't burned.'

Forester hardly seemed to hear. He was staring over Carson's shoulder, his unfocused eyes the only point of brightness in the unlit room. 'They decided I'd be no use to them, so they got rid of me. Or they think they did.' His attention returned to Carson like a searchlight's glare. 'You said you had to identify someone?'

'One of the lab assistants. They found her in a field nearby.'

'Girl-friend?'

Here we go again. 'Sort of.'

Forester's attitude changed slightly to include a hard and uncompromising element of fellowship. 'I was offhand with you before,' he said. 'I shouldn't have been.'

'That's all right.'

'The bastards. "If he can't help us, spin him a line and piss him off." Who do they think they are?'

'They've got a job to do,' Carson said non-committally.

'That's no excuse,' Forester said, pulling the door open. 'Who the hell are they supposed to be doing it for?'

He went through the lobby and out into the street. Carson followed him as far as the door, but Forester had disappeared into the twilight.

Carson held out his hand. The rain was starting again.

Chapter 5

Alison Wells looked out into the night and shivered. Through the gates and across the platform behind her the Intercity rumbled tensely and began to roll, water sluicing from its gutters as the carriages clattered and banged off towards Carlisle and the Scottish lowlands.

Penrith station always reminded her of a small boarding school or a convent. With its red brick and sandstone frontage it was in probably the prettiest part of town; the building itself was unpretentious and attractive, and across a wide tarmac forecourt and the road it faced the neat railed park which housed the castle ruins. But the picture was tainted by the ugliness close behind, the livestock market and the slaughterhouse – on warm days children played on the crumbled walls and rolled on the grass and bathed in the smell of fear.

There was somebody in the forecourt's only telephone kiosk and someone else was waiting, a youth hunched against the cold in an inadequate bomber jacket as he stood in the miserable shelter of the station's canopy. Alison decided not to phone ahead but to drive directly to the clinic. She smiled weakly to herself; nobody would worry if she was half an hour late, nobody would be particularly pleased if she was half an hour early, and the thought had been nothing more than a reflex.

Hampered by the pulling weight of her weekend bag she put her head down against the rain and tried to run. After a few yards she came to a gate in a white picket fence and fumbled it open, letting herself through into the old station yard. At one time it would have been filled by a gritty, glossy range of coal mountains, but the steam locomotives were long gone, replaced by urbane diesels. Now there was just a broken-down Post Office van, and a couple of heaps of tarred stones covered by tarpaulins, and her own Honda.

There was a diminishing two-tone blast from the train as it attempted to raise its spirits for the night run ahead, but it was a forlorn and lonely sound that rolled across the empty yard like the incoherent ravings of a derelict. Alison dumped her bag on the back seat of the car and climbed behind the wheel.

The engine turned over and fired first time on full choke. Not bad, she thought; two days standing in which the car's had plenty of opportunity to come up with reasons to be awkward and instead it starts up with perfect sweetness. Somehow, it didn't reassure her, almost as if it were treating her with exaggerated kindness knowing that something worse lay around the corner — but of course, that was ridiculous. She stopped outside the yard and left the engine running while she went back and closed the gate.

A couple of minutes later she'd crossed over the impersonal slash of motorway that separated Penrith from the main Cumbrian landmass and was driving west on the Ullswater road. The wipers set up a steady beat that was almost hypnotic, and when she'd left the overhead lighting behind, Alison found it difficult to concentrate on the flickering pool of road that flowed through the car's dipped beams. She reached to her side and opened the driver's window a couple of inches. The cold and rain-flecked breeze lifted her hair and fixed hungrily on the exposed skin of her neck, but at least there was now no chance of her drifting off into a daze.

After she'd taken the Ravens' Bridge turn-off she realised that she hadn't even been thinking about her route. Habit. Whenever you left the Jenner Clinic this was the road you had to take, the same when you eventually had to go back. Alison supposed that the weary unease and the general lack of focus that she felt were a consequence of the long and dull journey and the painful days that had preceded it. She was surprised to find that she was looking forward to being back in the little bed-sitter in the old farmhouse that she was coming to regard as home; far more so than the drab two-room suite in Ealing with its shared bathroom and meter that she called her 'permanent base'. She thought of her attic room with its hard polished wood and clean white plaster, the crazy angle of the beamed ceiling and the uneven lines of its walls; it was a small and warm haven where the objects around her were all personal items that she'd chosen with care – the books on the pine shelves, the Tolkien posters, the thick, heavy knit of the bedspread and rugs, the brass lamp that cast a milky yellow glow from the bedside table and made all the shadows big. Her section of the divided house in Ealing was fast becoming by contrast a place where she stored the material debris of her life that she'd never got around to throwing away.

She reached the lake, dark and almost invisible in the night, betrayed by the unsteady reflections of one or two points of light far away on the distant valley side. The pleasure boats moored by the slatted wooden tongue of the steamer jetty stirred apprehensively, lifting in the slop and dip of the lake water, and then the silhouettes of the first lakeside trees moved in to screen off the road.

She saw nobody in Ravens' Bridge itself, just the odd light in the upper storey of a shop or a cottage, and then she turned down by the chapel and was on the long and dead-ended road to Langstone.

Winding things up with Eddie had been painful, but it had been necessary. Perhaps what was really troubling her was the way that he'd taken it so well, the way that he'd simply shrugged and said okay and then finished his pizza and left. He could at least have had the decency to seem upset, but then she ought to be pleased at this confirmation of her action. Eddie wasn't conducting an affair, he was simply screwing by the railway timetable. You're working over this weekend? Shit, baby, no Hoggins for Eddie. It was a case of either knock it off or else soon she'd have to start faking orgasms, and she knew from every magazine she'd ever read since she was fifteen what *that* indicated.

Eddie would survive, no problem – it was better than having him become another habit, just another piece of Ealing debris. Tomorrow afternoon he'd be back in the British Museum coffee shop, some incomprehensibly studious text propped open in front of him while he eyed up the talent. He liked his girls to have brains, he said. It gave you something to talk about while you were cleaning up afterwards.

In fifteen minutes she'd be home, but then the windscreen shattered.

Forty miles an hour and there was nothing before her but a web, a crystal crazing that glittered with all the brilliance of her headlight beams and showed her none of the detail beyond. She stamped on the brake in reflex and the car pulled over to the left as the wet pads skidded and slipped, the seat belt biting into her shoulder as the reel locked solid. Two of the wheels were off the road and bouncing so hard they seemed ready to shake the car apart as she fought to get the vehicle back on to the unseen surface, but the steering wheel fought back harder; then for almost a full second it came completely free but the car was flying, two feet off the ground and out of control until it came down bang, and slammed into the stone upright of a farm gate.

The screen abruptly became a roaring, tumbling waterfall of colours as her head was whip-cracked back on to the Honda's padded rest, then the belt released and she slumped forward. After a few seconds the waterfall ran dry and let reality, hard-edged and painful, back in. She was still gripping the steering wheel. Two of her nails were broken. The car was still.

The broken screen was still together, each tiny piece gripping its neighbour and holding it in place. The crazing wasn't regular, it radiated out from a striped zone across the centre which under normal conditions might have given her a degree of visibility – enough, at least, to pull in safely. But at night, and in the rain, and with no lighting other than the angled glare of her own beams – no chance.

Alison undid the belt and immediately lost her grip on it. The strap rolled itself back across her shoulder quickly and efficiently, the buckle catching for a moment as it bounced across her hipbone. She opened the door and stepped out into the night, holding the car for balance. At the first touch of rain on her skin she bent and reached into the back of the car for the thin nylon cagoule that she'd left bundled under the seat three days before.

The car lolled drunkenly against the gatepost, one eye hanging out. Told you so, it gasped smugly, told you I had something worse lined up. The post was leaning and part of the adjacent wall had slid into rubble; the gate itself was lying a little further into the field, pressing its gate-shape into the long wet grass.

She dropped the cagoule; hardly noticed it falling. It lay, a splash of blood-orange, on the twilight edge of the one remaining beam. Then she moved around unsteadily to inspect the damage.

The nearside wing had been folded and crumpled by the impact so that it pressed on the wheel. The wheel itself was tilted at an unhealthy-looking angle. Alison gasped a little as she bent to look more closely – her right breast was sore where the belt had snapped taut across it. It seemed that the car was unlikely to move from the spot under its own power; she groaned and closed her eyes and rested her forehead on the cool metal of the wing, but despite her deepest pleading the situation didn't go away.

The mouse-hairs on the back of her neck rippled and raised as if stirred by a child's enquiring finger. Her eyes snapped open and her mind cleared. She was being watched.

She scrambled upright and looked around, keeping a hand on the reassuring solidity of the Honda. Beyond the throw of the headlamp there was no detail, just black shadows that bulked and flowed into one another. Up the hill about a mile away she could see the lights of a farm, and the extra-dense blackness of a run of trees which cut across the hillside and seemed to mark a farm track which joined the road just beyond the field; in the dark spaces between there was room for all the Watchers of Hades. And the cagoule had gone.

She had only the vaguest memory of the smooth material sliding through her fingers and on to the ground, but it had been there and she'd dropped it and it wasn't there now. There was no wind to move it. The headlamp flickered and weakened a little as the battery began to waver under the strain of full beam.

Alison backed around, keeping the car behind her, seeing her own shadow dance out across the field as she passed before the light. The innocent sounds of night began to acquire new and sinister resonances as she moved; the far-off swilling of the lake, the finger-breaking crackle of dead leaves in the trees, the tick and clank of the Honda's cooling engine.

The door was half-open and she was ready to get into the car and lock herself in when the lights hit. They raked across her three times, blinding her and pinning her like a rabbit, and then the noise and the brilliance were all around her and she was trapped.

'Get some light into that field!' Schaffer called, and one of the policemen in the Rover swung the spotlight that was mounted on the roof framework. Around the other side of the Honda uniformed men were spilling out of a Sherpa van and unslinging their torches as they trotted along the road and scanned the verges, some of them moving towards the gateway.

Alison cringed back without meaning to as Schaffer reached her. 'Are you all right?' he asked her.

'Yes . . . I think so.'

'Did you see anybody?'

'I thought there was someone watching me. I didn't actually see anyone.'

Torchlight was dancing like fireflies through the trees on the far side of the road. Schaffer said, 'Where would you be going at this time? The valley's a dead end, you know.'

'I work here,' she told him, still keeping her grip with difficulty. 'The Jenner Clinic, just above the village.'

'You're from the Jenner Clinic?'

'That's right. Is there something wrong?'

'You'd better get into my car,' Schaffer said, looking around into the night with a new anxiety.

'I'm all right. I'm a bit shaken because of the windscreen, that's all.'

Despite her protests he began to lead her away from the Honda. 'All the same, I'd like you to get into the car.'

'But what about *my* car?' she asked, resisting feebly, and he took a light hold of her shoulders and began to guide her.

'We'll see to it. Quick as you can, please.'

They arrived at Schaffer's saloon. 'Why?' she said. Policemen were climbing out of the woods, swinging over the wire fence that held the trees back from the road. One of them saw Schaffer and shook his head.

'You could be in danger, that's why,' Schaffer explained.

He almost had her into the passenger seat when she remembered something else. 'My luggage . . .'

'I'll get it for you. I want you somewhere safe.'

Schaffer locked Alison in, both doors. Then he crossed to where a sergeant was standing by the damaged car, watching for any movement in the field.

'Anything?' Schaffer asked him.

The sergeant didn't show any enthusiasm. 'No, nothing.'

'She said she thought she was being watched. Could there have been anyone?'

'I don't think so.' The sergeant raised his voice and shouted across to the searchlight operator, 'Just run the beam over that grass!' The slanted shaft of brilliance showed a deep, rich field of standing grass that waved slightly as air moved over it. One uniformed man was wading out, cutting an obvious furrow as he went. 'See what I mean?' the sergeant went on. 'Anybody running around would leave a trail. Probably just an over-active imagination.'

'Yes. But we can't take chances, can we?'

The sergeant followed Schaffer as he went to collect the girl's luggage. As Schaffer puzzled over the release lever which would let the seat spring forward and give him access to the back, the sergeant looked at the broken windscreen.

'Looks like a stone,' he said after a moment.

'Yes,' Schaffer's voice came muffled from the car's interior. Some of the men were climbing back into the Sherpa van, bone-weary after a long hard day and this unexpected interruption to their late journey home.

'You can see where it hit and spread,' the sergeant elaborated as Schaffer emerged with the weekend bag. He pointed to a spot on the screen where a large number of the shatter-lines came together. 'A stone, that's all.'

'Yes,' Schaffer said, unsatisfied, 'but where from?'

'No way of telling. I had a broken windscreen once, it just went. No stone or anything.'

An accident. Not enough to base a suspicion on. 'I'll drive the girl back into the village. Stoneley's staying overnight, and he'll want to see her. Can you hook up a towline to drag the Honda back to Penrith?'

'Don't you want to take it back with you?'

'No. The village is congested enough as it is, without dumping wrecks on the main street. Stick it in the yard for tonight and we'll get a garage to collect it in the morning.'

So a couple of the men were dragged out again to fix up the towrope. Schaffer put Alison's bag into the trunk of his car and then unlocked the driver's door. She looked up at him, confusion in her face as the interior light threw its pale glow over her; despite the unflattering illumination he saw clear eyes with a well-defined arch to the brows, a strong feminine bone structure, and shoulder-length hair that would probably be ash-blonde in daylight. The light winked out as he closed the door.

'Your car's being taken care of,' he told her. 'I'm driving you to the village.'

Alison had been sitting alone and trying to make sense out of what was happening around her, and she hadn't succeeded. 'What did you mean about me being in danger?' she wanted to know. 'Was there someone out there?'

'I don't think so,' Schaffer said, and managed to sound reasonably convinced.

'Then what . . .'

'When were you last at the Jenner Clinic?'

'The day before yesterday. I've been down to London.'

'With family?'

'I've got a flat. Most of us have. What's it got to do with anything?'

'Only that someone seems to have had a grudge against the Jenner staff. And because you couldn't be found, you were our main suspect.'

Alison's eyes widened. Schaffer could see their dull glint in the dark. '*Suspect?*' she said. 'Suspected of what?'

'I'm taking you to see my boss. He'll be able to explain it better than I can.'

'But what am I supposed to have done?'

'Obviously nothing, but for a while we weren't sure.'

His evasions were transparent. 'You're not going to tell me, are you?' she said. 'Is somebody dead?'

'Christ, this is going to be the worst-kept secret in Cumbria. Yes, somebody's dead.'

'Who?'

The Sherpa van's engine revved, and the Honda was pulled free of the wall. A uniformed man emerging from the field dodged as some of the unmortared stones slid and clattered over one another. He was carrying something, but Schaffer couldn't see what.

'Who's dead?' Alison repeated.

'Please don't ask me anything else. Stoneley will jump on me when he finds out that I've told you as much as I have. I'll drive you into the village and then we'll tell you everything.'

The constable tapped on Alison's window. She wound it down.

'This yours, miss?' he said, and held up her orange cagoule.

'Yes,' she said uncertainly. 'Where did you find it?'

'Slung over the wall, where you left it.'

She took it from him mechanically, and wound up the window again as he moved away. Then she slowly bundled the nylon up and put it on the saloon's back seat, as if it were somehow soiled, unclean. Schaffer started the car and made a turn in the road before heading back towards Langstone.

Chapter 6

If the loss of Alison Wells as his one named suspect bothered Stoneley, he didn't let it show – in fact he seemed quite cheerful the next morning despite the fact that he'd had less than five hours' sleep in his hotel bedroom. The good humour wasn't to last for long.

He was up early, keeping farmer's hours, and his first action was to gather his officers together and give them their instructions for a detailed farm-to-farm check. Later in the morning the bodies of the clinic staff would be moved under the supervision of the pathologist. Barry Lennox had received an offer the previous evening from the vicar in Ravens' Bridge that the bodies might be transferred to the chapel for the night. Lennox had passed the message on to Stoneley.

'Tell him no, and make it sound polite,' Stoneley had told Lennox, 'and then find out exactly how much the nosey old sod knows.'

As the farm survey team dispersed to their Rovers and vans and studied their maps, Stoneley prepared to take the two explosions experts, who had travelled up from Woolwich, to look at the site, in the hope that they might be able to add something to Clive Lord's analysis. It was a fresh, bright morning, and a strong breeze was holding the rain away. Stoneley was walking from the hotel to his car with the Woolwich men when he saw that Hennessy was moving to intercept him.

'Stoneley!' Hennessy shouted across the street. 'Before you go!'

'Excuse me one second,' Stoneley confided. 'I've got to bounce a bureaucrat.' He raised his voice to reach Hennessy, who was anxiously looking both ways before crossing the street. 'Better make it quick!'

Hennessy arrived, breathless and flushed as usual. There had been nobody available in the hotel to sponge his suit or press his travel-creased shirt, and breakfast had been pretty much a casual exercise in self-help. Not what he was used to.

'There's a message for you in the incident room,' he told Stoneley.

'An officer will tell me, if that's the case. Anyway, how would you know?'

'The message is only just arriving. It's because of me that it's being sent.'

Stoneley's good cheer began to seep away, to be replaced by a growing suspicion. 'Wait a minute,' he said. 'What is this?'

The two forensic men shifted uneasily as they sensed the changing mood. 'I gave you fair warning last night,' Hennessy said. 'You can't say you didn't have the chance to co-operate.'

Stoneley looked at him for a moment, but saw only a practised blankness. Then he pushed past and made for the school, leaving Hennessy and the two experts without another word.

The mortuary section of the schoolroom had been made smaller by the use of extra partitions, and in the L-shaped space that resulted the radio apparatus and two telex machines had been set up. New lines had been wired into the village's Post Office junction box to take the load, and these also fed a small switchboard with six extensions on a bare operations table. Stoneley walked directly to the working telex and surprised the blonde W.P.C. who was in the process of tearing the top sheet of a message.

'That for me?' he said.

She nodded and held it out. 'Just come in.' Another little fragment was added to the Chief's growing legend.

Stoneley scanned the flimsy once, and then again in disbelief. 'The bastard,' he muttered wonderingly. 'He can't!'

TO 5085 POLICE INCDNT
FROM 6440 POLICE PENRITH
0856 HRS. 16.10.87.
OPERATION TO BE SUSPENDED MATTER OF EXTREME NATIONAL
SECURITY. CEASE ALL LINES OF INVESTIGATION IMMEDIATELY
AND MAINTAIN TOKEN PRESENCE UNTIL ARRIVAL OF FORCES
SPECIAL UNIT.
SIGNED STANNEYFORTH CC'S OFFICE

Hennessy had followed him and was standing in the doorway, seemingly unwilling to cross the threshold into territory where he knew he was unwelcome. Fortunately he knew better than to appear pleased.

'All right, Hennessy,' Stoneley demanded. 'What's all this about?'

'It's not a matter for the local police, Stoneley. I'm sorry if it annoys you.'

'Annoys me? That's the understatement of the year. I'm bloody furious. What are you doing creeping around behind my back?'

Hennessy took a couple of cautious steps forward. 'I didn't creep around,' he insisted. 'I was as open with you as I'm allowed to be.'

'Well, I won't have it.'

'I'm afraid you don't have the choice.'

'We'll see about that. Who are you responsible to?'

'I told you, the Home Office. They processed the order, not me.'

'Then it's got no power,' Stoneley said triumphantly. 'Our force is responsible to the local authority, not to the Home Office.'

'I'm aware of that. It doesn't matter who you refer back to. The order sticks.'

The radio and switchboard operators were staring with exaggerated concentration at their consoles, trying hard not to appear to be listening. 'I'm not falling for it,' Stoneley said. 'You've got no constitutional sway over me. I didn't get this far without knowing how the system works.'

'I'm not pretending I've got any authority over you,' Hennessy pointed out. 'It's not my name on the order.'

This much was true. Hennessy couldn't give him instructions, but Stanneyforth certainly could. 'All right,' Stoneley said, 'Stop playing around with me.' He held up the telex. 'What do you know about this?'

'Nothing,' Hennessy said with tin humility. 'I'm just a civil servant.'

'Don't come that. That bastard Stanneyforth sold us up the river for you. What did you promise him, and why?'

There was a call on the switchboard. Reluctantly the operator tugged his headset back into place and opened the line to reply.

'You're not doing yourself any good, you know,' Hennessy advised. 'Call in your men and pack your gear before you make some real trouble.'

'Am I hearing this correctly? You're trying to tell a Detective Chief Superintendent what to do?'

'I'm suggesting, nothing more. It's your own Chief Constable who's given you the instruction. I'm only pointing out the wisdom of following it.'

Stoneley glared at Hennessy angrily for a moment. 'I'm going to phone him,' he said, but there was the desperation of defeat already in his voice.

'Good idea,' Hennessy agreed.

Stoneley indicated the telex. 'This could have come from anywhere.'

'I don't think so. Check the coding.'

'I intend to.' Stoneley looked at the six available telephones on the operations desk, and then at the studied indifference of the communications staff. Then he moved towards the schoolmaster's office, where the telephone was still on a direct outside line.

Hennessy moved after him. 'At the same time,' he said, 'ring the Lord Lieutenant if you can find him. And the chairman of the Police Committee.'

Stoneley stopped and turned in the doorway, blocking Hennessy. 'Why are you doing this?' he said, searching the civil servant's face without comprehension. 'What the hell was at that clinic that should scare you so much?'

'I thought you were going to make a phone call,' Hennessy said.

Stoneley kicked the door of the office shut and then telephoned his headquarters whilst Hennessy waited outside. He was told that Stanneyforth was in a meeting and couldn't be disturbed but yes, the instruction was genuine and had been logged at 0856. Stoneley put the receiver down with more force than was really necessary and then sat back in the chair, staring broodily at it. He wasn't going to make any more calls – not if it meant giving Stanneyforth ammunition to be used against him at some time in the future. He pushed the chair back and went through into the schoolrooom. Hennessy moved aside without comment as he crossed to the radio operator.

'Get on to all the cars checking out the farms,' he instructed. 'Tell them to come back here right away. No messing about.'

The operator reached for his list of vehicle codes. Stoneley looked up and saw Hennessy, still by the office door. At least he was looking a little embarrassed – but not much.

'Is it because we didn't grab him on the first day?' Stoneley wanted to know. 'Is that it?'

'That's got nothing to do with anything.'

'Police work isn't like that, you know. You don't leap in and tackle the nearest running thug, because there never is one. It's slow and it's methodical, and I'm good at it.'

'I don't doubt that,' Hennessy assured him smoothly. 'It's no reflection on you.'

'That's not much consolation. Given time and the opportunity to do our jobs, we'd have got him.' He straightened out the crumpled telex and reread it, smiling bitterly at the mention of a forces special unit. Then he abruptly screwed the thin paper into a ball and flung it in the general direction of a wastepaper basket. It bounced off the wall and rolled a couple of uneven feet across the floor, but Stoneley was already on his way out through the cloakroom with Hennessy hurrying behind.

The blonde W.P.C. exchanged a bemused look with the switchboard operator as she went over to collect the crumpled scrap. There was no reason to keep it because there was a bottom copy on a yellow roll in the machine, but she uncreased and read it with a puzzled frown before tearing it up and dropping the pieces into the basket. She thought she'd heard Hennessy muttering something to himself as he'd followed Stoneley. She thought it had sounded like, *that's what I was afraid of.*

Chapter 7

Ravens' Crag farm was high on the valley slopes, a rambling complex of old sheepyards and generally neglected buildings that had a view of the lake and of the road about a mile downslope. An old jacket and three pullovers protected Desmond Gaskell from the morning's chill; already he'd been up and working for a couple of hours. Long exposure had made him insensitive – he was a man who spent his days in grim cold and sleet winds, and he had a slow and patient temperament which resisted exasperation.

He'd been restacking a breach in one of the fold walls a mile away. Some of the walls dated back to the middle ages when they'd been laid under the direction of the monks from the Furness Abbey. They hardly needed any maintenance, but occasionally there would be a collapse that needed repair. If it were left unattended one or two sheep might try to struggle through the gap, enlarging it a little more until eventually there might as well be no wall there at all. Gaskell knew that his masonry was poor and that a hard frost might reopen the break, but it was the best that he could do – he couldn't afford the services of either of the two full-time masons in the valley.

The yard gate was old timber, secured by a loop of string that was attached to a nail in the post. The yard itself was an irregular shape, almost a triangle bound on two sides by the face of the house and the blind eyes of the barn. They looked across a low wall to a scattering of outbuildings, most of them too damp and derelict to be of any use to anybody or anything other than the chickens that picked around the yard and the adjacent stony field.

The farm was in a bad way. Deighton, the agent of the London shooting syndicate that owned the land, knew it and wasn't prepared to do anything about it; he was simply waiting for conditions to degenerate so far that Gaskell would leave of his own accord and give the vacant possession that was needed for the property to be managed with the next estate. Gaskell closed the gate behind him and whistled up the dogs as he crossed the yard.

Half-way to the house, just as the smell of frying bacon reached him, Gaskell saw that the barn door was open a few inches. It was old and warped, and the peeling wood leaned outwards dangerously if the latch was left undone. He'd forbidden both of the children to play in the barn because the loft was unsafe and the rat traps were always full, but he always got the impression from them that his orders were not so much taken as feared commandments as an indication that business as usual was fine, so long as stealth was employed. He glanced into the barn before he fully closed the door, seeing the sheeted and useless tractor in the strip of blue daylight. Summer had been difficult without it, winter was going to be impossible; the first snows at these heights would be arriving in a few weeks, maybe even before the end of the month.

The dogs hadn't come running at his whistle, but he barely had time to register the fact when his attention was caught by the police van that was climbing the hill towards the farm. It had been hidden until now by the trees that pressed together alongside the track, but as it came into sight the sound of its labouring engine came with it, an agonised moaning at the steepness of the hillside. Instead of going on towards the house Gaskell moved back to the gate and waited for the van to pull in.

Two men got out, neither of them Crichton, the local man; uniform behind the wheel, plainclothes on the other side. They left the driver's door open so that they'd be able to hear the radio, and as they walked over to the gate the plain-clothes man took out his warrant card. A formality; it wasn't there long enough for Gaskell to read it, and he didn't try.

'You own this place?' Barry Lennox said as he came near.

'Don't own it,' Gaskell told him. 'I'm the tenant, though.'

'That's near enough. Like to ask you a few questions and have a look around, if that's all right.'

'Something to do with the clinic, is it?'

Lennox looked at him searchingly, trying not to let his interest show. 'You know about that?'

'I should think every farm in the valley must know about it. Made enough of a bang when it went up.'

'Mind telling us what you saw?'

Gaskell shrugged, shifted his position slightly, glancing at the ground like a nervous child asked to recite. 'It was just before dawn, so I was up and around. I heard it go off, and when I looked over towards the village I could see the light of the fire on the hillside.'

'Did you call the emergency services?' the uniformed man put in. He was standing a few yards away, scanning the outbuildings and not appearing to listen.

'I couldn't,' Gaskell said. 'No telephone.'

Lennox glanced at the line overhead. It linked the house to a pole by the trees and then joined the Post Office network by a buried conduit. 'What's that, then?' he said.

'There's a line, but we couldn't pay the bill so they cut us off.' And then, almost defensively, 'We haven't missed it.'

'Didn't you do anything?' the uniformed man said. Over at the house a door opened and two small children emerged, a girl of about nine and a boy of around seven. They were both wearing duffel coats and wellingtons. They stood by the step and then watched from a distance.

Gaskell shifted slightly again, thrusting his long bony hands into his pockets. 'It wasn't ten or fifteen minutes before some of your fellows came tearing down the road. You get a good view of the approach from up here, as they turn in by the lake.'

Lennox nodded. He could see a section of the road that ran for more than two miles alongside the water. 'Did you see anything strange or unusual yesterday?'

Gaskell thought for a moment. 'Village was busy.'

'Besides that. Any strangers around, or anyone moving on the fells.'

'Not at this time of year. The valley's always quiet.'

'Mind if we have a look around the yard and the outbuildings?' Lennox asked.

'Not as long as you tell me what you're looking for.'

'We don't know, for sure,' Lennox told him as the uniformed man unlatched the gate and let himself through, and Gaskell stepped aside to let him pass. 'We're checking all the farms in the valley.'

'Just the two of you?' Gaskell said with mild surprise.

'And a few more.'

Gaskell turned and watched the uniformed man for a moment. Lennox had been right, he didn't seem to know what he was looking for. 'You're not from around here.' Gaskell observed. The two children, Peter and Sarah, still watched round-eyed from the doorstep, and behind them one of the kitchen curtains appeared to twitch.

'From the city,' Lennox said. 'We get about a bit.'

'I can see that. Somebody get killed, did they?'

'It was a big accident,' Lennox said carefully. 'It would have been a miracle if they didn't.'

Gaskell frowned, shifted about again. 'If it was an accident, why start looking for strangers?'

Lennox felt uneasy with the slow and purposeful grind of the farmer's intellect. 'We've got to cover all the angles.'

The uniformed man was over by the barn. 'Is this door locked?' he called.

'It's a stiff latch,' Gaskell didn't quite shout but his voice was loud enough to carry. 'Wait a minute.'

As Gaskell moved off to help, Lennox heard the crackle and spatter of the van's radio and then their own distinctive call sign. 'Hold on,' he called, 'there's a message coming through from ops.'

He ran to the Sherpa and reached under the dashboard for the transmitter mike. The temporary base desk was saying,

'Delta Four, please acknowledge,' as he thumbed the *transmit* button.

'Delta Four.'

'Fold your tents and back to the village, lads,' the operator's voice came through the distortion. 'The whole thing's suspended.'

'What do you mean, suspended?'

'Don't ask me, I'm only passing the messages on. Word of warning, though — keep out of Stoneley's way when you arrive.'

The uniformed man was coming through the gate and Gaskell was close behind him, his angular, weatherbeaten face showing unashamed curiosity. Across the yard the two children were still watching, and behind them in the kitchen — Lennox suddenly got the feeling that this was the most entertainment the family had probably had in a long time. 'Keep out of Stoneley's way?' he said. 'Why?'

'Little contretemps with that Home Office type, and our beloved leader seems to have come off worst.'

'The Chief? I don't believe it.' The uniformed man leaned on the van's wing to listen, and Gaskell hung back a few feet away.

'More than that I will not say. Anyway, cut the chat and clear the air. I've got another five calls to make.'

'Delta Four out,' Lennox said automatically, and rehung the mike by the radio set.

'They're recalling us?' the constable said, bewildered. 'What for?'

Lennox slid off the driver's seat and walked around to his own side of the van. 'Don't ask me,' he said. 'I only answer the phone around here.'

The uniformed man sighed heavily and turned to Gaskell. 'Forget the guided tour,' he said. 'Thanks anyway.'

Gaskell opened the gate so that the van could reverse in to make its turn, and then he watched as it bumped off down the track and disappeared behind the trees. Then he resecured the gate and walked over to where his two children were still standing.

'You two got nothing to do?' he said with the mock sternness that he usually employed to address them. They were too old for baby talk, and he couldn't feel comfortable talking adult-fashion to somebody so small. It was enough of an effort with adults.

'Yes, Dad,' they chorused, and then they skipped off, saving their questions for later when the eggs were collected and the chickens were fed and their parents had finished arguing. Little Peter's wellingtons clumped noisily as he ran across the yard; they were Sarah's hand-me-downs, still too big for him.

The kitchen table had been cleared from the children's breakfast and his own place had been set on the bare wood. June Gaskell was turning bacon in an oversized frying pan, making more noise than she really needed to and wearing a practised look of concentration and harassment. Gaskell's heart began to sink within him as he observed the familiar routine. He settled on to the bentwood chair and waited.

'What did they want?' June Gaskell said without turning around.

'They were police.'

'I could see as much. What did they want?'

'Just asking about that big bang yesterday morning.'

'And why would they want to ask you?'

Gaskell considered his answer carefully. It was probably loaded with weaknesses or invitations to criticism that only she would see. 'They weren't only asking me. They're asking everybody.'

'That's what they say.' She smacked a couple of eggs viciously on the rim of the pan and emptied the shells into the spitting fat. 'Then they try to catch you out.'

'Catch me out at what?'

'That's what I'd like to know.'

'They only said, have we seen any strangers around or anyone on the fells.'

'Who'd want to be on the fells at this time of year?' She made it sound as if the contention was his own, a weak and ridiculous concept, but he'd learned not to take the defensive line that spurred her on.

'I don't know,' he said. 'I haven't seen anyone, so I couldn't tell them.'

He got his breakfast as the children returned from their chores. Real country living; the bacon was from a vacuum pack, the tomatoes were tinned, and the fried bread was an indigestible slice of a bleached white loaf, all from the weekly order at Hamilton's store. Only the eggs were their own, and one of them had split and run in the frying.

It was ten minutes after nine, and the children were already late for school. June Gaskell gave them their sandwiches and apples, and then stopped by the door to check that all their buttons were fastened and their loose ends tucked in. Sarah pulled away, considering herself too old and independent for such fuss, but Peter submitted with an air of detached melancholy.

'They're looking for somebody, aren't they?' he said.

'Nobody round here,' June Gaskell told him curtly.

Sarah smiled knowingly. 'I bet they don't find him. I bet they don't.'

'It's nothing to do with us,' June Gaskell said, and turned Peter around towards the door. 'They were going past, that's all.'

'I know who they're looking for,' Peter said as he reached up to open the door.

'I know, as well,' Sarah said.

They went out and stood on the step together, sharing their secret; her own flesh. Her enemies. 'You're going to be late for school.'

'There might not be any school,' Peter said, laying on the disappointment too heavily in an attempt to conceal the hope. 'Sir might send us home again, like yesterday.'

'Yesterday was different,' she told them both. 'Get a move on.'

Gaskell was cleaning his plate with a folded rag of bread when his wife closed the door and moved across to the window. She watched the two children leaving the yard and walking off down the track.

'They've started again,' she said wearily.

'I heard.'

'I thought all that was finished with. I thought it was over.'

Gaskell crossed the knife and fork on his smeared and empty plate and reached for the mug of tea that had been cooling beside it. 'They're growing up, that's all. It's nothing to get worried about.'

'It's easy for you to say. You're not around them all day, when they're at home.'

Gaskell cringed inwardly as the self-pitying accusation echoed back down the years. It's easy for *you*. It's all right for *you*. 'It's only to be expected,' he persisted. 'Lots of kids invent friends to play with. It's not unnatural.'

'Just because a teacher tells you, that's what you believe? Did you do it when you were little?'

'That's different.'

'I know *I* didn't.'

'You didn't grow up on a farm. They don't meet many people, so they make someone up. There's no harm in it.'

'No *harm*?' she said, and moved abruptly away from the window. 'How do you know they're not going to grow up all twisted because of it?'

'They'll come out of it, as they get older.'

'You said they'd got over it already.'

'I thought they had. Look, if it makes you feel any better I'll have another word with the teacher next time I'm in the village.'

'Words won't do them any good. They need to get away from this place before it's too late.'

He should have seen it coming. He drained off the last of the

95

tea and pushed his chair back from the table. 'Not that again,' he said.

'Yes, that again. And don't just walk away from me this time.'

'I've got things to do,' he said, but there was an undertow of guilt in his voice, as if he knew deep down that she was right.

'We're being buried here. Every year we owe more and make less. Why won't you sell up and move to the town?'

Selling up would be a joke. Apart from the flock of tough Herdwicks everything belonged to Deighton, even the house furniture that still bore wartime utility markings. 'And what will I do in the town?' he said. 'I've no trade, and once I'd paid off the debts we'd have no money from the sale.'

'But why is it only us? Why is every other farmer in the valley running a big car, while we can't even afford to get the tractor fixed?'

'Because they haven't got Deighton for a landlord, that's why. He wants me out, so he won't invest.'

'Well, go to him!' she pleaded, and put both her clenched fists on the table. 'Talk to him, at least!'

Gaskell looked at his wife. Over the past few years she'd become wild-eyed and ugly, like a caged animal that constantly clawed and bit at itself.

'I'll crawl to no one,' he told her.

Misery turned to sudden venom. 'No. You'd rather see your children starve, first.'

'They'll starve and freeze in the town with no roof over them. There's no work for me there.'

'Only because you won't lower yourself to look. It's hopeless. Why won't you call it a day?'

'I've got things to do,' he repeated, and this time he meant it.

A couple of glossy red hens broke off their conversation and ran off squawking when they saw Gaskell coming. He was several yards away from the house when he remembered the dogs; he'd be needing them to bring sheep down to the lower pastures, and they hadn't come at his call. It wasn't like them – they were well-trained and responsive, so obedient that he didn't even tie them in their kennels under the lean-to at the back of the barn. He was about to whistle them again when he saw that the barn door was open.

He walked over towards it, puzzled. The policeman hadn't been able to undo the latch – you had to press and lift the door slightly at the same time – and Gaskell hadn't even arrived to help him when they were called over to the radio. Perhaps he'd got it right to the edge, and the metal pin had popped out since, when nobody was looking.

Gaskell swung the door open and took a couple of steps into the barn. It smelled of mice and corn dust, of stale feed and wet newspaper. He lifted a corner of the grubby sheet that he'd thrown over the tractor's body to keep dust out of the half-stripped engine, almost wishing that some magic might have been worked in his absence and that the engine would be whole and functional again.

Some hope. The vehicle's open heart gaped, black and slimy with congealed oil. It was beyond his abilities to fix it, and he couldn't raise a loan to pay for repairs; he was way over the line at the bank, and he had no collateral to put up for finance. He regretted that he hadn't made more of an attempt to enter the community of the valley during the ten years of his tenancy, but June had always felt that other farmers and their wives looked down on her because she didn't have a farming background herself. They weren't church people and they had no family in the area that they could call upon, so there were no favours to be traded.

There was something else in the air, a scent that he couldn't recall; an odd musky sweetness that danced beyond the edge of perception and wouldn't be identified. Something brushed at the back of Desmond Gaskell's neck, and . . .

Chapter 8

At about nine-twenty the teams started arriving back and found that they were to start loading up and moving towards home. The incident room was to be stripped out and all the information that had been collected so far was to be assembled into a single file. Hennessy was in the hotel on the telephone to his London office, presumably devising some plan for contacting the relatives of the clinic staff to ensure a minimum of public fuss; meanwhile Stoneley had taken him at his word and had even pulled the roadblocks in – if Hennessy wanted to keep people out then fine, let him make his own arrangements. Forester drove straight through without any trouble and found Stoneley in the schoolmaster's office, morosely contemplating a cup of cold tea from a hotel flask.

'You busy?' Forester said from the doorway.

Stoneley, who obviously wasn't, said 'Yes'.

'I'd like a word.' Forester stepped into the room and closed the door behind him. At least Stoneley was now being spared the sight of his incident room being torn apart and carried out in pieces, but then something occurred to him.

'Wait a minute,' he said. 'You're not press, are you?'

Forester shook his head, and Stoneley gave a disappointed sigh as the opportunity to foul Hennessy's lines evaporated.

'I was here yesterday,' Forester said, 'but you wouldn't see me. It's about this accident.'

'What accident?'

'Exactly. I want to know why I was spun that line when I asked about my child.'

Something knitted up in Stoneley's mind. 'I remember now, there was something said about it yesterday. Wasn't it cleared up?'

'To your satisfaction maybe, but not to mine.' Forester moved away from the door and his glance flicked about the room as if he were looking for spyholes and enemies. The second chair was before him, but he didn't sit.

'There were no children in the place,' Stoneley told him, feeling a mild unease at his prowling. 'There weren't *supposed* to be any children in the place.'

Forester stopped and looked across the desk. 'You wouldn't notice mine,' he said. 'He never made it that far.'

Oh, Christ, Stoneley thought as Forester's dark unblinking gaze bored through him, I've landed a nutter. 'Detective Inspector Schaffer told me he'd been through all this with you. You're talking about an egg in a bottle, is that right?'

'It's a pretty crude way of putting it.'

'I'm sorry, but I'm not in the mood for poetry this morning. You can think yourself lucky that it's all you lost.'

'All?' Forester echoed. 'What do you mean, all?'

'I mean that the clinic was full of living, grown people, sons and daughters and lovers and friends. Pull people like that out of the world without warning, and you're left with a sizeable hole.'

'You're saying that I lost nothing. Is that right?'

Outside the door something dropped heavily and made an expensive-sounding noise as it hit. Then a girl's voice, heavily muffled, said 'Aw, fug', and somebody else made solitary applause. Stoneley pushed the tea aside. He preferred it when it was cold; when it was warm he actually felt obliged to drink it.

'I'm saying that you lost damn little in comparison,' he told Forester. 'Think yourself lucky and go home.'

'That depends,' Forester said.

'On what?'

'On the kind of cover-up you're planning here.'

'Cover-up?' Stoneley said evasively. 'What are you talking about?'

'The accident story. I know damn well it was no such thing.'

'Who told you that?'

'Carson told me, in the hotel last night.'

'Carson?' Stoneley said dismissively, and got up from the desk to wander across to the window where he could be a little further from the heat of Forester's tightly controlled aggression. 'He's got too much money and not enough brains. I wouldn't take his opinion on anything.'

'You're still insisting this isn't murder? You're saying that you're not going to look for whoever's to blame?'

'In a way, I'm relieved to say that it's got nothing to do with me.'

'What's that supposed to mean?'

The small-paned office window was on the side of the building away from the road. It looked out over grass, long and washed-out and boring, untouched grazing that stretched to the sudden climb of the valley side. 'It means I'm no longer investigating,' Stoneley said. 'It means I won't have to juggle with the political complications of keeping a score of deskbound wonders contented and informed so that they can carve up my credit between them when I bring the killer in. Above all, it means I *won't* bring the bastard in.'

'He's going to get away with it?' Forester said, dismayed.

'I don't know. Anything else, ask the Home Office. But don't expect them to be very forthcoming.'

'So I was right.' Forester seemed to be talking almost to himself. 'The accident story was just the start. This whole thing's going to be buried, and no one will know.'

There was the scrape of a ladder on the gutter somewhere above; the teams must all be in, so the radio mast could come down. 'The story had nothing to do with it,' Stoneley said. 'That was just a clumsy excuse to turn strangers away from the valley so we could get on with our set-up. If you'd been here an hour earlier we'd have told you that the area was under quarantine.'

'But what now?'

'The army's coming in, I think. It doesn't really concern me.'

'No,' Forester said with sudden bitter malice, 'and I'll bet you're glad.'

Stoneley turned from the window, stinging with outrage at the low kick. 'You've got no justification for saying that. This is the worst crime in this region that I've seen in my whole career, and I don't let it go lightly. I wouldn't let it go at all if I wasn't forced.'

'Why do they force you? What are they hiding?'

'A word of advice. Don't ask questions like that. And don't get any ideas about going to the newspapers, either. I already told that to Carson, in case he had any ideas about filing the story. At that time we could only have asked the editors to co-operate, but Hennessy and his mob might go as far as a D notice.'

'Are you being pushed out altogether?'

Stoneley was tempted to say more, but knew he couldn't. 'I think I've told you enough,' he said, forcing himself into calmness. 'Please, Mister Forester, for your own good let it drop. Be thankful you didn't lose anything much. Wait for the official story to come out, claim back any money from the insurance and try again.' Take it any way you like, it all spelt *knuckle under*, and it ate at Stoneley like an acid. 'If I can't keep my head up in the face of this, I'm damn sure you can't either.'

Forester looked at Stoneley for a moment. He was distant, speculative. Then he said, 'The official story. Yes, I'll wait for it,' and turned around and walked out of the office.

Outside in the schoolroom they were folding the partitions back and exposing the line of ten grey meat sacks. The clothing and effects had gone for analysis the night before, and now two unmarked wagons had arrived from Carlisle to take them back for post-mortem study. When the corpses were gone the schoolroom could be restored to normality and reinhabited, and little pink faces would be singing morning hymns at the desks which were now serving as mortuary slabs. The irony wasn't entirely lost on Stoneley; poor little bastards, he thought, if only they knew what was waiting for them at the far end of the line. He was feeling old and wrung-out when he went to look for Mike Schaffer.

Schaffer was by one of the wagons, talking to the pathologist. When he finished and turned away he saw Stoneley waiting for him, alone like a child left out of a game. Schaffer hadn't yet heard about the enforced withdrawal — he'd only just arrived with the funeral convoy — but he immediately sensed that something was wrong. Better be careful, he told himself.

'Sorry I'm so late,' he said. 'But it took a while to get the big vans up the road. Part of it's starting to flood.'

'It would,' Stoneley said resignedly. 'We could have used that yesterday.'

'Can't we use it now?'

'No. We're to load up all the vans and send them back.'

This technique of incident control was completely new to Schaffer. 'Why?' he said, bewildered.

'Because it's all over, that's why.'

'You've got him?' Schaffer said, sensing a tiny growing fireball of mixed elation and disappointment, but Stoneley quickly killed it.

'We're not going to have the chance. Hennessy has taken control and he's throwing us out.'

'*Hennessy?*' Yesterday, the man had been a joke. 'Can he do that?'

'He's done it.'

'Oh no,' Schaffer said, shaking his head. 'No, that's too much.'

'Save the arguments,' Stoneley told him, 'I've tried them all. Hennessy is bringing his own men in, and that's that.'

'Amateurs, I'll bet.'

Stoneley glanced around as if he was afraid of being overheard and didn't want it to show, and Schaffer discerned a momentary rock-hard glint behind the despondency. The Chief gave a little follow-me nod and they began to move along the street, past the hotel and away from most of the activity.

102

'Amateurs is a fair guess,' Stoneley said. 'In which case we might be able to get our hands back in after all. Give them enough rope, and they may at least tie themselves in knots.'

'I don't follow.'

'I believe in letting a fool prove he's a fool.' They stopped by the telephone kiosk as two more meat sacks came out of the school, and then carried on. 'That's why I'm not putting up any more resistance to Hennessy. And that's why I'm not completely disbanding the incident unit. They can't object to me leaving one man here with a telephone and all the basic records we've got so far – not unless they're going to go the whole hog and declare a military emergency, in which case I suspect they'd need approval from Parliament.'

They were almost level with Hamilton's Store and Schaffer was grinning at the quiet aptness of the strategy. 'Pity that poor sod, whoever he is,' he said.

'Don't start feeling sorry too soon.'

Schaffer's grin persisted for a moment and then faded abruptly. 'Now, wait a minute,' he said, but Stoneley cut across him.

'You're the best choice. I know I can trust you.'

They stopped outside the store with its rusting enamelled signs for tea and chocolate and its dusty window display of tinned toffees and mintcake set out on faded wallpaper. 'But I'm a Detective Inspector,' Schaffer protested. 'You don't want to see me wasting my time warming a chair.'

'You wouldn't be wasting your time. And I need somebody of the rank and the judgement to know what's going on around him.'

'Anyway,' Schaffer said, 'I'm on leave,' but it was straw-clutching time, like trying to put off a hanging by claiming a dentist's appointment.

Stoneley shot it down easily. 'Leave's cancelled. That gives you another advantage, because your duties have already been covered. I'm not doing this lightly, you know. We may be getting the bum's rush down the valley road, but we're still sitting on a multiple murder and presumably the killer's still wandering around on our patch. You can't turn your nose up at that just because you don't get the chance to play Dick Tracey.'

They started to walk back. Schaffer said, 'Dick who?'

'Forget it, you're too young. Sort out the stuff you need and install yourself in the school. If the headmaster starts getting difficult, refer him to me. When Hennessy and his khaki thugs decide they need us, we'll be there. Anything special we can leave you?'

Sure, thought Schaffer, you could leave me Ellen O'Brien and a water-bed, but he only said woodenly, 'I'll get whatever I need.'

Stoneley slapped his shoulder approvingly and brightened. 'Fine,' he said. 'Now let's go into the hotel and have some of that boiled goldfish-shit that passes for tea.'

By the school a Detective-Sergeant was trying without much success to look avuncular and unforbidding as he told a small group of children that there was going to be no school today, either. They took the news and the little notes that he gave them and walked away. As soon as they were out of his reach they ran off down the street whooping and jumping and hollering. Schaffer watched them dodging around the parked trucks as he trailed in Stoneley's wake into the hotel lobby. Lucky little bleeders.

It was shortly after half past nine, and Carson was high above the village and looking down. He could just see the roofs of the cottages and the hotel over the trees, but as he climbed higher and the track road curved a little more they would be lost to him altogether. Already he could see as far as the lake, and further peaks and ranges were rising into view beyond, mist-shrouded and distinct like the paper layers of a chinese watercolour. When the cold ache in his chest had died down he turned his back on the scene and pressed on uphill.

Today he was wearing jeans and a ski jacket, and heavy rib-soled shoes. As long as he stayed on the surfaced track he knew he'd be fine, following the buried P.O. cable towards the clinic by the concrete marker posts that were jammed into the soft earth by the tarmac's edge, but he knew that he wasn't equipped for any rougher travelling through forest or fell. Under better circumstances, he thought, perhaps he could like it here; maybe even come to love it; not in the tourist season, but in the winter when the population was pared down to the bone and all the brittle edges were showing. Some day he would come back, and to give himself heart for the return he'd determined to get just a little closer, to see just a little more of the reality of the place than the village's confusion or the claustrophobic interior of the hotel. Up here the air was fresh and cold, and it seemed to blow through him as if his body was no more than a fine mesh.

Nobody in the village had seemed inclined to pay much attention to him or to stop him, so Carson had reached the junction unchallenged. A stack of abandoned plastic barrier cones was as good as any signpost, and after the first half-mile of climbing the big muscles in his thighs and calves appeared to realise that there was no point in complaining and settled into a steady, ground-eating rhythm. After another three quarters of a mile he came over the dip and into sight of the Jenner Clinic ruins.

Most of the tarpaulins and plastic sheeting had pulled free and wrapped and tangled around the buildings so that the effect was that of a large skull gift-wrapped in trash. There were no vehicles apart from the two battered shells half-buried in the courtyard, no people apart from the solitary figure of the girl who stood at the gateway looking over the rope barrier.

Alison didn't turn as Carson approached, and didn't even seem to be inclined to look at him as he came and stood beside her, a good stranger's pace away. She was wearing faded blue jeans and a thin anorak, unzipped and flapping. Her gaze seemed to be searching through the wreckage for something that wasn't there – ghosts, maybe.

Carson said, 'Aren't you cold?'

It didn't register for a moment, and then she seemed to come out of a dream. 'I hadn't noticed,' she said, reluctant to take her eyes away from the ruins. 'Who are you?'

'My name's Peter Carson.'

It faded from her memory as quickly as it was written. 'Are you with the police?'

'No. Are you?'

For a moment, she was struck by the oddity of the notion. 'Me? No.' She pointed to the upper level of the clinic's burnt-out wing. 'That was my room, over there.'

'You work for Jenner?'

'I did.' She looked beyond the sooty building to a sea of autumn-brown ferns, waist-high beyond the yard enclosure. 'They found Tracy Pickford in that field.'

'I know. I identified her.'

'I'm glad I didn't have to see her after the fire. I had to look at some of the others.'

That explained her unsteady grip on her surroundings, the Ophelian melancholy.

'She wasn't burned,' he said, and she looked at him directly for the first time.

'But they told me she was . . .'

'They've been saying different things to different people. The story changes every couple of hours. I think there's something they want to hide.'

She couldn't handle that, wasn't interested. She said, 'Were you the man that Tracy had been married to?'

'I didn't even know she'd *been* married,' Carson admitted uncomfortably.

'Oh. I hope I didn't say the wrong thing.'

The wind boiled up into a sudden gust, and some of the loose tarpaulins cracked like whips. Carson said, 'It's all right, I hardly knew her. We met a couple of times, that's all, and then she asked me to drive up. I never found out why.'

He was disappointed to see that he was slipping out of her attention again, as in her mind she drifted back to the dead buildings on the other side of the rope. 'I can't believe it,' she said.

'Did you work in the lab, as well?'

She nodded slowly, almost imperceptibly. 'I'd been down to London and I only arrived back last night. Otherwise I might have been in there.'

'You were lucky. Try to think of it that way.' Jesus, he thought, that sounds trite. Can't you come up with anything better?

'It doesn't help much, somehow. All I want to do is get away, but that . . . that Stoneley man won't let me go. He won't even let me in to see if I can find anything that's mine.'

'He probably doesn't want anything to be moved.'

'Why not, if it was only an accident?'

'I don't know. I told you, the story keeps changing.'

Alison seemed to make a determined effort to clear the fog of distress. 'Well,' she said, 'he isn't here now.' And she lifted the rope and ducked underneath, leaving Carson hesitantly staring after her as she picked her way across the yard. But she'd broken the spell; it was no longer a wall, it was just a rope, and Carson thought what-the-hell, and followed her.

She was in a blown-out doorway, looking up. 'It's a mess,' she said, her voice echoing in the empty space. 'The floor's fallen through.'

He squeezed into the doorway beside her. 'Which was your room?'

'Up there, on the attic floor.' She pointed, but it was no more than a shaft to the open sky. A sudden thought occurred to him.

'Is your name Wells?' he said.

'Yes, Alison Wells. Did Tracy mention me?'

Carson didn't think it would be wise to explain that he'd seen the name on the tag which had tentatively misidentified Tracy's body, but the thought had reminded him of something else. 'They collected a lot of loose stuff and moved it down to the village. I saw them carrying bags of it into the schoolroom.'

Alison shook her head. 'No point asking. Everything will have been ruined. You only have to look.'

They moved away from the wing, which still carried a lingering atmosphere of danger in its smoke-blackened walls and the ripped and hanging floors of its upper storeys. Carson said, 'What will you do now?'

'Get away as soon as I can. As soon as Stoneley will let me.'

'I think Stoneley's pulling out. That's why there's nobody here.'

Alison stumbled on a few loose rocks and Carson put out a hand to steady her, but she managed without him. 'Pulling out?' she said. 'So soon?'

'That's what I heard in the village, no more than half an hour ago. Somebody called Hennessy is taking over.'

The name obviously meant something to her. 'Hennessy? Is he here?'

'You know him?'

'Not exactly. I've heard of him, through the clinic.'

They moved towards the back section of the U, the largely undamaged farmhouse. In a peculiar way Carson was enjoying himself; the two of them alone together like this, they could easily have been friends, cousins, lovers. He could wipe out the pretence when they left and feel nothing; Alison would never even be aware. It was sanitised, irresponsible, and appealing.

Somebody coughed. Or at least, Carson thought they did.

'Wait a minute,' he said.

'What's wrong?'

'I thought I heard something.' It hadn't been from the buildings, it had been from the direction of the dying ferns beyond the yard's outer wall. Whoever made the noise — if there *had* been a noise — was keeping himself out of sight. Deliberately.

'I can't hear anything,' Alison was saying, but Carson shook his head firmly. He was thinking of knives and fire and twelve grey meat sacks in the schoolroom, two of them still warm.

'Come on,' Carson said, and started to guide her towards the nearest door. Her resistance was only feeble, and she didn't forcibly push him away. 'This is a lousy spot to be in when there's no cavalry.'

'I can't hear anything,' she said, bewildered. Her hand on his own was icy. The door was locked. 'I think you imagined it.'

'Maybe,' Carson said, and scanned the yard for cover. The only way out was through the jaws of the U, and then the walled-in track would become an easy rat-run for any fit pursuer. More than a mile – they wouldn't make it.

He pulled her towards the burned-out Toyota, and she tripped and staggered over the glass and the broken stone that littered the yard. He looked around for a hand-sized brick or a piece of sharp metal – anything that might make a weapon, something that he could at least hold and draw courage from. No stone was the right size, and the only metal that he could see was a flattened Heinz soup-can a few feet away from the car. Perhaps they taught you to kill with flattened soup-cans in the commandos, but it was outside Carson's experience.

'What do you think you heard?' Alison said, not as quietly as Carson would have liked.

'Somebody coughed,' he said grimly.

She stared at him and blinked a couple of times, incredulously. 'We're doing this because you thought you heard somebody coughing? Are you serious?'

'Ten people got knifed right here not much more than twenty-four hours ago – damn right I'm serious. And I would have thought that as the one surviving member of staff you'd be more concerned than me.'

From the other side of the wall came a wet sneeze.

'Did I imagine that?' Carson whispered triumphantly.

'I wouldn't exactly call it threatening,' Alison said, and she raised her head to look through the empty window-holes in the Toyota's shell.

A black, shapeless bag was thrown over the courtyard wall, dropping from the large top-stones four feet up and landing in a heap. There was a look of concern on Alison's face as she got to her feet, dust and glass falling from her jeans as she moved around the car. The bag stirred weakly and sneezed again. Alison was running towards it.

'It's Lucy!' she called back. 'But, look at her!'

Carson followed uncertainly at a distance. The bag unwound a little and wet, rheumy eyes looked up at him.

'But it's a monkey,' he said wonderingly.

'She's not a monkey, she's a chimpanzee.' The animal was an immense size, not at all like the cute little dwarves Carson had always imagined chimpanzees to be. 'But what's she doing here?'

Lucy sniffed and rubbed weakly at her nose with her wrist. Some of her fur was missing, showing patches of grey skin, and there was a shaved area across her belly around an operation scar which was barely held together by a row of torn stitches. The edges of the wound looked raw and unhealthy, and Lucy whimpered and held up her hands when she thought that Alison was about to touch the injury. It was an alien, unsettling sound.

'Somebody must have let her out before the fire,' Alison said. 'She's come back.' She tried to get Lucy to sit upright and the ape struggled gamely, but it didn't happen. Lucy lay back rasping hoarsely, her jaw hanging open and her lips rolled back into an exaggerated grin.

There were two more dark figures huddled together in the ferns, dead autumn leaves clinging to their wiry fur. Carson told Alison, and she stood up to take a look.

'It's Fifi and Bobo,' she said. 'We're going to need help.'

The two primates obviously recognised Alison. Carson said warily, 'Are they dangerous?'

'Not if you know how to handle them. They're lab chimps, fully humanised. But this one's in a bad way.'

'But where have they come from?'

Alison nodded back towards what Carson assumed had been a stable. 'The animal house. Over there.'

The two chimps were knuckling their way across the field

towards the low wall, linked by the hand of the smaller one tucked into the fold between belly and thigh of the leader.

'They're coming over,' Carson said.

'I'll get Lucy under cover. You go down to the village and get some help.' Alison's enchanted misery had disappeared. Carson was already missing it; he felt even less sure of himself with this capable girl who reacted so easily and readily to such a bizarre apparition.

'I'm not sure Stoneley's going to believe this,' Carson said. He wasn't sure that he believed it himself.

'Go to Hennessy, then. He knows the set-up here.'

'Let me give you a hand, first,' he offered, hoping she'd say no.

'She'll be too heavy for you. I can manage.'

Fifi and Bobo hopped nimbly over the wall and immediately helped Carson to decide that Alison's plan was a good one. These two were no sick weaklings, and a night out in the open hadn't hurt them at all. The larger of the two was almost mature with a long, pale face and heavily ridged brows, and she stood taller than the wall before she dropped to her hard black knuckles and loped over to sit by Lucy. The other one was a little over three feet tall and was more like the large-eyed and small-bodied media chimps of commercials and jungle pictures.

Lucy whimpered again, and the smaller chimp pouted and emitted a series of *whoo* sounds. Alison was obviously in no danger so Carson moved off towards the track. At the rope barrier he paused and glanced back; the two healthy animals were helping to carry the sick one towards the house.

Carson made it back to the village in less than twenty minutes, jogging most of the way downhill. Until he reached the valley road he saw nobody, the only life and movement a couple of rabbits that fled blindly before him for a few yards, finally getting wise and diving into the roadside culvert for shelter. It seemed that Stoneley's withdrawal was, indeed, complete.

The line of cars and vans that had been strung out of the

village was down to just a few vehicles, and by the hotel two of the incident caravans had gone and the third was being hooked up and wired to a Land-Rover. Entering the lobby he saw that the tall Australian girl was picking her way downstairs with an armload of bed linen. Her hair was tied back and she looked weary, unhealthy.

He stopped by the wooden banister and called up. 'Is there somebody called Hennessy staying here?'

She moved carefully because the carpet was what might kindly be called serviceable; in other words it was old and ugly and thin, and it had enough frayed edges and loose seams to be as deadly as a tripwire. 'I don't know,' she said, peering cautiously over her high bundle. 'What does he look like?'

'No idea. I've never seen him.'

'Don't ask me, then. This place is a mess.' She made it safely to ground level and then swayed around towards the kitchens.

Carson said, 'Where's the boss?'

'God knows,' her voice echoed back down the corridor. 'If you smell any money, you'll probably find him counting it.'

She slammed the kitchen door open with a swipe of her backside and disappeared through, leaving the doors to flap aimlessly for a few seconds like a busker's applause. She had a mean swing to her hips, a whole season's practice. Carson turned and was about to leave for the schoolhouse and Stoneley when he heard someone calling, 'Are you looking for me?'

There was a short fat man at the angle of the stairs. He'd descended a couple of steps in order to be able to see down into the lobby. He was in his shirtsleeves, and he was holding a rough white hotel towel in both hands, wiping at his neck; he'd obviously been shaving, because there were two little rims of soap just above his ears.

'Is your name Hennessy?'

'That's right.' Hennessy came down, making the old wooden treads creak and complain, *hey fatso, walk near the outside*. 'Who are you?'

'My name's Perer Carson. I've just come down from the clinic.'

Hennessy paused about three steps up and his pink, bald face became hard. 'And who the hell gave you permission to go up there?' he demanded.

'Nobody stopped me,' Carson said, and he was about to go on but Hennessy looked around himself and shouted at the top of his voice, 'Stoneley! What is this?'

There was a gap of several seconds and then Stoneley ambled without haste through from the hotel lounge. In one hand he held a teacup and in the other, half a biscuit. The corner of his mouth twitched slightly when he saw Hennessy's disarray, but otherwise his face was a polite blank. 'What's the matter?' he said.

Hennessy pointed at Carson. 'This man wandered on to the clinic site unchallenged.'

Perhaps Hennessy was expecting Stoneley to whip out the cuffs and shout *okay boys, let's nail him*, but he simply glanced at Carson and said, 'What's it got to do with me?'

'I want to know what you're playing at, leaving the place unguarded.'

'I'm doing as I was told.'

'Nobody told you to declare open house.'

'You want to borrow my men, you make a formal request. But if my team's off the case, there are things for them to do.'

Hennessy came down the three steps, and lost the slight advantage of elevation. 'But you're supposed to have left a token force.'

Stoneley looked behind him into the lounge. 'I did. He's around here, somewhere.'

Hennessy was winding up for another salvo when Carson said, 'Can I get a word in, please?'

Both men stopped and looked at him. He went on, 'There's a girl called Alison up there with three sick-looking apes.'

'Alison?' Hennessy said. 'Alison Wells?'

'That's her. She worked at the clinic.'

Hennessy turned on the senior officer. 'Stoneley, you closemouthed bastard, why didn't you tell me she was alive?'

Stoneley shrugged. 'It's in the paperwork. If you're not interested enough to read it, that's your problem.' He looked at Carson. 'Did you say apes?'

'Yes, chimpanzees.'

'Of course,' Hennessy said excitedly, 'The animal house! I never even gave it a thought!'

'Real ones?' Stoneley said with interest, still looking at Carson.

'Actually, only one of them's sick. She wants help to get them down to the village.'

'Stoneley,' Hennessy said in tones which suggested he didn't expect opposition, 'I need one of your vans and some blankets.'

Stoneley dunked his half-biscuit in what was left of his tea. 'I'm off the case,' he said, and then quickly got the wet mass to his mouth before it could sag and break up.

'Forget the personal angle for a minute, will you? This could be important!'

'I don't see why you should be so excited about a few monkeys.'

'These aren't monkeys, they're lab chimps. For Christ's sake stop behaving like a schoolkid and start acting like a policeman.'

Stoneley's eyes narrowed a little as he swallowed. The shot had reached his pride. 'I'll agree to lend you a van,' he said reluctantly. 'You can get blankets from upstairs.'

Carson said, 'What about a vet?'

Hennessy shook his head. 'An ordinary doctor would be more use.' He looked at Stoneley. 'Do your cars carry first aid? Penicillin, morphine, that kind of thing?'

'Yes. Nothing too complicated, though.'

'It's a start,' Hennessy said, and with a last rub around the jowls which got most of the dried-on soap he moved back towards the stairs. Stoneley looked around for a moment before setting his cup on a small half-round table which carried a vase of dried ferns and the inevitable Lake Steamer schedule. He was moving towards the door when Carson said to anybody who'd listen, 'Shall I come along?'

Hennessy was climbing the stairs with a speed that was surprising for his size. 'Sorry, Carson,' he called back. 'The clinic's out of bounds from now on. You shouldn't have been there in the first place.'

He disappeared, his voice tailing off along the upstairs landing. Stoneley was already out and half-way across the road to the schoolhouse, calling to a sergeant to organise a vehicle and driver.

Carson was alone in the lobby. Old dark carpet in bad taste, a few pieces of junkshop furniture that were no more than set-dressing, a couple of faded hunting prints on the plain and slightly yellowing wallpaper. Somewhere beyond three or four brick walls a hot-water geyser fired up and the plumbing started to shake. In the dark, wood-panelled bar there was the whining vibration of the bottle cooler as its thermostat kicked in.

'Don't mention it,' Carson said out loud.

The van was back in fifteen minutes, and it reversed alongside the hotel so that the animals could be transferred to a double garage which was tucked into the narrow angle between the back of the building and the neat rockery that marked the start of the hillside behind. The hotel's owner had agreed to move his Range-Rover and his wife's Renault into the car park for the moment; Carson stood on the fringe of the activity with his hands in his pockets and wondered if there was a going rate for the rental or whether the owner was ready to negotiate special terms.

Lucy was carried from the van, wrapped in blankets and looking around her feebly. Bobo, the larger of the two healthy animals, climbed out on her own and confidently followed Alison through the garage's side access door. Fifi scampered close after, nervous of being left behind, dragging her blanket on the ground behind her.

It seemed that on their release the chimpanzees had run for the nearest wood, but despite their fear of the explosion and the incomprehensible activity that had followed it they were too fully humanised to want to keep running. After a wet day and a night in the open they'd cautiously made their way back to the only place they were familiar with.

Fifi and Bobo seemed to be quite unharmed by their experience, but not so Lucy. She'd obviously been weakened by some operation shortly before the escape, and besides the sepsis of her unclosed wound she was showing some of the symptoms of pneumonia. After a few minutes Alison came out of the garage, closely followed by a young police constable who hurried past her and on towards the main part of the hotel.

'How are they?' Carson asked her, somewhat self-consciously, as they walked across the small car park.

'Lucy's in a bad way, she might die. The other two seem fine.'

'I'd always thought that animals were okay in bad weather.'

'Chimps are tough, but they can get any human disease that's going. Influenza has them dropping like flies if you're unlucky. They've no natural resistance. Hennessy is sending for one of the police doctors from Penrith.'

'Aren't you going to stay with them?'

She shook her head and kicked up a rainbow from a dirty puddle that had collected on the asphalt. 'Hennessy wouldn't let me,' she said. 'I just want to get away from this end of the country altogether.'

'Back to London?'

They had to wait as the chimp transport van reversed out into the street and turned itself around. 'As soon as my car's ready,' Alison said over the noise of the passing engine, 'whenever that is.'

Carson said, 'What's wrong with your car?'

'The windscreen shattered and I came off the road last night. I bent a wing against a gatepost and jammed the wheel. The police have towed it to some garage in Penrith for me.'

116

'You could go back now and have the car sent on when it's ready. Assuming Hennessy will let you go.'

'I think he wants everybody out of his way as soon as possible,' Alison said. The idea of getting away from the area with its unhappy associations – a complete reversal of her mood of the night before – obviously appealed to her. 'But that sounds expensive.'

'No more expensive than staying in the hotel. The owner's into his third exercise book as it is.'

'I suppose not,' she said as they passed the windows of the cheerless dining-room and came up to the ivy-covered porch. 'No Boots or Rucksacks, Warm Welcomes at Reasonable Rates.' 'And until one of the agencies can find me another job, I'll have no money coming in.' They stopped and she looked at him, directly for the first time. The daylight had worked on the blue of her eyes, changing their shade to an indefinable grey-green. 'Will you be driving back?' she said.

'As soon as I can get away,' he said, wishing he had the nerve and the confidence to return her gaze fully. He had to remind himself sharply that she was only asking him for transport, not inviting him into her bed. He said, 'I'll give you a ride, if you need one.'

She gave him a quick smile. 'I'll get my luggage,' she said. 'What's left of it, that is.'

Chapter 9

Roger DeLisle Forester was ex-Royal Air Force and a Bachelor of Science, in that order. He'd left school at the age of seventeen, a bright and promising pupil a year ahead of his class, and had entered the Service direct, much to the affected world-weary regret and disappointment of his friends. By his mid-twenties he was married to the daughter of an estate agent and serving on the aircrew of a Vulcan bomber which held back the Communist Threat from a base on Cyprus.

Whoever had designed the contract to which Forester had put his name, they'd known what they were doing. One signature and that was it, they'd secured not just a career but a life. There was a superficial illusion of fairness in the clause which gave you the option to renew or quit after a certain period, but when you reached the age of thirty – so far away at seventeen, and yet not so far that the idea of a new start seemed daunting if you hadn't quite made it as a hero – when you hit thirty and the contract came up, and you found yourself with no skills and no qualifications for anything other than what you were already doing, then you weighed all the advantages and disadvantages (what seventeen-year-old ever did *that*?) and you signed. You accepted that the world wasn't completely open to you any more and never really had been, and you signed.

Forester had seen it coming and had decided not to wait for his optimism to die. At the age of twenty-six he'd made a request to buy himself out. Naturally, it had been turned down.

The decision to apply hadn't been an easy one to take; they would watch you and suspect you afterwards, their confidence in you shaken. You were intimately acquainted with the capabilities and operation of one of their foremost pieces of defence weaponry (virtually obsolete) and you had shown that your commitment and enthusiasm were less than total.

There were other factors that had pulled him back as well, a growing warmth of ease and security that ate away at ambition leaving it no more than a heartless, tottering shell. They had a pleasant subsidised flat in Akrotiri, white plaster walls and red tiled floors with a wrought-iron balcony that gave them a view across the rooftops towards the Ladies' Mile and the Mediterranean beyond, and as long as you kept to the British community within the base the local friction of Greek and Turk wasn't too much of a worry. Marie had put her pills aside, and although she hadn't actually started a baby yet she was already feeling better; the headaches were gone and so was the dull, listless sensation that resulted from tissues that absorbed water and then refused to give it up. As far as getting pregnant was concerned, the base doctor told her not to worry, it often didn't happen for a while, it was simply the result of tension and she should stop worrying and trying so hard.

Forester persisted with his request. He searched back to find a precedent in the records, and reapplied with this in support. He knew that waiting a few more years for his option to arrive would undercut his self-confidence even more, and that if he delayed so long he would probably sign up again. He told them that he wanted to resume his education – a solid and irreproachable reason that had the added convenience of being true – and in the end they decided that such a disconsolate airman would be of limited use to them, and they let him go.

They moved back to England and spent the next three years in a grimy but pleasant seaport town as Forester studied for a degree in Sociology. Marie got a job in a solicitor's office to support them; all of their savings had gone in the buying-out and Marie's father had lent them the rest. Fortunately he wasn't in a hurry to be paid back, and they'd agreed on a strategy in which Marie would leave her job when Forester graduated and found work that he wanted to do, and they'd resume their plans for a family. It was lucky that she hadn't conceived yet, and because she didn't want to go back to the pill she visited a local clinic and came back with a dozen tubes of sticky cream and a contraceptive cap. It was the size of a small bucket and it squeaked when she coughed.

Those three years were fun, kind of. They lived in a rented terraced house in an area that was barely a step up from a slum, and Forester discovered that when you had an inevitable upheaval to look forward to it was impossible to feel trapped or depressed. Marie didn't share his outlook much; she worried about what they were going to do when the course was over.

After eight months of highly-qualified unemployment they got him at last. He conformed. Nobody seemed to need graduates, especially non-technology graduates, and under sheer financial pressure he accepted a job offer from Marie's father. Only for a while, of course, until he could find what he really wanted, but deep inside he knew he was beaten. Marie seemed content, almost relieved. They moved back to their home town, and Forester sensed a mocking victory in the old familiar streets. You thought you could get away from me? You thought you could escape?

With a regular income at last they started to repay Marie's father. They bought a cheap bungalow on a neat little estate of identical units and in the evenings Forester worked on a correspondence course to get some estate-agent-type letters after his name. It was easy compared to the intensity of study that he was used to, but it left him feeling heartsick and caged. As his personal goals dissolved and became no more than insubstantial and bitterly-remembered dreams, the desire to raise children through whom those dreams could finally be realised became an obsession.

Two years later, he went for tests. Any couple that tries for two years without success is considered infertile. Forester wasn't afflicted with a macho mentality that refused to accept that the trouble might be his; he'd gone into the literature carefully and knew that more than a third of the infertility cases recorded had been traced back to problems in the male, but the sperm count was adequate and so they paid for Marie to have tests at one of the private clinics.

The simpler procedures showed nothing; no obvious psychological inhibitions, no antibody reaction, her cycles were regular and ovulation seemed normal. The only thing left was to take a look. Culdoscopic examination showed that Marie's fallopian tubes were blocked by an accumulation of wastes, endometriosis. If it had been found ten years earlier it probably could have been cleared without much difficulty, but now the tubes themselves were damaged and closed, and the eggs couldn't descend to be fertilised. The examining doctor said that there was a good chance that surgery could correct the problem, but it wasn't cheap and they should go home and think about it.

They went home. Marie didn't do much thinking, but she cried a lot. After a while Forester got tired of watching her, and he started to go through the literature again.

Tube repair had little more than a twenty per cent success rate. Even if it was possible to remove the damaged sections and link up what remained, there was a possibility that growing scar tissue would form a new blockage. And as the examining doctor had said, the treatment wasn't cheap. Britain now led the world in fertility manipulation, but that was strictly business; when Steptoe and Edwards had done their pioneering work on *in vitro* fertilisation and reimplantation in the seventies, it had been without the support of the Medical Research Council. The grants and funding that had subsequently been made available for the set-up of clinics and practices had come through departments of industry, not of health. The clinics attracted more than forty per cent of their business from overseas – suddenly babies had become an invisible export.

Forester could just about raise the money through a bank loan – his father-in-law and his bank manager were fellow

Freemasons — but it was a one-shot chance with the odds favouring failure. He wanted better.

He faked a list of appointments in his office diary and spent an afternoon in the commercial library in the town centre. There were plenty of clinics which handled the basic stuff like donor insemination or sperm concentration or hormone treatment, but for surgical procedures you generally had to go for a clinic attached to a hospital practice, and the fees climbed alarmingly.

Lab fertilisation and implant was the most expensive item of all with the exception of genetic surgery, and that was so experimental that nearly every case was one of volunteer research with a high abortion rate as the foetuses developed malformed. But the advantage of the F & I procedure was that there was a recognised element of trial and error built in; it always took a number of attempts under subtly varying conditions of temperature and pH level to get the cells to merge at all, and then it was a matter of finely-judged timing of cycle and hormone levels to get the blastocyst implanted. So you paid a lot more, Forester reasoned, but it looked as if they kept on trying until they succeeded; with a simple tube repair, failure simply meant tough luck and no comeback.

There would be no second chance. With a loan repayment and their existing debts they'd never be able to afford it, and Marie would soon be reaching the age where child-bearing became risky and ill-advised. Forester combed through the yearbooks and directories and compiled a shortlist of commercial clinics, and then he went back to the office to type out letters to each requesting catalogues and current price lists. Within two weeks he had all of his replies, and he spoke to Marie's father; three days later, the loan was in his account.

Of all the services offered, two seemed the most promising. One was the Jenner Clinic in Carlisle, the other was the Sherborne Institute near Windsor. Both offered a partial refund in the event of a total failure; maybe even enough, if it wasn't too late, to sell the car and raise a little extra private finance on the house and go for a last attempt at the tube repair after all. He rang the two numbers from the office. Windsor had an eighteen-month waiting list – it was in the south-east catchment area for visitors from America and from the Catholic countries – but at Carlisle he could get in by the autumn if he applied straight away.

He told Marie, but she hardly seemed to want to listen; she threw in irrelevances about his job, and where would they stay, and who would look after the kitten – a pampered beast whose idea of hygiene was to go into the garden at night and shit amongst the vegetables.

Forester wasn't worried. He'd already forwarded a deposit and a booking to the Jenner Clinic.

After the news of the so-called 'accident', Forester had driven the twenty miles to Carlisle and told Marie. She'd already packed her hospital bags and was ready to leave; official word had come through that there were problems at the back-up facility and that complete refunds would eventually be made – depending upon the way in which patients complied with in indirect but unmistakeable request that there should be no publicity for the occurrence.

Marie was now dry-eyed and calm. The vast complexity and the extreme discomfort of the process had seemed, to her, to be far removed from what she instinctively understood to be the urges and satisfactions of motherhood, and so the loss was really no loss at all. Her pain and her feelings of incompleteness and inadequacy had come long ago, with the realisation that she was not the fully functioning organism that she had believed herself to be. But she was learning to cope with this and to understand it; her husband's obsession was a wave for which he alone had provided most of the energy.

He'd taken her to the station and put her on the evening train after telephoning his father-in-law and making arrangements for her to be met. Then he returned to the cheap hotel in the city centre where they'd been staying and spent the night with the lights on, staring at the yellowed ceiling overhead.

After his meeting with Stoneley in the disintegrating incident room, Forester had gone to sit behind the wheel of his car to think for a while. At first he couldn't find any essential track of logic amidst the feverishly circling tangle of ideas, and after a while he'd stopped trying.

The car was half off the road in an angle beyond Hamilton's Store; it was the closest spot to the centre that he'd been able to find, and he'd turned the car around so that it faced in towards the village. He could see what was happening, although he couldn't easily be seen.

He saw the arrival of the unmarked wagons, and the transfer of the meat sacks from the temporary mortuary. He counted them, grey and shapeless and unmistakable. He saw Stoneley and his young D.I. taking a walk along the street towards the store, pausing only a few yards away before they turned and walked back, obviously deep in some conspiracy. Ten minutes later he saw Carson jogging past from the valley road making for the hotel, and five minutes after that he saw Stoneley, along with a girl and a fat little man he'd never seen before, climbing with two constables into a van that had drawn up outside.

Forester wasn't sure what he wanted or expected. Not justice; he wasn't so naïve. There was no justice, only the most generally acceptable compromise negotiated by the most powerful interests involved. They were fixing it now. His interests weren't included – they thought they were buying him off with promises of refunds and compensation – and as the van sped past towards the clinic turn-off the basic essentials of an idea fell into place without any prompting or pushing.

The hotel lobby was empty. He lifted the flap of the reception desk and stepped around to consult the pegboard which carried the keys to all the rooms upstairs. Four of the hooks were empty, indicating rooms that were occupied.

Ignoring the junk under the counter, he opened the two shallow drawers at waist level. One of them contained a dog-eared romantic novel, half a bag of toffees and some hotel stationery, the other a glove, a pack of cards, a toy submarine and a large bunch of keys. He took the keys and closed the counter-flap behind him before he went upstairs.

The upper landing was dark and cool and quiet. It ran the whole length of the back of the building, and there were doors on both sides; illumination was from skylight panels above. Forester was only interested in those rooms which fronted the hotel.

The owner and his wife lived in a small flatlet down below so all of the rooms, with the exception of the bathrooms and a linen cupboard, seemed to be guest rooms. Forester listened for a few moments, but as far as he could tell he was alone.

Ten doors. Forester sorted out the passkey from the bunch, and went to the end of the landing. He tapped lightly on the first door and then, when there was no reply, he twisted the key and let himself in.

It was a small room. There was an old teddy bear on the bed and a couple of posters pinned to the wall; they were airline travel posters, one showing Sydney Harbour Bridge and the other a ski scene at some place he'd never heard of. There was a portable TV on the bedside table and a row of books on a makeshift plank-and-brick shelf under the window; the help's room, no use to him. He withdrew and moved on to the next.

The rooms were all roughly the same size and shape but they were furnished slightly differently, as if the pieces had been assembled through several visits to country auctions. There was a basin and a mirror in the corner of each, and a heavy spread on the bed. He ignored the fittings in every case and crossed to the window, looking out at the view of the street. There was little difference until he reached Alison's room.

It was in the middle, and larger than any of the others. Some of the extra space could be accounted for by the presence of a bay window instead of an ordinary flat casement. Forester looked out at the three-sided view of the valley road; he was almost directly over the hotel's entrance and opposite the school. He tried the sashes. They were stiff, but they raised and didn't jam.

He glanced around the rest of the room, but he was already satisfied. It was dominated by the overstuffed bed and a huge dark wardrobe. The wallpaper was a floral print, uninspired but inoffensive. There was a bundle of girlish frilly things on a chair by the bed, and a screwed-up rag of orange nylon that had been flung into the corner.

Outside in the street the van was passing again, returning from its hasty trip to the remains of the clinic. Forester left the room and closed the door behind him, noting the number before he walked away and down the stairs.

He returned the keys to their drawer and then searched underneath for the checking-in book. He'd seen Peter Carson using it the night before to make his own arrangements, so presumably as long as the police were around and running the catering resources of the hotel at full output, it was a case of see to yourself. He turned over the leaves. There were a few short bookings later in the month, mainly at weekends, and nothing beyond. What he had in mind would take at least a week before he could get back to Langstone; it sickened him to think that he might return too late, but he didn't see any way that he could reduce the time. He entered a reservation for the bay-windowed room for seven days ahead, and then took a hotel envelope from the stationery drawer and enclosed two notes from the small supply in his wallet as confirmation. He wrote his name and the room number and dates on the front.

As he was writing, he glanced up. Carson and the girl were standing just outside the entrance, and he heard the girl say, 'I'll get my luggage. What's left of it, that is.' Then she came towards the lobby, and Carson followed.

The girl didn't know Forester, and she went on past and towards the stairs without looking at him. Carson stopped at the desk and said hello.

'You're moving out?' Forester asked him.

Carson opened the loose-leaf folder at the tariff page and

pulled his cheque book out of the back pocket of his jeans. 'Hennessy says I don't have to stay, and his word seems to be the one to take around here. What about you?'

'I think I'll hang around for a while. See what goes on.'

'I doubt whether there'll be much to see. May I . . . ?'

Forester looked down at the ballpoint pen that he was still holding, and then said 'Sure,' and handed it over.

'You shouldn't make too much of this,' Carson said as he scribbled out the cheque, holding the folded book flat with difficulty. 'You should try to put it behind you.'

'Like you did?' Forester shook his head. 'Some of us don't recover quite so fast.'

Chapter 10

Forester had gone when Carson came downstairs with his luggage. Alison was sitting on the hard chair which faced the dining-room door, her weekend bag on the floor beside her. She stood up when he appeared.

Carson said, 'I left a cheque to cover my bill. Can I do the same for you?'

'Forget that,' Alison said flatly. 'Let Hennessy worry about it.'

They drove out of the village and back down the narrow lane which skirted the lake, and Alison pointed out the gateway where she'd left the road and damaged her car. After Ravens' Bridge the roads were more open, and as they headed east out of the central glacier-cut landmass they both began to relax a little. It was one of the oldest masses in Europe, a compressed blue-grey ash with deep-scoured valleys that radiated like spokes from the upland ranges at its heart. The place was too old and too knowing to seem any more than superficially benign.

He was about to tell her how to recline her seat so that she could lie back a little, but she found out anyway. The last few miles that would lead them to the motorway were a straight and easy run, four lanes and a central reservation, and now it was possible to feel that they were really travelling and not just touring; but they weren't to get away so easily.

Three miles before the motorway interchange, Carson glanced in his rear-view mirror and saw the white police Minivan. It was about a hundred yards behind, and it was pacing him. He didn't know how long it had been there – because the road was so good he'd been lazy in checking – and although he wasn't going particularly fast he eased off the accelerator and let his speed fall.

The police driver seemed to realise that the stalking part of the contest was over. The blue light on the van's roof abruptly came to life and the vehicle swung into the overtaking lane and pulled in just before the Mercédès, *STOP* sign glowing. Carson drew into the side of the road a few yards behind.

The policeman had an inelegant scramble to get out of the van with its low cramped interior, and when he straightened his uniform and walked down the road towards the Mercédès, Carson was out of the car and waiting for him.

Carson recognised him as the younger of the two men who had been on the roadblock in the valley on the previous afternoon. He didn't even seem interested in Carson; instead he looked along the length of the car with satisfaction, as if it were a piece of big game that he'd just brought down.

'Got your documents?' he said.

Carson took the licence and the papers out of his wallet. 'I wasn't doing more than thirty,' he said.

'*I'll* tell you what speed you were doing. Where are you from?'

'London.'

Forsyth stared at him. 'Don't get funny.'

'That's what you asked me,' Carson said, pleased at scoring a point but knowing better than to let it show.

'I want to know where in this area.'

'You know damn well I've been staying in Langstone. You were on the barrier when I drove in.'

Forsyth pulled a wad of forms out of a flat pocket on his overjacket. 'And don't get smart, either,' he said. 'You flash bastards are all the same. I'm booking you for exceeding the limit.'

'I can see there's not much point in saying that I wasn't.'

'That's right.' Forsyth looked up from filling in the details, a dull gleam of hope in his eyes. 'You been drinking?'

'No,' Carson said. 'Sorry.'

Forsyth tore off the completed top copy and handed it over. 'You'll get a summons and a form to fill in. That's where you can claim any mitigating circumstances. I wouldn't contest it.'

'I know the way it works,' Carson said, folding the paper in with his documents and returning them all to his wallet.

He got back into the car as Forsyth walked off. He started the engine and waited for a couple of heavy lorries to pass before he pulled out. Alison looked out of the passenger window at the police van as it slid away to the side; Forsyth was leaning across the seats and seemed to be writing something. She turned back to Carson.

'That was outrageous,' she said. 'You weren't speeding at all.'

'I know.' Carson glanced in his mirror again; the Mini-van was moving, indicating to pull out. 'It happens quite often.'

'But why?'

'It's the car,' he explained. The van was staying well back, trailing him, waiting for him to make a mistake. 'They resent me. It's the same when people spit on it or scratch the paintwork in the street.'

'You could lose your licence.'

'They don't usually book me.' This was true; generally they sounded off for a few minutes to fix him firmly in the hierarchy, and then let him go. But perhaps the police here were in a specially lousy mood because of losing the clinic investigation.

They were approaching the motorway interchange, a complex of roundabout and slip roads with the six carriageways running beneath. Alison said, 'I'd be tempted to change the car.'

Carson eased into the circle and indicated for the southbound exit. 'And let them win?' he said.

He took the sliproad and saw the side of the van flash white in the late morning sun as it was lost from his mirror. There was a steady flow of traffic heading south from Scotland, and as he picked up speed to join it Carson saw the Minivan again. It had stopped on the overpass. He knew that Forsyth was

130

watching him. A gentle pressure on the accelerator, and the Mercédès left it all behind.

Children have the purest conception of time. They know its true nature, that it is subjective and relative, and that pedantic measurement can have no effect on the most endless of hours or the briefest of days. But they learn.

It generally took Sarah and Peter Gaskell about twenty-five minutes to walk down the track from Ravens' Crag farm to Langstone and the schoolhouse, cutting across the fields before they reached the valley road to shorten the route. Today they had taken more than two hours over the return, delayed and distracted by the lonely fascination of the living countryside.

No school for an indefinite period. New premises to be sought and arranged. Neither of them could understand the exact nuance of the tortured English or the note they'd been given to take home, but they knew what it meant and the message was freedom. They giggled loudly as they ran across the deep grass to the track wall, with Peter tripping and stumbling in Sarah's old wellingtons despite two pairs of socks.

They climbed over the wall, jumping down from the top. The track was unmade and stony, worn down into twin ruts with a slight peak running up the middle. In places the ruts were dark with the remains of the previous day's rainfall.

Home was ahead. Their joy became more subdued, and tinged with guilt. Sarah wished that she hadn't lost the note along the way. It had fallen from the pocket of her duffel coat as she'd leaned out over a fast stream, stirring the mud with a twig to see if she could disturb anything, and it had been carried away as quick as thought, dancing primly on the boiling surface. Peter had reminded her at intervals since that she was In Trouble.

Their mother probably would not believe them, not without some talisman of evidence to hold back her scorn. Their father would withdraw and uneasily support her, avoiding the children's eyes and finding himself something to do before long, something that would take him out of the house, out on to the fells with his dogs.

Their protests would probably be ignored. They would be turned around and sent back. As they came within sight of the farm they began to compose themselves, to prepare to tell their story with straight-faced seriousness and exaggerated regret and concern.

The farmyard was quiet, the gate was open. Peter tugged at Sarah's sleeve. 'Look!' he said, and Sarah nodded.

In the middle of the yard the Strange Boy was waiting for them. Waiting to play.

PART THREE

London

16 October 1987

Chapter 11

After two hours of driving Carson and Alison stopped at a motorway services area, a cut-rate chunk of space-age that straddled the carriageway. The cafeteria was on an upper floor, and the rest rooms and sales kiosk were below. There was muzak echoing from cheap speakers, generated from a cassette somewhere that couldn't keep speed. As Carson waited for Alison he wandered across to the kiosk; the floor was wet from swabbing-down, and there was a faint smell of disinfectant rising from the glistening vinyl.

Even in the mid-afternoon there were still copies of most of the newspapers, and Carson picked up a couple at random. Outside in the concourse he looked through for any mention of the events at the clinic, but there was nothing. He dropped both copies into a battered wastebasket when he heard Alison approaching.

'Everything okay?' he said, and she wrinkled her nose in disgust and then smiled.

They returned to the Mercédès and refuelled before joining the traffic flow. Home was a little nearer, and with every few miles the countryside grew a little uglier. The motorway slashed on through fields and villages without regard for either, and after a while the villages flowed together and became towns, and the towns joined and merged to take on the appearance of a city. When the press of grey on either side became too much the motorway fizzled out and abandoned them to the early-evening commuter jam of the North Circular Road.

During the slow hops between traffic lights Carson stole sideways glances at his passenger. She'd reclined the seat again but she wasn't sleeping; her head was turned aside and she was looking out of the window, not really seeing anything. The last few miles to Ealing were covered in a jerking crawl which took more than an hour, and daylight was breaking down into darkness as Alison gave directions through the maze of streets and parked cars away from the main shopping area. Streetlight timers were cutting in and the lamps were glowing red as she pointed to a space and asked Carson to pull in.

Alison's flat was on the top floor of a large house, one which, in its own extensive grounds, might have been attractive; but it was packed into a close row of dwellings, its gardens disfigured into tarmac parking space. Carson carried her weekend bag through a brick archway to a side door, and waited as she looked for her key.

'Thanks again for the ride,' she said. 'What about the petrol?'

Carson shook his head. 'There's no expense. Forget it.'

'I can't just forget it.' Alison found the key and opened the door, reaching inside to switch on the hall light.

'You've got to concentrate your resources until you can find another job.'

'That won't be a problem.' She held the door open as he shuffled through sideways with the bag, and then closed it behind him and led the way up the stairs. The hall was neat and tidy, but it was bare in a way that betrayed its nature as common property. 'The agency will get me placed again as soon as I'm ready.'

'You're going to wait a while?'

She nodded. 'I think I might.'

A short half-landing gave on to passageways to different parts of the house. Alison led the way to where four doors lined a shallow cul-de-sac. Two of the doors were numbered, and Alison opened up the door bearing an eight.

The curtains in the flat were drawn, cutting down even the poor light that remained from outside. Carson heard the flick of a switch, but nothing happened.

'Looks like the bulb needs replacing,' Alison said as she

136

moved across the room, bumping some furniture as she misjudged her way.

There was another click, lower down; possibly a table lamp, but still nothing happened. 'There's no power at all,' Alison said with obvious annoyance. 'Excuse me for a minute.'

She brushed by him in the dark, and her closeness brought a sudden tingling which raised the short hairs on his skin for a moment; then she was gone, and light from the hallway spilled into the room from the half-open door.

Carson set down the bag and moved across to the dim grey square of the window behind the curtains. He pulled the drapes back, and it helped a little – the mixed twilight and yellow sodium light would at least be enough to prevent Alison from falling over the bag in the middle of the floor. On the far side of the hallway there was an insistent knocking on the opposite door.

What he could see of the flat told him nothing. There was a drop-leaf table under the window with a hard chair on either side, facing into the room like two stone lions. In front of that was a low sofa and a coffee table. The table was glass-topped, and there were several piles of magazines under it. On another low table by the wall there was an inexpensive stereo unit and some uneven stacks of records; he couldn't make out the details on the posters on the wall above the unit, but they might have been Escher prints. Across the hallway, a door was opened and an unfamiliar girl's voice registered surprise.

'Alison!' the girl said, 'I didn't know you'd be back so soon.'

'Why's the power off?'

'They did it this morning. I've been querying the bill.'

'But I'd sent you a cheque to cover my share of the quarter.'

'I know, but it wasn't that. I wasn't happy with the bill.'

'You mean you haven't paid it?'

The girl, although Carson couldn't see her, was obviously being evasive. 'I've got the money set aside,' she said.

'But why didn't you tell me about it when I was here two days ago?'

'I didn't want to worry you. I wasn't expecting you back, so I didn't think it would affect you.'

Alison sighed. 'I suppose this means there's no hot water and no cooking.'

'I'll go down and sort it out tomorrow,' the girl said with an attempt at eagerness. 'I'd have gone today if I'd known you were coming home. Sorry.'

Carson realised with a guilty start that he'd almost wandered uninvited into the bedroom, all his attention on the conversation outside. Despite a tug of interest he moved away, and after a little less than a minute Alison returned. There was something in her hand, Carson couldn't see what, but then she held it up; a box, and it rattled slightly.

'She's given me a box of candles,' Alison said, somewhere between resignation and disbelief. 'That's what I call consideration.'

'How comes she pays the bills?'

'It's a shared meter. I'd like it separate, but there's a common bathroom and kitchen between the two flats. I'm damn sure she hasn't queried the bill because she's said nothing about it before. She just hasn't paid it, that's all. She's supporting an unemployed Turkish waiter with my money while I sit in the dark. I at least wanted to offer you something to eat.'

'You can come home with me,' Carson offered, and the speed of her reply shook him slightly.

'You talked me into it. Let's go.'

This time, she insisted on carrying her own bag down the stairs, because it was no longer a social prop to precede an invitation. Carson's place was only a couple of miles away, in a vastly overpriced and overcrowded strip along less than half a mile of the river east from Kew Bridge. The traffic had thinned considerably by now, and most of the twenty minutes of the journey were taken up by Carson calling at a late-opening delicatessen on the way.

It was a huge house, too big to survive as a single occupied unit; a developer had stripped it out and done a thorough conversion to make it into four self-contained apartments with only the hall and stairs common to each. Of the three floors and the basement, Carson had all of the ground level and what had once been the garage on the side of the house, now a second bedroom which was reached by a slightly awkward twisting passage which cut under the stairway.

Carson parked the Mercédès on the forecourt off the road, and walked around to help Alison out. She seemed slightly awed by the size of the building, by the large white-columned portico and the four stone steps that had to be climbed to reach it, by the cleaned and refaced brickwork and the elegant white shutters on the windows. There was a light in the top-level flat, the smallest of the four.

The front door was heavy and solid, and it pushed back against the pressure of a slow-closing spring. Just inside the hallway, behind the speaker grille and the numbered bell-pushes, there was a shelf with a few pieces of mail; a couple of them were for Carson but they were junk mail, expensive waste paper from a motoring organisation. The door to his own apartment was the only one in the hall on this level, a few yards down and on the left. As Carson was opening up, the front door finally closed itself.

Alison said, 'You leave the hall light on?'

'It'll switch itself off in a few seconds.'

They were in a lesser hallway, an irregular square which opened out on the right into a short passage which turned under the angle of the stairs. There was a bedroom to their left, at the front of the house, and Carson pushed open the opposite door and led the way through into the sitting-room, switching on light as he went.

'I'm impressed,' Alison said. The room was long and plain, stretching down to french windows which gave on to a railed veranda and a view of the gardens and river beyond. The thick carpet was moss green and the walls were dove grey, and the only diversions from simplicity were a Regency fireplace with gas logs in the cast-iron grate and some ornate plasterwork in the angle between walls and ceiling. Outside the french windows the last redness of the day was draining from the sky.

Carson seemed to have been taken off-guard by her appreciation. He looked around as if he never really gave the place any attention. 'Thanks,' he said uncertainly.

Alison stepped forward and ran her hand along the green velvet covering of a Chesterfield in front of the fireplace. 'With all this and the car, those magazine articles must pay you pretty well.'

Carson shrugged. 'Not really,' he said. 'I don't sell many.'

'I don't understand . . .'

'The articles are just something to do,' he explained. 'Most of my money comes from a trust fund.'

She nodded, curious but too polite to pry. She said, 'I don't suppose there would be any hot water for a shower?'

'As much as you like,' Carson said. 'Gas heat, no problem. There's a shower just off the bedroom through there, or there's a full bathroom around the corner.'

'Shower will be fine.'

He showed her into the bedroom and put her weekend bag on the bed, and then went to get her some towels from the linen cupboard in the hall. She unzipped the bag and started to dig through the tangle of clothing for her soap case. Tomorrow she would have to do some shopping; she'd kept most of her other clothes at the clinic.

The room was sparse and tidy, as fresh-looking and tasteful as the rest of the apartment, and like the rest of the place it told her nothing about Carson – except, perhaps, that he employed somebody to clean up for him, because it had the impersonal neatness which could only be achieved by an outsider. There was a radio by the bed, and a full rack of books.

'It must be quite some fund,' Alison said, raising her voice to reach him. 'Prices in Strand are incredible.'

'I wouldn't know.' His voice came muffled from the cupboard. 'An agent fixed it all up for me.'

'Don't you even know what it cost you?'

Carson appeared with the towels, a bath-sized and two hand-sized, and laid them on the duvet by her bag. 'I wasn't really interested.' He moved back towards the door. 'My father wasn't exactly short of money when he set up the trust.'

'I can't imagine what that must have been like,' she called after him. 'As you grew up, I mean.'

'I didn't get anything until I was twenty-two.' Carson's voice was receding fast, towards the kitchen at the far end of the lounge. 'He left my mother when I was four and never gave her a penny after that.'

Alison was surprised and slightly pleased to hear a trace of feeling breaking through. 'Didn't he ever do anything good for you?'

'Yes,' Carson said, faint and distant from the kitchen. 'The old bastard died.'

She closed the door; she was going to close it completely, but she changed her mind and left it open a few inches. Then as she started to unbutton her blouse she moved around the bed and sat down, turning her head to one side to read the titles of the books in the mellow light from the table lamp. They told her nothing, paperbacks and hardbacks mixed indiscriminately, a wide variety of titles and subjects and a few back editions of *The Writers' and Artists' Yearbook*. She stood up and shrugged out of her jeans and pants.

Peter Carson stared hard at the open copy of *The Cookery Year* on the work surface before him. There was no problem with the recipe; he was simply having difficulty in concentrating enough to read two lines of text in sequence.

He was angry with himself for what he had let slip. Not because he'd been provoked or excited; on the contrary, it had happened because he'd allowed himself to relax, to lessen his control and to become open and vulnerable. There were parts of his life that he didn't want the world to see, Alison least of all.

Maybe it was pointless anyway. She'd probably looked around the flat and compared it with the two shabby and incomplete rooms that she'd just left, and the first foundations of the barrier would have been laid. This was the old slug's vicious inheritance, Carson thought bitterly, to dump the money on me before I'd had a chance to learn how to fight for it or to handle it – and too late for it to be of any *real* use. There was nothing to reach for, no sick aching energy of ambition to move him; as far as he could see, he was just kicking around in medium comfort and waiting to get old and die.

He should be getting used to it by now, but instead he was almost ashamed of the place where he lived. Perhaps there's hope for me yet, he thought as he unrolled the fillet on the cutting board. Blood oozed out of the meat and stained the carbon steel of the knife blade.

The shower cubicle was in a tiny room with a basin and toilet off the bedroom, and a luxurious steam built up quickly in spite of the efforts of the extractor fan to draw it away. When Alison stepped back into the bedroom the slight drop in temperature immediately sought out the damp patches on her back and shoulders that she'd missed with the towel.

All of the doors between her and the kitchen were open, and the aroma of the food was seeping through. She pulled the end of the bath towel across her damp shoulders, and the loose tuck that she'd used to secure it came undone so that the towel unwound and fell free.

Carson's bathrobe was on a hook behind the door. Alison contemplated putting it on, but wasn't certain. If the place had carried the distinct imprint of Carson's personality the action would have fitted in easily, but the apartment was strangely arid in its elegance and she was sure that she would feel unsettled.

But the breathless battering of the shower had done a lot to sluice away the weariness and discomfort of the past couple of days, and perhaps she felt bold enough to try. She lifted the blue-grey towelling from its hook, and sniffed delicately at the material; it was clean and odourless with no man-animal scent, as if it had been bought and hung but never worn.

She put it on, and stood before the dressing-table mirror. It was much too big for her, of course, but then that was probably rather appealing. All the same the effect wasn't quite right, and so she undid the Alice-band at the nape of her neck and let her hair fall to her shoulders, tousled and damp at the edges.

Still wrong. She tried loosening and retying the robe to be more revealing. Now she'd only have to sneeze and the whole damn thing would slide off her shoulders and into a heap on the floor, in which case she might fairly be accused of trying too hard. Finally she undid the sash and let the robe fall altogether.

She contemplated the long, pale shape of her body in the mirror, the angles that were softened into curves, the light dusting of talc on the clear skin. While she had been in the shower the bedroom door had drifted open a few more inches, and if Carson were to cross the lounge on the far side of the hallway he'd probably be able to see her; but there was still something wrong, and it was obvious that an analysis of her appearance would be pointless. The fault lay not with Alison but with her surroundings, soulless and uninviting. Peter Carson's camouflage, non-involvement guaranteed.

She sighed lightly and pushed the door closed before she turned to dress.

When she emerged, the wall-lights had been dimmed and the polished table by the french windows had been set for two. There were wineglasses and an open bottle.

'Be a couple of minutes yet,' Carson called from the kitchen.

'That's fine,' Alison said, and crossed to look out of the windows. She could just make out, beyond her own reflection, the night-shapes of a long garden with a flood-wall and a towpath at its end. She turned as Carson brought a dish of hot rice on a metal stand to the table. 'Is there a key for this?' she said, and Carson nodded.

'Catch.' He fished a small key-ring out of his pocket and tossed it to her. 'It's the odd black one that doesn't look like a key at all. Takes about four turns to wind the deadlock back, then it's the little key for the latch in the middle.'

He went back into the kitchen and Alison unlocked the window, stepping out on to the clay-tiled terrace. She could look down over the rail into a walled sunken courtyard belonging to the basement flat, a brick-lined niche with some white cast-iron garden furniture and some shrubs in open barrels. There was a large picture-window through to the apartment itself, and a wooden gate led to a flight of brick steps linking to the passageway down the side of the house. Overhead there was a smaller veranda jutting from the flat above; the October wind sang through the ironwork of the terraces, making a sound like women's voices plaintively calling. Across the gardens the river was wide, flat and moonlit, crossed some distance to the east by a railway bridge. Alison shivered slightly, and stepped back inside.

She relatched the window and looked for the deadlock key on the ring, but Carson said, 'I'll see to that later. This is ready now.'

It was certainly better than the sandwich and a can of beer that she'd expected; if this had been the late and unlamented Eddie she'd probably have been faced with a walk to the nearest carry-out to find that he'd finished off the beer in her absence. She glanced back towards the narrow terrace and said, 'It's very nice. But don't you get overlooked?'

Carson shook his head. 'Only for those few feet outside. And there's nobody living upstairs right now, anyway.'

'Someone moving out and selling up?'

'Sitting on an empty place and waiting for the price to rocket, more like.' He was about to add *that's how the old man made all his money*, but he stopped himself in time.

Alison noticed the momentary tension, but he seemed to

bring it under control pretty quickly. Time for a change of subject, although she wasn't sure why. She said, 'Tell me about the magazine stuff you write. Am I likely to have read any of it?'

'It's possible, but not likely. I haven't done all that many. I don't even do them very well.'

'That's not a very positive way to look at it.'

'But it's true. I'm not pushy enough to dig out real controversies, and I can't get worked up about red-hot issues. I commission most of my research from an agency, and apart from that I rely mainly on secondary sources.'

They sat and ate. 'Why do it,' she said, 'if it gives you so little satisfaction?'

'I didn't say it gave me no satisfaction.' He leaned across with the bottle, and she realised that she'd almost drained her glass at the first attack. She'd have to be careful. 'Sometimes my style's exactly what's needed,' he went on. 'I get lots of commissions from company publications, airline in-flight magazines, that kind of thing. My American agent once got me some stuff placed in the *Reader's Digest*.'

'Really?' Alison said, accepting more of the Stroganoff. 'I didn't think anybody actually wrote for *Reader's Digest*. I thought it was all done by a computer.'

'Well,' Carson said uneasily, 'that's the kind of thing I write.' There was a defensive undertone which seemed to say *you asked me, remember*?

The level of the wine dropped rapidly, and after the meal Carson scrambled around at the bottom of a stripped-pine cupboard and came up with a bottle of port. His uncertainty over what he had and where it might be seemed to indicate that he only drank when he entertained, and that he didn't entertain very often. He fired up the gas logs to supplement the background heating and they sat on the Chesterfield before the warm dancing fantasy. She agreed to one glass of the port, not because she was feeling at all drunk but because she knew that she ought to be.

Conversation was easier now, and although Alison noticed

that Carson managed to keep it centred around her life and background she no longer tried to push and probe. It would be unsubtle, and there must be better ways to find out. If Carson had been predictably agreeable and obviously interested she would have accepted the lift and that, apart perhaps from the promise of a follow-up lunch some time, would have been the end of it. Maybe she was reacting to the challenge.

She didn't mean to, but she finally came to terms with the lateness of the hour with a yawn; it was already happening before she could stop it. He seemed to understand.

'I'll run you home,' he said. 'Or there's a spare room here, if you can't face the blackout.'

It was a knife's edge of a mood, and by the merest fraction it had tipped the wrong way. A spare room, modest and demure; not just 'you can stay here', but all of the scandal and none of the fun.

She smiled. 'Thanks, but you've done so much for me already. There are things I have to sort out, you know.'

'Sure,' he said. 'I'll get your bag.'

Carson drove with extra care and an eye on the mirror, but they covered the distance on the noisy roads to Ealing without any problem. There was nowhere to park the car, and that solved any uncertainty about how to handle the parting; before she slid out she gave him a quick kiss on the cheek like a schoolyard dare, and was gone before there could be any reaction. Before disappearing through the brick arch she turned and gave him a final smile and a wave.

He brushed his cheek with his fingertips. It was a better ending than any he could have imagined.

Chapter 12

The morning sun came slanting through the corridor windows, making the airborne dust sparkle and filling the air with the scent of lavender floor wax. The courthouse windows were open but the radiators below them were hot; it took several hours for any changes in setting to make themselves felt through the massive heating system, and it was impossible to keep up with the irrational temperament of the month. A couple of days ago, Tony Donaldson thought, it was pissing with rain and half-freezing; now everybody was stamping around in wellingtons and three pullovers, about as appropriate as scuba gear on a parachute drop. It wouldn't last, because it never did, and the end of October might even bring the first tentative snows of winter – but until then people would continue to be caught out, and to shiver and sweat as a penance for their gullibility.

Donaldson side-stepped to avoid two solicitors in conversation, fairly young men who seemed to have made a conscious effort to propel themselves into a facsimile of late middle-age. He spilt some of the machine tea from the plastic cups as he moved, and one of the wizened youths glanced back for a moment in disapproval. Donaldson fought the urge to put his tongue out.

Mrs Balanchine was sitting on a hard chair outside the number two courtroom. It was a busy corridor with a constant traffic of clerks and assistants between the courts and the offices, a disconcerting place for an outsider to be, and Mrs Balanchine seemed relieved that Donaldson had returned. She was an elderly lady, small and frail-looking, wearing her best tweed overcoat and a small hat with some faded cretonne flowers on its side. She was clutching a large handbag on her lap as if it was a shield.

There was a radiator behind the chairs with a protecting shelf above it, and Donaldson set the plastic cups down on this.

Nervous? he fingerspelt, following it up with the fear sign but smiling to take the edge out of it.

Wish all over home she fired back in the rapid, un-punctuated shorthand of spelling and sign, blinking through the thick lenses of her glasses. A teenage clerk from one of the offices down the corridor was passing with a sheaf of rolled documents bound in ribbon, and he was staring at the exchange. He bumped into the double doors of the courtroom as they opened out towards him.

Easy Donaldson reassured her. *No fear just talk me. Take time no rush. Soon over.*

Mrs Balanchine was from the small village of Renwick, about ten miles north of Penrith. She'd had severe hearing impairment since birth and had become profoundly deaf in her mid-twenties, at a time when welfare services were mainly restricted to those provided by charities and ignorant and inaccurate phrases like 'deaf and dumb' were still common public currency. Her early education had been poor because of the misconception amongst her teachers that language ability and intelligence were somehow different faces of a single concept, and it was only in later life, with the help of her husband, that she'd been able to make up on the intellectual deprivation of those early years.

Edward Balanchine was now in hospital. He'd been hit by a car three weeks before, and he had a broken arm and pelvis. His wife had been comparatively lucky, thrown into the road and bruised but otherwise unhurt. Now the driver of the car had been traced and in a few minutes would be appearing at committal proceedings in the Magistrates' Court on charges of dangerous driving, failing to report an accident, and failing to stop at the scene of an accident. Tony Donaldson had rearranged his visits and his work schedule back at the Social Services department so that he would have most of the day free to serve as Mrs Balanchine's interpreter.

The clerk of the court was standing by the doorway and calling for Mrs Balanchine. She read Donaldson's expression and stood up with him, turning and leading the way through into the courtroom.

The room was a waist-high maze of rich wood panelling, staggered over several levels with the magistrates' bench at the highest. The senior magistrate was a large and imposing man with a round face and a bald head; the man and woman on either side of him seemed dried-out and lifeless by comparison, as if most of their energy had been diverted to sustain their companion.

Nobody appeared to have been told about the need for translation, and there was no copy of the interpreter's oath in the courtroom. Fortunately, Donaldson had his own copy in his wallet, written on the back of a creased and much-used card. As he was reading it out he became aware of a movement at the back of the room.

He looked over the card as he delivered the oath, which he knew by heart, and saw the incongruous green of an army uniform through the glass of the doors. The court usher was out there talking to the officer, and Donaldson was about to return his attention to the card when he saw the usher deliberately turn and point at him. The army officer turned to look.

Donaldson faltered. Several heads were raised, and one or two swivelled in the direction of the doors; the usher saw this, and started to hustle the army man away. The officer was saying something, but the usher was shaking his head firmly.

The oath was ended, and the prosecuting solicitor got to his feet. Donaldson wasn't too happy about his placing in the room – the light was behind him and against Mrs Balanchine, the complete opposite of the ideal – but they would probably manage. He repeated the opening question out loud, fingerspelling each word with an occasional supportive sign, breaking away for the sake of legalistic accuracy from their usual curtailed and compressed flow of pure communication. Mrs Balanchine frowned and concentrated, trying to hold the tortuous grammar in her mind as the question was formed letter-by-letter. Over in the dock the accused, a gangling boy of about nineteen, was smirking. He seemed to think that he had an idiot for an accuser, but his solicitor was not so happy; he didn't seem to like the idea of having to address a witness through an intermediary.

The army officer was back, his uniform cap in his hands as if he was in a church. He was sliding into an empty bench at the back of the public rows. Only a reporter from the local newspaper turned to glance at him.

The session was short, the smile fading from the face of the accused as Mrs Balanchine described in detail how the car had come storming around a blind corner and swung in close to the wall where they were waiting to cross. The defending solicitor tried to fault her on identification but she described the car as having a metallic paint job, wide wheels and a number of triangular stickers in the rear window; she also thought that she could remember a couple of fluffy dice hanging from the rear-view mirror, and she gave the first three letters of the registration number.

The rest of the proceedings was over very quickly. The accused had fixed a new glass fibre wing on his car the day after the accident, and he said he couldn't remember what he'd done with the old one. After a hurried consultation with his counsel it was decided that he wanted to alter his plea. The magistrates gave the go-ahead to the committal and would be prepared to consider a bail application in the afternoon.

There was coughing and shuffling and a lot of page-turning as the court prepared to move on to the next case, and Donaldson helped Mrs Balanchine down from the witness-box. As they moved across the courtroom the army man stepped out to meet them.

'Mister Donaldson?' he said. For a soldier he was casually, almost comfortably dressed, a heavy pullover and an old-fashioned thin tie just showing over the crew neck, pressed trousers and polished shoes. He looked younger close-up than he had from a distance.

Donaldson said, 'That's right.

'I've to ask you to come with me.'

'Where to?'

'I can't tell you here. It's been fixed up with your office. They know all about it.'

'So?' Donaldson said, and started to lead a confused Mrs Balanchine towards the door. The officer moved to block them.

'Please, sir. I've got my orders to get you to come along, no matter what.'

'At gunpoint?'

'No,' the officer said, obviously uncomfortable, 'of course not.'

The court usher appeared then and asked them to move out into the corridor. The army man reluctantly gave way.

'Look,' Donaldson told him outside, 'I'm not being deliberately awkward, but you can't appear from nowhere and expect me to go along with you without an explanation.'

The officer hesitated, and then said, 'It's to Langstone. Do you know it?'

'I know it.'

'We need someone to do some – ' he flapped his hand inarticulately ' – translating, or whatever you call it.'

'When?'

'Right away. I've got a Land-Rover outside.'

'Out of the question. I've got to get Mrs Balanchine to the hospital so she can see her husband.'

'That's all right. We can take her in the Rover.'

Mrs Balanchine was helped into the Land-Rover. She sat without protest in the passenger seat as Donaldson clambered into the back to sit on a narrow sideways bench, thinking to himself this isn't real, it isn't happening. The driver was apparently unfamiliar with the area, and the need to call directions forward made question and conversation impossible; the only responses he could get were Langstone, a promise of explanations later, and another reassurance that everything had been cleared through his office. The impenetrable lack of doubt in the military mind, he reflected; if it's been okayed on the next step up, further question becomes unnecessary.

The Land-Rover pulled into the ambulance unloading bay at the hospital and then moved off to wait in the staff car park while Donaldson took Mrs Balanchine to the men's ward. Her husband was on the free list, visiting at any time, which meant he was bad. Donaldson left Mrs Balanchine on the ward and found a pay phone to call his office.

They confirmed that the army's request had been approved by the head of department but no, he wasn't available to explain. He never damn well is, Donaldson thought, and asked what was to be done about Mrs Balanchine. Somebody's on his way over, he was told.

It was an uneventful drive to Ravens' Bridge, past the steamer pier and the small wooden jetties before turning sharply to cross over a shallow, slow-moving stream; a final view of the calm and sparkling waters of the lake and then they were swinging around into the village's centre – a wide area off the road painted into parking spaces, a couple of tea rooms, several small hotels and a marine shop with a yard for pleasure boats alongside. There was an end-of-season atmosphere; relief and sadness mixed. The fishing nets and the postcards were no longer on display, and the woollens and the charming useless pottery had been packed away for the coming winter and the new season to follow – then they were out of the village, passing through a scattering of newer and less substantial houses and following the narrow lakeside road to Langstone.

They met no other cars on the road and when they reached Langstone itself they didn't stop. They took the first turning after the hotel and began to climb towards the Jenner Clinic.

Tony Donaldson's first view of the clinic site was of a curious and ill-assorted hybrid of stone and canvas. Those parts of the complex which were neither intact nor totally destroyed had been covered and converted to shelter equipment, and the central courtyard was almost completely sealed in by an open-sided marquee top supported on braced poles. Two army lorries with hanging tailgates were parked nearby, and behind them was another Rover.

The officer led him into what had once been some kind of common room. The TV set and the vinyl chairs had been piled in a corner, and the room was now a field headquarters. The air still held the sharp, sooty smell of burning, now dampened and a little stale.

'Please wait a moment,' the officer said, and went out of the door.

Donaldson looked around. There was a noticeboard with safety messages and memos, some of them old and yellow. No carpet. A heavy wooden desk with a large-scale ordnance survey map of the area pinned out across it, and some papers which Donaldson was trying to read upside-down when the little fat man walked in.

'Sorry about all this,' he said, 'my name's Hennessy.' He turned to introduce a dark-skinned and compact officer who had followed him. 'This is Captain Robert Windeler of the Army Special Services Unit.' Windeler gave a slight nod, but didn't otherwise change his expression. He sauntered around the desk, leaving the show to Hennessy.

Donaldson said, 'Are you finally going to tell me why I'm here?'

'You mean, nobody's said?'

'Apart from someone needing an interpreter, nothing.'

Hennessy seemed satisfied, as if this was exactly how it should be. 'Good. We'll give you all the details in a moment, but first I'd like you to read something and sign it.'

Windeler slid a form across the desk. 'It's only a declaration under the Official Secrets Act,' he said. There was a trace of accent in his voice that Donaldson couldn't place. Mediterranean, perhaps, if the skin colour that he'd taken for suntan was natural. 'Just a formality.'

Donaldson read the form through and signed it; only his silence was needed to keep him from all liability. Windeler took the sheet from him and slipped it into a drawer in the desk. Then he locked it.

'All right, Hennessy,' he said, 'you can go through with him now. But I still think you're wasting your time.'

'Perhaps I am. We'll soon know, won't we?'

Hennessy led Donaldson out into the courtyard. 'You may find this job a little . . . unusual,' he said, choosing his words as carefully as he picked his way through stacks of jerrycans, bundles of wire, and anonymous green sacks. The canvas overhead snapped and cracked in the wind, the supporting poles quivering with the strain. 'In fact, it may not turn out to be a job at all, but without you we couldn't know for sure.'

The wet plaster smell and the white dust on the cobbles underfoot indicated that rubble had been cleared from the yard only a short time before. They reached the entrance to what was probably the least damaged of the buildings, long and windowless. There was a soldier in battledress and beret by the door, and he stood aside to let them pass.

The only windows in the building were narrow and high, and they washed the enclosed space in an opal gloom. For a moment Donaldson supposed that he was in a stable but no, the smell was wrong, dry and musty and not nearly so strong as the fertile stink of horses. There were cages against the long wall and dark, manlike shapes were moving towards the bars; the tiled floor glistened wet from a recent hosing-down, the walls were rough and whitewashed, and at the end of the room there were some battered grey lockers, a large enamel sink, and a bare wooden butcher-block table with a greengrocer's scale on it.

The larger of the two chimpanzees stood upright and grasped the bars of the cage. Her coarse fur was bristling with ready aggression. There was nobody else in the room. Donaldson turned to Hennessy.

Hennessy said, 'Please don't look at me like I'm a fool. I suspect I'll feel enough of one anyway.'

'But who am I supposed to be talking to?'

154

Hennessy was obviously embarrassed. 'To them, actually. Their names are Bobo and Fifi.'

The larger chimp had settled down. The smaller peeked around from behind her. Donaldson said, 'Is this a joke?'

'No joke, I assure you.'

'But they're monkeys.'

'Chimpanzees. There's quite a difference.'

'Not *that* much of a difference.'

Donaldson looked again, keeping well beyond Bobo's brawny reach. She was black and well-built and obviously powerful. Hennessy said, 'Please, Mister Donaldson. I asked for you to be brought here to do a specific job. Will you at least please make an effort?'

'To sign to a chimpanzee?'

'There's nothing ridiculous about it. They're lab chimps, and before they were acquired for the Jenner Clinic they were part of a language project. I want you to find out whether they've kept any of their signing ability, and if so how much.'

Bobo was watching Donaldson, not attempting to meet his eyes but reading his body and his posture instead. He said, 'But how – how do I start?'

'I don't know. The same way you'd open a conversation with a child. You're the expert, Mister Donaldson.'

Donaldson had got over being self-conscious about his signing quite early on in his training, but as he squatted down before the cage and made a greeting sign he felt that early embarrassment returning. Both of the chimps looked at him without reaction. Fifi yawned and scratched herself.

Donaldson straightened. 'You can't be serious about this.'

'Please. Just try.'

He tried again, spelling *Bobo*. The larger chimp pulled herself up and rested her face against the bars, watching him sideways, while Fifi grinned and shook her head from side to side. Hardly a great display of comprehension. He said to Hennessy, 'What do they like?'

'Like? How do you mean?'

'Sweets, chocolate, anything like that?'

'I don't know. I thought they only liked bananas.'

'Can you get me some stuff from the village? There must be something we can use to get their interest.'

Hennessy thought for a moment, then nodded. 'I'll fix it up,' he said, and moved towards the door.

Whilst Hennessy was talking to the soldier outside, Donaldson found a light switch for three unshaded bulbs high in the rafters. They didn't do much to cut the gloom, but they were a help. He went back to the cage and concentrated on Bobo, because she seemed to be giving him more attention and was sitting close up to the bars. He fingerspelt *Bobo want chocolate?* and got what he thought might be an expression of interest as Bobo made a couple of deep *whoo* noises and rocked from side to side. He repeated the query, substituting biscuit, ice-cream, banana; there was the same level of response, but nothing more.

Donaldson sensed that Hennessy had returned and was behind his shoulder, and he said, 'Are there any bananas around?'

'I think they have them in their feed,' Hennessy said, moving away again. 'Let me check.'

As Hennessy was opening up the grey lockers at the end of the room, Donaldson spelt *Bobo* again. Fifi had wandered off and was throwing small handfuls of straw around at the back of the cage but the big chimp stood up and grasped the bars, still rocking.

Hennessy arrived with a handful of bananas, blackened and ripe. Bobo responded immediately by reaching out with a begging gesture, palm upwards and fingers slightly curled. Fifi shuffled over and stood behind her, eager to share in the bounty.

Bobo want banana? Donaldson signed as Hennessy watched anxiously. Bobo continued to reach out, but Donaldson held the banana beyond her grasp.

'This isn't going to work,' he started to say, but Bobo pulled her arm back into the cage and made a vague two-handed gesture.

'Was that something?' Hennessy said hopefully.

Donaldson was doubtful. 'I'm not sure. It could have been a variant on the banana sign.' Watching Bobo he repeated the sign in full, a stylised outlining of the fruit with thumb and forefinger followed by an exaggerated peeling gesture.

Bobo touched her crooked fingers to her lips and then lowered her hand, palm upwards. Then she brought both hands back to her lips and spread her arms expansively, before bringing them back together and pushing her fists forward at waist-height as she rocked on her haunches; then the banana sign, clearer and more distinct this time, both hands finally coming together with the fingers bent, a rough but distinct letter B.

The signing was crude and approximate, but the meaning was unmistakeable; PLEASE TRAINER GIVE BANANA BOBO.

Donaldson gaped numbly. Bobo was reaching out with her begging gesture again, and he realised that he was still holding the bananas. He broke one off the bunch and held it out tentatively. Bobo pursed her lips and began to pant and chomp her jaws in appreciation as it came within reach. As she took the fruit her hand brushed Donaldson's, rough and dry and warm. Then she knuckled off to the back of the cage and Fifi followed, her eyes fixed on the banana although she wasn't trying to snatch.

Hennessy said, 'What are you getting?'

'I'm not sure. They know some signs, all right, but I'll need time to find out how many.'

'But you'll be able to ask them questions?'

'That's expecting a lot. I don't think so.'

Bobo was breaking off pieces of the banana, rolling them around with her lips. Fifi was sitting patiently by, hand outstretched in the begging gesture. Bobo broke off a piece and magnanimously handed it over.

'There are a lot of claims about chimp language ability,' Hennessy said. 'See what you can find out.'

Donaldson took the bananas over to the butcher-block table and found a knife and a dish, He chopped the fruit into pieces; Bobo and Fifi were now at the bars again and getting quite vocal. He needed to keep the rewards small to maximise his results, or he'd quickly end up with two bored and sick chimps and no means of persuading them to co-operate.

He set the dish before the bars as a visible inducement. Then he started to make progress with simple objects in the room, rewarding each correct identification. Bobo was doing all of the signing and collecting all of the fruit, while Fifi watched each transaction anxiously but made no effort to communicate. The signing was unorthodox, many of the gestures modified and difficult to read; there was no fingerspelling at all other than of first letters of names. It was more than a simple indication of wants, because with a little prodding Bobo was starting to make sentences with a logical construction to them. In some ways Donaldson realised that it was he that was actually doing all the learning – Bobo was using a vocabulary that she'd already acquired, whilst he was struggling to adapt himself to it.

'I don't believe I'm doing this,' he muttered.

The thrill of the bananas started to fade after a while. Bobo gave every other piece to Fifi, and after that she rolled away from the front of the cage and started to throw straw around. Fifi stayed, her hand stretched through the bars, looking from the bowl to Donaldson and back again, but otherwise not signing.

'What's the matter?' Hennessy said.

'She's getting bored.'

'You should be making it more difficult.'

'Not with the conversation, with the food. It's hard to get a real exchange going. As soon as she gets what she wants, she stops signing.'

Hennessy moved in closer now that he knew that he wasn't placing communication at risk. Bobo was lying on her back, her short legs waving in the air. 'Can't she understand what you're trying to do?'

'She understands it. She's milking it for all it's worth. How long is it since they were taught to sign?'

'A few years, but the handlers kept it up – that's what I've been told, anyway. It made the chimps easier to manage. They were already used to using signs, and over a period the handlers picked them up.'

There was a knock on the door at the far side of the room, and after a moment the soldier entered with an armload of goods in striped bags. He dumped them on the table by the scales, and Donaldson went over to sort through them. There were bags of boiled sweets, several blocks of chocolate, some assorted bags of toffees, some cartons of flavoured milk, and a block of ice-cream that was starting to melt and ooze through its wrapper.

The soldier said to Hennessy, 'Could you sign this, please, sir?'

Hennessy looked down at the slip of paper that he was being offered. 'What is it?' he said.

'An expense voucher. They wouldn't give me credit in the shop.'

'Trusting of them,' Hennessy observed as he put the slip down on the table and reached for his ballpoint pen.

'I didn't press it. I felt bad enough as it was. They probably think we're all having a Smartie party up here.'

Donaldson dropped the leaking ice-cream into the sink and emptied the rest of the bags into the tray from the scale. He left the toffees on the table, not wanting to have to wait through five minutes of loud and appreciative chewing between replies. He carried the curved steel tray over to the cage and set it down just out of reach, leaving it in view as he went back for a chair.

Hennessy looked up from replacing his pen in his jacket pocket, and called out a warning. Donaldson turned and saw that Bobo had her arm through the bars, prodding at the basin with a straw and rocking it so that it came close to spilling its contents within her reach.

Donaldson rescued the bowl and placed it between his feet as he sat down. 'Smart monkey,' he said.

Bobo tapped her head, the *think* sign.

Hennessy brought a chair of his own and set it down some distance away. 'Don't underestimate them,' he said. 'They can pick locks when they want to.'

'All right, I'm ready to give this a try. What do you want to know?'

It went slowly, with Donaldson struggling to transform Hennessy's questions into logical chains of linked concepts that Bobo might grasp.

Bobo remember fire?

FIRE (a dead end; she was simply recalling the sign, not the occasion. Try again.)

Bobo remember when big fire Bobo scared Bobo run?

BOBO RUN COLD GREEN STRAW (Cold green straw? 'The grass outside,' Hennessy supplied. 'It was deep and wet. There was another chimp that night, an old one, got pneumonia and died afterwards. Ask her who opened the cage.')

Who open cage Bobo Fifi?

PLEASE TRAINER OPEN CAGE BOBO

Trainer no can open cage. Who open cage?

PLEASE TRAINER OPEN CAGE

If Bobo tell who open cage, trainer ask open cage. Who open cage?

PLEASE TRAINER GIVE CHOCOLATE BOBO

Who open cage so Bobo run from big fire, run cold green straw? Tell trainer, trainer give chocolate Bobo.

BIG FIRE BOBO RUN, BOBO HIDE

Who open cage Bobo, so Bobo run?

LUCY OPEN CAGE BOBO

'Keep at her,' Hennessy urged.

Bobo tell trainer who open cage big fire?

DIRTY SHIT TRAINER

Bobo ran to the back of her cage and Fifi had to scamper out of the way to save herself from being trampled, and then Bobo was storming back with a handful of straw and dung which she hurled at Donaldson before slamming herself into the bars and screaming loudly as they shook. Her fur was bristling and erect, and she was grinning furiously to show her yellow uneven teeth. Then she abruptly dropped back and walked away.

Donaldson had jumped from his chair and stumbled back a couple of paces, and Hennessy had removed himself even further. The guard from outside was at the door, but Hennessy waved him away.

'You want me to try again?' Donaldson said. Fortunately the dung had been dry, and it brushed out of his hair easily. Bobo at her most literal.

'No, I don't think it's worth it. Thanks for trying at all.'

'I'll carry on. I don't mind.'

'It's getting late. Thanks anyway.'

Glancing at his watch, Donaldson saw that it was after five; seven hours since he'd been picked up at the courtroom, during which time he'd skipped lunch and spent his afternoon handing tidbits to a bright primate. Fifi was back at the bars and stretching out her hand in a vain attempt to reach the steel tray. Her fingers were crooked, but she didn't seem to be attempting the begging sign. Bobo was muscling up and down morosely at the back of the cage.

'Looks like the little one's making a "C",' Donaldson said. 'Could that be anybody?'

'No,' Hennessy said, and he kicked the tray so that the contents spilled within reach of the bars. 'Come on, I'll get a car to take you back.'

The Land-Rover was waiting, but it took a minute or so to find a driver. As they stood by the covered courtyard Hennessy said, 'Remember, please, not a word to anybody. It's been cleared with your office.'

'Who would I tell?' Donaldson said in a voice which suggested that he even doubted it himself. 'Who would believe me?'

'You might be tempted, but it wouldn't be wise. Thanks for your help.'

Evening mists were starting to fill the valley as the Rover began the steep descent to the village and the lakeside road. It all seemed disjointed and unreal to Donaldson, as if his world had suddenly taken a lurching sideways step. He felt both elated and frightened. For a few brief moments he'd been able to forget the room and the bizarre encampment and Hennessy at his elbow, and he'd conversed in a language that came to him now almost as readily as his first; he'd conversed with a dark-eyed alien.

Hennessy watched the Rover go, following it until it was lost behind a fold in the uneven green that provided a covering for the harsh crags underneath. Then he looked across to the far side of the valley, softened by the twilight into a cascade of blue silk; it was going to be another damp and lousy night of drizzle. Tomorrow he would have to make a visit to Penrith to get himself fixed up with some more appropriate clothing for this unsympathetic and unreasonable patch of country. He turned and looked back at the half-covered clinic, at the low exposed walls of the animal house.

'Lying bastards,' he said softly under his breath.

Rennie Hamilton came from behind the counter of the village store and picked her way across a floor that was crowded with display stands and boxes, craning to catch a glimpse of the Rover and its occupants as it sped on past the hotel and towards the lake. The army trucks had passed through in convoy the previous evening, and any new fact or assumption about the happenings at the clinic's ruins were now conversational gold-dust.

She was too late, there was nothing to see. She was lowering herself from the tip-toe that she needed to look over the panelled backing of the window display when something else caught her eye, further down the road.

'I don't believe it,' she said.

'Believe what?' her husband demanded, levering himself with difficulty out of the empty space of the refrigerated bacon counter. He dumped the wiping cloth back into the sulphite bucket, and some of the liquid slopped on to the linoleum. Finished, the job that that he'd been putting off for most of the day. He switched on the refrigeration unit, and as it shivered into life the counter lights came on under the glass.

'One of the Gaskell children's coming down the road with a shopping bag. The little lad. Nobody with him.' She moved away from the window. 'I've seen everything now. Eight weeks of collecting the order and still they haven't paid a penny. Now they send a child rather than face us.'

'Don't serve him,' Billy Hamilton said decisively, stretching his dog-lean, fifty-year-old frame and feeling some of his joints popping.

'I can't not serve him,' she said as she moved around the counter and back on to home territory. 'And his father knows it, too. That's why they've sent him on his own.'

'I'm going to go up there and ask Gaskell what he thinks he's playing at.'

'It's not for us to chase. It's for him to come down here and settle his debts, like everybody else in the valley. Not to send the little boy in his place so he doesn't even have to offer excuses.'

The door swung open and the bell bounced on its spring. Peter Gaskell shuffled through in his oversized wellingtons, a large empty canvas bag flapping against his knees. His hair was rumpled, and the toggles on his duffel coat were done up wrong. He could only just reach the handle to close the door behind him.

Hamilton had disappeared through the connecting passage which led to their living quarters. The door was more or less permanently wedged open, and Rennie Hamilton could hear the abrupt gush as the sulphite was emptied away.

Peter Gaskell placed a half sheet of exercise-book paper on the counter and said, 'Can I have the order, please?'

'Are you on your own, Peter?'

'There's no school.' He didn't seem as elated as he might by the idea.

'I know, but that's a heavy bag for you to carry on your own.'

'Only going back,' he pointed out with incontestable logic. 'It's empty coming down.'

'Couldn't your father come down with you?'

'He's out on the fells. I can manage it all right.'

She looked down at the undersized and ill-clothed child, and was warmed by an ache of loving despair. She had no children of her own. For a moment she wanted to say that her husband would run the order up to the farm in his van, but something else quickly stepped in and said no. It wasn't the valley way. People paid their debts and when they needed help, they asked and it was never refused; it was the way that the small and widespread community had always lived, and as a system it was dignified and efficient. Perhaps the Gaskells behaved like outsiders but the community was there, ready and open to them; all they had to do was to slip into the place that was offered.

She looked down the list. All the standard items, but there were a couple of puzzling additions in a childish hand at the bottom. She turned the list around on the counter and said, 'What does this say, here?'

'That's fruit. We need apples and oranges this week, that kind of thing.'

'Did you write it in?'

'Yes. Dad asked me to.'

'Well, there's an "i" in fruit. It's not very easy to recognise without.'

Hamilton came back into the shop, rolling his shirtsleeves down and buttoning the cuffs. 'Give it me,' he said, nodding towards the list. 'I'll make it up.'

He moved off along the shelves, reading as he went. He was a slow reader, and his lips moved as he followed the words. Figures he could handle, quarterly returns and VAT, but words danced along almost beyond his reach.

Peter Gaskell thrust his hands into his pockets. He didn't wander over to the rack of imported American comic books as he usually did, but he seemed to be watching the street outside. It would probably be dark for the last half-mile or so

164

of his walk home. What could his parents be thinking of, sending him out alone like this?

Rennie Hamilton said, 'How are your mother and father, Peter?'

'All right,' he said. No details.

'Has your father managed to get his tractor fixed yet?'

'Not yet.'

Hamilton called from the far side of the shop, 'It's end of season, you know. These apples are a bit expensive.'

His wife motioned to him to be quiet as she moved around the counter. 'Come here a minute, Peter,' she said. 'You've got your toggles done up wrong.' She squatted down to his level, and he stuck his chin up in the air so that she could rebutton his coat for him. 'You can tell your father,' she went on in a low voice, 'there's plenty in the valley willing to help. But nobody wants to pry, that's all.'

'I'll tell him,' Peter promised.

Hamilton added loudly, 'You can tell him we'd like a word next time the order's due, as well.'

'That can wait,' Rennie Hamilton said sharply as she straightened up. 'Haven't you finished yet?'

'Just the bacon. I suppose it's to go in the book.'

Peter said, 'Yes, please.'

The bacon and the cheese had all been transferred to the room-sized storage refrigerator behind the shop, and whilst her husband was out of the way Rennie Hamilton loaded all the groceries into the canvas bag and did a quick addition on the list and noted the amount on the end of the growing column in the credit book.

When the bacon arrived she tucked the greaseproof package down the side and gave the bag to the child. It seemed almost too heavy for him to lift but he managed it, resting it against his leg and swinging it along as she held the door open for him.

'And what was all the hushing about?' Hamilton wanted to know as soon as the door was closed.

'It wasn't the time,' his wife said.

'Not the time?' The open book was on the counter before him. 'Have you seen how much we're owed?'

Down the street, she could see that Peter was level with the schoolhouse. He set the canvas bag down and walked around it, changing his grip to put the weight on his other side for a while. 'It won't break us. Not yet.'

'But when are we going to get it, if we ever *do* get it?'

Reluctantly she turned away from the window. 'You can't take it out on the child,' she said.

'That's exactly why Gaskell sent him down. To play on your sympathy. Seems like it worked well enough.'

'Don't you start,' she warned, glancing up at the old clock above the shelves. Another half-hour and they'd be closing. 'You do enough mumbling to yourself at the back of the shop when the child's around, but when it comes to something constructive . . .'

'I said I'd go up there, didn't I?' he protested.

'Only as long as you knew I wouldn't let you.'

Hamilton said, 'Gaskell won't last another year in this valley.'

'Not with the landlord he's got.' She looked down the darkening road again. Peter Gaskell was out of sight. 'But we can't interfere.'

Chapter 13

As Desmond Gaskell's son was walking out of Langstone village with his difficult load, Roger Forester was sitting in a hired car just outside another village some three hundred miles to the north. He was off the road on a forest track, little-used and thick with dead leaves, and he was watching the failing light through the branches of the trees overhead. He knew that he ought to be trying to sleep – he'd managed no more than about five or six hours in the last fifty – but he was edgy and alert with the cold-water clarity of near-exhaustion. He'd sleep later when he returned to the track, curled awkwardly on the back seat of the car under an overcoat.

He'd sold his own car for cash in Carlisle, and he had more important uses for his funds than a guest-house bed. The hire car would be running up a heavy bill, but apart from the advance that he'd had to hand over Forester had no intention of paying it. Petrol, food and a few tools had been his biggest expenses so far, and if the budget started to tighten he'd have to stop buying food and see what he could find in the woodland around him.

Forester had chosen his area carefully. He'd begun from Inverness and started to work his way westward, around Beauly Firth and towards the forests of Corriehallie and Lochrosque. He was interested in the hamlets and villages on the fringe of the deer country, the cottages and the farmhouses that might provide bases for dedicated stalkers. Anywhere that was obviously occupied he drove on past, as he did with any place that was exposed or too close to the main road, but deserted-looking buildings on village outskirts and elevated rows that were set back from the road generally rated at least a circling-around and a second look.

He thought that he'd found what he wanted in a village so small that it wasn't even marked on his petrol-station roadmap. He drove on through and then turned around in a gateway and cruised back more slowly. Two sets of cottages had caught his eye. They were several hundred yards apart and hidden from each other by a bend in the road, and they were both set well back and reached by private tracks which were better maintained than the road itself. Clean whitewash and straight rooflines of new-looking slate showed through the trees. Promising. He drove a few miles out of the village and then pulled off the road to wait for dusk.

It was a calculated guess but sooner or later he expected to hit lucky, and here on the fringe of a large private estate the chances were better than anywhere. The kind of place that he was looking for was the second home, the petit-bourgeois country retreat which is usually sparsely and cheaply furnished and rarely occupied. The area was about four hours away from Edinburgh or Glasgow – near enough to be accessible for weekends, far enough to be considered remote. Perfectly placed for the man from the city whose idea of a good time was to get a Roe or a Red in his telescopic sights and blast it with a soft-nosed slug.

At seven-thirty he got out of the car with a flashlight and pushed through the undergrowth to a nearby stream. The last traces of day were gone and the blackness was total, perfect. The air carried a reviving chill which Forester reinforced with a couple of splashing handfuls of cold stream water which made the skin of his face sing and drove out the dull ache behind his eyes. Then he filled his cheap vacuum flask and took it back to the car where it completed a meal of dry crusty bread and cheese.

The turning of the car's starter motor was an ugly and unwelcome sound in the stillness of the forest. He backed up all the way to the road, squinting to make out the track behind in the faint glow of the reversing lights. When the car bumped out on to the tarmac he swung the wheel hard across and turned the car around to face towards his chosen village.

He slowed as he came to the first of the two rows, leaning across the dashboard in order to be able to see up the slope. Besides the long access drive that climbed into the trees alongside the road there was a break in the wall by a drain culvert, and a flight of narrow stone steps which climbed towards the cottages.

Lights glowed dimly through the woodland. He drove on.

Further on around the bend there were no lights and no signs of occupation in the second row. He carried on past and found a place to pull off the road, and then he collected together his flashlight and a roll of tools and set off to walk the short distance back.

Steps had once linked this row to the roadway as well, but they were overgrown and unusable. He had to go the long way around, but it gave him plenty of time to watch for any indication that there might be anybody at home.

It was a terrace of three stone cottages, with a cobbled clearing at the front and a common area with a few small outbuildings at the back. They'd been builder-restored as a unit, and they looked too picturesque to be true. One of them had window-boxes and a twee cartwheel propped against the wall by the door. All of the curtains were open, and none of the rooms were showing any lights.

Forester put his flashlight to each of the front windows in turn and peered through the glass as the distorted beam slid around the rooms. Each was low and irregular, plain white plaster walls with prominent wooden spars bracing the ceiling and an open stone fireplace. In two of the cottages he could see glass-fronted rifle display cases. Empty, of course, but then he hadn't expected it to be *that* easy.

The back of the row was similarly standard, low-cost fitted kitchens with plain flagged floors. The doors to the kitchens seemed to be the originals, stripped and revarnished and rehung after being fitted with modern Yale locks.

Forester set the canvas roll down on the ground and undid the tape that bound it up. He had a pry-bar amongst the tools if he needed it, but ideally he wanted to get in without it being obvious. Metal pinked against metal as he opened out the roll, and a sheaf of little plastic cards fell out of the middle. They were joke-shop membership cards of fictitious organisations – Alcoholics Unanimous, recruiting secretary for the Pudding Club, Registered Lecher. They were about the same size and thickness as credit cards.

The second door was the most badly warped of the three, and around the lock a gap of about a sixteenth of an inch appeared when he put his weight against it. Holding it back with his shoulder and managing the flashlight under his arm, Forester took one of the cards and forced it into the gap, feeling it bend stiffly as he pushed it around the edge of the door. When there was little more than half an inch left protruding from the frame he gripped it with thumb and forefinger and started to work it around.

After a minute or so the plastic card split where it bent, and Forester had to pull it out carefully. He pocketed it, leaned on the door a little harder, and tried with another. He could only guess at where the angled metal of the sprung bolt might be, and hope that with sufficient working around the card would eventually ease it back. He kept up the pressure with his shoulder to give himself the widest gap possible.

The door opened unexpectedly, and he would have fallen into the dark kitchen were it not for the fact that after four inches it jarred and stuck. The flashlight showed the silver gleam of a length of plated chain stretched taut just above the lock. He took a pair of bolt-cutters from his kit and applied the jaws to the chain, and thirty seconds later he was inside the kitchen. Obviously the owner of the cottage had never been burgled and didn't really believe that it might happen; there was a new-looking bolt at the bottom of the kitchen door that hadn't been shot.

Forester checked the drawers and cupboards before he moved through into the main room. The china was market seconds, and all of the pans and utensils were unmatched oddments. In a drawer by the sink he found a billspike with a number of receipts, and he took these with him. A short

170

passage linked the two rooms together and gave access to the stairway.

He found the meter and turned on the mains, and then switched the lights on after closing the drapes – it would look a lot less suspicious than the occasional flicker of torchlight across the glass. The gun case had room for six hunting rifles and there were two drawers underneath which were not locked. One contained only an empty ammunition box, the other a number of receipts from firearms dealers and some guarantee cards. He put these with his haul from the kitchen and crossed the room to where a pile of mail lay on the mat inside the front door, pausing on the way to look at some of the framed photographs and certificates that were arranged along the mantelshelf. The photographs showed sporting groups posing with their weapons, except for a couple which showed a man – the same in both – on one knee by a dead stag. He was holding the animal's head up by its antlers and looking shyly pleased at the camera. He had protruding ears and a thatch of curly hair that sat on his head like a woolly beret, slightly off-centre. The stag's eyes were rolled back and its nostrils were clotted with blood. Both photographs seemed to be of the same occasion, as if the hunter was so proud of his kill that he couldn't choose a single image to commemorate the event. The death weapon was by his side, propped against the animal's cooling flank.

There was nothing of interest upstairs, even though Forester went through the pockets of some expensive-looking rough country wear that he found in the bedroom wardrobe. He went back down to the kitchen and assembled his information on the table.

The mail was uniformly trivial, but he read it all and then stuffed the torn envelopes and their contents into his pockets for disposal elsewhere. The firearms receipts were probably of the most use to him, and the guarantee cards all carried the purchaser's signature, *Ian P. Sampson* in a leaning scrawl that shouldn't be too hard to imitate. The *P* stood for Paul, he learned from another of the documents.

171

He reached into an inside pocket and took out a form which he placed on the table. *Application for the Grant/Renewal/Variation of a Firearm Certificate.* He scribbled a few lines on a scrap sheet to get the hang of Sampson's cramped style, and then he started to fill in the form. On Sampson's behalf he denied that he had any history of criminal activity or mental instability – not much point going on if he didn't – and then with the records from the gun case drawer he compiled a list of the weapons that Sampson already possessed.

He was making out a case for the purchase of a .308 rifle as an extra weapon for deer hunting on the nearby estates. It would be a serious game rifle with considerably more punch than a target toy, a guaranteed killer of the same gauge as the 7.62mm NATO standard issue Service weapons with which Forester was already familiar. It was a reasonable plaything for a sporting thug like Sampson to hunger for.

There were still gaps on the form when he'd finished, mainly relating to Sampson's personal details. Forester had an idea of how he might get the additional information, but it would have to wait until tomorrow.

Forester returned the billspike to the kitchen drawer and the receipts and guarantees to the gun case, and then he took a screwdriver from his canvas roll and unscrewed the cut end of the doorchain from the frame and slipped it into his pocket. At some time over the next couple of days he could call into a hardware shop to find a match, and replace the missing part on his next visit. Sampson would simply assume that he hadn't put the chain on at the end of his last stay. It might not matter in the end – Forester fully expected to be traced and caught – but every difficulty and delay that he could strew behind him could make a final difference of hours or even minutes that might determine the distinction between success or failure.

He took a last look around. There were a few places where he'd disturbed dust, and he blew on them hard to blur the marks and redistribute the deposit. Two or three days, and they wouldn't show. Other than that, the place was as he'd found it. He switched off the lights and opened the curtains; the night was still as black as a stone. He cut the power by the meter and collected his roll and the half-completed form from the kitchen table before he let himself out through the back door. The lock snapped into place behind him, and he set off down the hill towards his car.

Chapter 14

Carson was in his bathrobe, messing around the apartment at the slob things that people always do in bathrobes, when the telephone rang. He padded barefoot across the carpet and lifted the receiver. It was Alison.

'Hello, Peter,' she said.

He'd been thinking about her, but he didn't want it to show. He said, 'Alison!' and sounded surprised.

'I'd be offended if you didn't remember me after only two days.'

'I was going to ring you.'

'Why didn't you?'

Good question. 'You never gave me your number.'

'You never gave me yours, either. But we're both in the book.'

Ah. There was an uncomfortable silence for a moment and then she went on, 'Is this an example of your research? No wonder you don't sell much.'

'I had the idea you'd be busy.'

'No, I told you I was going to take it easy for a while. What about lunch?'

'Today?' he said, thinking of the scramble he'd have to get showered and dressed and hoping that the panic didn't show in his voice.

'Did you have something else fixed up?'

'Nothing at all.'

'What about one of those cute pubs on the Strand towpath? You won't have to rouse yourself to go far.'

'I'm not quite the sloth you imagine me to be.' Oh yes you are, he thought, tightening the tie on the robe as it threatened to slide undone. 'Shall I pick you up?'

'I've got a couple of things to do, first. I'll meet you by Kew Bridge in an hour. We can walk down from there.'

'Fine,' Carson said, and she hung up.

He arrived a little before twelve and waited below the bridge at the riverside, across from the peeling frontage of the old Thames Road laundry. Above him, traffic rumbled noisily towards Richmond and Kew. The towpath proper didn't start until a few yards further down where it angled away from the road and followed the river; here it was marked by a narrow strip of waterside grass and trees that would immediately raise the cost of any overlooking property by two or three thousand.

Carson was aware that he wanted to see Alison again, although he wasn't sure why. The best that he could conclude was that she was, somehow, *clean*; nothing about her had so far offended or disappointed him, and there had been nothing to detract from the engaging pull of her looks and personality. Even when she'd been tired and limp on the journey down from Cumbria this inner cleanliness had still radiated through.

Alison reached the bridge a few minutes late, and she apologised. Carson said it didn't matter. They started to walk and he said, 'Why today, in particular?'

'Because it's the first decent break in the weather we've had. And because I owe you a meal from a couple of nights back.'

'Look,' he started to assure her, 'I don't keep accounts and have to be paid back . . .'

'Relax,' she said, 'I was joking!'

'Of course. I'm sorry.'

They stepped around a duck which wasn't about to move for anybody. This section of the towpath was about six feet wide, with the riverside cottages to their left and an iron railing to the right. The tidal waters beneath were low, exposing slick grey mudbanks which would be swallowed during the afternoon. Some of the cottages behind their stone sea-walls had real charm, others were plain and cramped and only borrowed a little grace from their situation.

Alison said, 'You know, Peter, I think I'm starting to make you out. You're really sensitive about being well-off, aren't you?'

'I wouldn't say that.'

'You assume it slams up some kind of barrier around you. You're expecting people to resent it so you hold back before they can get any ideas about hurting you.'

'There are disadvantages,' he admitted. 'But nothing I'd want to complain about.'

'Well, don't complain when I buy you lunch. And don't worry about whether I can afford it, either. The agency have agreed to pay me a retainer for a couple of weeks while I think about what I'd like to do next.'

'A retainer? Sounds like a pretty enlightened agency.'

'Lab staff are pearls without a price these days. We're getting into a science economy, didn't you know?'

'The fact was passing me by until now.'

They came to a pub which was low and dark and already starting to get crowded. Two bearded young men in tracksuits were standing by the door, beer glasses in hand and bellies stretching their Adidas sweatshirts. They were watching Alison with innocent interest, and trying to appear not to.

'There's a better place on the other side of the bridge,' Carson told her, and they walked on.

The bridge carried the rattling old carriages of the District Line Underground from Gunnersbury to Kew Gardens. As they passed in its shadow Alison remarked on the low floodwalls before the cottages. Carson said that in theory his own place was within the flood basin, but there had never been any trouble as long as he'd lived there; places right on the towpath used to get flooded regularly when the tide was high.

They came to the pub that he'd had in mind and climbed

the steps to the door. Inside the bar they descended again into the dining alcove, and they sat at a table by a small-paned window which was back on a level with the path outside.

Carson placed the edge of his hand against the glass, about two feet above the sill.

'I was in here once,' he said, 'and the water was this high up the glass.'

'I don't think I'm jealous of people with houses on the riverbank any more. I'll stick as a visitor, thanks.'

She said that she'd be happy with wine so he caught somebody's eye and asked for a carafe of the house red. Then he said, 'How long do you get to spend in London?'

'It varies. There's usually live-in accommodation with the jobs; but there's no continuity to it. I like to keep in touch with my own place.'

'How long had you been at the Jenner Clinic?'

'To be honest, I've lost track. Don't make me start counting the years up, please – it'll ruin my whole day.'

The wine arrived in something resembling a hospital urine bottle. As he filled their glasses, Carson said carefully, 'How do you feel about it all?'

She didn't reply for a moment, and he glanced at her anxiously. She was hesitating, getting her thoughts into order. Then she said, 'I don't, really. I suppose I still haven't grasped it, and I don't want to. It's like . . . well, the longer I leave it, the less it will hurt when I finally face it. What about you?'

He set the carafe down. 'I was hardly involved. I'd feel guilty if I started looking on myself as a victim.'

'For God's sake, Peter,' she said with a small and surprising explosion of irritation, 'why don't you let yourself go for once?'

'I don't know what you mean,' he said, and then a girl was by their table with her notebook. They ordered, and as soon as the girl was walking away Alison started in again.

'Of course you know what I mean. You're defending yourself by being indifferent again.'

'I don't do it on purpose.'

'I'm not so sure. You're always going for the safe line, no involvement and no chance of damage. Do you find me attractive?'

The question took him off-guard. He glanced around, uneasy. 'Well, yes,' he said.

'I'll try to discount the element of evasion and take that as sincere. Would you shrink from the idea of sleeping with me?'

'It would depend.'

'On what, for Christ's sake?'

'On whether you came on with the aggressive line you're using now.'

'Peter,' she pleaded, 'I'm not attacking you, I'm only trying to reach you!'

'No need to reach me. I'm here.'

'The front's here, but where's Peter Carson? Two nights back, in your flat, I needed comfort. I got a damn fine meal and a hell of a lot of elegance, and that was it. I had to get a lift home with the richest virgin in London.'

Salad plates were slipped before them, but Carson hardly noticed. He said wonderingly, 'You've really been storing this up, haven't you?'

'I need to know,' she insisted. 'Are you rejecting me, or did I really make such little impression on you?'

'Listen, Alison, I'm sorry.' He wanted to say, I don't really know how to read people, and every time I've tried I've got it wrong. But all he said was, 'I haven't wanted to hurt you, and I'm sorry if I did. Can we go on from there?'

She was about to say something, but then she changed her mind. She smiled and loosened, and to Carson it was like the warm sun falling on his skin. 'I'm sorry, too. I went over the top. I think you've been plying me with wine to get to my virtue.'

'I don't see how you can accuse me of that, when you're paying.'

'You cunning swine, Carson. You've got me financing my own downfall.'

178

They started on the salad. After a while, Carson said, 'You know, I had an idea earlier. You've just confirmed it for me.'

'I have? How?'

He had to hitch his chair forward to make room for a party who were moving in around the table behind him. Four men of different ages, all wearing medium-cost suits in bad taste, a lunchtime ritual to pass an hour of freedom from the office. He said, 'You were right, I've been holding what happened to Tracy at arm's length. I shouldn't close my eyes, I should try to find out more.'

Alison was guarded, suddenly sober. 'Like what?'

'I'm going to write a piece about the Jenner Clinic.'

'That's not confronting the problem, Peter. That's making a game out of it.'

'If I approached it the way I usually work, I'd agree. But I'm going to make a break from that crappy airline magazine style, ditch it altogether.'

She frowned and looked out of the window. A train was crossing the bridge, and its thunder drummed against the glass. She said, 'I'm not sure it's a good idea.'

'But it's the kind of thing you're trying to push me towards. And I'll need your help in setting out the basic research outline. There's a lot I don't understand – like, how come Jenner picked such a remote and inaccessible spot for his labs?'

'He liked the view.'

'And, you know, I haven't the faintest idea of what actually goes on at a baby farm. Where did those chimpanzees come into it, for instance?'

She took the paper napkin from her lap and crunched it up into a tight ball, dropping it on to her plate. 'I've got to go,' she said.

Carson looked at her blankly, and she went on, 'I've stayed longer than I intended.' She took some notes from her pocketbook and laid them on the table by her plate and her half-empty glass. 'These should cover the bill. See to it, will you?'

Carson watched uncomprehendingly as she stood up and edged sideways from between her chair and the table, looking down and not meeting his eyes. He said, 'But you were going to tell me about the fertility business.'

'Some other time. Please, Peter, forget the article.'

'But why?'

'Don't ask, just believe me. It's better forgotten.'

He wanted to follow, but he was trapped by the money on the table and the hard chair that was jammed against his back and wouldn't move. The office fellows on the table behind laughed abruptly and in unison. It was social laughter, an attempt to hammer out a common weapon against despair. Alison was up the steps and away, lost in the press of people that had filled the bar since they'd come in.

Well done, Carson. Screwed it up again, haven't you?

Chapter 15

He was almost home before he thought to look at his watch. It was only just after one o'clock. As he stood on the steps before the heavy front door and dug in his pocket for his keys he could hear the ringing of a telephone, blanked and muffled by several layers of brick and plaster. In the hallway with the traffic noises pushed into the background it was a little louder, and when he opened the door to his apartment the sound became rounded and alive in the empty rooms.

Carson let the door swing behind him, hurrying through into the sitting-room and reaching for the receiver. As he started to speak he heard the line go momentarily dead and then break into a callbox paytone.

The line cleared, and an unfamiliar voice said, 'Carson? Peter Carson?'

'Who is this?'

'Roger Forester. Don't you remember me, from Langstone?'

Forester. How could he forget the intense little man in that crypt of a dining-room? He said, 'Yes, of course I remember. I wasn't expecting to hear you, that's all.'

'I've been working through all the Peter Carsons in the London directory. I got it narrowed down to your number.'

'What can I do for you?'

'I need some help. Did I hear that detective say you were a reporter?'

Carson hooked his fingers under the phone base and carried it across to the Chesterfield. 'I don't know what you heard, but I'm not.'

Forester seemed thrown. 'He said something about you phoning the story in,' he insisted. 'About stopping you.'

'He'd got it all wrong. I do features for magazines.'

'Isn't that the same thing?'

'No, nothing like.' The time-pips were sounding on the line, and he added quickly, 'Do you want to give me your number? I can call you back.'

'It's all right,' Forester said after a moment. 'I've got a bag of change. Those features, do you have to do research for them?'

'Sometimes. Look, if you can tell me what it is you want to know . . .'

'I need somebody to get some information for me. I don't know how.'

'What kind of information?'

'It relates to that business at the clinic.' Forester was being careful. 'Please, don't ask me to go into details.'

'If you won't give me details, I don't see how I'm supposed to help.'

'I need background on someone. I thought you might have contacts.'

'Someone from the clinic?' Carson asked, intrigued.

'No. And nobody famous, either. It really needs someone who can get the information unofficially.'

'I told you, I'm not a reporter.'

It wasn't what Forester had expected to hear. 'Please,' he said, 'at least give me some idea of how to go about it.'

'I'm not sure I should. What are you trying to do?'

There was another break as the pips sounded and Forester fed the callbox again. 'I told you not to ask,' he said when the line was grudgingly given over for another fifty seconds. 'They've made the accident story official, and now they're covering up like mad. The village is back to normal, but the army's sealed off the ruins.'

'I know you're still upset, but . . .'

'Upset? And what about you, Carson? You lost someone, too. Or have you forgotten already?'

'You need to be careful,' Carson told him. Forester was sounding pretty obsessed over . . . well, an egg in a bottle.

'Look,' Forester said urgently, and Carson could imagine his knuckles going white as he gripped the payphone receiver hard in an attempt to get his point across, 'my child's been murdered, and the police and the government have got their heads together to cover up for the killer.'

'But why should they want to do that?' Carson said, and he wished that he could be as confident as he was trying to sound.

'Because there was something foul about the set-up at the Jenner Clinic, and they don't want it made public.'

'Something foul? Like what?'

'I don't know. Maybe bad publicity for the fertility business could make waves on an international level.'

'That's a bit far-fetched, isn't it?'

'Not at all. This is the only country in the world with an organised fertility industry. There are a few places in the States, but there's no federal policy to get them organised on a big-money basis and all the little local pressure groups keep them harassed and staying small. Same over most of Europe with the religious organisations. If some sheikh wants a son and he needs a push from technology, he sends over a couple of wives and a bottle of frogspawn. The sons are assembled for him, and he even gets a genetic guarantee of health. And he pays for it.'

Carson leaned back into the Chesterfield. He said, 'I don't see what that has got to do with murder.' But his tone said *carry on*.

'You don't understand how *big* it is. Income from eugenics equals income from arms sales.'

'Arms sales are down.'

'Hardware, maybe.' This was – or, at least, had been – Forester's field. 'Now we concentrate on research and exporting technology. So nothing goes through the docks, the income's still there and it's getting bigger. I suppose now you're going to get timid, and tell me not to rock the boat.'

'I don't want to walk in with my eyes closed. It doesn't mean I've been frightened off.'

'Can't you see the scale of it, now? Can't you see that they might find it worthwhile to bend the truth and sit on justice when there's so much at stake?'

The money ran out. When Forester had fumbled another coin into the machinery, Carson said, 'Tell me what you need to know.'

'Are you going to help me?'

'I probably can't, personally, but there's a research agency I use. I'll put them on to it.'

'I'll pay whatever it costs.'

'That doesn't matter.'

Carson got a pencil and a reporter's notebook from a drawer in the telephone table. He rested the book on his knee and wrote as Forester gave the details.

'It's a man called Ian Paul Sampson, and I think he lives somewhere near Edinburgh. Could be Leith, but I'm not certain. Early middle age, and not too badly off although you wouldn't call him rich, either. I need to know his home address, his occupation, and his business address, and if any of these have changed in the last five years. Then I need to know his date and place of birth.'

Carson wrote *B.D. – when and where?* and then said, 'Anything else?'

'No, that's it.'

He frowned at the pencilled details. 'I don't see how this ties in with the clinic.'

'He doesn't, directly. But that's all I'm prepared to say.'

'I'll see what I can do. Where can I get hold of you?'

'I'm moving around,' Forester said quickly. 'I'll contact you . . . how about tomorrow afternoon?'

'It might take longer than that.'

'I'll call anyway, see how you're getting on. Thanks, Carson.'

'Don't mention it.'

'I mean it. And I'm sorry about the way I spoke to you before.'

There was the same note, the same feeling of hard comradeship that Forester had shown once before towards Carson, back in Langstone. Carson found it strangely

184

warming. He said, 'That's all right. I think I'm starting to get used to it.'

With the call over and the notebook still open before him, Carson stared into the cold gaslogs in the fireplace. Forester had been perfectly correct, the happenings at Langstone had been gross and illogical; he'd chosen simply to deny involvement and ignore them. When Alison had pushed him he'd started to gather the momentum to ask the same questions that were obsessing Forester – apparently not the reaction she'd expected, judging from the way that she seemed to have slammed the lid back on the mixture before it could boil over.

He went back over to the telephone drawer and took out his slim and little-used address book, flicking through to find the number of his research agency. He'd found them through an ad in *Private Eye*, and they always welcomed his business – but then, the tottering co-operative would welcome anybody's business. The line was engaged.

He tried re-dialling two or three times, but either it was a long conversation or he couldn't time it right to slip in between calls. At least they still had a phone. He hung up and got the last volume of the bigger directory from the rack under the table. There were hundreds of entries under *Wells* and a dozen or more *A*'s; none of them matched with Alison's address as he remembered it; and yet she'd told him she was in the book. He put the directory back and tried the agency again, but it was still engaged.

What the hell, he was up and about and dressed for the road. He returned the phone to its table and slid the notebook into his pocket; it took some forcing, but it went.

First call was to Ealing via the Underground. Carson knew better than to use the Mercédès as in-town transport – traffic and parking problems made a car into a liability during the daytime.

The side door to the house swung in when he touched it – probably only locked at night. He climbed the stairs and knocked on the door to Alison's flat, but there was no reply and the sound had a hollow ring which said *nobody home*.

The door opposite was trembling in its frame from the loudness of the music behind. He went over and banged on the panel so hard that his knuckles hurt – even so, he knew that he'd be lucky if he were heard. Then the record shifted into a quieter phase and he heard something falling over inside the flat.

After maybe half a minute, the door was opened and Carson was hit by the rise in the music level and a sickly aroma which billowed out around him. The unemployed Turkish waiter stood in the doorway and peered at him; he was muscular and squat, and he was wearing only pyjama trousers that were creased and stained. His olive skin seemed to glint in the soft light of the hallway; the flat behind him was almost totally dark.

Carson said, 'I'm looking for Miss Wells. Do you know when she'll be back?'

The Turk didn't reply, but turned and disappeared. Sinews bunched and moved under his skin like oiled spaghetti; Carson guessed that he'd been posing and flexing in front of a mirror. Shapes moved against the drawn curtains of the room beyond, and a few seconds later the girl came forward into the light. She was barefoot and wearing a man's shirt over jeans, the sleeves rolled back on her thin arms. No make-up, hair a mess, tired-looking. She said, 'Is something the matter?'

'Nothing like that. I'm looking for Alison Wells. I was wondering if you'd know where she is.'

'I heard her go out around eleven this morning. Then I think I heard her come back and go out again about an hour ago.'

The shadow of the Turk passed across the room behind her, eyes glowering at Carson like twin red coals. He persisted, 'You don't know if she'd be at her agency?'

'What agency's that?'

'I don't know what it's called. The one which finds jobs for laboratory workers.'

The girl seemed blearily surprised. 'Is that what she does? I never knew.'

Carson said, 'Well. Thanks, anyway.'

She flashed him a brief and insincere smile, her eyes puffy and filled with her own worries. She closed the door.

The Researchers' Co-Operative was just off Leicester Square, reached through an alley alongside one of the big prestige cinemas. All of the Hollywood gloss and glitter was up front in the Square where the lines formed and the buskers milked, but the alley was just a mean crack with high walls of featureless brick, somewhere to hide the trash cans and somewhere for the tramps to sleep. The ground was a mush of litter banked up on either side, and overhead the sky was blanked out by the narrow crowding of the strap-iron ladders and landings of fire escapes.

The offices were in a high building, one which may well have been neat and prosperous around the time that Dickens was labelling bottles in a boot-blacking warehouse; now its main value lay in the soaring price of the land on which it stood. Its frail old shell served little other purpose than to squat on the ground and prevent any adjacent developments from creeping across it. The original entrance foyer on the main road behind the square was barred and boarded and papered over with layers of handbills; Carson walked up a few steps near the end of the alley and pushed open the door of a tradesman's entrance.

The floorboards inside were bare, although they still carried the black tack-heads which had anchored linoleum. The strong smell of damp and cats gave a quick explanation of why the first two floors of the building were uninhabited. Carson started to climb the stairs, passing some stacks of yellow newsprint and a bicycle which was chained to the rotting wood of the balustrade, before turning and starting up the next flight. Rooms gaped empty on the next landing, their doors gone for firewood, paper stripped and plaster crumbling away from the lath walls.

R.C.O. had tried to brighten up their corner of the third floor with a few gallons of inexpensive paint. The bright crust over the decay was better than nothing, even if the job-lots of emulsion clashed badly. In its own way the co-operative was quite a success story if only for the fact that it had kept going more or less continuously for almost five years. It had been started with two friends by Adrian Cotterell, Polytechnic journalism drop-out, and although the two friends had themselves dropped out after the first twelve months Cotterell had managed to keep enough people together for the place to stay in business.

Carson looked into the outer office. Furnishings and fittings were strictly junkshop, stacked with box-files and scribbled notes and second-hand reference books that were mainly bought cheap and out-of-date when libraries renewed. In the next room along, a telephone was ringing. Cotterell was at his desk, a large mahogany monster that had been inherited with the premises because nobody could face the idea of carrying it down the stairs.

'You busy?' Carson said from the door.

The telephone stopped ringing, chopped in the middle of its signal. Cotterell looked up blankly for a moment, and then Carson and his wallet slid into a niche in the young man's mind and he smiled. 'Nothing that can't wait, Peter,' he said. 'Are you working on something?'

Closing the door behind him, Carson said, 'I'm making a start.'

Another man who was unknown to Carson put his head through from a connecting office. Under a dark pullover without elbows he was wearing a Levi shirt that appeared to have been sucked colourless by some dog. His hair was cut close into a fringe, to make the best of the fact that he was losing it. He called to Cotterell, 'It's the Royal Veterinary College, that fellow you wanted to ask about horse doping.'

'Can you see to it?'

'I'm supposed to be at the Holborn library in ten minutes,' the researcher objected.

'It won't take a second. I was only after a couple of references.'

Co-operative or not, Cotterell was obviously in charge and not to be messed about with while he set up a commission. The researcher stopped hanging on to the doorframe and stepped into the room. He said resignedly, 'Where's the file?'

'On here, somewhere.' Cotterell lifted some Manila folders, and they slid around and spilled across the desk. They'd been re-used many times, titles and references and hasty notes making it difficult to see any sign of what the current contents might be.

'Got it,' the researcher said, and pulled one out from underneath. Cotterell made an attempt to push the remaining files back into a stable heap.

'Sorry about that,' he said to Carson when they were alone again. The researcher could be heard in the next room, stalling on the telephone while he looked through the file for the references. Cotterell said, 'Do you know David?'

'I don't think so.'

'David Reynolds. He joined us a couple of months back. It must have been after the last job we did for you.'

'Probably.' Carson moved two bound runs of *American Cinematographer* magazine off the office's only spare chair so that he could sit down. 'I've got another one for you, now.'

Cotterell nodded and started looking around for a piece of paper. 'What's the subject?'

'It's medical. Fertility treatment as practised in State and private facilities.'

'What's the slant?'

'I don't know yet. I'll have a better idea when I can see the background. I want as many concise and informed references as you can find, but nothing so technical that I can't understand it.'

David Reynolds passed through, dropping the horse-dope file on to Cotterell's desk and pulling on his jacket. As he stepped past Carson he gave a quick, tight smile of acknowledgement. Cotterell said, 'Do you have a limit, or do you want us to give you an estimate?'

'An estimate will be fine. I want something deeper than the stuff you usually do for me, so don't look for ways to cut corners. There are some specifics, as well.'

'Fire away.'

Carson pulled out his pad and tried to read the shaky notes that he'd made on the Underground. 'Background and biography of a Doctor Jenner. I don't know his first name, but he was a consultant in some hospital in Carlisle and he ran a backup laboratory near Langstone in Cumbria.'

'How about an interview?'

'That might be difficult to arrange. There was some kind of explosion at the clinic and all the staff got wiped out. You might find out for me what the official version is.'

Cotterell was writing in a mixed shorthand, spelling out some words and substituting personal symbols for others. He said, 'Sounds like it calls for a trip up there.'

'I'd rather you didn't. I don't want to make the interest too public – not at this stage, anyway. Next I'd like whatever you can find on someone called Hennessy. I don't know his name either, but I think he's a medium-range civil servant.'

Cotterell said doubtfully, 'Jenner should be straight-forward enough, but that one's a bit thin.'

'Sorry, but it's all I've got. I only know that he turned up a few hours after the accident and got into some row with the head copper. The next day the police had to fold their tents and leave.'

'We'll see what we can do.'

Carson flipped back a page, to the first entry in the notebook. 'That's it for the moment, except for one other thing.' He tore out the lined sheet and passed it across the desk. 'Can you get these details about somebody called Ian Paul Sampson?'

Cotterell nodded as he looked at the list of biographical queries. With a middle name and an approximate area, it shouldn't be too hard. 'Is this connected with the other business?' he asked.

'It may be, but I'm not sure. If it is, I'd like to know how.'

Cotterell chose his next words carefully. 'We don't usually ask questions, but is this one sensitive?'

'I don't know. Assume that it is, and go from there.'

'It's quite a departure from the usual kind of thing you do.'

'I wouldn't worry about it, if I were you. I'm expecting it to cost me.'

Cotterell put his pencil down and rocked back in his chair. It groaned in disbelief. 'I'll put some feelers out and then ring you tonight with the outline proposal and estimate,' he said.

'You can start so soon?' Carson said, getting to his feet and returning the notebook to his pocket.

'No problem, it's slack time.' Cotterell bumped the chair squarely back on the floor before coming around the desk to see Carson out. 'Whoever heard of anything interesting happening in October?'

'The Russian revolution.'

'Well . . . it depends what you call *interesting*.'

Cotterell was in touch that evening, at around eight. Carson had only just put the phone down after trying to get Alison's number from Enquiries, but as he'd waited for his call to be taken he'd thought of her, perhaps contemptuous of his anxiety and annoyed by his persistence, and he'd hung up without even making his request.

Whatever she'd told him, he would go ahead. Not because of the article – that idea was just something to get him moving – but because he wanted to know.

There was no preamble. 'Got the estimate for you, Peter,' Cotterell said. 'I reckon, with what you've asked for, there won't be much change out of four hundred.'

'And what will I get for it?'

'Well, fifty's gone already in backhanders to a couple of the girls at Central Records. We'll bill it as expenses. We'll have

Anne tied up in the libraries for two or three days going through the periodical indexes, that'll be another hundred plus whatever the xerox charges are.'

'That fifty. Does it mean you've got something for me already?'

'Just the basics on Hennessy and Sampson. You want them now?'

He'd kept the notebook ready. 'Go ahead.'

Sampson, it seemed, had been the easiest. He was an Edinburgh solicitor who had two houses, two cars and had commuted between two women before one of them found out about the other. Carson scribbled down all the details that Cotterell gave him and commented, 'That was fast.'

'Thank the silicon chip. Just bang in the name, and the whole lot comes spilling out like a Sealink breakfast.'

'What about Hennessy?'

'A bit harder, but I think we managed it. You said he turned up a few hours after the event, so it seems likely he left London at short notice. Plus the fact that he was throwing his weight around with the police seemed to say Whitehall and no small potatoes, so we started with that. We tried Education and Science first. They've got a Hennessy, but according to his secretary he hasn't been away from his desk for a week. So I went on to the Home Office; they've got two employees with the name, but one's a woman and she's off having a baby. The other one went North on business three days ago – no number or address being given out, but his office is relaying messages.'

That sounded like the one. Carson said, 'What does he do?'

'He's the Deputy Commissioner for Genetic Control. It's a Home Office post, attached to the Medical Research Council on Park Crescent. He's the executive part of a committee whose main function is to review and license proposals for experiments with DNA. They grade the proposals according to danger, and lay down sets of conditions for the experiments.'

'Has that got anything to do with fertility?' It didn't sound like it.

'I don't know, but we'll find out for you. I was going to put Dave Reynolds on to the Jenner part of this; will that be okay with you?'

'Whoever you think's best,' Carson told him. 'I won't argue.'

'That's where the main expense comes in. When I checked in *Who's Who* I found that Jenner held down a post for several years at David's old university. He's got friends there who've moved on to the staff, and he reckons he can pump them for information without making any official waves. Didn't you say you wanted it low-profile?'

'That's right. Go ahead with the trip.'

'Have you got any ideas yet for a particular direction?'

'No, just carry on as you are. I don't want to start setting up patterns just yet.'

Cotterell's experience so far had been that R.C.O. had virtually pre-written most of Carson's material for him. This kind of broad attack was something new. He said, 'We'll get going on it first thing tomorrow. We should have something for you in a couple of days.'

They said their goodbyes, and Carson left Forester's material by the telephone, ready for his call.

Chapter 16

As the first grey slivers of dawn were filtering down through the trees, Roger Forester climbed stiffly from his hire car and stood on the track beside it, stretching his sore limbs and trying to beat some warmth into himself. The temperature had dropped during the night, and the dead leaves underfoot were bearded with ice; they broke and crackled as he limped around the car and opened the trunk to get his kit.

The vapour of his breath feathered in a trail behind him as he moved through the cold bushes towards the stream. For the first couple of days he'd used it to shave and wash but now he was finding it too icy. Instead he'd fill his aluminium container and take it back to boil on his small gas cooker.

The can of soup that he'd left on top of the flame was starting to bubble when he got back. Chickeń soup for breakfast was a lousy way to start the day but at least, it was hot. A chill mist was rising through the woodland as he lifted the open can away from the heat and replaced it with the water container. He could feel the glow through his gloves.

Half an hour later he was crouched in the bushes upslope from Sampson's cottage. He had a good view of the main road and the side track that climbed to the row, and he could see a part of the buildings themselves, small and neat and quiet.

Fifteen minutes before eight. A bicycle came into sight on the main road, and the rubber honk of its brakes cut through the air as the postman slowed and dismounted. He held on to the machine by the handlebars as he turned off the road and started to push it up the steeper incline of the track. Forester sensed a worm of tension, deep in his belly and fighting to get free.

The postman was a tall, skinny man with near-white hair and a permanent stoop; this brief caricature of an impression was all that Forester had been able to make out from a distance. He was probably as tough as old leather, cycling his rural route with a heavy sack every morning. Over the three days that Forester had been observing, his schedule had been consistent to within a few minutes either way.

Today he was slightly late. He'd probably had an extra delivery to make, perhaps at the occupied row further along the road. Forester waited until the postman had come freewheeling down the track, and then as the momentum was spent and the postman pedalled off into the morning Forester started to move downslope towards the cottages.

He used another of his plastic cards to let himself in through the back door. He was getting quite practised now, and it was faster than using a key. The new chain that he'd fixed brushed against his sleeve as he entered the kitchen. There had been no problem in finding a matching replacement for the cut piece; a hardware shop in Inverness had supplied it, and it had taken only a few minutes to fit.

There was only one piece of mail behind the door. Forester glanced at the envelope once and dropped it back. It was advertising mail, like most of that which he'd opened on his first visit and later burned in the forest. He sighed heavily, and forced himself to relax.

He'd scattered a few items around the place so that anybody looking in through the window would get the impression that the owner was in residence but out for the day or the evening: a box of tissues and some magazines in the main room, a half-empty bottle of fresh milk and some crockery draining in the kitchen. Now he collected them together. They'd served their purpose, as a handwritten note pushed through the door on the Saturday afternoon had shown; *Mr Sampson – Appreciate your haste and will get things moving as quickly as I can for you*. It referred to a note which he'd included with the Firearm Certificate application form and the fee, saying that he (Sampson) had a chance at a

Weatherby Magnum Deluxe rifle at a price that was madness, but only if he could wrap the deal up within a few days. Forester had delivered the certificate and the other papers by hand to the country police station; it wasn't much more than a converted garage alongside the local man's house, and it hadn't been difficult to pick a time when it had been unattended.

The policeman's note had promised action some time during the next two or three days, which could no doubt be split into a fraction of a second for a data check to establish that Sampson was a worthy and responsible citizen and neither a pervert nor a dangerous lefty, and then many hours of waiting in a paper tray to be shunted and shuffled and finally put into an envelope. It was the time taken for this bureaucratic grind that chewed at Forester's patience the most – each day away from Cumbria increased the chance of his missing the conclusion of the investigation.

When he was satisfied that everything was straight, he let himself out of the back door. For the rest of the day he would go into Inverness, take his spare clothes into a launderette and then perhaps try to find a public baths with hot showers. But he would be back tomorrow.

As Roger Forester was closing up the cottage behind him D.I. Mike Schaffer was swinging his legs off a creaking camp-bed in the office of the Langstone schoolhouse and sitting groggily upright. His situation was not unlike Forester's in that he was cold, sleeping badly and eating out of tins warmed on a small portable stove. He also had a telephone, a telex machine, and a roof, but none of these was much consolation.

It was worse than being in the C.I.D. room with its battered furniture and wire baskets and overcrowded notice boards. At least, things *happened* there; it was obvious to Schaffer that his presence in Langstone was nothing more than the merest nod towards protocol, but Stoneley had refused to let him return and make the police withdrawal complete. At least try to keep an eye on what they get up to, he'd told his inspector, and then made some vague and undefined promise about arranging a relief. So Schaffer sat with a stack of paperback books from Hamilton's corner rack, and occasionally tried to catch Hennessy to pump him for information.

He turned on the gas and put a match to the stove so that it could warm the office. He had an electric bar fire, but unless you actually stood over the mesh it was a cheerful glow and no heat. When he felt brave enough he took off the old pullover and the tracksuit pants that he'd been sleeping in and started to dress.

Schaffer was still young enough to find his job largely exciting, but to find appealing the idea of being the force's lone representative in the shadow of a major incident was not the same as embracing the reality. He'd applied to join the police in his final year at university; it had been an unfashionable thing to do but he'd given it a lot of careful thought. After his selection and Police College training he'd been slightly surprised to find himself not to be a component of an irresistibly righteous machine, but a member of an organisation that was as flawed and human as any other. It depended for its success on the motives of those involved, like Jerry Crichton's need for the satisfaction of peaceful authority or Toby Knight's wish for a permissible framework to act out his resentment of the world.

Because he'd been a graduate entrant, accelerated promotion had been guaranteed. He could handle the fast rise now, although he'd had some trouble along the way from non-graduates who had looked for every opportunity to declare their own superiority. He knew that his abilities had been recognised above, not by the glory-seekers and the empire-builders, those who 'shaped policy' and 'formed long-term strategies', but by the old wise hands whose influence was most effective in the end. When the time came, they would elevate him to become another Stoneley.

This was the dark cloud that every day was banked a little higher on Mike Schaffer's horizon. After his long, slow climb Stoneley had found himself to be a novice at office in-fighting, some examples of which could make the brutal intentions of a common criminal seem almost harmless. He had a small mousy wife, and two grown sons who came home to drink all the beer out of the refrigerator and tell him that he was a strong-arm man for a decrepit and decaying society. Worst of all, he was beginning to suspect that it might be true. And this was the prized position that was being prepared for Mike Schaffer.

He wished they'd left him the radio mast, so that he could at least listen to some music and pick up the news. A little transistor with a tin spike for an aerial was useless so far up the valley. The only sound that broke the quiet of the cavernous schoolroom was the occasional hum and spatter of the telex.

He ambled through to take a look at the machine. He'd heard the daily summary coming through some time after midnight, but he hadn't bothered to check it; anything important or relevant and Stoneley would have telephoned him direct, and there were too many big shadows and dark corners in the schoolroom for his liking.

The two-layered paper had spilled in a heap off the back of the printer. He tore it off and rolled it up to glance at later. The room was still in the mess in which the incident squad had left it, the desks pushed together to serve as mortuary slabs and the movable screens stacked to one side to make way for the meat sacks being carried out.

Schaffer paused to look at some of the bright crayon drawings that were pinned to the foremost partition. Soon his own children would be making similar pictures for him to admire, so maybe he'd better start getting into practice. Some were competent and some were barely recognisable, but each had its unique charm. He bent to get a closer look at one drawing that had been fixed lower than the others, as if the teacher had somehow tried to segregate it off and pretend that it wasn't part of the display.

There was a strip of green and brown along the bottom, and a house crammed into a tight space on one side. There were three figures in the foreground, with a boy on the left and a girl on the right. They were holding hands with the figure in the middle.

After staring for a moment, Schaffer straightened and blinked. Perhaps now he could see why the drawing was in a space by itself. Any child that could produce such a disturbing vision from within its own mind probably needed psychiatric attention, and fast. He looked again, and read the name in the corner of the sheet. *Peter Gaskell Aged 7½.*

Sounds of a Land-Rover in the street outside. Schaffer was going to move into the cloakroom and take a look through the window, but as he grabbed his binoculars from the office there was a polite knock on the thick outer door which resounded through the hollow space of the building.

Hennessy was waiting outside by the railings. He wasn't wearing the ridiculously inadequate suit in which he'd first appeared in the village on that same spot. Instead he was in tweeds and brogues, his idea of a country outfit. There was an army man by the Rover behind him.

'Hope we didn't wake you,' Hennessy said, and Schaffer was reminded that he was unshaven and unwashed.

He said, 'Good God, a human face. Well, near enough.'

Hennessy turned to the army man. 'This is Detective Inspector Schaffer. He's one of Stoneley's men, which accounts for the courtesy.'

The army man seemed pained. 'Don't try to get me involved in a departmental dispute, Hennessy. I don't have the time.' He looked towards Schaffer. 'I'm Captain Windeler, in charge of the special unit based up at the clinic.'

Schaffer nodded. 'I've seen you driving past.'

'I think that's one of the reasons why Stoneley chose to hang on to the school as an observation point,' Hennessy said. 'Anything going in or out of the valley has to pass along this road.'

'We've nothing to hide from the police,' Windeler said.

Schaffer didn't readily swallow the P.R. 'Or from the public?'

'Strategy demands that we be wary about the information we release at this stage.'

'Is that why you persist in calling the clinic incident an accident?'

'We've never called it anything of the kind. I understand that the accident story was the idea of your superintendent, conceived shortly after the quarantine story. We've done no more than fail to alter it.'

'It was only intended as a short-term measure,' Schaffer objected, 'to keep the valley clear and give us the best possible chance for a manhunt.'

Windeler smiled politely. 'As it continues to do. I'm grateful, I assure you.'

'But why does it need the army?' Schaffer demanded. Hennessy was looking around and trying not to seem too pleased with himself. 'This is a straight police assignment.'

'My unit's a special unit, we do very special work. This is no ordinary manhunt, Inspector.'

Schaffer almost snorted. 'I'll agree with that. Nothing much seems to happen up at your camp.'

'I'm glad to see you're putting those binoculars to good use,' Windeler said, indicating the Zeiss that Schaffer was still holding, 'but I doubt that they'll tell you much. On the other hand, there is something you can tell me.'

Schaffer said warily, 'Oh, yes?'

'Don't be difficult,' Hennessy advised. 'It's not worth it.'

Windeler went on, 'Before your force withdrew, you checked on a number of the valley farms, is that right?'

'Some of them. The check was never completed.'

'If you can give me a list of the visits made by your men, the list will be completed now.'

'You may as well start again from the beginning,' Schaffer said. 'Anything could have happened over the last few days.'

'Perhaps, but it hasn't. I'd have known. You see, we haven't been completely idle, Inspector. We've been moving at night. Now nothing and nobody can travel for any great distance in the valley without breaking a laser path which will tell me exactly where he is.'

'*If* your man's still in the valley. The chances of that must be nil by now.'

'That's where you're wrong, Inspector. Probably the only assumption that we *can* safely make is that "our man", as you call him, is still in the area.'

This was enough for Hennessy, who seemed to think that the policeman and the Captain were starting to get on too damn well for his liking. He said, 'I think we've said enough, Windeler. The list, please, Inspector.'

Schaffer gave a little shrug and went inside, leaving them to follow or not, as they wished. Windeler came in straight away, Hennessy a moment after.

He found the list of farmhouses along with the radio operator's log in one of his file boxes. There were ten listed, and four of them had been checked off. Schaffer held the paper out to Windeler and said, 'You know that you're throwing it all away. You can't just wait and expect him to come to you.'

Windeler looked at the list for a moment, and then folded it neatly. 'Whereas the police, no doubt, would continue to draft in innumerable squads of men to trample the landscape and inspect the ground, and exude such an aura of busyness and continuous reorganisation that even the most cynical observer could not fail to be impressed.'

'It's the system, and it works.'

'Most of the time, but not here. That's why my unit has been brought in. Waiting can be quite constructive if you have a clear idea of what you're waiting for.'

Schaffer was unconvinced. 'And what are *you* waiting for?'

'Snow,' Windeler said simply, and walked out of the schoolroom.

Even Hennessy was taken by surprise at the abrupt departure, and he stood in a moment's confusion before turning and hurrying out. The Land-Rover's motor was already running when he arrived in the street, and when Hennessy had clambered in on the passenger side Windeler moved off without even waiting to see if the door was secure.

Schaffer stepped down from the railed entrance-way and watched them going. Then he looked up towards the softly-defined slopes, high above the village. No movement that he could see, with or without the aid of the binoculars – but then he didn't really know what he was looking for, whilst Windeler had seemed far more assured.

He slung the binoculars over his shoulder by the carrying strap, and went back into the schoolhouse to throw together some breakfast.

'Snow?' Hennessy said incredulously as Windeler took the clinic turnoff without slowing. 'Are you serious?'

The Rover bounced stiffly on its springs, but it held a tight grip on the road. Windeler said, 'Why shouldn't I be?'

'I'm sorry, obviously I'm no strategist. We save our energies and wait for pneumonia to get him first, is that it?'

Windeler paused, as one might when humouring an over-ambitious suggestion from a bright child. 'It's an idea,' he conceded. 'If we could be sure he's having to hide out in the open, it might even be a good idea.'

'Oh, come on.'

Windeler glanced across before giving in to the slope and changing down through the gears. The Rover rumbled with new life, and he said, 'Schaffer's getting to you, isn't he? Come on, Hennessy, admit it. You're impatient to see the whole valley turned upside down and shaken to get him out.'

'Of course not. We don't want to arouse so much interest.'

'Exactly. So we maintain the illusion of a low-manpower exercise, and we wait for him to show himself.'

'And where does the snow come into this?'

'Tracks. We've had a few scares from the lasers so far, but when we get on the scene there's nothing to see.'

Hennessy was caught off-guard. For a moment he forgot his

attempts to look dignified in the Rover's utilitarian steel cabin. 'The laser network's genuine, then?' he said.

'It certainly is. That's how we know he hasn't slipped over into the next valley. The weather reports indicate that we may get a light fall some time over the next few days. After that, all we'll need is one definite alarm and we can follow him wherever he goes.'

'Pray to God it happens away from the village.'

'It'll be fast and quiet, I promise.'

Hennessy wasn't wholly reassured. 'If word ever got out, my career would be over.'

'There are broader issues than that to consider,' Windeler reminded him.

'Maybe, but that's the one I get all my energy from. I had word last night, there are ripples in London.'

'What kind of ripples?'

'More danger signals from Central Records – somebody's been milking the system from inside, trying to get hold of data on Jenner and the clinic. I've started a quiet enquiry to find out who's making money from being an unofficial outlet.'

'Could it not have been something innocent?'

Hennessy didn't think so. 'There were enquiries made about me, as well. That's the part that really bothers me.'

'Then it's in your interest to find out who is asking the questions,' Windeler said. 'Find out, and divert him.'

'Sit on him hard, you mean. I get the impression that it's some sort of systematic research, maybe a response to a leak. I've put through a request for all the technical libraries to run the Jenner reference list through their own databanks at the end of each day. Any withdrawals or xerox applications on books and magazines that might worry us, and we'll have a straight printout of the names and addresses of all the applicants. If any name appears more than once, then we'll know it's time to move.'

The clinic was now in sight, some way ahead. Windeler said, 'What if he turns out to be working for the Americans?'

'Don't say it. I don't even want to think about it.'

Windeler grinned. 'You're in the wrong job, Mister Hennessy. The way you worry, you'll drop dead when you're fifty.'

'If the Americans ever find out what we were doing at the Jenner clinic,' Hennessy told him gloomily, 'I won't even make it that far.'

Chapter 17

The Tuesday morning was overcast and dull with none of the compensating crispness that had helped Forester to crawl back to an alert state on previous days. His head ached as he made towards the observation point above the cottages. It felt like somebody was trying to poke his eye out from the inside with a pencil.

He should have sensed that something was wrong, but he saw the thin trail of smoke above the trees and it hardly registered in his mind. Only when he broke through into sight of the track and the buildings did the realisation hit him.

There were two cars on the cobbled forecourt. A Range-Rover before the end cottage with the cartwheel and window-boxes, and a blue Volvo Estate by Sampson's door.

What the hell was this? The weekend should have been the danger period, not a *Tuesday*, a nothing day of the week when nobody did anything other than look back wistfully on the pleasures behind them and look forward to the unformed pleasures ahead. Sampson had no damn right to appear on a Tuesday and fuck everything up. Who the hell did he think he was?

Forester was staring at the cottages and the cars, his fists bunched up hard, trembling with rage. He took a couple of deep breaths and forced himself to calm down. He had no more than ten minutes before the postman would come cycling down the road. Maybe he wouldn't be bringing the certificate today, but then again in ten minutes' time Sampson could be on his way down to the police station with an open envelope. Forester could simply melt away and leave the area, but his own freedom wasn't his main concern; he'd already spent a week away from Cumbria, and he had a sick fear of returning to find the clinic ruins empty and the valley returned to placid normality. He couldn't move to another part of the country and start the process over.

He had to get to the postman before he reached the cottage. He started to push his way downslope towards the road.

He recalled his first day in the area, when he'd stopped off at Conon Bridge to browse around a sporting store and listen to the gossip. As he'd studied the tackle and the nets and the green canvas bags on display he'd listened to the gunsmith behind the counter taking telephone enquiries. Nothing around the twentieth, the gunsmith had repeated for each caller. Both of the safari buses were booked up solid for the month after that. Forester had moved to the window and looked out into the yard where the two long-wheelbase Land-Rovers stood side by side, somehow managing to be tough and elegant at the same time in their rough-country rig with full-length roof racks and mounted searchlights. Nothing for him, so he'd wandered over to pretend an interest in the shop's felt-covered notice board while he tried to overhear the conversation of two men who were trying on shooting jackets.

Today was the twentieth, the end of the closed season on hinds. The females had dropped their young and reared them to the point where they could survive to be next year's prey. Sampson, like many others, had come looking for an easy kill before the numbers fell.

Forester scrambled over a low wall and on to the road. He glanced at his watch; less than five minutes, and as he trotted along to intercept the postman's route he couldn't come up with any plan that seemed remotely workable. Threaten the old man and take the letter, or even the sack and the bicycle; he would remember what deliveries he had yet to make, and after some simple detective-work the word would go out and Forester's certificate would be useless. And what if it wasn't in today's delivery? He'd have blown it all for nothing. Somehow he had to stop the man, distract him. But how?

He had to dodge in to the roadside as an open-backed van loaded with milk-crates passed, its brakelights glowing as it slowed to take in the bend. Any time now, the bent figure and the bicycle would be coming into sight. And Forester had no idea of what he would do then.

The noise of the van receded and Forester expected its place to be taken by the measured squeak and clank of the old machine, a sound that he'd so far heard only through still air at a distance. There was only birdsong, and a splashing of water somewhere off in the woods. Then he came around the bend and saw the bicycle.

It was propped against the end-post of a break in the wall, the same break that gave on to the cottage steps which Forester had passed before. Obviously the postman preferred the short climb to the longer haul up the access road. There was no delivery sack with the bicycle.

Four big slabs of grey-green stone formed the opening of a drain culvert beside the post, and the bicycle had been placed squarely across this. There was no bubbling of water from inside, and the culvert seemed to be disused and silted up with debris. Forester moved the machine aside and leaned forward to look into the dark space that was uncovered.

The brown canvas delivery sack was hidden around the corner on a stone shelf, several inches above the rotten humus that blocked the culvert. Forester lifted it out. Thinking that it was heavier than it looked, he undid the straps and buckles and threw back the flap.

The envelopes were packed together in bundles and secured with thick elastic bands. He rested the sack on the flat top of the culvert; high above him on the slope he could hear somebody whistling. He pulled out a bundle and looked at the first address, but he didn't recognise it. He tried another. He thought he could hear footsteps now, nailed boots scuffing on worn stone.

How could he know if there was any mail for Sampson at all? He had only a few seconds before the postman came into sight through the trees above the road. He could hear the grinding of the boots on the steps distinctly; the postman was on his way down, whistling as he descended.

Surely the bundles must be in some kind of order. He'd pulled two out at random, but the one that he wanted would be the next on the route. He reached for the packet that was nearest to the front of the bag.

It was one of the slimmest, and the envelopes in it were pinched in slightly by the pressure of the bands. He fanned it out and tried to read the addresses inside.

Forester pulled out a single white envelope with Sampson's name on the front and stuffed the bundle back into the bag, throwing the flap across and fumbling to thread the straps into the buckles. He couldn't remember whether they'd been fully done up or simply pushed through loosely. He looked up, expecting to see the grey skinny man staring down at him from the steps. Nobody there, but he couldn't be more than a few yards away and Forester's fingers wouldn't obey him enough to get the buckles properly secured.

Maybe they hadn't been secured anyway. He slung the bag into the culvert and replaced the bicycle, remembering to lift it clear of the ground so that the whickering of the freewheel gear wouldn't give him away. Then he jumped on to the wall and missed his footing, banging his shin hard and falling headfirst into the bushes on the other side.

He had a soft landing on rough ground, and the foliage closed up again behind him. He held his breath and didn't move.

The footsteps came to road level, and then there was a pause. The bicycle moved back and rattled against the wall, and then there was a soft scraping of canvas across stone. Then a long silence. Forester could visualise the postman frowning at the interference with his sack, looking around angrily, seeing scuff-marks in the moss on the wall where Forester had stumbled over, the broken twigs and an uncovered shoe or a sleeve glimpsed through the leaves; he didn't dare even raise his head.

The whistling resumed, some way down the road. The postman was gone.

Forester allowed himself a quiet groan of relief. Twigs dug

into the palms of his hands as he pushed himself upright. Sampson's letter was underneath him, and he picked it up and straightened it out. Dirt had obscured the postmark, but it was machine-franked with no stamp. He tore open the envelope.

It was his certificate, fully made out and legal.

Chapter 18

David Reynolds had arranged to meet Diane Rohmer in the Science block, because unlike the Union building it had open access and he wouldn't have to be signed in. The style of the place was very much mid-seventies, a long open-plan corridor of painted brick which was saved from cheapness by the rich texture of the veneered doors and woodwork of the offices down its length. Down below were the lecture theatres; above, four identical corridors and several hundreds of labs and offices that were made barely personal with books and posters.

An increase in the traffic marked the end of a timetable period. Reynolds moved out of the way into an alcove. It had been set aside for no obvious purpose with a low table and several padded vinyl seats; they were old and split with yellow foam bulging out, and on the walls were two art-school lithographs bearing optimistic prices. A girl in a duffel coat and jeans was taking an early lunch in the corner, reading a magazine and eating a sandwich from an open plastic container on the seat beside her.

Reynolds looked out of the window across the campus. He didn't want to watch the quiet parade of students – they made him feel so damned *old*. If it wasn't for them, he'd be feeling like he was home again.

He wondered how many of those around him were there for what he would call the right reason: the feeling that it was simple, playful fun to know things, an eager delight at the discovery that each piece of learning was a key to greater complexities of understanding. Probably about ten per cent, if his memory of his own days still held; perhaps less, considering the government's attitude that the universities could only justify their existence by pre-packaging high-level robots for industry.

Diane Rohmer had been an unspectacular student, chugging through the system along a safe, marked trail, and it wasn't surprising that she'd gone into research. He'd managed to track her down on the Friday evening, waiting for several minutes as she was summoned to the communal phone in the hall where she was now a deputy warden. She'd been surprised and off-balance on hearing his voice, but her subsequent enthusiasm and willingness to help him out had been well-feigned. He could remember the hall well. It was an old house in its own tidy grounds, all parquet and notice boards, three floors of quiet cells inhabited by ungainly girls who wore long skirts and tucked their legs under them when they sat on floor cushions drinking coffee. There were a few stunners, true, but they always moved out after their first year whilst the ungainly ones became permanent fixtures. Diane hadn't been a stunner, but she'd had a pleasant face and a more than tolerably decent body.

Would she have allowed him the use of it in any outside circumstance, anywhere that open sexual contact would be anything other than common and unremarkable, and was he being honest in trying to tap some dry spring of old feelings to further his own ends now? No, he told himself firmly, you're a working professional. And besides, don't forget, it was *she* who dumped *you* in the end. There was no pressure on her to help him, but still she'd agreed to get together as much information on Jenner as she could over the weekend.

'Sorry I'm late,' she said, and he snapped around from the window in surprise, almost forgetting to smile for a moment.

'Only just got here myself,' he lied. 'Good to see you again. How've you been?'

'Fine. What about you?'

'You know. Okay.' He wanted to study her without it being obvious, to match her up with his memories of the girl he'd known. A few years had improved her considerably,

211

firming up the soft and rather indecisive lines of late adolescence to a more attractive overall effect. Her hair was as he'd remembered it, chestnut brown and long.

She said, 'I managed to get some of the information you asked me for.'

Reynolds glanced at the file under her arm, pressed against the stiff white of her lab coat and the softness beneath. 'Any problems?'

'Not really. I knew a lot of it from way back, when Doctor Jenner was still here. I remember seeing him a couple of times.'

'Did you have to spend anything?'

'Nothing that matters.'

'I told you, keep the receipts. I'll pay you what I owe and then get it back off the agency.'

She shrugged. 'It was only pennies, really. Three or four science articles I had copied for you in the library.'

'It doesn't matter how little. It's more than enough that you should be helping me.'

'I didn't even keep the receipts. Honestly, it was nothing. I made you some notes, as well.' She unshipped the file and held it out. 'Dates, the people he worked with, that kind of thing.'

He took the folder. 'You've gone to a lot of trouble,' he said, opening it out.

'Half an hour, that's all. It was quite useful from my point of view.'

Reynolds looked at the first page of the notes. They'd been typed on an old portable with a faded ribbon, so badly laid out that it was obvious Diane was no typist. It must have taken her most of an evening.

She said quickly, 'Would you like me to go through what I've done for you?'

He smiled, and closed the folder. 'Why don't we go down to the refectory and look at it there? They'll be serving morning coffee, won't they?'

They were now into the next lecture period, the last before

212

lunch, and the campus had quietened down again. As they were walking down the paved way to the Union building, Reynolds asked, 'How's Michael, these days?'

There was a silence, which told him he'd scored a bull's-eye, and then an over-bright tone in her reply that confirmed it. 'I haven't seen Michael in ages. We split up years ago.'

Which means, Reynolds thought, he dumped her shortly after she dumped me. For some reason it seemed to kick down some of the barrier of strangeness between them.

There was no porter manning the reception desk, so he didn't have to be signed in after all. In the refectory a queue was already forming alongside the hissing Espresso machines and perspex lids of the snack counter, so he sent Diane off to find a table. He insisted that the least he could do would be to pay for the coffee, and he always tried to do the least that he could. She smiled and relaxed a little, even though he was sure that he must have used the joke on her before. Face it, he used the same joke on *everybody*.

He got a coffee for her and a tea for himself and then made his way through expanding groups at undersized tables, stepping over canvas bags, overstuffed briefcases, sliding piles of ring-folders. Diane had got them a table in the corner and had spread the notes and articles out. She moved a couple of the sheets to make way for the saucers.

'Am I allowed to wonder why you need all this?' she said as he pulled a chair in and sat down.

'There's nothing secretive about it, if that's what you mean, but I don't know myself exactly where the information will finish up. The agency takes on any kind of job – you just name the subject and give us some indication of the kind of thing you want to know, and then we go out and get it for you.'

'And is it a good job?'

'It's not really a job, in the accepted sense of the word. We run the agency as a workers' co-operative, and we all share in the profits.'

'Some sort of commune?'

'Not really. It's a registered company, as capitalist as you can get.'

Diane indicated the pages before her. 'It's just that I was surprised that you should be doing something scientific like this. Or don't you have specialists in different areas?'

'We're not so big,' he admitted. 'And there's really an advantage in having a layman on something that's going to be a bit convoluted. You're less likely to end up with gaps and assumptions.'

All of the tables and chairs around them were now taken, but the coffee line was no shorter. She said, 'Will you be wanting to look around the labs afterwards?'

'If you think it will help. I don't have to be back until tomorrow.'

'You're staying somewhere?' Diane asked, and Reynolds detected a slight anxiety in her voice.

'I'll find a hotel,' he assured her.

'You could have had my sofa, but I'm afraid it's a bit difficult, with me being a deputy warden now . . .'

'Don't worry, I remember. I did my share of late-night drops from the fire escapes.'

'Sorry,' she said, and smiled weakly.

'No need to be, the client pays my expenses. My dossing days are over.'

'As long as you understand.'

He understood more than had actually been said, and he wanted to find some way to ease her embarrassment. He said, 'Why don't you tell me what you found out?'

'Well,' she said with relief, 'Doctor Jenner left the university in 1982, that's the year I first came here so I never really got to meet him. Besides which he never really lectured, he was more pure research.'

'What kind of research?'

'He was part of a team under Professor Liawski. They were trying to isolate the gene that produces insulin and insert it into the nucleus of a bacterium, so that you could get a self-replicating life-form which could then be used in the treatment of diabetes, or else it could provide a source of insulin that wasn't animal-derived and didn't give you rejection problems. Is that too complicated to understand?'

Almost, but Reynolds reckoned he could just about handle it. 'That's fine,' he said. 'Have you any idea what Jenner's specific job on the project might have been?'

'Not really. It was a sponsored project, probably by one of the drug companies but I'm not sure. Anyway, that meant that the whole thing was top secret, because they didn't want to risk any leaks in case somebody followed up the work and got in first with a patent.'

'Could you make a guess?'

'I suppose he'll have had something to do with the animal house. He got his Ph.D. through animal experimentation, but he wasn't qualified when it came to recombinant DNA technique. He was really an M.D. – kept up a second income from some sort of consultancy at the teaching hospital. Did you know that?'

'No, I didn't.'

She sorted through the papers and pushed across some stapled xerox sheets. Sugar grains crunched and gritted on the table beneath it. 'This is a report on the Ph.D. work he did, if you're interested. I had it copied from a microfilm of the *Journal of Comparative and Physiological Psychology* for 1975. It's a pretty poor piece of research.'

Reynolds looked at the title of the piece, but he couldn't make much sense of it. 'In what way?' he said.

'Jenner took the easiest way he could. It makes you quite annoyed if you're doing genuine research yourself. It's a trick you fall back on if you can't really do any original thinking – you devise a new research procedure to "confirm" an already established theory. All you have to do is make a sufficiently methodical presentation and you can get away with it.'

'You don't approve,' Reynolds said.

'Because it's bad science, that's why. Dressed up as "basic" research.'

'What exactly did he do?'

215

She looked down at the xerox and shook her head. Her disgust was obvious. 'Read it for yourself. You wouldn't believe me if I told you.'

'How did that kind of line get him on to the insulin project?'

'Probably because of the sponsors. If it *was* a drug company, they rely pretty heavily on impressive animal test data to put the product over. But that's really a marketing thing, it isn't too scientific.'

'Why not?'

'Because animal results rarely apply to human beings.'

'So why rely on them?'

'It's cheaper than experimenting on people, and there are far fewer risks and restrictions. The simple fact that it's not an adequate form of research doesn't count for much in the commercial field. Look at LD-50 – that's a mandatory test to establish the concentration of a product which will kill at least half of a test group of animals. It's worthless. It's no guide because no two species react to substances in exactly the same way.'

Reynolds said, 'That's the commercial side. What about the academic side?'

'Sorry, I was including that. When you're seeking a grant for your pet project, you have to sell it to the sponsoring body as if you were touting it on the open market, because there are so many pet projects and only so many grants. You're in a competitive situation, and you've got to either learn the salesmanship or else start getting used to failure.'

'But how come you still get animal experiments if that's the case? Surely they only take place when the data's known to be applicable to people.'

She sighed heavily, as if she'd often met this concrete wall of misconception, and she leaned forward and looked at him intensely. 'Thalidomide was proved by three years of animal tests,' she said, 'and these were confirmed in every country of its use except for Turkey. They didn't rate the animal results, and they did lab tests instead. They didn't like what they saw,

216

and they prohibited it. Everyone else went ahead on the basis of the animal data, and then found out the hard way that if it's taken during pregnancy you get damage to the foetus.'

'Presumably that discredited animal testing?' Reynolds hazarded, but he should have known better.

'Not at all. It was used as an argument that more should be spent on development of technique. The vivisection approach is incredibly entrenched, it's been going since Claude Bernard started the whole thing back in the 1840s. You're not going to brush aside a tradition like that with a few facts. Look at the amount of resistance stirred up when it was first suggested that operations should be carried out in aseptic conditions. It's like anything else, most of the people who make it through into professional science don't really have the commitment or the imaginative fire to be there. Ninety per cent of them just slog along with their heads down, following the established line and being intellectual conformists because it's the easiest way to win peer approval. Why are you smiling?'

They were off the subject of Jenner – at least, in any direct sense – but he wanted to go on watching and listening to her talk. She was unlike the girl she'd been or the girls he'd known since; she had a rare energy, and it was good to be near. He said, 'I'm reeling at the way you're shouldering my prejudices aside.'

'I wish it was always so easy. I'm working on the production of a culture from placental tissue which can give reliable results in toxicity tests. I have to fight for every penny I get, I've no assistants, no commercial sponsorship, and I'm always last in line for equipment and computer time.'

'I would have thought that if you were offering something better, people would rush to take it up.'

'Not the case. Not unless you've got somebody very high in the scientific establishment with enough swing to make the lesser lights take notice. It's not as if the evidence wasn't hefty enough – there's an endless list of drugs and substances which show how results can't be extrapolated across species barriers. Penicillin kills guinea pigs, but strychnine doesn't..

217

Chloroform kills dogs, and if you give them digitalis it raises their blood pressure. That's the opposite of its effect on man. Two of the commonest experimental animals, and the examples are typical. But then, I'm not in too much of a position to complain. If I'm honest I'll have to admit that the major application of my research will be for commercial drug production. I'm really only looking for my place on the bandwagon.'

'Now you're being unfair to yourself,' Reynolds told her.

'Not really. There's a third world study which lists a minimum of drugs and medicaments essential to public health. There aren't more than fifty products on it.'

'Why stick with it, if you don't believe?'

'I suppose I'm weak,' she said, regarding him evenly. 'I climbed upon the science train because it was the only door that swung open for me after I got my degree. I'd come so far without looking from side to side, only seeing the next qualification up, that by the time I began to feel closed in it was too late. I envy you, David, I really do.'

Now it was his turn to be embarrassed. 'Envy *me*? By your standards I'm probably a workshy tramp.'

'Perhaps once. But I'd have been wrong.'

Wow, Davy boy, this is starting to get too deep for comfort. Better suggest a move.

The refectory had almost emptied, the snack counter had closed, and the tables were being wiped down. It was Diane who proposed that they should go over and take a look at the labs where Jenner had worked and Reynolds agreed, more than a little relieved that they were returning to the main subject; he was made uncomfortable by Diane's self-revelation and the way in which it had begun to erode his easy preconceptions of her and her 'type'. As they walked back along the paved way between the Union building and the Science block he said, 'Did the insulin project ever come to anything?'

'No, it wound down and ran out into nothing. It hadn't been the greatest operation anyway, because it seemed that

Jenner and Professor Liawski had some big argument around seventy-nine.'

'What about?'

'You'd have to get hold of someone who worked on the project to tell you the details. I'm not aware of anyone who's still around. Presumably it was something to do with the way that Jenner approached his work. Because it was a secret project there were several phases being developed separately, and it's possible that Professor Liawski didn't like the forms of experimentation that Jenner was using. He didn't much approve of animal experimentation in the first place, so I'd guess that it was forced on him by the sponsor.'

They stood aside to make way for a blind Indian youth in a parka who was confidently striding down the way with his cane held out before him. Reynolds said, 'You say that of all the people who worked on the project, none of them are still here?'

'Jenner took most of them with him,' Diane said as the youth passed and they moved on towards the doors of the Science block. 'He went up North somewhere to set up his own unit, I don't know where.'

'Cumbria,' Reynolds supplied triumphantly, pushing open the glass swing door and standing aside for Diane.

'What?'

'That's where he moved to. He bought up a farm complex and converted it into a private lab to give specialised service to his medical practice. Any idea why he should decide to do that?'

'There was no secret about it. He got quite a hefty government grant, cashing in on the fertility boom.'

Ready-money karma, indeed! They passed the entrances to the lecture halls and Reynolds said, 'It was being handed out, just like that?'

'Obviously Jenner's work aroused more interest than Professor Liawski's. This way, I'll show you the animal house.'

The animal house was actually a section of the basement,

reached by a wide staircase at the end of the concourse. There was a heavy entrance door that looked as if it might be airtight, but it was wedged back.

'This was always kept locked when Jenner was here,' Diane said. 'You could only get in with a pass if you were a member of the project. The rats had to be kept in another part of the building.'

They were in a corridor that was lined on one side with a six-foot-high bank of cages. Each cage was about the size of a wire basket for office mail, and in the corner of every one was a pellet hopper and an inverted water bottle. They were tagged with colour-coded labels bearing experiment numbers and feeding instructions. Each cage held at least one white rat.

They shuffled around on the wire, blinking at Reynolds in their hundreds as he was led past. Some of them had pink shaved patches on their heads with electrodes that stuck up like a second pair of ears, and here and there were dark grey rats that seemed bigger than any of the others. They were soulless little beings, numerous and uniform, no more than a commercial product bred to a standard, and Reynolds was slightly disturbed to find that they didn't evoke any feeling of sympathy from him.

Diane exchanged a couple of words and a smile with a young man who had emerged from a side door carrying a clipboard and what looked like a litre bottle of clear water. Reynolds hung back and looked around self-consciously, determined not to feel any irrational stabs of envy. He nearly managed it.

The young man moved on, and Diane led the way through into the room that he'd left. It was a large tiled room, brightly lit and with the dry, rich smell of animal feed – it made Reynolds realise that there had been no noticeable odour in the corridor at all. White lab rats make good neighbours. Robert Frost?

Apart from the sacks of feed and the table and scales, the room held four large cages. They were heavily barred and on wheels, somewhere between a luggage trolley and a circus sideshow. Reynolds said, 'What are these?'

Diane glanced across as if she'd momentarily forgotten that they were there. 'Those are the primate facilities,' she said, 'but they're not used. Primates are expensive to buy, there's God knows how many regulations attached to keeping them, and you have to employ two full-time handlers to look after them. Most projects don't run to that kind of budget – not for the big chimps, anyway, which is what these were for. Rhesus are cheaper but they're bitches to handle.'

One of the cages had a movable inner wall which could slide along rails the full length of the interior. Reynolds asked about this, and Diane explained that it was a crush cage, a means of restraining an animal for injection or biopsy. 'You transfer them across from their regular cage and then close the door behind them. Then you slide the inner wall across and use it to pin them against the side of the cage so they can't move or fight. Then you can do what you like.'

The cages were dusty and unused. Reynolds wouldn't have been able to stand upright in one of them, and the open-mesh floor would have made it even more uncomfortable.

There was an anteroom and an empty office on the other side of the disused primate facility. More doors, and they emerged into the empty vastness of a darkened theatre.

They were at floor-level, and beyond the empty ranks of seats above them the only light came from two dim green *EXIT* signs. Then Diane found a switch and threw it, and a weak pool of illumination washed down a white screen on the back wall. There was a diagram on the screen and a few dried-out felt pens on the wooden ridge under it. Far from brightening the place the light only increased its menace, like a guttering campfire in the middle of a bear forest.

Reynolds turned to Diane. She was a black silhouette against the screen. The diagram seemed to show bones, veins, turned-back flaps of skin. Or perhaps that was only his imagination.

Diane said, 'Demonstrations.'

There was no lectern, just a big table on a swivelling stand. Diane's shadow fell across it, and as she moved forward Reynolds saw a dull gleam of stainless steel.

'Demonstrations of what?' he said, not sure that he wanted to hear the answer.

She lifted a buckled strap from the table's edge. He couldn't tell if it was leather or canvas webbing, but it looked broad and strong. The table's steel surface was ridged with a network of channels that led to a drain-hole in one corner. 'You name it,' she said. 'Did you see that stuff in the room we just came through?'

He'd looked, but most of the items on the Dexion shelving in the anteroom had been no more than shapes under canvas sheets. 'Didn't mean anything to me.'

They went back into the anteroom, but the door through to the theatre remained open. If Reynolds glanced back he could still see the dark bulk of the table against the light, its straps hanging.

It seemed that the room was an equipment store for the theatre demonstrations. Everything was kept to hand, ready to be rolled out when needed. She took the covering from one of the nearer pieces, revealing what looked like an old-fashioned letterpress.

'A smaller version of the Blalock Press,' Diane explained. 'Used for crushing tissue on a limb without crushing the bone.'

There were more, doll-sized restraints to prevent the struggles of monkeys in response to massive trauma, sets of electrodes with a variable current supplied by a rheostat, a stock for immobilising a medium-sized dog. 'This isn't for research, as such,' she told him as they moved along the rows of apparatus. 'This is straight lecture stuff, experiments to be repeated even though the results are known in advance. You see what I mean? Pseudo-science.'

It was calculated and clinical, the worst kind of violence – that with the stamp of a society's approval. Reynolds said,

'What about the animal welfare movements? Can't they at least bring pressure for control?'

She put the cover back over the Pavlov stock. 'Not as long as they're sentimentally motivated, which unfortunately most of them are. It leaves them wide open for dismissal by anybody with a basic knowledge of debating tactics. All right, so you design a cup and rod device to compress a cat's testicle and crush it, and when you've done it a few thousand times over word gets out and you have protests and pressure. It happened at New York's Museum of Natural History in 1976, and the experiments had to be wound up because the funding stopped. But say you use brown rats from the sewers instead. You think you're going to get the same kind of opposition? There's only one way you can cripple a bad scientist, and that's to demonstrate how bad his science is. Then the *really* hard part is persuading the public to listen, because the last thing they want to believe is that the charlatan in the white coat isn't going to give them a cure for cancer, a promise he's been renewing at regular intervals for the past two hundred years. They don't want to lose sight of the miracle around the corner that will let them go on pumping their bodies full of chemicals and preservatives, most of which were okayed by animal experimentation in the first place. Anyway, this is Jenner's territory.' A wave of the hand covered the shelving and the dark theatre beyond. 'Does it give you some idea of the kind of man he was?'

Reynolds hesitated for a moment, then said, 'I don't see how this ties in with his medical practice.'

'There would have been some degree of overlap. Have you never seen a fertility clinic catalogue?'

'It's not something I've ever really needed,' he said, trying not to make it sound assertive.

The warmth of an old memory seemed to stir in her eyes, but she quickly dampened it down. 'Let's go over to the library,' she said briskly. 'They may have something on file.'

She wanted to check on some of her cultures before they left the building, so they went up to the third floor and along a corridor lined with rooms numbered for experimentation and behavioural study. Reynolds waited in the small office that Diane appeared to share with four others; after the windowless basement it seemed almost palatial. He'd misjudged her, he reflected. The strait-jacket role of middle class, middlebrowed fugitive from reality wouldn't fit and couldn't be forced. He no longer felt as confident and secure as he had on his arrival.

Diane came back without the lab coat. It had been shapeless and unflattering, and she looked a lot better without it.

'There's always an endless wait for the lifts,' she said apologetically, so they used the fire stairs.

As they were descending, Reynolds said, 'I get the impression that you didn't much rate Jenner.'

She was a couple of steps ahead. Her voice echoed in the stairwell as she raised it to carry back to him. 'I told you, I hardly knew him. But if the way he treated Professor Liawski was anything to go by, I bet his mother would have had trouble finding something good to say about him. It's obvious that Jenner only used the insulin project to further his own work.'

'Which was?'

'Who knows? The locks didn't come off the animal-house doors until Jenner had cleared out.'

Another landing when they were close together for a moment, and then another descent. Reynolds said, 'Is Professor Liawski still around?'

'He died a couple of years after the end of the project.'

'Family?'

'He didn't have any. They were all killed in the concentration camps during the war. He escaped and managed to get to England while they were still alive, but nobody took his stories seriously and by the time they knew better it was too late. He hadn't exaggerated and he hadn't tried to make the S.S. seem worse than they really were, the way everyone had assumed.'

'So he settled over here.'

'The Academic Freedom committee helped him resume his studies at Cambridge. He went back to Nuremberg in 1946 to testify, but as far as I know that's the only time he ever left the country.'

The library was a tall wedding-cake of a building on the far side of the campus, unofficially reached by cutting across a couple of weak-looking lawns. A chill October breeze forced its way through countless gaps and alleys in the structures surrounding them, tugging and pushing when it was least expected, lifting Diane's hair and flicking it across her face.

'Liawski must have had papers, notes, things like that about the insulin project,' Reynolds said. 'What would have happened to them when he died?'

'I've no idea. I expect his notes went into the university archives, and the rest of his belongings would have been sold off. I don't suppose he had much.'

'Any idea where he lived?'

She pushed back a straying wraith of hair. 'You remember the Evergreens? He was the warden there. But the housekeeper looked after most of the administration and discipline for him. Look, I thought it was only Jenner you wanted to know about. If you'd like me to ask around again for Liawski . . .'

'I wouldn't dream of it,' he reassured her quickly, 'you've done too much for me already. It's getting so I'm almost ashamed to get paid. Let me do something for you, instead.'

'What?'

'Dinner, tonight.' As soon as he'd said it, he thought how unbearably old-fashioned it sounded.

Diane said, 'Isn't that stretching your client's generosity beyond reasonable limits?'

'Not on the client, on me.'

'Much as I admire your unstructured lifestyle, on the evidence of the knees in those jeans I'd think twice before I traded bank accounts with you.'

He glanced down. Wait until she saw the elbows of his pullover. He said, 'How do you know I'm not an eccentric millionaire?'

'I might believe the eccentric part. Dinner's fine, but it's on me, as long as you don't get picky and expect anything too complicated. There's a limit to what can be done on those little caravan stoves they provide us with.'

He said, 'Deal,' and they went into the library.

Security was tighter here than it had been in the Union building, and Reynolds had to be signed in by Diane before he could be issued with a visitor's pass. He showed this to the porter who watched over the entrance turnstile, and Diane produced her staff ticket. Once inside they went to the card index. The system seemed quaint and inefficient in comparison with the microfilm and computer displays used by the library staff behind the checkout desk, but it was still the most convenient way of satisfying reader enquiries and it was a useful backup in case of computer failure. At one time the cards had been relegated to a storeroom to await incineration, but the power strikes around the middle of the decade had left the facility without any index at all. The cards had been rescued and reinstated, and the error-tempting V.D.U.'s removed.

Most of the country's fertility clinics were listed, although none of the catalogues was up to date. They were on reserve, which meant that they weren't on the shelves but had to be ordered from the stock by a librarian. Diane filled in an order form for a Jenner Clinic catalogue and took it over to be processed while Reynolds waited, arms folded and leaning against a pillar by the card files.

Diane came back. The computer had located the catalogue, and it would arrive in a few minutes. Reynolds said, 'How could Jenner make the leap from insulin to fertility?'

'Because they're both fringe studies on genetics. Or molecular biology, if you want to be more specific.'

'You're losing me.'

'DNA, the double-helix molecule that carries the genetic blueprint which tells any organism how to build itself. Right?'

'Right.' At least, he thought so.

'It can be broken down into sets of signals, each signal with a specific function. Some of them can be isolated.'

'Like the signal that triggers insulin production?'

'See? You know more than you thought. Early fertility treatments were mainly mechanical, like fallopian reconstruction, artificial insemination, concentrating sperm which had a low count and then, when things started getting a bit flashy, *in vitro* fertilisation.'

'In what?'

'Test-tube babies. All of this involved taking both parents' sex cells with their half-complement of DNA signals in the chromosomes, and bringing them together so that the cells could clamp on to each other and start dividing and growing. The trick was then to get the newly-formed zygote back into the mother so it could attach to the inside of the womb and develop normally.'

Several books from the reserve stocks were being put out for collection, but none was theirs. Reynolds said, 'And this is all part of this molecular biology thing?'

'A lot of the techniques are common to the two fields. The big boost came when the recombinant DNA programme in the States suddenly folded before it had ever really got going. Kennedy was fighting on the issue of public accountability for scientists, and the Friends of the Earth were pressing for the withdrawal of Federal funding for recombinant experiments. Anybody scheduling an experiment was likely to find himself faced with a lawsuit if he didn't make the environmental impact statement that was required under the National Environmental Policy Act. And since it's usually the case with an experiment that you don't *know* what the exact outcome is going to be . . . well, a lot of the top men moved out to where conditions were easier. Quite a few wound up in the private labs in Switzerland. Not so many came here. Two main points about Britain at this time: the science unions were putting pressure on the government to shift economic policies from an industrial to a scientific base, and the health service was on the point of collapse. Within the year there was money made available for projects which could take the broad skills of a science like genetic manipulation and give them a saleable medical application. It was a fast move to corner the market, and it worked.'

Most of the books that had been set out on the last delivery had gone, and now more volumes were being added. One of them was a slim pamphlet that looked as if it might be the catalogue. As they moved over, Reynolds said, 'And that's where Jenner came in?'

'Exactly. Just about every fertility clinic in the country was set up with a government grant. And most of the services they offer aren't readily available outside Britain.'

Reynolds thought that Carson would probably want to see the catalogue, so he asked if it would be possible to get it copied. As he wasn't a registered reader it needed Diane's signature on a xerox form. After she'd made out the application for him she said, 'Can you manage if I leave you with it?'

'I expect so. Thanks for your time.'

'You're welcome. About eight tonight?'

He nodded. 'That will be fine. Gives me the chance to get a few things done.'

'Do you know where to find me?'

The question had a strange and almost forlorn appeal. He said, 'I've an idea. Don't worry, I'll get there okay.'

She went off to attend to her cultures, and Reynolds handed in the form and the catalogue to the copy clerk. Another delay as the work train was slowly shunted along, and as there were no seats on the customer side of the counter in the tiny room he went out into the periodicals area. Low comfortable chairs had been set out in a square; too comfortable for some, because there was a distinct buzz of snoring from the other side of a rack of trade journals, broken only by the bats' wing rustle of folding and refolding newspaper.

He opened the file out and spread the papers across his lap. First he looked through the typed notes that Diane had done

228

for him. They gave the bare details of Jenner's life and career as far as she'd been able to check it out – dates, addresses, all the useful stuff that Reynolds could work from – followed by a surprising amount of straight campus gossip. His early academic record was unimpressive, and his private life had been a disaster; whilst he worked late hours in the animal house or grudgingly fulfilled occasional lecture commitments, two senior geography students and half the fencing team were back home screwing his wife.

Surely not all at the same time, Reynolds thought, and turned to the summary of Jenner's thesis work. *Observations on the Responses to Systematic Stimulation of the Caudate in Mammals.* It took some puzzling to deduce that a *caudate* was actually a tail, rather less to see that Jenner had used cats in his experiments. No explanation of where he got them from.

The test model displayed extreme hyperactivity, and as curare was not immediately available (and would, in any case, have tended to invalidate subsequent observations) the more traditional method of a minute's hanging was employed to subdue the animal. Handling by kidney squeeze overcame any further resistance so that it was then possible to secure the model in the Pavlov stock. Jenner's stiff and stilted prose then went on to describe how the 'model' – the first of a number – had been allowed to recover before the serrated plates of a Kocher clamp had been placed around its tail. A measured degree of crushing pressure had been applied, and Jenner had noted the animal's reactions on a Richter-like scale of his own devising: loud crying, sweating paws, panting. *Ideally it would have been wished to leave the model in the stock overnight, but as the equipment was required by another experimenter the animal was removed. By the next morning its hyperactivity had returned, and to make future ease of handling possible it was decided to employ the Walther method of de-clawing.*

Some surprise managed to shoulder its way into Jenner's turgid writing. It seemed that he'd expected the animal's response to be more intense on the second day, but it actually scored lower on his scale. Jenner wondered if the unanaesthetised de-clawing may have had some effect on this, and he offered the theory that an alternative source of pain might cause a distraction from the tail-crushing effects of *caudate stimulation*. Maybe, he suggested hopefully, a promising new area of investigation had been revealed.

He pushed the idea for a few more pages, but Reynolds didn't read them all. Recurring words and phrases caught his eye: extirpation, sacrifice, light anaesthesia. He'd got the message.

His photocopies would be ready, and he had things to do.

The Evergreens had been a large and comfortably rustic dwelling, too big and rambling to be a house but too small and unpretentious to be a mansion. It was a good half-hour's walk from the campus, standing in its own grounds on the fringe of the green belt. What remained of the gardens was now given over to the university's botany department, and so the building had been able to retain much of its outward character. Inside it had been converted to make a dozen study bedrooms with shared facilities and a self-contained warden's flat, painted a bland cream throughout and carpeted with the tough fibre matting that was a feature of all the student halls and houses.

Reynolds decided that a ring-file and a couple of paperbacks were all the disguise that he needed – it was early in the term and the place was full of strangers. At this hour of the afternoon there were few signs of life in the house. There was no car in the warden's reserved parking space, and when Reynolds walked openly into the entrance hall there was no one to challenge him.

He'd been in the house once before. It was for a party in one of the upstairs rooms, but it had been a long time ago. Perhaps even when Liawski had been warden, but that wasn't something that Reynolds could expect to remember. He pushed through a regulation fire door and found himself in a narrow passageway that ran along by the stairs to the kitchen.

230

One of the first rules of house and hall parties had been to scout the building for dark corners that might make useful retiring-places if the evening went well — preference was given to anywhere that had a lock on the inside. Reynolds had only the vaguest memory of his search of the Evergreens, but he thought he could find what he was looking for.

The door under the stairs was as he recalled it, low and cut on a slant to fit in under the balustrade. He opened it, reached in, switched on the light. An unshaded fitting glared weakly down the cellar steps.

The cellar was four large connected rooms of whitewashed brick. The one nearest the back of the house contained the old-fashioned central heating boiler and had ground-level access through two angled flap doors. The other chambers were less well-frequented, and it showed. They were used to store trunks, suitcases, large misshapen cardboard boxes and broken furniture. The light switches clicked but nothing happened. Reynolds went back and found an electric flashlight by the boiler, and with this he began to stab and search through the first of the three rooms.

Everything was dusty and sticky with lacy cobwebs. He tried to knock some aside but they clung to his fingers and a spider danced across his knuckles and disappeared up his sleeve. He shook his arm vigorously for more than a minute, but it was impossible to tell in the uneven twilight whether it dropped out or not.

It was in the second of the rooms behind a damp stack of spare mattresses that he found what he'd been hoping for. It was an old tin steamer trunk, its corners reinforced with iron shoes. The lid had been battered out of shape and the locks no longer met, but a leather strap held the whole thing together. The initials H.P.L. had been hand-lettered on the side, and the ink had almost faded to invisibility.

Reynolds leaned the mattresses away. He didn't want to drag them, because even though it would give him more room there would be a risk of noise which might attract the attention of the housekeeper. On the other side of the thick wall, the boiler fired up in response to some secret signal. He undid the strap and lifted the lid.

Most of the stuff in the trunk was personal trivia, robbed of its meaning in the absence of the one who valued it. There were framed photographs, ribboned bundles of letters, awards and certificates. Nothing for the archives and nothing that could be sold off, this bric-à-brac had obviously been stored against the possibility of some surviving and previously untraced relative appearing to claim it. Once stored, it had been forgotten.

He moved aside the folded *Tephillim* and uncovered five neatly-bound books. When he lifted out the first and looked through the handwritten pages he found that he was holding Henryk Liawski's personal diary covering odd and irregular dates between 1952 and 1958. He put it aside and looked through the others. He had no way of carrying them all off, but two of the volumes were dated to cover the period of the insulin project as Diane had described it. On a random dip into one of these Reynolds's eye was caught by the name *Jenner*. Gold dust. He returned the other three books to the trunk and replaced the mattresses. There would be no reason for the trunk to be disturbed, and if Carson decided that he wanted to see the other diaries it would be a simple matter to get hold of them.

He listened before he let himself out of the cellar, but there still seemed to be nobody around; Reynolds felt gritty and smeared, at an unhappy disadvantage if he should have to lie his way out of an embarrassing situation. He only started to relax when he was out on the stone-chip drive and walking away from the house. Back to the campus and a free shower in the sports annexe, then kill some time in the Union before going on to see Diane. And maybe he'd be able to save himself something out of Carson's expenses.

It was early evening when the manager of the Langstone Hotel came to the reception desk in response to the ringing of the bell. Forester was waiting there, and he looked tired and worn. By the counter were a suitcase, a fishing bag, and a green canvas rod case.

Seven days. He'd timed the reservation pretty neatly. Forester's fear was not so much that the room might not have been available, but that if Hennessy had moved out the hotel might be closed down for the off-season altogether. Elsewhere in the Lakes the tourist industry was having a last determined autumn fling, but not here, not in this quiet and relatively undiscovered cul-de-sac. Winter came early.

'On your own?' the manager said as he shuffled around to get Forester's key.

'For a few days. Come to get my thinking straight.'

The manager nodded and handed over the key. 'Will you be all right with your bags?' he said. 'I can call Lesley.'

'Don't bother,' Forester said. 'I know where it is.'

The manager watched him as he wearily climbed the stairs. Sly bugger probably planned it this way, he thought. No child to save the marriage, so he sets up some fishing straight away instead. Who does he think he's kidding?

In the bay-windowed room Forester locked the door behind him and closed all the curtains before turning to the rod case that he'd laid on the bed. When he was sure that there was no chance of being disturbed or observed he undid the flap at the top of the bag and reached inside. Slowly and carefully, he withdrew the Steyr-Mannlicher .308 hunting rifle that he'd bought that same afternoon using the cash from the sale of his car and the Firearm Variation certificate that had been issued to Ian Sampson. It was a second-hand weapon, but it was in good condition. From the fishing bag he took a scope sight and two boxes of ammunition, one of them depleted from the sighting-in that he'd carried out in a deserted glen on the drive south. He'd daubed a rock with paint and used the tell-tale splashes to correct a slight right-hand drift, and then he'd taken a rasp to the elaborate Monte Carlo grip, reshaping the stock to approximate to the military form on which he'd been trained and binding it with tape when it was as he wanted.

The ammunition was soft-nosed, not what he'd been used to but the only kind that was allowed for hunting. It didn't worry him, because over a distance the soft-nosed rounds would break up on entry and be considerably more destructive, splattering meat in exactly the same way as a hard point carved into an illegal dum-dum. He fixed the scope into place and then loaded up.

Over by the window there was a wardrobe that had been built to fit into the corner, tall and heavy, mirror-fronted with small brass teardrop handles. He leaned the Mannlicher inside against the back boards and turned the small key in the door. The wire hangers rang together like bells and kept it up for almost a minute.

As he waited for the noise to die down, Forester looked around the room. On his last quick visit he'd been more interested in the situation than in the fittings. He had two chairs, one hard and one padded, both of them small. A chest of drawers with teardrops that didn't match the wardrobe's, and a thin metal wastebin next to a modern formica bedside table. The sink was squared-off and old fashioned, with a white splashback and a tilting mirror; Forester switched on the fluorescent shaving light and tried to tip the mirror to look at himself, but it wouldn't stay in place until he found out how to tighten a chrome-plated hexagonal nut on the hinge.

He looked like something you'd frighten children with on Hallowe'en. His eyes were bloodshot, his skin was grey and waxy with fatigue, and there were small patches of bristle in hollows where he'd missed shaving. He knew that he was going to have to give himself one night's sleep at least, one night when he wouldn't be bent into the back of a freezing car or upright on a chair. He'd have to leave the window slightly open and hope to be disturbed if anything happened.

He lifted back the drapes and looked out into the road. The darkness was almost complete. There was a light in the schoolhouse.

Chapter 19

Early on Wednesday afternoon the telephone rang. Carson answered immediately. Yet again, it wasn't Alison.

'Carson?' David Reynolds said after the money had been rammed home and the tone had cycled, 'Carson, are you alone?'

It was a moment before Carson was able to place the researcher's voice – after all, he'd only heard it once before – but he said, 'Yes, I'm alone. Why?'

'Trouble, that's why.'

'What do you mean?'

'You've started something, I don't know what. But when I got back to the agency this morning, the place had been cleared out.'

Carson frowned. 'I don't understand.'

'Turned over, raided, the whole operation. There was a van by the door and they were loading up the files, the contracts, documents, everything.'

'The police?' Carson hazarded, apprehension growing.

'I didn't stop to find out. It's because of this Jenner business, I'm sure of it.'

'Just hold on.' This way they were going to generate a lot of heat but not much reason. 'Where are you?'

'Euston. I've got a ticket, and I'm using it as soon as I've seen you.'

'You've got something about Jenner.'

'I've got something, all right, and the sooner I can get rid of it the happier I'll be. It'll cost you four hundred.'

Carson hesitated. He didn't know Reynolds, and this sounded like a shake-down. He was tempted to hang up and call the R.C.O. number to see if this was the case, but something told him no; there was an authentic quality to

Reynolds's agitation that couldn't be defined but was nevertheless persuasive. Carson said carefully, 'That was the estimate for the whole deal.'

'This is worth it. Worth more if anything, but I'm not going to stay around and haggle. I'll want it in cash.'

'I usually pay through the agency.'

'There *is* no agency now, and I need that money. You've about an hour before the banks close.'

'Shall I come to the station?'

'Christ, no,' Reynolds said quickly, 'not with cameras everywhere. Somewhere nearby.'

What was near to Euston? 'Regent's Park?'

'Too open.'

'For God's sake . . .'

'Look,' Reynolds said, 'you obviously have no idea of just how nasty this could turn.'

'I asked for a biography of a dead scientist, not a list of missile sites.'

'You'd better take this seriously.'

'You don't make it easy.'

'I'm not going to tell you about it over the phone. I'm not going to tell you about it at all. You bring me the four hundred and you'll get what I found. Whatever you do after that, I don't want to know.'

'And if I don't think the information's worth the cost?'

'Sue me.'

It wasn't a matter of money – four hundred was enough to be missed, but it wouldn't break him – it was the risk of finding that he'd been duped and made a fool of that made Carson wary. But there was sincerity in Reynolds's fear, and so he said, 'All right. If the station's too enclosed and the park's too open, where do you want to meet?'

'Somewhere I can see if you're being followed.'

'How about the zoo?'

'No, it's too . . .' Reynolds seemed to realise that such objections could go on for ever, so he said, 'Yes. Okay, make it the zoo in the park. Do you know the Sobell pavilion?'

236

'No.'

'You can find it, buy a map or something. The garden area in the middle. It's appropriate.'

Reynolds hung up.

Carson arrived at the zoo an hour later and bought a layout map from a kiosk just inside the South gate. The day was miserable and the animals were likewise, with very few people around.

He took a shortcut through the Lion terraces to reach the Broad Walk down the zoo's centre. Two lynx, sleek and amber in the first enclosure that he passed, were disregarding the tourists and staring possessively at the peafowl across the way.

The buildings and the greens were well laid-out, modern in style and agreeable to look at. Carson had been before, but the place had always made him uneasy; it was so Victorian in its assumptions. If there were a colonial mentality that could covet territory across the species barrier, this was it. A declaration of dominance, of the attitude that had accepted Darwin only so long as his ideas could be misrepresented in shuffling the animal kingdom into a league table with man several steps above its head, almost within touching distance of God. Children came to laugh at the animals as they rocked autistically or broke into irrational tantrums; creatures accustomed to marking out miles of territory in a single day were now constrained to prowl and circle in a few narrow yards.

He was aware that present-day zoos were no longer dedicated to this ideal, although he wasn't so sure about some of the visitors. More than a hundred years of systematic captivity had created a whole new genus, animals that had none of the skills and few of the desires of a wild habitat. He could appreciate that a collection might become the last refuge and hope for survival of an endangered species, but the knowledge did little to modify his response; apart from the dogs' home where he'd once been bought a sick puppy, it was one of the saddest places he knew. He was starting to wish that he'd suggested somewhere else.

The Sobell pavilions were a number of wire enclosures designed to seem as open as possible, linked to glass-walled brick chambers which held the zoo's collection of apes and monkeys. Appropriate, Reynolds had said. Carson stood in the open quadrangle of tended plants and empty benches that he assumed to be the 'garden area in the middle', and looked around. A keeper in a loose green uniform and wellingtons walked past, carrying a yardbrush and a bucket. Otherwise he was alone.

Reynolds arrived a couple of minutes later. Presumably he'd been watching from somewhere. He looked hunted and haggard, and he was carrying a small parcel wrapped in brown paper.

'Got the money?' he said. A baboon shrieked on the far side of the pavilion.

Carson said, 'I want to see what I'm buying, first.'

Reynolds seemed offended. 'I'm not trying to cheat you.'

'I didn't say you were.'

'Please,' Reynolds said, 'please don't get me into any more trouble.'

'You don't know for sure that this is why the agency was raided. You're only assuming. I could be buying expensive junk.'

'No,' Reynolds said, and he shifted his grip on the brown paper as if it were getting hot in his hands. There was desperation under his attempt at reassurance. 'It's what you were looking for, and more.'

'I'll decide that.'

'All right,' Reynolds exploded, 'stuff your fucking money. But you've got to take the parcel off me!'

Carson was surprised to see tears of anger and frustration glistening in the corners of Reynolds's eyes. After a moment he reached into his jacket and produced a thick envelope. 'Four hundred,' he said. 'It's in tens.'

Reynolds blinked and wiped his nose on the back of his hand. 'And three.'

'What?'

'It cost me three pounds to get in here.'

Well, it *had* been Carson's idea. He took out his wallet and handed over three more notes. Reynolds took them and gave him the parcel. He seemed glad to be rid of it.

'Good luck with this,' he said. 'You're going to need it.'

'What have I bought?'

'Professor Liawski's diaries, 1978 to 1983. And if anybody ever catches up with me and starts asking questions, that's all I know about it.'

'Who's Professor Liawski?'

Reynolds shook his head firmly. 'You've got your money's worth. Don't follow me out.'

He was backing off and looking around when Carson said, 'Where will you go?'

He shrugged. 'Somewhere safe and cheap. It'll only cost me a couple of lies.' And then with a final glance to either side he turned and walked off towards the main gate.

Carson took a peek into the brown paper on the Tube. By now it was the rush hour and he was squeezed into the corner of a carriage by a family of Swedish tourists who talked loudly and without vowels and continuously trafficked maps and guidebooks across him, so there was no chance of getting a look at the diaries or the few folded sheets of paper that were wedged between them. Beyond the Swedes was an impersonal sea of heads and hats and magazines and knuckles on hanging-straps. Forget it.

Frequency of the trains had been increased but the swollen crowds filled up the tunnels and the escalators at the interchanges. It was almost dark when Carson emerged from Gunnersbury station. Some of the streetlights were still glowing red but most were at full sodium yellow. The worst of the evening traffic was already over.

Habit shouldered curiosity out of the way for a moment

when he got back to the house, and he checked around the Mercédès for damage. As he'd told Alison, spitting and scratching were nothing new but that was mainly when the car was on the road. Here on the asphalt forecourt tampering was far less common. Besides the discouraging glow of the porch light he supposed that some invisible demarcation held vandals back to the pavement; that was their territory, this was his. Maybe he had something nasty waiting for them. The car was untouched.

It was easy enough to get the front door open one-handed, not so easy to switch on the hall light with no hands at all. The spring-button was too high for his elbow so he didn't bother. Enough light would spill inwards from the porch as the door closed slowly on its damper, enough at least for him to get to his own door and line up the key; but when it came to it he hurried too much and was trying to shake out the Yale when the front door put him in darkness.

But not quite. There was a bar of light under his own door.

He couldn't remember leaving a light on. When a shadow passed across the bar, he knew that he hadn't.

He started to back off, and the parcel shifted smugly against his side. Because of me, it said. All because of me. Whoever was in the flat must have heard the muffled sound of the closing door and was going through into the bedroom to have a look out of the window.

When Carson reached the stairs at the end of the hall he kept on going, feeling for the first riser with his heel and wincing when the step creaked under his weight. There was some glow from the tiny window on the half-landing above and behind him, but not enough to do much for the hallway; the sliver of light under his door was hard-edged, bright, unmistakable.

He could feel it as a line of cherry heat across his back when he turned and began to climb the stairs more carefully. The only wooden stairs that never seemed to make any noise were those inch-thick slabs in modern public buildings; house stairs always took pleasure in announcing to everybody what you were doing. Just like the plumbing. He walked on the carpet at the outside of the treads and the noise dropped away to almost nothing. Cheat, came the muffled accusation.

On the next landing he could hear a TV set on the floor above. The top storey was a one-bedroomed apartment, rooms that had once been servants' quarters in the tight spaces where the house narrowed towards the roof. It had been bought by a middle-aged nursing Sister who'd had to sell her car to raise the deposit on the place. She'd lived without carpets for the first few weeks and it had been nearly a year before she'd been able to ditch her old and undersized curtains. Carson liked her because she seemed to display the ideal mix of warmth and distance that made a good neighbour. For a moment he was tempted to keep on climbing, to knock at her door and tell her that something was wrong; but what then? He'd simply have acquired a spectator and a potential liability.

He stopped at the door of the flat directly above his own, the empty place. The key was on top of the frame where the lazy agent had left it, another Yale on a big paper tag. Open up – watch the hard rasp as the key slides into the lock – and step inside.

The rooms were cold and empty, and they smelled of dust and glue size. Because the converting builder had demolished most of the internal walls there was no correspondence in the shape and layout of the rooms to the flat below, but the lounge was still at the back to take advantage of the small terrace and river view. Carson stayed close to the walls and trod as delicately as he could on the bare boards. The french-window keys were in their locks.

From the outside terrace he looked down on to his own tiled patio, no more than about twelve feet beneath. He'd been right when he told Alison that he wasn't overlooked, because he could only see a narrow slice of his lounge from here; but when he got down on his hands and knees and peered through the wrought ironwork the angle improved and he could see almost half of the room.

Alison was sitting on the Chesterfield, staring in front of her. There was a man in a dark overcoat and gloves standing by, apparently talking to somebody just out of sight. He turned slightly and said something to her. Slowly, she shook her head.

Bait? Or hostage? Carson couldn't know which. He scrambled upright and went back into the empty flat.

At the door which led back on to the landing he was looking around for a prop or a wedge to pin it open when he thought of the parcel that he'd been hugging since the zoo. Well, why not?

With a line of retreat set up, Carson went back down the stairs and got ready to stir up a few wasps. Still in darkness, he pulled open the big front door and leaned outside. The second bell up had his name against it. He pressed twice and heard the buzzer sounding deep inside the house, then he dived back into the hallway and past his own door.

The hot shine must have cut to black as he was soft-footing it up the stairs, because when he turned around on the half-landing and crouched behind the angle of the banister the only light in the hall was the inward spill from the porch, and that was getting less as the door slowly closed on its hydraulic arm.

The all-weather speaker by the bell-panel crackled as the internal phone was lifted. There was a moment's hesitation and then he heard Alison's voice, filtered and distorted and too distant to make out what she was saying. The speaker scraped and clicked a few more times, but after half a minute of no reply the phone was rehooked.

There was a muted metal sound from the apartment doorway, followed by the sigh of wood across wool as the door was opened. A pasty white blob seemed to float out into the darkness, and then the laser brilliance of a pencil flash in the hand below it. The blob looked towards the door, and as

242

the flash emerged further into the hallway another blob drifted out behind it.

The outer door thumped shut, and the lock that had been holding back and resisting went home. The pencil light spun around, raked up the stairs, and speared straight into Carson's eyes.

The world exploded into popping blue circles as his irises clamped shut and his retinas screamed with the shock, like somebody who'd dived into Caribbean waters and found them as cold as Arctic slush. Carson pushed himself blindly to his feet. They were coming for him.

He went up the landing by memory, one, two, three. When he reached the open doorway he booted the parcel into the room and whirled around to slam the door behind him. The two men were at the top of the stairs and almost within grabbing distance, but if either had tried it he would have left his fingers in the frame as the bang echoed through the house and Carson thumbed the deadlock button, just in case they had any ideas about picking their way in. There was a soft double-thump as they piled up on the panels.

Pick their way in? They didn't even consider it. After no more than five or ten seconds' pause the door shivered under a hard kick, and then another.

Carson knuckled his eyes and blinked. His sight was coming back but he still seemed to have some uneven blindness, as if he were trying to look at the world through a ragged hole in a postage stamp. He turned his head from side to side, trying to line up his patchy vision with the brown paper package – wherever *that* was.

The door was solid and would hold up for quite a long time. Unfortunately the locks and hinges wouldn't. Under the sixth or seventh kick they started to splinter and break inwards. Neither of the two men outside had spoken or shouted.

Could there be more than two? Carson hoped not, as he made out the shape of something like Liawski's diaries over by the skirting board of the opposite wall. He scooped up the solid little parcel. If there had been only two men holding

243

Alison in the room, this meant that they'd left her unguarded and she'd be able to slip away.

The door bounced inward again. Carson tucked the diaries under his arm and went through into the empty lounge. Two men had followed him up the stairs. One was trying to kick his way into this flat. And the other?

The french windows were still open by a few inches. Carson stepped out on to the terrace and looked over the rail again. It hadn't looked an easy distance before, but now it looked impossible. It wasn't even a very big target. He held the parcel out and then let it fall, and it had time enough to turn lazily over before it landed with a solid smack on the terrace below and bounced towards the rail. It skidded to a halt just inside the edge. The door burst inward and crashed back against the wall.

Maybe it was best this way, he thought, no time to consider, no time to get scared and piss down your pants leg. He vaulted the rail.

From inside the room it must have looked like he was just hopping off into empty space, say goodbye to Buck Rogers, a suicide leap over a thirty-foot drop. For a fraction of a second it looked as though it were going to be just that, he'd vaulted too hard and he was going to overshoot the small terrace and land on the ugly hard shapes of the garden furniture in the basement courtyard beneath.

Twelve feet. Four or five can jar your legs badly and shake your guts up into a momentary dysentery if you land wrong. Six or seven has the same effect if you land *right*, leaving you with an aching crotch and bruised joints if you're lucky. He wished he'd hung from the rail and reduced the distance, but that would have taken several seconds to set up and his pursuer had already been half-way across the room. He hit.

His legs were bent, unintentional but lucky because they folded neatly under him and stopped his tail from slamming down hard on the tiles. His spine was saved but his knees punched into his chest and he pitched over sideways, scraping his elbow and knocking his head as he rolled on to his shoulder.

Still in one piece. He tried to get up, and fell over.

No bones gritted or grated, even though his ankles now felt miserably weak, it was just that his muscles wouldn't firm up enough to keep him straight. He grabbed the wall for balance, and it spun him around.

One of the men was re-emerging into the room, heading across Carson's lounge. Up above, the other man was clambering over the iron rail of the terrace, a dark and uncertain shape against the night sky.

The man inside reached into his coat. He brought out a gun.

Carson tried again and got to his feet. He held on to the rail. His legs were quivering and his insides felt like mush, but he stayed up. He was facing the man in the lit room with only thin wood and a lot of glass between them and the man was still moving, the blue-black automatic squat and ugly in his fist. It might have been the man that he'd seen before or it might not; his face was no more than a characterless oval with a few spare lines drawn on it for features.

Alison wasn't in the room.

The man grabbed the inside handle with his free hand and began to shake the windows. *Is there a key to this? I'll see to it later. This is ready now.* He'd never got around to closing the deadlock.

It was academic in any case, because the man reversed the automatic and used the butt to punch out one of the panes. Carson skipped back nimbly enough when the glass cloudburst fountained out past him, and for a moment he felt something soft push against his foot. He looked down just in time to see Liawski's diaries disappearing over the edge.

The man in the room withdrew his arm and shook it free of slivers before turning the gun around ready for use. Carson had nowhere to hide, and he was about to be joined from the upper terrace.

Jumping into the dark was easier. Imagination contracted the distance and made it surprising to fall for so long, and then he was tearing through dogwood and elder bushes and tumbling in a shower of twigs and leaves on to the ground. He rolled against the legs of a spiky cast-iron chair. Better under it than on to it.

There was a flat impact twelve feet up, a squealing skid and a howl of pain. The dropping man came up against the wrought iron, and glass powder sifted like fairy dust down into the courtyard.

For the second time, Carson was looking for his parcel. There were no lights on in the basement flat and precious little illumination spilling into the enclosed yard from above; he banged and scraped his hands on table legs and chair legs as he groped around, and he even cracked his head a couple of times. When he knocked one of the seats he heard paper shift on painted metal, and he grabbed for it.

The man on the terrace was groaning. It was a deep, inhuman sound. Carson ran up the brick steps to the courtyard's wooden side-door, rattling the bolt free and stepping out into the narrow alley that ran down the side of the house. Up ahead, the lights and sounds of the road were a thin vertical slice of freedom. As he edged past the dustbins he reached in his pocket for the keys to the Mercédès.

On the forecourt he unlocked the car and threw the diaries across on to the passenger seat before sliding in behind the wheel. On his first attempt to start he pumped the accelerator too hard and almost flooded out. He glanced in his mirror as he reset the key. The front door to the house opened, and the man with the gun stepped out.

Carson was putting the shift into *Drive* almost as the engine caught. In the mirror the man had stopped and his hands were coming up, clamping together to steady the automatic, feet apart ready to take the recoil. Carson didn't wait to admire the artistry.

He hit the accelerator so hard that for an appalling moment the wheels spun on the asphalt and the car didn't move. Then the car leaped forward and the driver's door that he'd forgotten to close swung out and hit the stone pillar at the entrance to the forecourt. It bounced back hard and left the pillar splashed with paint and some of the trim as Carson fishtailed the Mercédès out into the road and away from the house. Behind him the man was running out into the roadway, already too far off for a useful shot. Carson saw him slow and stop, the gun hanging down by his side, a dark silhouette with a white featureless blob of a face. Carson switched on his lights.

The yellow metal box that was fixed to the brickwork on the greengrocer's shop reminded Leigh Sorvino of his infant son. It made a lot of noise for its size, and there was no obvious way of stopping it.

Sorvino shook the folding rail across the shop doorway again, but it held firm. The burglar alarm shrilled on like a Sunday-afternoon drunk in a park. Looking back at the bell-box Sorvino was tempted to find a half-brick and try to put it out, but that would be fun and not duty. Duty said that the police wouldn't interfere with the property as long as they could be sure that no criminal entry or damage had taken place. They'd attempt to trace the owner and inform him, and that was it. Until he arrived, the poor bastards in the area would have to sit with their fingers in their ears.

Lenny Campion appeared from around the end of the block. One gloved hand held a flashlight, and with the other he was beating grey dust from the front of his uniform.

'Nothing out back,' he said. 'It's probably set to go off if the cat pisses on the potatoes.'

The loud ringing was starting to give Sorvino a headache. They walked away from the shop, across the broad sloping pavement to where their area car was hitched up with two wheels off the road, hazards flashing. Lenny Campion climbed into the nearside observer's seat and Sorvino walked around the big Ford. Passing cars on the southbound carriageway slowed and came close to bumping as drivers rubbernecked for a spot of interesting carnage, but they drove on disappointed.

With the car doors closed the noise was cut considerably. Sorvino massaged a tight little muscle on the plate of bone above his ear. Sometimes it thickened and pulsed with blood and felt like it was going to rip something. It had to be the cold air and the bright lights against the darkness. On winter night shifts it was at its worst. Maybe he should follow up Lenny Campion's suggestion, have his eyes tested for strain.

Campion had unhooked the mike for the multi-channel radio from under the dash, but he wasn't speaking; base desk was giving out a priority call and he'd stopped with the mike on his knee and the coiled flex hanging loosely. Leigh Sorvino treated his eyes to a final squeeze shut and then listened in.

The call was for a silver-grey Mercédès with a damaged offside door. Distinctive, at least. The even, tedious voice of the base desk operator went on: '*Last seen heading north on Kew Bridge Road at 19.20 hours. We're asked to apprehend and detain the driver, who is not thought to be armed but who may resist arrest.*'

Sorvino said, 'That's only five minutes away.'

'Mercédès with a smashed-up door. Can't be many about like that.'

Sorvino couldn't think of a better reason to get away from the ice-pick drone of the alarm. He said, 'Nothing worth sticking around for here. Let's cruise and see if we can pick him up.'

For a moment Campion didn't answer. Sorvino glanced at his observer and saw that he was half-turned in his seat and looking out towards the back of the car. 'Christ, Leigh,' he finally said, 'look at that!'

Sorvino hitched around in his seat so that he could follow. He caught a last glimpse of a grey Mercédès on the far side of the central barrier railings. It was moving unhurriedly. There was a deep vertical crease in the driver's door, and the door wasn't hanging right.

It was carnival time, lights and siren, and Sorvino's migraine disappeared like a popping soap bubble. They took

248

off at three Gs and cars behind had to stand on their noses to make way as the big Ford burnt rubber off towards the next junction south and a break in the central barrier.

Traffic ahead dodged and scattered as Sorvino got across into the overtaking lane and stayed there. Lenny Campion raised the mike to his lips to report.

'Base desk from Lemur Sierra November,' he said, 'we are following the reported Mercédès north on Hanger Lane.'

'Acknowledged, Lemur Sierra November, do you have confirmation of the registration?'

'The colour and the damage check out. We couldn't see the plate.'

They were a hundred yards short of the junction. The lights were red and all three lanes were blocked with waiting traffic. The crossflow of cars had stopped at the sound of the approaching siren and now drivers and passengers and a small number of pedestrians were all looking around, uncertain of the direction. Leigh Sorvino had every warning light on the car operating except for the headlamp flash, and he pumped this now as he was forced to slow behind the blockade.

There were two cars in the overtaking lane. The second flashed the first, and they both jerked out of the way. Sorvino punched through the gap and into a U-turn against the red light.

He nearly took it too fast, and Lenny Campion put a nervous hand on the padded dash as the car tipped sideways and the rear end tried to break away. The tyres screamed and fought for grip and then the whole car did a little wiggle like the backside of a pouncing cat and stormed on, back in the direction from which it had come.

Sorvino killed the siren but left the lights. He gave it a few more seconds to get him through the next traffic signals and then killed it again. Lenny Campion gripped the Bakelite microphone so hard that it began to hurt his hand.

A long empty stretch, and the Mercédès was in view ahead. Expensive, sporty-looking thing. Must be quite a villain

No sudden spurt, no scramble to get away. They came up alongside, and Lenny Campion was almost within arm's length of the young driver. The driver glanced over and seemed only mildly surprised to see them. Campion stabbed his finger twice, once at Carson, *you*, and then towards the road shoulder, *over there*, and then Sorvino put the Ford across the Mercédès' bows and slowed him into the side of the road.

With the age and general appearance of the driver and the obvious wealth behind the car itself Campion was sure it had to be either hard drugs or pornography, maybe a sweep operation somewhere and one of the fishes had struggled through the net.

They both got out of the car. The carriageway was empty and sealed off from the world by chipped grey railings down the centre and either side. The Mercédès had almost rolled to a halt about fifty yards behind them. They started to walk back, one either side, pleased with themselves but still ready for trouble.

'Wait a minute,' Campion said. The car was still rolling.

Nobody was driving.

Lenny Campion ran forward and Sorvino hung back, ready to sprint for the car if this should be a trick to shake them off. Campion came level with the Merc and looked inside. It was empty and the automatic shift was in *Drive* so that the car continued to creep forward under the gentle pull of the engine. The broken door hung open a few inches. He looked down the road but could see nobody; the driver had hopped the fence but it was impossible to say where.

He turned back to look at Sorvino. The police driver was still waiting, still uncertain.

'He's pissed off!' Campion said incredulously.

Most of the lights in the underpass had been kicked out and what showed of the green and white tiling had been generously sprayed with graffiti, *Hendrix* and *Are Gay Militants Limp Fisted?* Carson waded across the newspaper on the undrained floor and climbed the concrete stairway into the night.

Along the road in the far carriageway he could see the two-car tableau under the bright lights, but he didn't linger to watch. With his much-abused parcel still under his arm, he started walking back towards the city.

When he reached an Underground station he bought a ticket without even thinking of where he might want to go. Inside the system and moving, he could at least feel safe. It was tempting to think that he might live down there for ever, occasionally emerging to dodge through the empty quiet streets; watching for the armed patrols of the faceless men in black. They had Alison, and he couldn't hope to reach her.

He got a corner seat in an empty carriage. The doors sighed and closed with tender regret, and the whole train growled and shook itself like a dog coming out of the sea. Reality began to slide away outside, and a sphincter of darkness drew tight around the windows.

Carson started to open out the parcel. It was actually a brown paper bag, oversized and wrapped around its contents. Some twigs and leaves fell out of the folds.

The books had taken their battering well, although the covers of one were bent and crimped inwards from a hard landing. He looked through the xerox sheets that had been pressed between them but there was nothing too controversial there, just a Jenner Clinic catalogue and price schedule and a few dates and details. He opened one of the diaries. It was handwritten on fine lined paper in a series of dated entries, and somebody – presumably Reynolds – had marked the locations of a series of entries with folded slips. The second book was the same. Carson looked for the earliest date, and started to read.

Chapter 20

7 November

I have to write something of the general path which the project seems to be following. It is beginning to disturb me. We are well out of those vigorous early stages of feasibility testing and speculative planning which mark the beginning of any project, the times when everything appears to be possible and the process of discovery beckons irresistibly. Now each department and each individual researcher is having to live with the decisions that he has made and the procedures he has laid down. Some are less happy than others, nobody is particularly elated – but that was to be expected. We're not the first research group to tackle this problem.

What I find disturbing is the way in which the research group seems to be fragmenting. The weekly review meetings are poorly attended, and they hardly ever run for the full hour. Doctor Jenner, in particular, hasn't been to one yet. I suppose that I ought to call him about it, but the need is hardly urgent; virally-induced diabetes in test animals is easily achieved, and none of the other researchers has yet reached a stage where the conditions of sponsorship demand animal tests. Which makes it far more strange that he should spend so much time in the animal facility; the written reports that he sends in place of attendance at the weekly meetings indicate that he's devising new procedures that are specially planned to suit the needs of the project. How he can presume to know what those needs are when he won't attend the meetings, I have no idea.

This morning I went into my office in the science block. I took along my keys to the side door because the building is always locked on Sundays, but when I arrived the door was open.

Bob White was emerging from one of the labs as I passed. He's a spare, easy-going young man whom I somehow find it difficult to like. He makes me wonder if it's possible to be too eager, too confident of the path one is following. When I asked him what he was doing – a perfectly open question, no accusation or suspicion – he seemed at first surprised and then embarrassed. As we spoke, a stranger emerged from the lab and joined White.

I was concerned, and I suppose it showed; security of the project is one of the conditions fixed by the sponsors. White hastily introduced his friend – I forgot the name immediately – and explained that he'd driven down from one of the Northern Institutes of Science and Technology for some friendly pooling of results. When I showed interest I was told that it was work for Jenner, some test methods that weren't yet sufficiently developed to be worth describing; if anything came out of it, he told me, he'd present it at one of the weekly meetings.

I was going to press on and say that, as head of the project, every aspect of the work no matter how little developed is of interest to me, but something in White's manner dissuaded me; there was something shifty, almost guilty, and as it has never been in my nature to be imperious I let it go.

18 November

Another blind alley this week, the fruitless culmination of several months of work for the mapping team. Only Jenner's research area seems to be flourishing; the fact that we have no product for him to test doesn't seem to discourage him, nor do the low demands placed on his facility by the present stages of experimentation. Yesterday I received an application from him for the acquisition of a number of rhesus monkeys, and I used it as an opportunity to get in touch. He invited me down to the basement to take a look around. Of course, I could have done this at any time, but I have to remember that I'm not just another researcher and that a visit from me could have resounding political implications in our little hierarchy.

Now I can see why Jenner's work has drawn such a steady amount of our total funding; besides setting up containment areas for treated and control groups of animals he's also been working on a means of inducing diabetes by the chemical destruction of large areas of the pancreas in test models. This, he argues, gives more reliable and consistent results than viral methods, which are only inferred from clinical observation and haven't been given sufficient animal trials.

I am far more inclined to argue the effectiveness of the clinical method above any amount of what I am still inclined to call vivisection, but Jenner's credentials are impressive and I have to acknowledge the part that they played in getting the project set up in the first place. He wants to apply to the Dean for a closed facility; did he want me to have a word about it, I asked, but he said no, he knew how busy I was and would go direct.

I actually found myself apologising to him because I didn't spend as much time as I felt I ought with the various heads of department within the project. Whilst my general grasp of the overall detail of our work is good, I'll admit that the animal house is, for me, one of the least attractive locations in the university, and a day spent without speaking to Jenner is a day from which nothing vital has been lost. His confidence reminds me of that which is growing in Bob White, a self-assurance which regards the world as an infinitely adjustable mechanism and himself as being fully qualified to adjust it in accordance with his own judgement. It hit me as I was led through the ranks of cages, past the rodents and the cats and the four dogs that he'd acquired from a local pound; they hustled around and looked up as he walked by, and I thought, this man wants to play God.

I don't believe that Jenner is going to contribute anything at all to the success of this project, but he is crucial to its viability. What we eventually deliver to him for testing – if we deliver anything at all – will be known to be without dangers because it will be a precisely-defined product derived from human tissue. He'll administer it to animals with extreme and abnormal diabetic conditions that have been induced by chemical trauma, and he'll experience repeated rejections; animal tissue will reject human insulin in exactly the same way that human tissue can reject the animal insulin that we now use – one of the main reasons, other than freeing diabetics from the needle, behind our project. He'll have to extend the sample enormously before his results can confirm that it is safe to proceed, and only then will we be able to go on to the testing that we know will be of any value.

Also, I find the animal house offensive. I know as a scientist that it shouldn't affect me, but it does.

12 December

When I returned to my office this morning after the Edinburgh symposium, among the memos in my IN tray was an impersonal note from the Dean telling me that the basement is to become a closed facility for Jenner's containment experiments, and that students' animals will be moved to the first floor. No doubt there will be complaints, but Jenner seems to have sidestepped all of that.

The last project meeting over-ran, according to my secretary; almost three hours, four flasks of coffee, two plates of sandwiches and a bowl of peanuts. I think the sandwiches and the peanuts impressed her more than anything. The discussion over-ran the booking in the conference room so they all moved downstairs, she doesn't know where. Bob White offered to handle the minutes for her, but when I glanced through the mimeographed sheets that were left for me, it seems that he didn't pay much attention to the job. If I had the time I'd follow it up, but tomorrow I'm in London; we're barely through the first term of the academic year and I'm already having to play salesman to ensure funding for the next. The only decision that came clearly through Bob White's minutes was one to apply for a number of junior research assistants; no indication of where the bursaries are to be drawn from on a budget that's already drum-tight.

Anyway, I've an idea where the meeting may have moved to after the first hour. Jenner attended.

2 February

I was with the Dean today. He told me that I don't socialise enough around the campus, and it affects the prestige of my department; I was tempted to say that I've never considered prestige of that kind much worth having, but I let it go and claimed pressure of work.

I was casual when I showed him the papers, although I must admit they'd been worrying me considerably. He looked at them once and said yes, he'd given the authority in my place while I'd been in London and couldn't be reached. Probably some administrative hitch had stopped the information from getting to me; I was about to answer when I looked up and saw him with his head slightly to one side, the light catching the lenses of his spectacles and masking his eyes from me, and I could almost see myself as he saw me; too solitary, he was thinking, always a misfit, backing into his shell and starting to believe that his own department is working up a conspiracy against him.

My department is, as far as I can make out, working perfectly well. But apart from my indispensable services as a fund-raiser, they're doing it without me. I retrieved the advertising receipts and the check copy of the text offering bursaries for junior research assistants on the project, and tried to seem reassured and unworried as I withdrew. I doubt that I succeeded.

25 February

Whether or not it was right at the time, I agreed quite early on that Jenner should be free to buy in animals without first having to refer to me. He's built up his collection of dogs considerably over the past month – apparently there's always a surplus available at this time of year as mongrel puppies lose their Christmas appeal – but the orders that passed across my desk this morning alarmed me. He's ordered no fewer than five large primates, not the rhesus he wanted and got a couple of months back, but actual chimpanzees. The orders were fully processed and needed no action from me; they had the Dean's counter-signature as authorisation. If the papers hadn't been shuffled in with the research assistants' application forms I might never have seen them.

I broke one of my own rules, and went down to the animal house uninvited. It's a pointless rule anyway; I haven't been invited to observe work in progress for some time, and my own practical contribution to the project since those early procedure-devising days has been negligible. There was a security guard on the door to the facility, and my credentials were insufficient to impress him. I had to wait until Jenner himself came to the door to escort me in.

The area was little changed, although the main corridor had been cleared of rat and rabbit cages and there was no longer any access through to the lecture theatre. By this time Jenner had collected about forty dogs, and their sharp signature was in the air; during my brief visit I didn't hear a single bark.

Primate cages had already been installed in a room of their own. We passed them as Jenner took me into his office. I grabbed the opportunity to produce the order forms and ask what was going on.

He told me that he'd approached the sponsor direct and with the Dean's approval. It would have been done through me, he assured me, but I hadn't been available – the Edinburgh symposium providing yet another convenient excuse – and the chance to bid on the chimps couldn't wait.

The animals were going to cost three thousand pounds each, of varied ages and in guaranteed good health. It's always struck me as ironic that such concentrated care should be taken of an animal whose sole purpose in life is to be maimed. Jenner anticipated my argument that it was ridiculous to spend so much in an area of research that had such limited usefulness, saying that it was precisely because of the dissimilarity of dogs and rhesus to human metabolism that he needed the apes. So why, I said, do you need forty dogs and two dozen rhesus? He smiled and told me that he had to test his procedures before he could put one of the expensive apes at risk. By the end of the interview he almost had me

257

convinced that I was attempting to interfere with experimental method and damage the whole project.

I couldn't fight him, not on his home ground and without the support of the head of the Faculty. As I sat in his office feeling lost he reached across his desk and pulled a sheet of paper across. He'd need a handler for the apes, he told me, and he thought that one of the research assistant applicants would do nicely and could he have her? He handed me the sheet of paper, which turned out to be a form identical to those that I'd left in my office. I didn't even bother to ask how he'd got it; obviously the Registrar's department had been instructed to let Jenner have first pick of the would-be researchers. The girl's name was Catherine, and the photograph on the front of the form showed that she was extremely pretty. No doubt this had influenced Jenner in his decision but her record was good, too. There wasn't anything I could say.

On the way out I met Horsley and Collison. They stood aside to let me pass and nodded amiably. They, it seemed, didn't need Jenner's personal authority to get access to the animal house.

3 April

The dreams continue. Time hasn't dulled or softened them at all.

3 June

Catherine, Jenner's new assistant, telephoned me today. She had been promised an interest-free resettlement loan by the university and she needed the signature of her head of department. Jenner was at his consultancy and she was rather desperate for the money, so she was wondering if I could help. I told her to bring the papers up to my office.

As I waited for her I began to think that this might be my chance at least to gain some intelligence on the project that carried my name. I was no longer needed even to raise the bankroll, Jenner had seen to that by establishing direct communication with the sponsors. Reports reached me infrequently, and those that I was sent were short and uninformative. The weekly meetings had stopped altogether.

Isolation of the insulin-producing gene and its subsequent attachment to a plasmid seemed more remote than ever. On paper my project had run itself into listless inactivity, but in practice my researchers were drawing increasingly large funds and expanding their operations throughout the Faculty. Bob White's liaison with the Northern I.S.T. had become official, and I was occasionally asked to initial his expense vouchers after visits. I was never given details — by now nobody was even bothering to lie to me.

When Catherine arrived, the first thing that I did was to give my authorisation for her loan. I didn't want her to suspect that I was using it as an unfair means of pressure.

Because she was new on a team that I still supposedly headed, there was a legitimate excuse for me to want to chat to her for a while in my office. It would look like simple everyday staff relations, and it would give me the chance to find out how much she'd so far been told — which was, as it turned out, very little. She'd applied to do lab work — she had some experience of DNA manipulation in high-containment facilities — but she'd taken the handler's job because there were so few opportunities that came up in the middle of the academic year, and the competition was consequently stiff.

I sensed that she wasn't particularly happy with the idea of doing animal work; she actually flinched when I referred to it as vivisection, and I quickly apologised for my old-fashioned ideas. Then I told her everything.

I made no requests, no demands. If she comes back to me it will be of her own accord, because what she sees and hears will confirm what I have told her.

5 August

More than two months, and Catherine has never returned. This afternoon I was walking across the paved way through the middle of the campus when I saw her in the distance. I wondered if she would acknowledge me or speak, but I never found out; before we met she disappeared behind a crowd of friends and I saw her a few seconds later, head-down and hurrying across the grass towards the science block.

There seems little point in my even coming into the university any more. I spend the days sitting in my empty office with nothing to do, whilst my secretary keeps herself occupied by taking some of the workload from her friends down the corridor. I've worked on some papers but they're old ideas, old material. I haven't completed any of them.

30 September

Last night, there was a quiet knock on my door. There was loud music upstairs, and I almost didn't hear it. I suppose that I could have gone up and asked him to turn it down – even told him to turn it down, since that's the kind of thing that wardens are supposed to do – but the sound didn't irritate me anywhere near as much as it comforted me, and some of the music wasn't at all bad. I could let it seep in and fill all the empty spaces. Better that than anything else.

When I opened the door, Catherine was standing there. She was wet and shivering and she'd apparently walked all the way from the university. She was wearing a light raincoat and it had become soaked through; I got her a towel for her hair and spread the coat on a radiator where it began after a while to steam gently.

During all of this, she said nothing. When I turned around from the radiator and looked at her she was standing with the towel in her hands. Her eyes were screwed shut, but fat tears were squeezing from the corners and running into the cold rain on her cheeks. I guided her to the sofa and she dropped on to it heavily and buried her face in the towel.

I sat on the chair across the rug. If I've learned anything in my life, I've learned patience. There was nearly a whole side of Ralph McTell from upstairs before she was ready to speak.

She told me that she'd finally found out what the project was about. She hadn't come to me before because she'd seen nothing unusual, nothing that suggested that the aims of the insulin project were being diverted; as far as she knew she was simply working to keep the experimental models prepared for the time when test substances would become available. In the meantime she helped Jenner with the occasional biopsy or prepared samples for him when he was too busy to do it himself, but otherwise she was frustrated when she thought that she'd trained in lab research techniques but was working as a small-time zookeeper.

I discovered why she'd actively avoided me. Jenner had told her that I was losing my grip, that I was unable to cope with my responsibilities any more; only the loyalty of my staff covering all of my duties amongst themselves saved me from an undignified trip to a sanatorium. He explained that I imagined myself persecuted and that I saw conspiracy in the most innocent actions, and she'd been duly frightened off.

I almost laughed at this, and not wholly through bitterness, but the agony and confusion in Catherine's eyes quietened me. She stopped, uncertain of how to go on. I tried to get her to tell me about the real work of the project that she'd discovered, but she said that she couldn't explain it and she'd have to show me.

She had her own key to the animal-house doors. They were locked but unguarded at night. We would have to walk down – I have no car – but her coat was still wet so I lent her one of mine. It was unflattering and the sleeves were too long, but it was better than nothing. She pulled the belt through the loops and knotted it around her waist, and that at least gave her some kind of shape.

On the long straight road that led along to the back of the university campus she walked ahead of me, leaning forward slightly into the wind. There were lights in the sports centre but the track alongside the games field was dark. We passed long rows of parked cars behind the Union building, where despite the cold every window was open and twenty different kinds of noise were blasting out, and then we cut under an archway and found ourselves beside the science block.

I used my key, and we entered by the side door on to the fire stairs. We crossed the silent concourse to the basement stairway; there were low green emergency lights and enough of a spill from outside reflected up from the waxed floor for us to see where we were going.

Straight through into the primate facility, and I got my first view of the chimpanzees in the shadows, sooty black and slow and massive as they stirred and came awake. Catherine switched on the room lighting and they all started to grunt and roll over, covering their eyes. All except one.

'That's what the project was for,' Catherine said.

The infant came unsteadily forward and tried to grasp the bars. It was scrawny and almost hairless, a wizened little gnome of a creature with bright black eyes and badly misshapen hands and feet. Its back was twisted out of true, as if at delivery the obstetrician had given it a casual wrench before tossing it into the cot and walking away.

It got its bent fingers around the bars and pulled itself upright, staring at me and grinning fearfully. The large chimp in the cage behind it started to rock back and forth and make warning noises, but Catherine calmed her. She called her Lucy.

This child had never been born, not in any normal way. 'Jenner made him,' Catherine told me.

She'd been presented with her new charge that same afternoon. His name was Chad, and he was a chimeric hybrid of man and chimpanzee. I was both horrified and fascinated; I couldn't begin to imagine the number of difficulties that lay behind his creation, difficulties that obviously hadn't been fully surmounted. The malformation of his limbs was probably repeated in his internal organs and his glands; how could hybrid haemoglobins and enzymes work? The creature seemed to hover on the very brink of viability.

Its legs gave way and it sat down abruptly. There was a white

262

line of scar tissue across its throat, and I guessed that Jenner had devocalised it, probably as a matter of course as he appeared to do with his dogs. Chad reached out a hand through the bars, and Lucy pulled him back. She was the oldest of the female chimpanzees, and it seemed that she'd promptly adopted this ugly orphan.

Catherine had shown me what she'd needed to show me, and now she wanted to leave. I agreed with mixed reluctance and relief.

We walked back to the Evergreens, a little more slowly this time as the pace and the distance began to get to me. I often covered this route twice a day in the summer months, but then I didn't have to face the rain and this harsh, rasping air. We didn't talk.

I gave Catherine my spare room for the night. Mrs Donoghue would no doubt be heartily shocked in the morning whatever reassurances I gave her — she has the moral flexibility of a Standing Stone — but Catherine was clearly too exhausted and confused to go any further. I didn't go to bed, not for several hours; I took a stack of texts from my shelves and sat looking at none of them.

Natural hybrids are rare, never occurring outside the same genus. Mules are the only hybrids that could in any way be called common, and they're crossed from within the same species; a cross of yak and buffalo is the most disparate successful hybridisation that's so far been achieved. Anything more complex and you would have to move right away from any ideas of 'natural' fertilisation — artificial insemination included — and into the laboratory.

Cell fusion is nothing new, nor is the creation of artificial chimeras. But these are no more than cultures, little colonies of cells in a pampered environment, and they invariably end with the rejection of one set of chromosomes. At least forty genes would have to be tracked down and either removed or suppressed before that incompatability reaction could be overcome, and then you would still be a long way from raising a working creature; you would have nothing more than a blueprint.

This in itself was a considerable achievement. Human and primate chromosome complements are radically different — forty-six for man, forty-eight for the chimpanzee, the orang and the gorilla. There could never be a one-to-one hybridisation of genes because there is no one-to-one correspondence; I'd guess that Jenner would have to be satisfied with the insertion of a small portion of genetic material from one species into the genetic makeup of the other. Removal of the nucleus of a fertile sex cell and its replacement with the new material would bring the hybrid a step closer to viability; some kind of host would then be needed as it progressed to the embryonic stage.

Whilst a part of me could admire the elegance of the science, I was shocked by its audacity. An early and impressionable period of my life had passed in the presence of men who had the arrogance to class their fellows as sub-human; Jenner, I felt, had managed to equal them. He had created one.

The reason for Chad's existence was clear to me. Jenner had already admitted that the lack of standard reactions between species invalidated animal test results, but it didn't seem to deter him from constructing elaborate procedures; presumably he expected his results to be more reliable when taken from a model with a major human component. With this he'd managed to impress the sponsor and his fellow-researchers. He knew that he would never have impressed me – not in the way he might want, anyway – so he'd kept me on the outside, a project figurehead with a cover story about insulin to shoulder off controversy.

I awoke in the chair. It was dawn, and Catherine had gone.

3 December

Catherine still wants to go for immediate publicity, and I still believe that it would be unwise. We have no evidence other than our own testimony, and we are too easily discredited.

She calls on me infrequently, sometimes only once a month, always at the Evergreens. As far as Jenner knows she is dedicated and enthusiastic, and he has no idea that she's passing me information to compile a dossier on the hominid. Whilst it was difficult for her at first – being in the same room as the animal made her angry and frightened, and this wasn't easy for her to hide – she's now far more settled and says that Chad's touch no longer repels her and that his emerging personality is not unpleasant. Jenner, now well into the second stage of his project, shows no interest in Chad at all.

I was right in supposing that the insulin project staff undertook the manufacture of the genetic hybrid with the co-operation of the Northern I.S.T. One of the chimpanzees was used to host the growing embryo in its early stages, but it was then transferred to a human host; Catherine says that it was implanted into one of the women being treated in Jenner's private practice. The woman believed herself to be normally fertile as a result of his care, but at a late stage of her pregnancy the foetus was removed to an incubator and the mother was told that she'd miscarried.

Jenner's priority now is to devise a method through which his results can be endlessly duplicated. The breakthrough is useless if the hominid can't be produced in commercial quantities, but Chad is sterile and the chances of repeating his exact hybridisation are remote; the obvious answer lies in a clone group of animals which will be identical in size, weight and metabolism. So far, Jenner's expectations have been reversed – he thought that production of the chimera would be the most difficult part of the operation and that the cloning would follow naturally as an extension of technique. I think he was surprised to get the viable hybrid so soon, but he hasn't yet had a single successful clone. Catherine tells me that his frustration shows on his rare contacts with Chad; he refuses to use any kind of anaesthetic when he takes tissue samples for benchwork, even though they may be from the liver or intestine. When this happens she has to hold Chad in what she calls the 'crush cage', but she says that he doesn't struggle much and, of course, he can't scream although he often tries.

Chad is developing fast, much faster than any human child. One of Catherine's duties is to chart his growth in physique and ability; she estimates that he'll probably reach adolescence around the age of ten years. Already he's picked up a few of the hand-signs that the other chimpanzees still use from their previous experiment. It's an advantage for Catherine, because she can give them simple commands which make her job easier.

13 July

This latest visit from Catherine comes after a long absence. She arrived late, and didn't stay for long.

Her last report had been that Chad was starting to show signs of regression and withdrawal. She'd been as upset at this change in his behaviour as if he'd been a human child, probably encouraged by the fact that his almost nonexistent fur cover made it necessary for him to be clothed. He was too frail for the rough play of the group in the confines of the cages, and he took to huddling in a corner and refusing to answer hand-signs except with the swearword-groups that he created for himself.

Now Catherine's attitude is noticeably different. She tried to treat him like a child, and he responded as a chimpanzee. When she reached into the cage and tried to entice a response from him, he roused himself into a rage and displayed at her, throwing himself against the bars and biting her hand. She now thinks that she was wrong ever to see him as a maligned human being, and I readily agreed with her; I tried to point out that the offence lay not in Chad's existence or some biologically calculable degree of his humanity, but in the appalling arrogance of Jenner for supposing that he had the right to create Chad at all.

I don't think she agrees with me. She drew most of her energy and indignation from sympathy with Chad, and that sympathy has been shaken. As long as he was pathetic, she could see Jenner as evil; now that pathos has been pushed aside by aggression her attitude to Jenner has begun to change, to lose its emotional focus.

I've had no luck in tracing the woman who unknowingly carried Chad. Of all Jenner's offences, I feel that the use of her was the worst and it is likely to be the most potent argument of any public condemnation of his actions. But if I eventually find her, will I be able to bring myself to tell her? I could not imagine the intimacy of revulsion that the news would bring.

A note from Catherine. She's decided that she can no longer be committed to opposition of Jenner's work, and that she'll pass me no more information; she feels that her early reactions were immature and unprofessional, and she wouldn't want to be responsible for an unfounded public controversy. I must admit I've been expecting this, or something like it.

I can't blame her. She hasn't really made a conscious choice, but then so few of us ever do; we simply fall in with the drift of our moral environment and then look around to be reassured by approval. Without her help I can never hope to know any more than the little I know now, so I decided to go to the Dean.

I didn't have any illusions about his impartiality, not when I knew that he'd been instrumental in taking away my power as head of the insulin project. That had been after he'd acted as one of my keenest supporters; obviously he and Jenner and the sponsors had considered it a useful piece of misdirection. When I walked into his office, Catherine was with him.

He listened patiently as I told him that I wanted a voluntary moratorium on further work within the project and an enquiry composed of equal numbers of scientists and non-scientists. If he wasn't prepared to initiate this, I would have to use what I knew to generate publicity.

My case was weak, and I knew it; without Catherine I could be easily discredited as unhinged and paranoid. My withdrawal from the life of the campus would tend to support this, and I didn't doubt that many suitable rumours had been spread; meanwhile I didn't even have a photograph of Chad, nor had I seen him since the night that he had stretched his bent claw through the bars of his cage towards me.

The Dean politely explained that there could be no moratorium, because there was no longer any project. It had been wound up with the agreement of the sponsors a couple of weeks before. Jenner had gone up to Cumbria to arrange the premises of the private clinic he was to open there, and when I showed disbelief the Dean invited me to visit the animal house and see for myself.

Numbly, I followed him down. Catherine came a few paces behind and neither looked directly at me nor spoke to me. The animal-house doors were open and there was a smell of blood and disinfectant and burning hair; many of Jenner's dogs had been destroyed and were heaped in the incinerator room at the end of the corridor, whilst those still fit enough to undergo further experimentation had been passed on to other researchers.

The primate cages were empty. Chad's physical reality was the only support for my claims, and they had moved him out of my reach.

It's too big for me. Again, I'm unheard. Jenner even has government money behind him now, and there's nothing I can do that won't be either forestalled or ignored. My intellectual integrity is generally said to have crumbled, and this is given as the reason for the project's failure — at least, its public failure. Jenner's work will continue — most of his staff are following him to Cumbria. Catherine is to be his head of animal experimentation.

Now I know that there can never be justice, not as long as men like Jenner arrange and shape the world for their own benefit. I can only hope and pray for some higher retribution.

PART FOUR

Cumbria

22 October 1987

Chapter 21

The day was struggling gamely to raise enthusiasm for the dawn when the mail train to Carlisle made a brief call at Penrith. The air was several degrees colder than it had been in London, and a light snow was feathering down in a continuous shower through the beams of the platform lights.

It wasn't a scheduled passenger stop, just a pause for the quick transfer of canvas bags way back in the belly of the train. Peter Carson lowered himself on to the wrong side of the track as the line of rubber-wheeled wagons was pushed in alongside the mail coach, and seconds later he was hidden by the cast iron pillars that supported the station's Victorian glass awning.

First snow of the season. The ground wasn't yet sufficiently chilled for it to stick, and the flakes blurred and melted away as soon as they landed. Carson wondered if he was expected. A carriage door banged loud and sharp in the still morning air, and the train began to roll.

Carson stayed behind the pillars as he walked along to the platform's end and finally came out from under the awning. This open stretch was bound in by a low wooden fence, beyond which was the wide dark pool of the old station yard. Nobody was watching. He pulled himself up and scrambled over.

The night mail was no more than a dying echo and a pastel smear which was fading down the track as he approached the picket gate and looked over it to the station forecourt. There was an army Land-Rover painted in drab camouflage colours with its nose almost into the station entrance. Its engine was running for heat, but some of the snow had settled white and powdery on its canvas back. All of its windows were thoroughly steamed and there were no runny peepholes rubbed on the glass. Carson unhitched the gate with care and eased through.

The grass and the stones of the castle ruins were dusted with the sugar of night frost, glittering like a sea of fallen stars as he walked past towards Castlegate and the town's centre. When he glanced back, the Land-Rover was moving.

For a moment he thought that he'd been seen, but then the Rover pulled up and swung around to get back into the shelter of the station a few yards along. One of the railway porters in uniform and a shapeless blue donkey jacket was going back under the canopy – he'd probably asked them to move aside for the mail van. Carson turned and walked on.

He walked around for an hour or so until the town started to come awake. It stirred slowly but early, which was fortunate because there wasn't much for him to look at. When the first newsagency put on its lights and opened its doors for the morning delivery Carson went in and bought some notepaper and airmail envelopes. Then he went to a transport diner on a main road just outside the commercial centre and got himself a rickety table in a corner before he ordered breakfast. As he ate he sketched out a letter to his American agent, and then he pushed the empty plate aside and asked for more tea (which he didn't really want) so that he could claim the table for long enough to make a fair copy, this time without the grease spots.

By now the diner had filled up and the waste ground outside was nose-to-tail with big trucks and lorries. Carson checked his watch and then went out to look for a post office.

He had a ten-minute wait on the doorstep before he could get an airmail stamp and get rid of the letter. Then he made a telephone call to London from a booth outside the office, and only then did he begin to relax a little.

The relaxation was relative. He was still wanted, and he didn't know how long he could stay mobile; he didn't doubt that they could freeze his bank account, and without it he had only the cash that he'd drawn from late night facilities around

Soho. Even Hennessy couldn't hope to get word around while the banks were closed. He had half a day, a day at the most, before his cheques would come bouncing back and a warning would go out to traders in the area; in short, he couldn't run, and Hennessy would have an immediate fix on him wherever he might be.

Well, Saint George, you're in a tight spot here, any ideas on how you're going to manage with a broken sword? Well, I thought I might try running up to the dragon and pissing down his throat. Step one of the exercise would be to get to Langstone without being stopped along the way.

The post bus wasn't the best idea. He watched it setting off empty for its first trip of the day, a little red Commer van with room for about ten people inside. It was bright and regular and conspicuous as hell, even if it did go right up into the valley to make deliveries and collections. He'd thought of something better, if he could get it to work.

He went back to the post office and got hold of a copy of the local yellow pages and a bag of change. In the booth again he started to work his way through the entries under *garage services*. He'd lost count of the number of calls he'd made before he was told yes, Miss Wells's car was ready for collection; there had been some trouble getting the replacement wing but the paint shop had finished with it yesterday. Fine, Carson said, she's gone back to London but she's asked me to pick up the car and settle the bill for her. The garage owner seemed wary at the idea of Carson picking up the car, far less so at the idea of him picking up the tab. Carson said that he'd be around within the hour.

His next call was at a sportswear shop, overcrammed with boots and wax and laces and bright nylon. He was still dressed for London, where unease of the soul was ignored and overshadowed by the exaggeration of physical discomforts; cheaply made shoes and a thin jacket had no place here. He bought a thick wool shirt with a pattern like a TV testcard, a ribbed pullover with leather patches on the elbows and shoulders, walking trousers, coarse knitted socks, and a cagoule. There was a wire rack with a small number of pairs of second-hand boots on display; some of them were reinforced mountain boots, the kind where you could jam a toe into a crack in the rocks and stand upright without too much effort, but there was also a pair of lighter Italian boots in Carson's size. The price made no difference to him, but buying second-hand meant that he was less likely to have trouble breaking them in. He couldn't afford the luxury of a couple of hours a day until the leather softened up and stopped rubbing.

He added some basic safety kit – map and compass, Swiss Army clasp knife, and a whistle. He took all of this and some fresh underwear into a stockroom behind the shop where the girl who'd served him said he was welcome to change. When he emerged she'd processed his cheque – he felt guilty about it, but it was written in good faith and would only bounce if Hennessy rigged it that way – and she gave him a carrier bag for his other clothes.

Back on the streets he felt, if not transformed, at least more at home. He was freed from the canned environment of cars and heated rooms; the sensation would probably last until he climbed his first hill and felt his body starting to complain. Until then it was look, Ma, top of the world.

Alison's blue Honda was parked behind the pumps outside the garage when Carson arrived. He went in through the open double-doors to the service bay and stepped over the dead black snakes of airlines to get to the office at the back. At the counter inside he pretended to study the itemised bill as a concerned friend should, and then to save time he said that he'd looked at the work outside and that it seemed fine. He paid with two cheques over two dates so that he didn't exceed the one-day limit on his guarantee card, and then he collected the keys.

There was a film of white dust over the black vinyl upholstery of the car and a grey thumbprint in primer on the padded dash. Carson threw his carrier bag onto the back seat and got behind the wheel.

He tried the engine first without choke, but it was cold.

More than half a tank of fuel, he noted as the needle swung up on to the gauge. He gave it full choke and tried again. The engine caught immediately.

The pedal pressures and arrangement were unfamiliar – it was a couple of years since he'd driven a car with manual shift – and the vibram soles of his boots made them more so, but by the time he was crossing the motorway overpass he felt that he was getting the hang of it. He was on a good road, better than any of the battered city tracks around home, and after only a few miles the land to either side began to lift and fold into the rugged contours of the Cumbrian interior.

He'd only driven the route once before, and this wasn't enough to make it immediately recognisable. He hadn't thought to check his new O.S. map, but there was nowhere to pull off the road and he never felt safe driving and trying to navigate at the same time. In the end it wasn't necessary – the road split and the Ravens' Bridge sign was obvious, directing him left around the lake shore. From there on he knew what he was doing; the chapel and the road with the police breakdown warning at its head, the climbing hillside and the stand of trees with their roots awash between the road and the lake, the chained gates of the country house hotel, the narrowing alley of stone and wire broken by the occasional farm track or gateway. He met no other cars, and no other cars tried to pass him.

Two miles before Langstone, the windscreen shattered again.

It still had the yellow chinagraph marks of the garage's order number in one corner and already it was useless, a quick *splat* and the whole damn thing was an opal spiderweb with a small toughened zone of half-transparency across its centre. Carson knew better than to try any stupid macho heroics like punching the glass out – fingers could be useful sometimes, and he wanted to keep all of his – so he just leaned in close to the cleared area to get the best view that he could as he braked.

He managed to stop without hitting anything, and when he

cut the engine and dropped back in the seat with relief the broken screen was ticking and clicking as it settled and tried to flex. He opened the door carefully – he didn't want to trigger off an inward fall and shower himself with fragments – and stepped out on to the road.

He'd pulled up ten yards past an open gateway. The stone wall on one side of the opening had been toppled over into the field of waving grass beyond, and the gate itself had been propped in place to cover the gap and secured with orange string.

Carson walked back along the road. There were long fresh marks of scrubbed-off rubber behind the car, but there were older marks on the tarmac beneath them that wove from side to side and then angled away towards the grassy base of the wall, continuing as black trenches gouged out of the earth. They came to an abrupt halt at the demolished stone, as neat a replay as anybody could wish. Just in case there was any further confirmation needed, when Carson stepped up on to the verge and looked over the wall he could see that some of the sharper-edged stones had carried off trophies of the Honda's blue paint.

He heard a scrambling from the road behind him, and he turned around so quickly that his foot slipped on the wet grass and he half-fell and half-slid to the road. All that he glimpsed was a movement just on the other side of the car, and when he managed to get his balance back there was nothing.

Carson circled the Honda warily. The driver's door was still open and a few of the stray flakes of snow that still danced in the air were drifting inside; he put out a hand to push it closed as he passed.

A short distance ahead there was a track joining the road, its emergence visible as a break in the wall but otherwise screened by trees. It wasn't the only cover – there was the wall itself, and the bushes on the other side of the wire fence opposite – but it was the only cover that could have been reached so quickly and with so little noise.

He kept going, slowly. He listened but there was nothing, just the wind trying to shake the last dry leaves out of the trees and the cold lake heaving and dropping beyond the bushes. Perhaps he'd been mistaken, and there hadn't been a movement after all; the more he thought, the more certain he was that he'd glimpsed only a momentary swirl of flakes that came together and then broke up, or a sheep that had struggled through the break in the wall and couldn't find its way back and that ran when it sensed it was being watched. You're going to feel like an idiot stalking a dumb ball of wool up the track, he told himself as he edged along towards the opening, but dumb ball of wool or not his heart was hammering and all his senses seemed to be screwed up to their sharpest. He hesitated, and then took the last step that would bring him out into the open before the track. He looked down for the sad-stupid expression of a stray Herdwick and found himself staring into the barrel of a gun.

'Hands on your head,' the soldier said promptly as he straightened up and kept the heavy rifle level. He was in combat field kit and a small hand-radio danced on a strap from his belt.

There was a breaking and crackling sound behind, and Carson looked around to see that two more armed men were wading through the bushes towards him. One of them raised his radio and spoke into it as the other held his rifle high and stepped over the wire fence.

'You deaf?' the first man demanded, and Carson quickly put his hands on his head. All three rifles were trained on him now. It didn't seem like a good idea to point out that if he made a break for it and they fired at him, they were quite likely to shoot each other; maybe it also wouldn't be a good idea to try it out.

'Rover's coming,' one of the men said, at which point the Rover arrived.

Carson was hustled into the back where he sat under the canvas canopy with all three rifles trained on his neck. He flinched at every bump in the road. Nobody spoke. The cover had been dropped down over the back of the vehicle so that there was no way of seeing where they were going; he guessed that the sharp corner meant that they were through Langstone and turning towards the Jenner Clinic, and the almost immediate climb confirmed this.

'I think you might be over-reacting,' Carson suggested hopefully. 'I got a broken windscreen and I stopped, that's all.'

Three stony faces looked back at him in silence.

Windeler came out of the clinic camp to see what his lasers had netted. He wasn't over-excited because over the past week he'd become used to false alarms; he was confident that he had the ridgetops fully covered, but within the valley the ground was too irregular and uneven for total surveillance. He could only sample the tracks and the fells, but even then it took no more than a sheep or a bird to interrupt the beam and the turnout team would be scrambling off on a pointless mission. This time was different, because at least the team had bagged a man – but then, a man wasn't what they were looking for.

Hennessy came and stood behind Windeler's shoulder as the Land-Rover braked noisily and Carson was propelled out of the back. The three soldiers came out around him, rifles lowered but still held ready. They no longer needed to intimidate. That was an officer's job.

Windeler said, 'Who the hell's this?'

'It's Peter Carson,' Hennessy supplied, and he stayed well behind Windeler as if it made him feel protected. He seemed annoyingly pleased.

'I'm surprised you remember,' Carson said.

'We've been expecting you.' Hennessy beckoned to the Section Leader who stood by Carson. 'Bring him inside,' he said.

The Section Leader didn't move, didn't even acknowledge Hennessy. 'He says something stopped his car,' he told Windeler, and he didn't sound as if he believed it.

Carson was going to point out that he'd said nothing of the kind, but Windeler got in before him. 'The ground surveillance would have picked it up if anything had been moving around by the road.'

'That's fine for the ground,' Carson said, 'but what about the trees?'

There was a pause, the only sound being the settling of snow on canvas. The fall was no heavier than before, but it was starting to remain where it landed instead of melting off. Windeler might soon have the betraying cover that he wanted. He said quietly to Hennessy, 'How much does he know?'

'Enough, from the sound of it.'

Windeler turned and led the way through the courtyard to the field headquarters in the old common room. This time, everybody followed apart from the two non-ranking soldiers who climbed back into the Rover to return to their scramble point and wait for the next alarm. There was a smell of cooking drifting across from the area that had once been Jenner's private apartment. The army had made themselves at home.

Windeler indicated a chair and told Carson to sit. The Section Leader was posted outside the door in case of trouble. Anything that might have made the room homelike had been stripped out or torn down, and Carson found himself facing Hennessy and Windeler across a broad table. There was no lamp in his eyes, nobody at his shoulder slapping a length of rubber hose into the palm of his hand, just Hennessy and Windeler taking their seats as if this was going to be a tough job interview and he was a candidate who didn't rate.

'We know you've got Liawski's diary,' Hennessy said. 'Now we know that you've read it, too.' As he spoke he glanced at a sheet of paper on the table before him, as if he needed the strength of a report or a summary before he'd commit himself to anything.

'What makes you think so?' Carson said.

'We got David Reynolds last night, about the same time that

you were doing your disappearing act on the North Circular Road. He went straight back to his girl-friend, and we had someone waiting.'

Windeler was leaning back, prepared to let Hennessy handle the flow of the questioning and to interrupt to learn more that was relevant to his own preoccupation, finding the chimera and catching it. 'Why did you come back here, Carson?' he said. 'Do you think that you can get your own revenge for Tracy Pickford, do better than us?'

'Revenge?' Carson said, surprised. 'Is that what you think I want?'

Hennessy came in again. Already the interview was moving neatly and logically, the way it should in a perfect world. 'All right,' he said, 'tell us what you *do* want.'

Carson thought for a moment. 'Well,' he said, 'I wouldn't mind seeing you get embarrassed about it. Preferably in public. Just to see what it feels like.'

'You're a fine one to talk about feelings, Carson. Your girl-friend was murdered and you took the news like a racing result.'

'And what lets you think that you've got access to whatever goes on in my mind?' Carson demanded. 'Just because I don't act out my thoughts in some easy shorthand for you to read?'

Hennessy tapped the paper on the desk before him with a soft pink forefinger. 'We know you better than you might think,' he said.

'I doubt it. You may have a file inches thick, a mile of computer tape and an office full of clerks to work out the cross-references, but don't for one minute suppose that you know me at all.'

'We have more than that,' Hennessy persisted.

'No,' came a voice from behind Carson. He didn't turn. 'That's all we've got, probably all we'll ever have.'

Alison closed the door and picked up one of the lightweight hardwood chairs stacked beside it.

'I borrowed your car,' Carson told her as she carried the chair around and set it by the end of the desk. It spoiled the interrogation set-up, but nobody commented. 'I paid the bill, but you'll need another windscreen.'

'You're not surprised to see me, then?' She seemed tired, moving slowly. When she sat down she tried to rub away an itch at the side of her nose, looking absently across the room and not at Carson.

'No,' he said, and he tried not to sound harsh or accusing. It reminded him of the unfocused airiness that he'd seen in her the first time that they'd met. 'It didn't take me long to realise that you were the handler who sold out Liawski.' Not long at all; a memory of a paper tag on the bag which contained the remains of Tracy Pickford, tentatively identifying it as *Wells, CA, F (?)* Catherine Alison.

'Where's the diary, Carson?' Hennessy wanted to know.

'Somewhere you can't reach it.'

'Wherever it is, we'll get it.'

Carson shook his head. 'And when you get hold of the book, that's it. You're free to bury me along with the bodies you dragged out of this clinic.'

Hennessy was suitably shocked. 'What kind of people do you think we are?'

'I know exactly what kind of people you are.'

'Please, Peter,' Alison said, looking straight at him for the first time. 'I can't tell you how important this is.'

'That's right. You can't, never will. You sold more than Liawski . . .' now he looked around at all three of them '. . . you sold yourself to cheap gods who asked too little and offered not much.'

Hennessy shrugged. He'd heard nothing so far that could convince him that he was vulnerable. 'So you don't like the ideas we live by. Tough. What makes you think that you can change them?'

'I'm not blaming you. We all live down to whatever we think we can get away with.' Carson had the satisfaction of seeing Hennessy's smile become fixed and start to fade. 'Changes always start with someone saying no.'

'And you're going to be the first?'

'The second.'

Windeler was less than impressed. 'Much as I enjoy a philosophical debate,' he said, 'I've got a job to do. What about the diary?'

Alison glanced at Hennessy. 'I didn't even know it existed, until last night.'

'It exists,' Hennessy assured her. 'After talking to Reynolds we found Liawski's trunk and got the other books in the sequence.'

'Mister Carson,' Windeler said with a mild but unambiguous warning in his voice, 'I suggest you tell us where it is.'

'No secret. I put it in the mail.'

'Can we get to it?' Alison asked, and Hennessy nodded slowly.

'It's possible. We could raise a bomb scare and have it held at the sorting office.'

Carson was relieved that he hadn't underestimated the scope of Hennessy's deviousness. 'In New York?' he said.

'Oh, shit,' Hennessy said stonily.

Windeler leaned forward. 'There's still a chance. If it were posted this morning, it can't have got further than the airport.'

Carson disappointed him. 'It was posted last night care of a freight agent, and I paid an outrageous price to get it in the Concorde bag. Unless the flight was delayed — which it wasn't, because I telephoned this morning and checked — the package should now be on the mail train from Washington to New York.'

Now Hennessy was starting to perspire, like a cold apple in a kitchen. He said, 'Why New York?'

'He's got an agent there,' Alison told him.

'Get to him,' Windeler said promptly.

'How?' Hennessy wanted to know. 'We can't ask for co-operation to recover a document which details how we've broken the rules of the Washington Convention!'

Alison said, 'Haven't we got people in New York?'

Hennessy shook his head bitterly. 'Not the kind of people you're thinking of. They're supposed to be our allies, for God's sake.'

'Not for much longer,' Windeler said, 'if they find out that **we've** not only been carrying on the scientific practices that they've voluntarily abandoned, but we've been using them to engineer production-line subhumans.'

'The whole thing will blow up.' Hennessy stared accusingly at Carson. 'We'll have a witch-hunt.'

'It might be worse,' Carson comforted him insincerely.

'It couldn't be worse.' Already Hennessy could hear the baying of the hounds, faint and distant on the trail behind him.

'Don't underestimate the Americans,' Carson advised. 'They kicked out recombinant DNA, and it wasn't a cheap decision to make. You've not only given them something to be outraged about, you've even manufactured them a brand-new oppressed minority to champion.'

'Something which is half an ape?'

'And half a man.'

'You can't make that kind of comparison.'

'Why not? Because it raises a side of the issue you'd rather not face?'

Hennessy banged his fist on the table with enough force to stun a butterfly. 'Why the hell do you have to be so needlessly destructive?'

'Now you've seen it twice, two different ways. You get it because of the way you treat people. It's the only answer you invite because disagreement is nothing more than a difficulty to be worked around by political means.' He turned to Alison. She was listening without expression. 'And I suppose it works on all kinds of lands' he said.

'You were starting to get curious,' she said simply. 'I thought if I left you alone, you wouldn't bother following the idea. You needn't think I liked it.'

'That doesn't really matter much. You still did it.'

'We thought that Tracy Pickford was trying to set up some public exposure of the clinic. We thought that's why she'd contacted you.'

'You were probably right. I suppose I should be used to being wrung for what I'm worth.'

Hennessy pushed his chair back. 'I've got to warn the Commissioner,' he said. 'He'll probably roast me alive.'

Carson turned to follow as Hennessy hurried around the desk to the door. 'Jenner probably had a special apparatus for it,' he said.

'Watch him, Windeler,' Hennessy said with lap-dog savagery from the doorway. 'If he tries to get smart, shoot the bastard. Somewhere painful.'

Windeler glanced at his watch, but he didn't seem inclined to take over the chairmanship of the interrogation; as far as he was concerned, there wasn't much Carson could tell him that he actually wanted to know. Policy and the political implications were the worry. Windeler knew the true bliss of amorality.

Alison was stroking the edge of the desk absently, running her fingers lightly across its age-roughened texture. Carson said, 'What about Chad? What made him so "needlessly destructive"?'

She seemed to be startled for a moment by hearing the name from a stranger – or, at least, an outsider – but she recovered quickly. 'He was getting big, and he could be a swine sometimes. That's why Jenner moved the operation to here, somewhere there would be less attention if Chad threw a tantrum. At first we let him have the run of the place, but he went off a couple of times. He always came back, but we couldn't risk him being seen. One time he was out overnight, and that really started a panic.'

'You mean he was rebellious? Did that make your attitude any easier to keep up?'

She didn't respond to the baiting, not straight away. 'I was doing my job. And no, he wasn't really rebellious, just difficult to handle. He didn't know whether he was a chimp or a human being, and you could never be sure which way he'd react to anything. Most of the time he was docile, even when Doctor Jenner was hurting him. Anyway, after a while we had to keep him in the animal house permanently. He didn't like that.'

'You noticed?'

Now she looked up angrily. 'Stop trying to make me feel a shit, Peter. I may have been lousy to you and I'm sorry, but I believe in the job I do.'

'You think you were lousy to *me*? I got off lightly.'

'Chad was an animal, Peter – *is* an animal. If you saw him, you'd know what I mean. Anything about him you might call human, it was only superficial.'

He wanted to hurt her, but he didn't want her to be hurt. She seemed to have aged three or four years since they'd last met but there was something more, something of the sensitive girl who'd cried into a towel in Liawski's sitting-room for a misshapen baby.

Carson said, 'Liawski mentioned a language that the chimpanzees could use. Did you ever teach it to him?'

'The hand-signs? No.'

'Did he ever use them?'

'He picked up a few.'

'Liawski said that the signs made the chimps easier for you to handle. Why didn't you teach them to him?'

'I don't know.'

'Because he was already too good at it for comfort? Is that why?'

'No,' she insisted, 'he was a good mimic, but then all chimps are. Stop assuming they're like people!'

'I'm not assuming that. I simply want them to be respected

for themselves, not to look at them the way Hennessy looks at me. To him I'm just an element that fits in somewhere with his needs and intentions.'

Windeler spoke for the first time in minutes. He said, 'Not quite, Mister Carson. I don't think you fit in with his needs at all.'

Carson smiled. He dressed it up as regret, but the triumph was obvious. 'Not any more,' he said. 'Sorry about that.'

'He tried to write.' Both men turned to look at Alison; she was frowning and staring intently at nothing in particular. She went on, 'The afternoon before I left for London, he got my notebook and tried to write something. He didn't know how because I'd never shown him – it wouldn't have been worth it, because his hands were too deformed to hold a pen properly. But he got hold of my notebook and pen, and he tried to make letters.'

Carson said, 'What did you do?'

'I took them off him and pushed him back into his cage. He was trying to make the *sorry* sign, but I took no notice. When I locked him in he went straight back into chimp behaviour, jumping and screaming and hammering on the bars. I suppose I was frightened. Not of him physically – I'd known him for most of his life and I could dominate him without much problem – but more of what I might do if he succeeded in getting a couple of words down.'

'And what would you have done?'

'Nothing, probably. That's what's so frightening. I'd convinced myself that Chad was no more than some kind of biological mechanism, the way Doctor Jenner had always taught us. I thought that my first reactions had been childish and sentimental. Now they were all coming back to me, just when we were on the edge of a big breakthrough in the cloning programme. Lucy – she was the chimp who died – Lucy was carrying an embryo that was due for implanting on the same day that it all happened. A patient called Marie Forester was going to get it. Doctor Jenner was going to use the same story that he'd used before.'

'Miscarriage?' Carson said, and Alison nodded.

Windeler said, 'Why did you wait until now to tell us all this?'

'I've been trying to keep it out of my mind.' She looked at Carson. 'Damn you, Peter, I'd nearly managed it.'

Hennessy returned, red in the face and somewhat moist. As he pushed the door closed behind him he said to Windeler, 'The Commissioner's furious. He's started cleaning up the records in case there's an investigation.'

'No point in expecting Carson to co-operate,' Windeler told him. 'Now the diary's out of his hands he's got nothing to bargain with.'

'What are we going to do?'

'Didn't the Commissioner give you any instructions?'

'Not unless you include praying for a miracle. We're on our own.'

'Then we'll have to try to get our own laundry done before it's too late. We'll bring in the copters and cover every inch of the valley. We can think of a public explanation later. First we've got to find that animal and burn every trace of it off the face of the earth.'

Alison was taken aback by this sudden switch of policy from *capture* to *kill*. She said, 'There's no need to go as far as that, surely.'

'There is now.' Windeler turned back to Hennessy, and indicated Carson. 'What do you want to do with him?' His tone indicated that, had it been a matter of purely military expediency, he would have preferred a quick shot and an end to the worry.

'Put him somewhere safe.' Hennessy gave Carson a venomous glance. '*Very* safe.'

'What about the animal house?' Alison suggested quickly, and Carson thought, thanks kid, we're performing way up to standard, aren't we?

'Good idea,' Hennessy said, obviously more attracted by the indignity than the security. 'Fix it up, will you, Windeler?'

Windeler called for the Section Leader, and Carson was escorted across the courtyard to the undamaged animal house. Alison followed a few paces behind, unable to stay in the field H.Q. because Windeler was drafting his plan for saturation-coverage of the Langstone valley. She stood back and watched as Carson was put into one of the barred chimpanzee pens, the door banged closed and was secured with a heavy tamper-proof padlock. Carson was at the end of the row, and Bobo and Fifi were two cages along. They seemed to become nervous at this strange activity, scuttling back and forth and panting loudly; Alison went over and calmed them, signing without speech.

The Section Leader hesitated half-way to the door. He wasn't prepared to let Alison stay, so she turned to Carson and said, 'Do you think there's anything else I could have done?'

He was about to take hold of the bars before he realised how B-Western it would look, Cottonmouth Carson slung in the cooler. Instead he put his hands in his pockets and said, 'On your own, perhaps not. But you've got an unfortunate habit of turning your friends over to the opposition.'

She nodded — she could hardly disagree — and allowed herself to be ushered out. The Section Leader closed the animal-house door and then there was the sound of a key being turned in an outer lock.

The cage gave him room enough to stand, but only just. It wasn't so much a cage as a divided-off section behind a wall of bars that ran the length of the building, rough wood for a floor and a back wall of whitewashed stone. In the back wall at intervals were floor-level openings about three feet square, blocked by heavy steel shutters without handles or hinges. There was no opening at the back of Carson's cage, but there was one in the irregular narrow enclosure next to him.

It was custom-built, solid ironmongery. No catches to rattle loose, no bolts to undo, and the forward bars — the ones that really counted — were set in concrete. Bobo and Fifi, reassured by their handler, were watching him with interest. Something of a reversal of the usual situation.

After a moment, Bobo got up and hunkered over to the back of the cage. She took hold of the bars, braced herself, shook her head a couple of times, and pulled. The ironwork started to groan immediately and there was a grating sound as the tongues of metal which fixed the bars into the stonework of the back wall slid out. There were two tongues, one for each crosspiece, and as they came away the nine-inch gap between the end-bars and the stone spread to a foot. The infant Fifi clambered past Bobo and squeezed through the opening without much trouble.

Carson flinched back as the small chimpanzee jumped at the bars of his own cage and climbed up to the ceiling, shaking them with her compact weight. Bobo had released the bars and was watching. Fifi put a long arm up and out through the front of the cage, and after a moment a steel pin dropped free and hung on a short length of chain.

Fifi danced back down the bars. The dividing wall rolled back a few inches. Carson put out a hand to try them as Fifi went back through the gap that Bobo was again holding open.

There were bearings in the corners of the dividing panel, and they slid along grooves in the front and back walls. Carson was in a crush cage. Now that the securing pin was removed, the barred panel coasted easily back and forth.

Bobo and Fifi were back in their places. There was no sign of Bobo's interference with her cage, no indication that Fifi had ever been out. Whatever Alison's message to them had been, it had contained more than anybody other than the chimps had understood. They watched to see what Carson would do next.

Their observation made him edgy, on top of the strange mixture of fear and outrage that had kept him going for most of the past twenty-four hours. His gamble with Liawski's diaries had been only half-successful; there would be international indignation and scandal, but the twisted hominid that Jenner had created would benefit from none of it if Windeler was finally able to track him down. And on a more pragmatic level, the evidence of the diaries was insubstantial if there were no living specimen to back it up.

He pushed the moving wall, and it rolled back without much noise. As the floor space of the cage was enlarged it came to include the blocked-off opening in the stone. Carson knelt before it and looked for some kind of gap in the steel shutter; it obviously came down like a guillotine, and whilst it wasn't quite as sharp as a guillotine blade, the edge that he felt when he tried to jam his fingers under it was enough to persuade him that he'd need leverage.

He checked his pockets. They'd pat-searched him for weapons, but the clasp knife hadn't been bulky enough to attract their attention. Opening out the toughest-looking blade – a stubby screwdriver – he put it under the edge and tried to lift. Although he couldn't actually raise the shutter he found that by working the blade he could get it to lift and drop by about half an inch; enough, at least, for him to jam open with a wadded cagoule.

With a widened gap he could get more than his fingertips through, and the material gave him enough padding to attempt a lift. Cold air was streaming in and washing around his knees and then, as the heavy plate rasped and scraped upward, white daylight.

Carson crawled out into an enclosed courtyard. It was small, barely enough room for the chimpanzees to exercise, and although it was open to the sky the outer wall was topped with three layers of silvery wire that were connected to a junction box in the corner. This, he thought as he straightened up and dusted himself off, must be attached to the outer wall of the complex, although it couldn't be seen from the Langstone approach. Before anything else, he turned and replaced the sliding shutter. He didn't want to show his gratitude to Bobo and Fifi by giving them pneumonia.

There were four bald tyres and a few pieces of rotten fruit heaped together in the corner. Snow was collecting around them and giving them an illusory permanence, as if they'd been fixed in plaster. The cobbling of the courtyard floor only showed through in patches. Carson tried the wooden gate, but it was locked; then he stood up on tiptoe and gingerly tapped at the lowest of the three wires, a brief touch at first and then with more confidence when there was no crackling shock.

Carson threw his cagoule over to get it good and tangled, and then he used it as a rope to pull himself on to the top of the wall. There he unwound the material and threw it down into the field on the other side before dropping after it.

As he'd expected, he was at a corner of the farm complex away from the approach road. A rough stony path led from the courtyard gate around the outside wall, but beyond that was nothing more than coarse ferns with their thickening cover of grey-white. When Carson pulled his cagoule over his head he could see little rips and pinholes of daylight where the fabric had torn on the wire, but it was still an extra layer against the cold and better than nothing. He pulled all the drawstrings tight before he made his way cautiously along the path.

Most of Windeler's men were scattered around the valley in small bivouacs, turnout teams waiting for a radio signal and a map reference from their command centre, and although the clinic had been set up to serve a complete unit the courtyard was deserted. Carson watched for a minute before he risked moving out into the open, and although he could hear the faint signs of life within the buildings he saw nobody.

Ten seconds later he was on the road and heading for the rise which would take him out of sight of the clinic. Nobody yelled and nobody fired, and the sick burn of apprehension within him settled and became controllable. As long as no one checked his cage he wouldn't be missed; not as long as the security of the animal house seemed unviolated. His only immediate worry would be another brush with Windeler's patchy and inadequate laser network.

There was probably a beam set somewhere along the road – surely Windeler would want to be warned of anybody approaching or leaving. Carson tried to marshal together his knowledge about the properties of lasers but his memory went no further than an impression of unswerving directness

291

and undiluted coherence; that is, they couldn't turn corners and they didn't weaken over distance. The first of these properties would limit the siting of the gear – the laser and its aligned receiver or reflector – and the second would place a limit on its accuracy. Windeler might know that a beam had been interrupted, but he'd have no way of telling exactly how far along its path the interruption had taken place. For something as crucial as an approach alarm he'd probably keep the beam short and low, three or at the most four feet above the ground. With this in mind, Carson watched the walls ahead of him as he descended towards Langstone. A hundred yards before the junction with the main valley road, he saw the disc of a lens buried in the stone.

If he looked hard he could even see the beam itself, a greenish whisper of light that was like an after-image of solidity. It was easy enough to duck under and carry on.

When he passed through the village he pulled the hood of the cagoule to cover as much of his face as he could, just another bad-weather walker heading for home. Away from the hotel and the school he dropped the hood again; he didn't rate the extra warmth as much as the need to hear any vehicle that might be approaching along the road behind. Nothing came, though, and he was alone with the wet road and the dead leaves and the thinned-out winter birdsong.

Alison's Honda was as he'd left it, the milky windscreen still in place with little drifts piled on the wipers and around the bonnet mouldings. He stopped a few yards short of the car and looked around for the alarm beam that had betrayed him; the falling snow showed it up, lancing across the field and missing the top of the drystone wall by no more than an inch.

Two identical accidents, both without obvious cause, both within a few yards of each other in open country. It couldn't be coincidence. Chad had slashed and carved his way through Jenner's entire staff with a single lucky exception, but he could recognise Alison's distinctive car and he didn't want to see her get away. Twice he'd stopped the Honda, and twice he'd been unlucky.

Perhaps Windeler hadn't made the connection yet, or perhaps he didn't know the extent of the overlap. The hominid had to be somewhere that he could see the valley road, somewhere near enough for him to watch for the car he wanted and to get down to the roadside fast enough to stop it; a building or a barn, some place that he might have discovered during one of his extended absences.

There was only one group of buildings in sight, high above on the valley slope. They were ideally placed to give the hominid a good view along the lakeside and the road, and they were close enough to give him the chance to scramble down at the approach of a recognised vehicle. Carson began to walk up the track towards Ravens' Crag Farm.

Hennessy stirred the gearshift on the Rover and tried to slip the clutch, but all he could get from the engine was horrendous mashing noises of metal on metal.

He raised his voice so that Alison could hear him. 'You ever driven one of these bastards?'

She nodded, and slid across the seat when he got out to walk around. Windeler wanted them both out of the way, and it had been Hennessy's idea that they should go down to the Langstone Hotel. The army man had been engrossed with his maps and pins and had given a sharp refusal to Hennessy's request for a driver, but after the mute incomprehension that had met his suggestion of walking he'd compromised and released a car.

Alison put the Rover into gear and released the handbrake, swinging around and out of the courtyard. She glanced in the rear-view mirror; it was angled wrong, and as she readjusted it she could see the flipped-around reflection of the animal house. Maybe Carson was in there or maybe he was out; there was no way that she could have checked without raising suspicion, no way that she could know whether Bobo and Fifi had understood and followed up her urging for them to repeat a trick they'd played on her more than once.

In an hour or less, Windeler's units would be starting a steady sweep to cover the length of the valley. They would be backed up by Sea King helicopters that were already on their way inland, and wherever Chad was hiding he would be found and killed, cremated on the spot by a concentration of flamethrowers. When Windeler had said that he would burn every trace of Chad off the face of the earth, he had meant it. From that moment on, the pressure of necessity would begin to push truth and history into new configurations; Liawski would be remembered for ever as pathetic and deranged, Jenner as a bold researcher and a compassionate healer, and the killings at the clinic would be the consequence of some obscure accident. Alison would be locked for ever into the contemptible framework of personality into which association with Jenner had set her; the only hope of release lay in Peter Carson finding Chad before Windeler could.

If only Carson was out.

The gate to the farm stood open, and the yard was empty. Dogs should have been barking and fowl should have been scratching, there ought to be washing on the line and smoke from the chimney. But there was nothing.

Carson left the gate and went over to the farmhouse. The sound of his footsteps was somehow soft and gritty at the same time, and the dark and melting trail that he left was the only mark on the yard's snow cover.

Most of the curtains had been pulled together without much care, and there were gaps which spilled a little light into the rooms beyond. Carson could see the dark shapes of old furniture. No detail. The inside doors were all open. The only room where there was anything to see was the kitchen, and here the impression was of general untidiness and neglect; there were plates and raggedly-opened tins stacked around the sink, and there was an overturned shopping bag on the table with two blackened bananas half-out of its unzipped maw.

Carson turned away from the glass and looked around, his breath hanging in the cold air. There shouldn't be any reason for him to feel unsafe – his tracks were still the only feature on the otherwise virgin yard, and he was half-disappointed and half-relieved to find the house apparently deserted – but there were too many angles and alleys between the slate outbuildings for comfort.

The barn door was open a few inches, warped and leaning outward. He went over and looked inside; there was light filtering down from the upper loft, straw-coloured and dusty, and the lower edge of the door dragged and rasped along the ground as he opened it far enough to step in.

Before him was the shrouded tractor, almost filling the barn. There was a smell of wet hay and mice and something else that made him uneasy, but which defied identification.

The tarpaulin seemed to be draped oddly for the shape of the machinery underneath. He lifted a corner of the cover to expose the half-assembled engine, and a white arm dropped out loosely and slapped him on the chest.

He staggered back as the whole tarpaulin began to slide and the woman slipped out headfirst and face-upward, moving a couple of feet before she caught on the angles of the machinery and hung upside-down. Her mouth was open and her eyes were dry, and her arm was outflung as if she were begging. Her kitchen apron had been doused in blood that had now dried and blackened, and as Carson looked on horrified a tiny white something wriggled off into the folds and shadows under the tarpaulin's edge.

Carson started to back towards the door. There was a man as well, leering out from under the cover with his pale face pressed against the apron. His lips were parted, and his teeth were black and clotted. The tarpaulin snagged and stopped its slow ride.

The cold air helped to keep the sickness down, but he had

to get out of the barn. Something hard thumped in between his shoulders and he spun around; he'd backed into the wooden door, and it shuddered as he kicked it aside and stumbled out into the yard.

The hominid was waiting for him.

It was taller than the girl-child it was holding, but only just. An arm was clamped around her neck with difficulty whilst the other hand was bent around the handle of a rusted kitchen knife, the point resting against her throat. She swallowed nervously, and the blade bobbed up and down.

The hominid was watching Carson, button-black eyes staring without expression from its bone-white face. A slight flaring of the flat nostrils was the only movement; the mouth was narrow and lipless and clamped shut.

There was a boy in a duffel coat and oversized Wellingtons standing a few paces back. His hair hadn't been combed, and there were dark circles under his seven-year-old eyes.

Nobody moved. After a glance at the boy, Carson couldn't look away from the hunched animal that was holding Sarah Gaskell. It had been dressed in castoffs that had been cut to fit its odd shape, and its feet were bound in layers of dirty rag. There were a few long wisps of hair clinging high back on its rounded skull, and when it turned its head briefly to order Peter Gaskell forward with a wordless jerk Carson could see the jagged line of the devocalising scar across its neck. Sarah gasped as the movement pushed the point of the knife a little harder against her skin, and as the rigidity of her fear was broken a tear started to cut a clean line down the grime on her cheek.

The boy came forward. He was shivering. His Wellingtons lifted and dropped as he shuffled. He said, 'Please. Please, you've got to do as you're told. He's sent Mum and Dad away and if you don't do what you're told he won't let them come back, ever.'

The hominid was staring, watching for his reaction. The boy was still shuffling, still pleading as he came towards Carson in the open barn doorway. 'He won't hurt us if we help

296

him to hide, he's promised. I asked him and he promised.'

The boy was about to speak again, but he faltered. Carson realised why and tried to move to block his view, but it was too late. Peter Gaskell wailed for his mother and ran past Carson and into the barn.

Carson managed to grab at the hood of the duffel coat, but he couldn't keep hold; the move opened up the scene to the rest of the yard, and Sarah forgot the knife and started to scream.

Peter Gaskell was tugging at his mother's cold hand, crying loudly and begging for some sign of recognition, putting every ounce of his negligible weight into the effort to get some response from her. The shaking dislodged the rest of the tarpaulin which uncovered his father as it folded on to the ground on the far side of the tractor. Dark with his own blood, Desmond Gaskell grinned lovelessly down at his son.

Carson stopped himself from running forward. and grabbing the child for long enough to glance out into the yard. The hominid was still holding the girl, but he was looking around in desperation. As the pale head swung from side to side, Carson took a running dive at the knife.

He skidded on the snow, and the three of them went down together. Carson had his hands around the blade, and he tried to keep his palms pressed hard against the flat of the metal whilst the hominid struggled to pull it free. The carbon steel was rusted and the edge had gone, but he could still feel it biting into the soft flesh near the heel of his hand as it slid along an inch or more. Then there was another pain as the animal tried to get its teeth around his knuckles to gnaw at them; Carson lashed from side to side and felt a hard smack of bone on bone, and the hominid rolled free and staggered to its feet holding both claws against the flat bridge of its nose, still holding the knife.

It stumbled across the yard, heading for the enclosing wall and the open fell beyond. Carson tried to get Sarah to her feet, but she sagged helplessly. The animal skipped over the wall. Carson couldn't turn and walk away from two hysterical children in freezing snow; he gathered the girl up into his arms and looked into the barn for the boy, but he was no longer there. The sliding punch-marks of his tracks led out of the barn and around the cleared patch of the struggle, across the yard and out through the gate.

The kitchen door was locked, but a couple of kicks broke it in; he didn't even have to put the child down. He left her on a threadbare 1940s sofa in the sitting-room and looked for the telephone, but when he found it the line was dead. As he rattled the cradle up and down it occurred to him that, even if he couldn't call the village, Windeler would soon know that something was happening at Ravens' Crag because the boy would interrupt one of the lasers on his downhill run.

Carson would probably be marched back to the animal house whilst the turnout team followed Chad's clear trail. He no longer found it so easy to pity the hominid, not after the display of callousness and cunning that he had seen; even the horror of the clinic murders hadn't really touched Carson, because he'd arrived when the blood had been cleaned up and the bodies tidily packed for transport. It's easy, he thought, to see the issues clearly when your hands aren't dirty.

But he knew nothing now that he hadn't known before; he'd known that Chad was violent and unprincipled, known that he was running scared. He'd also known that Chad was manufactured. Jenner had wanted to create a body, a convenient hunk of animate flesh that could duplicate human biological reactions closely enough to be commercially viable; he'd given little or no attention to the fact that, in order to create the body, he would also have to create a being. The tarpaulined gore in the barn was the work of Jenner's hand, devised not by intent but by a wilful ignorance.

Carson found an overcoat behind the kitchen door and took it through to put over the girl. He didn't want to leave her alone, but Windeler's men would soon be arriving and he couldn't stay. A torn strip of towel from the kitchen bound the shallow cut on his hand, and then he stepped out into the yard.

The hominid's footprints were still visible, but the wind was bringing lacy hanks of loose powder to fill and obscure them. After a glance downslope towards the lake and the road – nothing happening yet – Carson clambered over the yard wall and started to follow.

Peter Gaskell broke no laser tracks. He unthinkingly followed the route that he knew best, down the rutted approach road to about half-way and then on to the field path which was their shortcut to the school. The path was covered by a beam, but because of the rough lie of the land it couldn't get closer than four and a half feet from the ground. Peter Gaskell passed straight under it.

Cold and wet from the snow, breathless and sobbing from the run, he arrived in the village and made straight for the only building that he knew really well. Mike Schaffer heard his hammering on the door of the schoolhouse and went to take a look.

The boy stood wide-eyed and open-mouthed; he'd run without thinking to the nearest authority that he was familiar with after his parents, but this was a stranger, not the schoolmaster. He tried for a moment to come up with something else, but then his whole apparatus of action broke down.

Schaffer squatted down – less intimidating – and took hold of the boy. Peter Gaskell was swaying and crying and babbling at the same time, and nothing that Schaffer said could calm him for the simple reason that he wasn't listening. The usual movie treatment for hysteria seemed to be a hard slap, but Schaffer had never tried it and didn't trust it and the child was so small and frail. All he could get was something about the boy's mother being hurt and, repeated several times, the word *knife*.

It was enough. He swept the boy up and carried him across to the hotel.

The lobby was empty, the bar was empty, the dining-room was empty. Schaffer didn't waste time with searching around, he just stood in the lobby and shouted. Within seconds the manager appeared from the kitchen passageway, ready with an expression of annoyance.

Schaffer didn't wait for it. He said, 'Where does this boy come from?' and he turned slightly so that the manager could get a look at the crumpled, shoulder-hugging face. The manager hesitated and then frowned and seemed to be giving the matter some deep thought, and as he was doing this Hennessy and Alison appeared in the doorway to the lounge.

'I think it's Peter Gaskell.' The voice came from above, from the angle of the stairs. Lesley, the Australian girl, descended to get a closer look. 'Yes, it is. He's from Ravens' Crag farm. Mrs Hamilton was talking about him a couple of days ago.'

Schaffer said, 'His mother's hurt, or something. I'll have to go and look. Can you take him from me?'

Lesley nodded and held out her arms, and Peter Gaskell was transferred across. She was no more familiar to him than Schaffer had been, but he seemed to be more comforted. Schaffer turned to Hennessy.

'This could be it,' he said. 'The boy was talking about a knife. Get on to Windeler and have him meet me at this Ravens' Crag place as soon as he can.'

'I think it's best if you let Windeler handle this,' Hennessy started to say, but Schaffer had already gone.

There was an army Land-Rover waiting outside the schoolhouse when Schaffer emerged after a brief stop to collect his anorak and a map. He looked at the vehicle with suspicion – was Hennessy trying to pull some stunt to get him out of the way? But Alison leaned across the passenger seat and beckoned to him, and he stepped down and opened the door.

'You don't even know where it is,' she pointed out, and after a moment he nodded and climbed in. Alison put the Rover into gear and they headed out of the village.

Peter Carson was following a wall. Snow had piled up against its windward side and filled up the old hard tractor ruts, and there was only the line of stone and the hominid's shuffling, sliding footprints to guide him. There had been sheep here only a few minutes before and their droppings were still scattered on the white like handfuls of olives; there was no sign of them now.

It had been a gentle but steady climb. A mile or so ahead the valley side began an abrupt rise to overhead crags, and there the going didn't look so easy. After another hundred yards the wall angled away and ran out into nothing, the stones pushed over and not restored, and the ruins of a cottage stood almost as a final marker of civilisation. Chad's tracks went straight through the low piles of rough slate and the massive cornerstones, across the dark cut of a stream and on into the open valley beyond.

The stream coughed and guttered over the broken land, swirling cold around Carson's boots as he forded it; a creeping chill down his left foot told him that it had lapped over his ankle. Looking back from the bank he could just see the pixie-village roofs of Ravens' Crag with the first of a small Rover convoy rolling through the open gate; looking ahead he could see the figure of the hominid, shrunken and blurred by distance as it galloped doggedly on uphill. It seemed to be following another black thread of water; perhaps too wide for the slithering jump that it had used to cross this one, whilst wading in bound rags would be an invitation to frost-bite.

Carson set off again. He tried to raise his speed without exhausting himself early; it wasn't quite so hard now that his body had begun to tighten into the rhythm, but the first half-mile had been hell. That was the distance that separated them now, but Chad would soon be slowing as the ground began to rise more steeply. He was still keeping close to the stream, only breaking his irregular pace to glance back; soon he'd be seeing more than Peter Carson on his trail.

Carson checked back. There were figures along the far side of the wall near the farmyard, half a dozen at the most. He moved on.

301

Now he could see what Chad was heading for. Two or three watercourses joined at a common root, the slash of a narrow gorge in the fellside; it was no more than a ragged slit in the rock, almost invisible until viewed from head-on. To a running animal it would look like shelter, a bolt-hole. It might also prove to be a dead end giving no choice other than to turn and attack. Chad paused at the foot of the ghyll; then he scrambled in and was lost to sight.

It was like an open door to an unlit house, dark and uninviting after the laundered whiteness of the fells. The ghyll sides were lined with inward-reaching shrubs and thin trees that anchored themselves on any excuse of a crack or a ledge, and through these Carson looked up and saw glimpses of the falls, three steep drops of foaming water. Each raged down into a standing pool, each pool fed the torrent below it. The stream that emerged at the bottom was wide and clear and looked deceptively slow, rocks under its surface tearing long white feathers in the otherwise unblemished skin. Through a haze of airborne spray he glimpsed Chad, half-way up the second of the falls already, but then the hominid clambered around a tilted rock and was gone again.

Autumn rains and the melted runoff of the first winter snows had fattened the waters and made them spread. Grasses at the edge of the stream had been swamped and drowned, lying flat and plastered like dead women's hair, and Carson had to be careful not to slip as he edged into the chasm. The darkness and the soft roar of the falls came around him like a hand clamped over his nose and mouth.

It wasn't hard at first, and he could see how the hominid had advanced so quickly. The stream's million-year retreat through the rock had left it split and broken, and Carson could scale alongside the force itself as if he were climbing an irregular stairway. The fall thundered down only a few feet to the side, but it was impossible to feel threatened by it; instead Carson felt sustained by its energy. When the route became less of a gift and more of a challenge there were still plenty of hand and footholds, cracks full of grass and angles full of moss, determined little pockets of life hanging on wherever they could.

There were few choices to be made, which was fortunate because there was no longer any trail to follow. There were rims of snow and frost on the rock edges and the occasional flurrying fall from the branches overhead, but there was no still blanket cover to hold obvious prints. It didn't really matter – Chad could only go on up the rising corridor.

Carson stopped to catch his breath. There was no point in looking back any more because he could only see a narrow section of the valley chopped out by the sheer walls of the gyhll, and much of that was obscured by foliage. He couldn't even guess how long it would take Windeler's men to catch up; presumably they were fitter than he was, but then Carson wasn't carrying arms and equipment. He wiped some of the beaded spray off his face and scrambled over a lichen-covered lip of rock to find himself on the edge of a scooped-out basin, the foot of the second falls.

It was higher, louder, and faster. The water boiled white with a frosty green beneath when it hit, spreading and billowing out across the basin to tear at the creamy silt that was backed-up in side pools. There was a way around but the rock walls seemed to lean inward a little, and if he lost his hold he might fall back into the icy water as it gathered and squeezed over the edge to nourish the fierce drop below.

The basin was deep and its rim was narrow, too narrow for anything more firm than a stance using three or four inches of sole. Carson got a handful of tough heather and used it to swing himself within reach of the next foothold, shuffling along the ledge a few inches at a time until he could step across on to a flat rock that was almost awash. Then he was back on the natural stairway, more steep and wet and slippery now. Deeper into the ghyll, and darker.

He was within reach of the second falls, scratched and dirty with his breath coming in ragged gasps, when the gorge was filled with a clattering roar that drowned even the noise of the force alongside him. Carson looked up the vertical chimney of rock and saw the underside of the Sea King helicopter as it slid across the sky. Seconds later it had gone, the beat of its blades muted and suddenly distant. Perhaps it would be dangerous to drop a man into the chasm – or perhaps Windeler's closeness made the risk unnecessary. Another few feet, and Carson was again in the hollow at the head of a drop.

This time there was no obvious and easy way up. In fact, if he stayed on the same side of the gorge there would be no way up at all. The rock face was sheer and close, dripping with nets of runoff water from above. Across the pool it was a little more promising, but not much; a steep and gravelly scree that was running like a stream, the only way that the hominid could have gone.

It shouldn't be too difficult to get across – Chad had managed it, after all. There were plenty of big rocks standing out of the water near the edge of the falls, and although they weren't close enough or flat enough to be stepping stones he ought to be able to clamber from one to another. Carson stepped on to the first rock and then crouched and reached out for the next.

Everything was fine until half-way across – he didn't have to stretch dangerously from one stone to the next, and he hadn't allowed himself to be too worried about the long drop that was only a couple of feet away. It was when he tried to put his weight on to a small and innocent-looking hump of stone wedged between two others that it broke up under him.

His foot went straight into the dead sheep and through into the nest of maggots that was exposed by the broken crust of its skin. Even though he pulled back and scrabbled for his balance they came with him in a squirming white rain, and then he lost grip and fell forward into the headwaters.

Carson floundered and stumbled but managed to stay upright, splashing against the persuasive tug of the current that was guiding him backwards towards the concentration of the force. There were loose stones underfoot rounded to bearing-smoothness by constant abrasion as they jostled against one another, and they threatened to pull his legs from under him in the cold and bitter flow. He staggered on, boiling up a froth in his haste, and flung himself on to the scree bank before him.

He rolled over and anxiously looked for crawlers, but they'd been stripped from him by the current. The dead animal must have been there for several weeks or even months, fallen and jammed into the cleft. It had been washed by the falls until the skin was bare and grey and stretched to blend with the stone. Now that he looked back he could see a few giveaway strands of wool teased out along the adjacent rock, the hanging head with its empty eyes, the legs that bobbed as they were flipped lightly by the water rushing underneath. Still recognisable, but hollowed-out and rotten.

His clothes were cold and soaking wherever they touched, and he winced when he stood up and the material plastered new discomforts across his chilled skin. When he looked up, the hominid was watching him.

Chad still had his rusty knife, and the deformity of his claw made him hold it at an odd angle so that he seemed to be nursing the blade, his only true friend. He was no more than ten yards up the scree and he was staring down at Carson, a fearful white rim showing around his eyes. He was shivering in his thin and ill-fitting clothing, and the rags that bound his feet had been almost shredded.

The hominid waited. Carson took a breath, and then a step forward. Chad turned and tried to run.

At first he slid back more than he advanced as the scree moved under him, but then he got a hold and started to move. Carson tried to follow and had the same difficulty but Chad was doing better now, his stooping posture an advantage for once as he hugged the path four-footed. Knife and knuckles rattled over the stones and then he paused and looked back; Carson was still there, still following.

Fifty yards up, the path stopped. Water and wall pinched together, and there was no longer room to climb between them. Here it wasn't so much a fall as rapids, but there was still no way across and no far bank to reach if there had been; Chad looked first at Carson, then at the closed path ahead, then at the inhospitable flow, and then he jumped.

His short and powerful legs gave him a lot of distance, so much that it wasn't immediately obvious what he was aiming for; the knife turned over in the air as it fell and was swept away, and Chad caught an overhanging branch and bobbed back and forth over the rapids. Then he caught his balance and started to climb up through the shaking-down snow, and there was no way that Carson could hope to follow.

The branch started to dip. The whole spindly tree started to lean into the chasm as its roots were dragged out of their crack.

Chad threw back his head and screamed. There was no sound. He screamed again, and a blood-flecked run of spittle appeared on his white lips.

'Keep climbing!' Carson shouted, but the words swirled away in the general roar. Chad struggled and kicked in an attempt to get to a firmer handhold, but his grip was limited. A shower of earth and moss erupted from the rock overhead as roots sprang free, and Chad dropped and disappeared into the foam.

Carson turned and started to run downslope. He could see the branch being carried along by the water, turning around and tilting as the downstream rush guided it around the rocks. At one point it jammed for a few seconds, but the force was too heavy to let it stay; it was lifted end over end to be dropped and swept on. Chad was no longer holding it.

Carson arrived at the basin just in time to see the hominid come tumbling over the last few feet and be dumped into the moving pool. Chad disappeared under for a few seconds and then resurfaced, face-down and heading straight for the edge.

He couldn't be reached in time, but still Carson waded out and tried. Chad was pushed about by an eddy for a moment, and then he was thrown up against the dead sheep.

The animal broke up, the carcass fragmenting and tearing

apart as it was sucked away, and Chad jammed into the gap and stopped, his head under water.

The hominid's arms were waving weakly in the current when Carson got to him and took hold of the collar of his oversized shirt. He lifted, and Chad came up and out of the water coughing and retching; Carson tried to get a better grip around his chest, one that would let him fight the inexorable tug of the rapids and wade back to safety. He pulled the hominid free and took a couple of slow steps, and Chad swung his head from side to side in an obvious attempt to get some idea of where he was. Then he squirmed around and tried to sink his teeth into Carson's hand.

Carson slipped and went down on to his knees in surprise, but he didn't let go; Chad was ducked under the surface again, and he started to thrash. Carson got his feet back under him and hauled Chad up; once more the hominid bared his teeth and tried to bite him.

That was it, the end of sympathy. Chad was a killer and a kind of kidnapper, and Carson had risked life and liberty for him; in a cool moral assessment he'd be able to say why, but the conditions weren't ideal and he wasn't inclined to stand there in the raging waters and reason it out whilst the hominid tried to chew hell out of him. He didn't have a hand free, so he lifted Chad as much as he could and then bit his ear, hard.

Chad covered his head with his arms and screwed his eyes shut, and this at least made him less difficult to carry. Carson dumped him on the shale and then dropped down a few feet away. Let the hominid do whatever he liked now, Carson was beat.

Chad cautiously unwound his arms and sat upright. He was dazed and battered but didn't seem to have been injured by his downstream tumble. He hooted and coughed a couple of times, and then looked expectantly at Carson.

At least he wasn't up and running again. Carson half got up and moved towards him; Chad grinned nervously, a white Hallowe'en mask of supplication, but he didn't back away.

'Move aside, please, Carson,' Windeler called from across the pool.

Windeler was in rough-country gear, the hood of his parka thrown back and his mittens dangling from the ends of his sleeves. He'd bared his hands to get a two-fisted grip on the flat automatic that he was now levelling at Carson across the water.

Carson realised that he was blocking Windeler's aim at the hominid. 'Sorry,' he said, and shook his head.

Another of the army men scrambled into view behind, and as soon as his hands were free he brought his rifle around to bear. Windeler warned, 'I'll shoot through you if I have to.'

'Like hell you will,' came a voice from behind the second man, and Mike Schaffer climbed up on to the rock. 'Where do you think you are?'

Chad tried to peek out from behind, and Carson had to move to keep him covered. He saw Mike Schaffer stare and swallow as he got his first sight of the hominid, but he'd obviously been given some of the story already.

Carson said, 'Not going to be so neat, is it, Captain? No quick under-the-carpet job after all.'

There were two more soldiers on the opposite side of the pool now, altogether about as many as the bank could hold. The last man carried a hand-radio, and he raised it to speak.

'I've got emergency powers,' Windeler said, and he had to raise his voice as the Sea King came into line overhead. 'I'll use them.'

A wide hatch in the copter's side was open, and somebody was looking down at them. The man with the flamethrower for Chad? Carson told Windeler, 'You'll be sorry if you do.'

'Forget it, Carson. You threw in your hand when you parted with Liawski's diary. You want to commit suicide, that's fine by me.'

'Don't waste your only chance.' Carson pointed at the men with rifles. 'Call them off and put your gun away.'

'Why should I?'

'Because I didn't tell you the whole truth, that's why.'

Windeler hesitated. 'You didn't send the diary?' he said, and there was a thinly-disguised trace of hope in his voice.

'I sent it, but not straight to my agent. It went to an accommodation address. I sent a letter by ordinary airmail to my agent, telling her where to collect it. That gives you a full day's grace, could be even longer. Depends how you play it.'

'And what are you asking?'

There was a sneeze from behind Carson. He said, 'Safety for the chimera. Permanent and assured.'

'And?'

'A public declaration, nothing hidden. I'll let you organise that however you like.'

It wasn't exactly the kind of concession that would make Windeler gleeful. He said, 'I haven't got the authority to negotiate. But I'll forward your proposal.'

'Shove that. What about your "emergency powers"?'

'It'll have to be the Commissioner's decision.'

'The Commissioner's sitting by the fireplace right now, making bonfires out of anything that's got his name on it. I wouldn't look to him for rational judgement.'

Windeler wasn't happy. His was executive power, only indirectly affected by the mysteries of policy. He said, 'Suppose we make a deal. How will you know I won't break it?'

'We've got a police witness.'

'And you think that will count for anything?'

'I'm damn sure it will. The Commission doesn't have any direct power or influence over the police here – that's why you had to have them eased out. Is that right, Schaffer?'

Schaffer managed to drag his awed attention away from the patch of hominid that he could see behind Carson, and he said, 'That's the way it looks. I'll back you up, and I'm certain Stoneley will back me.'

Carson looked back to Windeler. He was still gripping the automatic, but with less conviction. Carson said, 'How about it? Don't be put off by the fact that I'm offering you something honest and above-board. I know you're not used to it.'

There was a moment in which the only sounds were the rushing of the falls and the battering of the copter, and then Windeler lowered the gun. 'If you'll drop the patter,' he said wearily, 'it's a deal.'

'And you'll handle Hennessy?'

Windeler nodded to his men, and they stood easy with their rifles. 'Hennessy will grab any opportunity to save face, but we'll have to watch him. He's built a career on broken promises.'

Carson smiled. 'Three cheers for good old blackmail, then.' He turned to Chad, who was hugging himself against the cold and shivering. 'I'm looking after you,' Carson said. 'Understand?'

Chad nodded.

The copter swung around and headed off up the valley; a few moments later another followed it, and then the radio man stowed his set and came across the rock bridge to help with the hominid. Chad was too exhausted to walk so they wrapped him in a lightweight foil blanket and improvised a stretcher out of four rifles; Carson was offered a blanket as well, but he found that he couldn't walk and keep it wrapped around himself. Most of his gear was wool and would supposedly carry on trapping his body heat even though it was wet, so he accepted some waterproof overtrousers to go with his cagoule in cutting down on wind chill, and hoped for the best.

'Couldn't you call us back a helicopter?' he asked Windeler as he struggled into the light nylon, but Windeler shook his head.

'Different service. The less they know at this stage, the better.'

Alison was waiting in the Ravens' Crag yard with the Rover when they arrived, parked alongside the other army vehicles She'd taken Sarah down to the Langstone Hotel and left the child with her brother in the care of the Australian gir and the local doctor, and then she'd gone across to the schoolhouse for Schaffer's binoculars before driving back to keep an anxious watch on the fells. She'd seen the inert bundle slung between the rifles and watched for some movement from it, but she couldn't trust her own imagination not to attempt to please her. She had to wait for the tired column to come tramping back into the yard and for Carson's reassuring smile and wink before she could know how the chase had gone.

'You want to go back to the camp?' Windeler asked.

'No,' Carson said firmly. 'He'll think we're taking him back to the animal house.'

Schaffer indicated Alison's Rover. Obviously he was considering it as police property for the moment. He said, 'Bring him to the schoolhouse, please.'

'The schoolhouse?' Windeler said in surprise, and the two men who were carrying Chad looked to him for instruction.

'Whatever that thing is, it's responsible for the deaths of a dozen people.'

'What about the deal?'

'I'll see it's kept, but not at the expense of the law.'

Windeler turned to Carson with a regretful *you-can't-blame-me-for-this* look. 'You hear that?' he said. 'It'll have to be destroyed after all.'

'Animals are destroyed,' Carson corrected him. Chad was a twilight being, and the laws would need some considerable refinement to take account of him. It would be public and painful, and it wouldn't be the exclusive province of some laboratory chief.

Chad was tired of being carried, and he showed it by attempting to struggle out of his thin foil wrapping. They let him clamber into the back of the covered Rover after Carson; Alison got into the driving seat, Schaffer beside her. As the convoy started to roll towards the village Schaffer turned round to Carson and said, 'Better cover him with something.'

Carson pulled his tattered cagoule over his head and put it around Chad's shoulders. The hominid seemed puzzled by the arrangement, but he accepted it. They bumped and shuddered down the hill, and when they turned on to the good road that meant the village was near, Carson persuaded Chad to draw the cagoule over his head and hold it there like any furtive suspect under delivery. It wouldn't stop the rumours, but it would at least delay the worst of the truth.

Windeler arrived first, and he and two of his men were climbing out of their transport when Alison drew up by the schoolhouse door. The other army vehicle pulled in behind as Carson stepped out and then turned to help Chad, who could only see a few square inches of the ground directly under him. Alison came around to give a hand.

She staggered as she came level with the rear doors, and Carson reached out to steady her. The sound of the shot came just as he saw the blood that was splashing up his arm, and then Alison's shoulder rammed into his chest as she spun. All three of them went down.

Combat response. Windeler's men were already under cover and shouldering their rifles. In the first-floor bay of the Langstone Hotel Roger Forester pumped the action of the Mannlicher to put another round into the breech and then raised the sight to his eye for a second shot. As the crosshairs roved wildly along the magnified slate in search of a target, three bullets punched through his chest and slammed him back against the raised sash of the window. His head banged on the wooden edge and broke the panes out, and as the glass showered down around him he tipped forward and fell headfirst into the roadway. He was dead when he hit the tarmac.

Carson tried to roll Alison over. The shoulder of her jacket had burst out into a reddening flower and she was staring at it in amazement. Windeler was with them then and he knocked Carson's hand aside before it could do any well-meaning damage. He called for a field kit and then peered into the wound.

'It's messy, but it's clean,' he said after a moment. 'Barely nicked the bone and went straight on through.'

'Oh, Christ,' Alison intoned dully, still staring at the shredded material around the hole. Then she passed out.

Two men were over with Forester's body, one of them prodding it suspiciously whilst the other eased the Mannlicher from underneath.

Straight on through?

Chad was a few feet away, over by the railings. There was a hole in the cagoule that covered him. It was leaking red and spattering on to the white of the snow, slow and thick as if it wanted to spurt but lacked the energy or the vitality. As if there were nothing left to push it out.

Carson reached for the corner of the cover to pull it aside, but Windeler prevented him. It didn't matter, he'd seen enough. Alison's shoulder hadn't stopped the soft plug of metal, but Chad's body had. He'd given it enough resistance to break it up into a tiny cloud of shrapnel, and he'd contained it.

Windeler was looking over towards Forester. The two soldiers had pulled the rifle away, and now one of them was turning the body over. The team's medic was arriving with the field kit for Alison when Windeler said to Carson, 'I hope you'll remember. We had a deal.'

Carson looked at him evenly. 'Don't think anythjng's changed,' he said. 'It hasn't. Not a damn thing.'

A selection of bestsellers from SPHERE

FICTION

NIGHT PROBE!	Clive Cussler	£1.95 ☐
CHIMERA	Stephen Gallagher	£1.75 ☐
CALIFORNIA DREAMERS	Norman Bogner	£1.75 ☐
PALOMINO	Danielle Steel	£1.75 ☐
RAILROAD	Graham Masterton	£2.75 ☐

FILM & TV TIE-INS

SHARKY'S MACHINE	William Diehl	£1.75 ☐
WHOSE LIFE IS IT ANYWAY?	David Benedictus	£1.25 ☐
GREASE 2	William Rotsler	£1.25 ☐
CAT PEOPLE	Gary Brandner	£1.50 ☐

NON-FICTION

TOM PILGRIM: AUTOBIOGRAPHY OF A SPIRITUALIST HEALER	Tom Pilgrim	£1.50 ☐
YOUR CHILD AND THE ZODIAC	Teri King	£1.50 ☐
THE PAPAL VISIT	Timothy O'Sullivan	£2.50 ☐
THE SURVIVOR	Jack Eisner	£1.75 ☐

All Sphere books are available at your local bookshop or newsagent, or can be ordered direct from the publisher. Just tick the titles you want and fill in the form below.

Name _____

Address _____

_____

Write to Sphere Books, Cash Sales Department, P.O. Box 11, Falmouth, Cornwall TR10 9EN

Please enclose a cheque or postal order to the value of the cover price plus:

UK: 45p for the first book, 20p for the second book and 14p for each additional book ordered to a maximum charge of £1.63.

OVERSEAS: 75p for the first book plus 21p per copy for each additional book.

BFPO & EIRE: 45p for the first book, 20p for the second book plus 14p per copy for the next 7 books, thereafter 8p per book.

Sphere Books reserve the right to show new retail prices on covers which may differ from those previously advertised in the text or elsewhere, and to increase postal rates in accordance with the PO.